The Obsidian Crown

The Obsidian Artifacts
Book 2

Whitney L. Spradling

To you. Thank you for giving me the opportunity to bring this story to life. I appreciate you.

Content Warning

This book contains contains adult themes, including graphic on page sex, language, and violence that is not suitable for readers under the age of 18. Reader discretion is advised.

Recap

Need a reminder of what happened in book one, The Obsidian Sword?

Wren found out the man who raised her, General Bishop, was not her father. Her mother, a Light Fae, escaped from her captor, King Deimos of the Dark Fae, when she was pregnant with Wren. She sought sanctuary with General Bishop, where she died giving birth to Wren. Wren was raised with Gabriel, the general's son.

Wren's Light Fae powers remained dormant until King Deimos attempted to have Wren kidnapped. Her magic emerged when she was protecting herself and her brother, thus prompting the general to admit the truth to her.

Wren and Gabriel set out on a mission to Valasia, the land of the Light Fae, to discover more about Wren's history as well as for her to learn how to handle her magic. On the way, they met Silas and his cousin Jerricha. They traveled together, until they became separated during an attack on Wren.

As Wren and Silas continued on their way to Valasia, their feelings for each other began to grow.

In Valasia, Wren learned who her mother was, daughter to the queen of the Light Fae (Queen Elowyn). During her stay in

Valasia, Wren learned Silas was really her enemy (a Dark Fae), and she panicked. She ran and got kidnapped by the Dark Fae.

Wren was taken to Morygg Keep, where she learned her real father was King Deimos of the Dark Fae. During her captivity, Wren learned of Deimos's plans to find the Obsidian Artifacts (Sword, Crown, Eyeglass), in order to take over their world (Sorentiv).

Silas helped Wren escape, and they reconciled their differences. When Wren found out King Deimos was in possession of the Obsidian Sword, she came up with a plan to get "captured" in order to steal the Sword. While in the Keep, Wren met Aeron, Silas's friend, who helped her find and steal the Sword.

When King Deimos found out, he brought his armies to Hillwood Manor (where Wren lived with the general and Gabriel), and the first battle took place. During the battle, Wren and Silas combined their magics (Light and Dark) and found out they were bonded mates. Silas was shot during the battle and died. Wren was devastated, and unleashed her magic, ending the battle. In the process, her magic also healed Silas and brought him back to life.

Wren told her grandmother, Queen Elowyn, she did not want to take up her birthright as princess of the Light Fae.

Book two, *The Obsidian Crown*, begins three months after the battle.

Who's Who and What's What

- **King Adriel:** First king of the Light Fae.
- **Aeron:** Dark Fae.
- **Avisten:** One of the human realms in Sorentiv. Ruled by King Trion.
- **Prince Balor:** Dark Fae. King Deimos's appointed heir, but not his son.
- **King Bhardyl:** First king of the Dark Fae. Stole the Obsidian Sword and Obsidian Eyeglass from the Elementals.
- **Prince Castain:** Crown prince of Avisten. Was initially arranged to marry Wren.
- **Dark Fae:** Dark Fae are Fae of the night. Their powers range from darkness, mist, and turbulent weather, such as storms and wind, to communicating with nocturnal animals, silence, and cold.
- **King Deimos:** King of the Dark Fae. Wren's father.

- **General Edward Bishop:** General of the Ellendyr armies and Gabriel's father. Brother of King Rodion. The man who raised Wren, but didn't tell her he wasn't really her father.
- **Ellendyr:** One of the human realms in Sorentiv. Ruled by King Rodion.
- **Elementals:** All powerful Fae, capable of controlling raw magic, the very essence that makes up the magic Light and Dark Fae possess. The Elementals live on Edein Island, surrounded by magical barriers to keep others out.
- **Queen Elowyn:** Queen of the Light Fae. Wren's grandmother.
- **Gabriel Bishop:** General Bishop's son. Wren's brother, but not by blood.
- **Hawthorne:** Light Fae. Advisor for Queen Elowyn.
- **Jerricha:** Dark Fae. Silas's cousin.
- **Library of Knowledge:** Where the Light Fae store and protect all artifacts, history, and culture to keep it out of the hands of the Dark Fae.
- **Light Caster:** The rarest Light Fae. They are direct descendants of King Adriel. Sun Casters harness the power and energy of the sun.
- **Light Fae:** Light Fae are Fae of life. Their powers range from light, warmth, and fire to healing, growing, and communicating with animals of the day.
- **Morygg Keep:** Where the Dark Fae live in the Morygg Mountains. Ruled by King Deimos.
- **The Obsidian Artifacts:** Three magical artifacts (Sword, Crown, and Eyeglass), created by

the Elementals and infused with magic from both Light and Dark Fae. The Sword was infused with Dark Fae magic and the Crown infused with Light Fae magic. The Eyeglass was not infused with magic. Whoever has control of the objects can wield unimaginable power.

- **King Rodion:** King of Ellendyr.
- **Shadow Caster:** The rarest Dark Fae. They are direct descendants of King Bhardy. Shadow Casters harness the darkness of shadows.
- **Silas:** Dark Fae. Shadow Caster. Bonded mate of Wren.
- **Sorentiv:** The world this story takes place in.
- **King Trion:** King of Avisten.
- **Valasia:** Land of the Light Fae. Ruled by Queen Elowyn.
- **Winston:** Wren's pet wolf.
- **Wren Bishop:** Light Fae and Dark Fae. Light Caster. Bonded mate of Silas.

Chapter One

Pain erupted in Wren's stomach from the invisible force that hit her so hard it threw her backward. Her breath left her lungs in a rush as she collided with the ground. Gasping, she groaned in pain and closed her eyes, blocking out the stars swirling in her vision. Boots thudded on the ground as her opponent slowly approached.

"Ow," Wren whined and peeked an eye open. The bright blue eyes of her companion stared down at her.

Aeron shook his head and reached his hand out to help her to her feet. "That is the third time today, princess." He looked her over with a critical eye. She must not have passed his assessment as his mouth pulled down in a frown and his brows lowered over his eyes. "What's going on?"

"What's going on is you mercilessly throwing your magic at me." She rubbed her backside and grumbled.

He chuckled. "You asked me to help you train. You can't complain when I knock you on your ass a few times."

She *had* asked him to help her train. He was the only one who didn't pull his punches. Which was weird, considering he thought of her as his princess. Even so, he had no problem throwing his Dark Fae magic at her so hard it left bruises.

Aeron had become a good friend since he had helped her steal the Obsidian Sword from Morygg Keep three months ago. They spent many days in the training field working on Wren's magic and hand-to-hand combat.

"A few times?" she exclaimed. "That was three times today and four yesterday." Wren lifted her hands over her head and stretched side to side. She groaned as her muscles pulled in a pleasant pain. A different feeling than the throbbing in her rear end.

"My point exactly." Aeron stared at her with uncharacteristically solemn eyes. "What's going on? You usually avoid my hits. You've been more distracted the past few days." His eyes widened and clarity shone in his gaze as he crossed his arms over his chest. "Is it Gabriel?"

Wren sighed. "Partly. I always worry when he's gone. I know the risk of danger is low on this mission, but I can't help it." Knowing her brother was out in the world with only Hawthorne as backup left her feeling twitchy. It didn't matter if he wasn't her brother by blood. Her worry was compounded by the fact he was following a lead that might provide information on the whereabouts of the Obsidian Crown. "I guess I'm just worried about everything, and the Dark Fae have been too quiet. We haven't heard from them since the battle. What are they planning?"

Aeron looked to the north, eyes going distant. "Their silence is troubling, but there isn't much we can do about it until they make a move." His gaze returned to Wren. "Let's see what Gabriel and Hawthorne find. Maybe they will bring back good news. Until then, all we can do is what we have been doing. Training and preparing."

Wren nodded and looked around the training field she and

Aeron had been using. The training field at Hillwood, her childhood home, was always bustling. Soldiers trained daily under the supervision of Gabriel and the general when they were there. Now, as the sun began its slow descent to the horizon, the sounds of clashing weapons and men shouting were becoming less frequent. A steady stream of soldiers headed to the barracks to wind down for the night.

"Are we done for the day? Dinner will be served soon." Wren waited for Aeron's nod before she began the trek back to the manor with him at her side.

It had been three months since the battle at Hillwood Manor with the Dark Fae. Three months since Wren had joined her magic with Silas's and discovered they were bonded mates. Three months since she had almost lost Silas before she ever really had him. She still woke at night, screaming and crying, reaching for her mate to make sure he was still there.

Their bond had strengthened even more. Besides sensing each other's emotions and location, they could now communicate through the bond as well. After that development, they had to learn how to keep their thoughts to themselves instead of automatically projecting it down the bond. Of course, Silas being Silas, he had learned to keep Wren out of his head before she learned to do the same to him, much to her dismay.

Wren had spent those first few days in a state of perpetual embarrassment, which had amused Silas to no end. She had had difficulty keeping her thoughts to herself, and Silas had learned quite a bit about what went on inside her head.

"Can you do me a favor?" Aeron asked Wren, interrupting her thoughts. "When you see Silas next, make sure you don't tell him you were training with me."

Wren shot him a curious look. "And why would I do that?"

He shuddered dramatically. "Because I prefer to live and

he will kill me if he knew how many times I knocked you on the ground."

Wren snorted, an unladylike habit she had never broken. "He's not that violent, Aeron."

He gave her an incredulous look and asked, "Have you met him?"

"Once or twice." Wren laughed. "Besides, he probably already knows." She tapped her temple, smirking at his expression.

"That is just too weird for me," he mumbled. "Just make sure he knows you asked for it. I'm too young to die." He pushed open the large wooden doors at the front of the manor, holding them open for Wren.

Her laughter echoed off the high ceiling of the grand foyer. "He won't kill you and you know it. Silas would be lost without you."

She wasn't exaggerating when she said that either. Silas depended on Aeron for so many things. For the longest time, Aeron was Silas's eyes and ears in Morygg Keep, the Dark Fae stronghold, when he was away on missions. Silas had entrusted Wren's life to Aeron when she was purposely captured in order to steal the Obsidian Sword.

Aeron's eyes narrowed doubtfully at Wren's statement as they climbed the grand staircase. "I'll take your word for that and hope I never have to find out."

They said their goodbyes and parted ways at the top of the stairs, each headed for their own rooms to freshen up before dinner. Wren rubbed her backside again—Aeron really packed a punch with his magic—and limped into her rooms. The sight that greeted her stopped her in her tracks. Equal parts admiration and amusement rose within her as she watched Silas admire his shirtless reflection in the mirror while flexing his muscles.

"Really? Is that necessary?"

Silas whirled around, his eyes wide. A hint of pink tinged his cheeks and he smiled at her. Brushing his hands down his chest and abdomen, he said, "When you look this good, it is absolutely necessary."

She rolled her eyes and limped over to him. His skin was warm and smooth under her fingers as she ran a hand down his muscles until he grasped her hand in one of his.

"Why are you limping?" he asked darkly.

"I was training. Getting knocked on your ass three times is one risk that goes with learning how to fight."

"Three times?" He narrowed his beautiful green eyes. "I'm going to kill Aeron."

She traced her other hand over his chest in an attempt to distract him. "He is the only one who doesn't go easy on me. How else am I to learn to better defend myself? Our enemies will not pull their punches, so why should my trainers?"

He grabbed her other hand, stopping its pursuit as well. "Why do you have to get hurt at all?" He walked forward, pushing Wren backward as he went. "I would prefer you to stay out of harm's way at all times."

"You know that won't happen." She kept stepping backward with her hands trapped in his steady grip.

"Yeah, but I can dream, can't I?" He pushed her, letting go of her hands.

Wren shrieked as she fell, landing on the bed with a bounce. She narrowed her eyes at him as he prowled closer. The wicked look in those green eyes she loved so much made her heart skip a beat. His warmth and scent invaded her senses as he climbed over her and lowered his mouth to hers. Wren made a noise in the back of her throat, urging him on. Looked like they would be late to dinner. Again.

* * *

"How's it going with the Sword?" Jerricha asked Silas between bites of food.

Wren was sitting at the table in the small dining room listening to the conversation her friends were having while trying to sit lightly on her bottom, which turned out to be an impossible task. She missed Gabriel and hoped he would return soon and bring back good news with him.

"As good as can be expected." Silas shrugged and answered his cousin. "Queen Elowyn is helping as much as she can, but considering no one really knows much about the Sword, it's more trial and error."

Wren's grandmother had stayed at Hillwood after the battle. With Valasia currently under siege, and the people of Ellendyr hesitant toward anyone with magical abilities, Hillwood seemed the best place for the Light Fae to remain. Her knowledge of magic, along with Hawthorne's, had been invaluable for Silas as he learned the ins and outs of the Sword.

Wren had spent many days watching Silas train with her grandmother, learning how to use the Obsidian Sword. No one knew what its true purpose was, but Silas had figured out how to use it as a conduit for his magic. The Sword appeared to concentrate his Dark Fae magic, letting him use less of it but making the little he used more powerful. Watching him train with it magically as well as physically had become quite the event at the manor. She teased Silas mercilessly at the number of female servants who always found a reason to be outside when he trained.

Jerricha turned her gaze to Wren. "How about you, Wren? How is training coming along?"

"Good," she replied, then threw in because she couldn't resist, "when I'm not being knocked on my ass."

Silas glared at Aeron across the table and Wren had to stifle a laugh as her trainer shifted in his seat, unable to look the Shadow Caster in the eyes. She elbowed Silas until he lowered his gaze to his food with a grimace. Silas threatening Aeron's life would never get old to her because she knew he would never follow through on it. Aeron was one of Silas's closest friends.

Jerricha chuckled, but before she could say anything that would further anger Silas, the dining room door opened.

"Gabriel!" Wren jumped to her feet and rushed to her brother. Instant relief swept through her as she wrapped her arms around him and squeezed tightly. Gabriel looked over her head at the spread of food on the table and his stomach growled. Laughing, Wren pushed him into an empty chair and filled a plate for him.

"Where is Hawthorne?" Silas asked as Gabriel shoveled food into his mouth.

"Reporting to Queen Elowyn," Gabriel said around a mouthful. He swallowed before continuing, "there is a lot we have to discuss. I'm sure Father will call for a meeting."

"What can you tell us right now?" Wren returned to her seat and anxiously perched on the edge. "Please at least tell us you have good news."

"I have good news," Gabriel said, much to Wren's relief. "But also bad news."

"Of course," Jerricha murmured. "It can never be easy."

Gabriel smirked in her direction. "We believe we know where the Crown is."

"And the bad news?" Wren asked, hope flaring in her chest despite knowing Gabriel was going to say something she didn't like.

"The Elementals have it. In Edein."

The room let out a collective breath at Gabriel's statement. Edein Island. The mythical land of the Elementals, the supreme beings from whom the Light and Dark Fae descended. No one really knew where Edein Island was located. All maps that depicted the island had been destroyed by the Dark Fae or locked away in the Library of Knowledge in Valasia, currently under siege by Prince Balor.

"Aren't the Elementals just a myth?" Jerricha asked, echoing the question Wren was thinking.

Gabriel shook his head. "We don't believe so. Not after what we found."

"What did you find?" Wren asked impatiently.

"Hawthorne and I will discuss everything once we have everyone together. No point in repeating ourselves multiple times."

Wren groaned under her breath, her knee bouncing up and down from nervous energy. Silas chuckled and squeezed her leg under the table.

What's so funny? she snapped at him through the bond at the same time she smacked him in the chest with the back of her hand.

Silas feigned innocence with raised brows and wide eyes. *Nothing, love. I would never laugh at you.*

Wren glared at her mate and the smile he fought to hide from her. *Uh-huh. Sure, you wouldn't.*

At those words, his smile broke free and despite her playful annoyance, Wren soaked in the feeling his smile gave her. It was like being bathed in the sun's rays.

Gabriel's confused gaze bounced between her and Silas in the growing silence of their private conversation,

"You'll get used to that," Aeron said. "Or maybe not. It's incredibly weird."

"They can now communicate through their bond," Jerricha

supplied for Gabriel, who looked beyond confused. "And Aeron is right. It is incredibly weird."

Gabriel turned to Wren and peered at her intently, as if he could look under her skin and see the golden chain that connected her to her mate. "That is fascinating."

Wren shifted under Gabriel's stare. "Well, if you are done looking at me like a science experiment, then let's head to the study and get this over with."

* * *

Everyone crammed into the study once again. Wren looked around the small space—the large desk with two chairs in front, the bookshelves filled with books she had spent her childhood reading, and the floor-to-ceiling window behind the desk with views of the manor grounds. She hated this room. After her arranged engagement, every conversation that took place in this study had further turned the room into a place of dread. She had a feeling this meeting would be no different.

Gabriel and Hawthorne were ready to share what they had discovered on their monthslong journey. The general and Queen Elowyn were seated behind the desk, while Jerricha and Wren were in the chairs in front of the desk. Silas was perched on the armrest of Wren's chair and Aeron leaned casually against the fireplace, his arms crossed over his chest.

The tension in the room was suffocating as everyone waited impatiently for the news. Silas's hand on her knee prevented her from bouncing it, so instead she worried her bottom lip between her teeth.

"We believe we have found the location of the Crown," Hawthorne began with no further ado. "Based on what we found, we think the Crown never left Edein Island. It is still in the hands of the Elementals."

Hawthorne's eyes shone with excitement. This was his element. Teaching and learning new facets about their world are what Hawthorne lived for. When Wren first arrived in Valasia, he was the one to educate her on the history of the Fae and how to use her magic.

"What proof do you have of this?" Queen Elowyn asked. Her silver-gray eyes were sharp as she leaned forward in her chair.

"There is a guard at the manor who came to me with a suggestion." Gabriel shifted on his feet. "One of his ancestors had pulled as many books and maps as he could from his town's library before the Dark Fae destroyed it. They killed him for it, but he never gave the Dark Fae the location of the hidden stash." He sat on the edge of the desk before continuing, "That secret has been passed down from family member to family member. The guard thought we might find something useful in the collection they had saved."

"And we did." Hawthorne took up the story. "There are books and scrolls in the collection older than what we have in Valasia." He rubbed his chin in thought. "It makes me wonder if there are more hidden stashes throughout the kingdoms. If any other brave souls attempted to save their histories before the Dark Fae destroyed them." He shook himself out of his thoughts. "We found a book with very detailed descriptions and explanations of the Elementals. Too detailed to be made up. What we read coincides with the little we know of them. It also mentioned the Obsidian Artifacts, the Crown specifically, and the location of Edein Island."

"Give us the details," his queen demanded. "Everything we need to know in order to find the Crown."

Wren listened intently as Hawthorne explained what they had found in the book. The Elementals were powerful Fae, capable of controlling raw magic, the very essence that made up the magic that the Light and Dark Fae each possessed. It is not known how the Light and Dark Fae were descended from the Elementals and the book did not explain it.

King Adriel, the first king of the Light Fae, and King Bhardyl, the first king of the Dark Fae, requested the Elementals create the Obsidian Artifacts. They infused their magic in the Crown and Sword, respectively, and the Elementals created the Eyeglass but did not infuse any magic in it. The book did not explain the purpose of the Artifacts, only that the Fae kings traveled to Edein Island in secret.

"And how do you know the Elementals have the Crown?" Silas asked, draping his arm around Wren's shoulders.

"The book mentioned something about a disagreement," Gabriel supplied. "The Elementals didn't want the Artifacts to leave Edein Island. King Adriel agreed, King Bhardyl did not. Adriel left the Crown in their possession, but Bhardyl stole the Sword and the Eyeglass." He shifted his weight on the desk to look at Queen Elowyn. "Somehow, Adriel got the Eyeglass from Bhardyl, which is how the Light Fae came to possess it."

"So, we still don't know a lot," Wren mused aloud. "Just that the Elementals created the Artifacts, and they currently have possession of the Crown." She stopped and looked at Hawthorne. "How do we know the Elementals are even still alive? It was so long ago anything could have happened, and no one has heard anything about them in hundreds of years."

He shrugged. "That is a risk we will have to take. One of many, if we are to travel to Edein Island."

Gabriel stood from the desk and rifled through some maps until he found the one he wanted. He spread it on the desk and they all gathered around to hear what he had to say. "The map we found depicted Edein Island here." He pointed to a spot in the ocean, southeast of Alynthi Harbor. "We estimate it would take two weeks to travel there."

"That's it? Two weeks isn't a very long time." Silas studied the map, brows furrowed. "How has no one discovered the island yet?"

"That is where more of the risks will come into play," Hawthorne answered. "The Elementals have set a perimeter around the island, a magical barrier. Not too unlike the wards we have placed in the pass to Valasia."

Wren shuddered, remembering the magic of the pass and how it had tried to taunt her off the path into the mist. "What kind of magical barrier?"

"Storms," Gabriel said. "Violent storms and raging seas."

"And sirens and sea dragons," Hawthorne murmured, almost too low for anyone to hear.

"Excuse me?" Aeron leaned forward, eyes on Hawthorne. "Did you say sirens and sea dragons?"

"I'm afraid I did."

"Well, that sounds like a splendid adventure," Aeron exclaimed, rolling his eyes.

"And my guess is it is like the wards in the pass. We won't be able to access our magic, and Wren and Silas won't be able to feel their bond."

Nerves flared at the thought of not having the bond. Wren locked gazes with Silas. *How in the world will we ever make it to the island?* she asked.

Silas didn't answer, instead he looked at Jerricha and a wicked grin split his face. "I think we need to pay Captain Cassidy a visit."

Jerricha groaned and slunk farther into her chair.

Aeron looked between Silas and Jerricha, eyes wide. "You cannot possibly be thinking of sailing to Edein Island. With a pirate, no less!"

Wren raised one brow and looked at Silas. "A pirate? You keep strange company, mate."

Silas sent a surge of warmth through the bond at her use of the word *mate*. "Cassidy Lochlan is an old friend."

Aeron snorted. "If that's what you want to call it." He approached the desk and eyed the map. "How do you propose we get good ol' Captain Cassidy to agree to sail through a magical barrier containing storms, sirens, and sea dragons?"

"Oh, I have no doubt he will agree." Silas smiled confidently. "He owes me."

Chapter Two

"Well, I've stayed in worse places." Hands on her hips, Wren looked around the Eagle's Nest, the inn the group was staying at overnight. They had left Hillwood a week ago, traveling through Ellendyr to Avisten. They had just crossed inside the border of Avisten, when Gabriel decided to send word to his men along the border. He wanted more up to date information before heading any further into the country. As a result, the group had stopped at the inn to meet with him, and take advantage of the food and beds the inn could provide.

Wren was travel-worn and more than ready for a night at an inn. She looked around the room again. It looked like a typical inn and dining room—battered round tables were scattered around the well-worn room. A few patrons were already settled into the rickety wooden chairs, mugs of ale in hand.

Gabriel gave Wren a questioning look at her statement and Silas chuckled, remembering the run-down inn they had briefly stopped at on their journey to Valasia.

Silas slipped his hand into Wren's and led her across the

floor to an empty table. "The floors at least look like they won't collapse."

Wren shuddered as she sat. The memory of Lendyr's End was not a memory she wanted to relive. "Hopefully, the townsfolk are more welcoming," she murmured.

Seated around the scarred wooden table, Wren, Silas, Gabriel, Jerricha, Aeron, and Hawthorne ate their dinner while waiting for Gabriel's informant to arrive.

"What is the plan from here?" Wren asked as she sipped from her water cup.

"Depending on the information we get," Gabriel said, "we will keep heading toward Addler's Cove, where we will hopefully find Silas's pirate."

"Addler's Cove is where Cassidy stays when he's not on the seas," Silas confirmed. "We may have to wait for him, but he will eventually end up there."

"Why exactly does he owe you a favor?" Hawthorne voiced the question they had all been wondering.

"I'm not sure you want to know." Jerricha snorted. "Ow!" she exclaimed when Wren felt Silas kick his cousin under the table.

You really have to tell me this story this sometime, Wren said through the bond, giving Silas an exasperated look.

He just chuckled and pressed a kiss to her temple.

The door opened and Gabriel's man approached. "Sir," he said, bowing to Gabriel.

"Jenkins, it's good to see you." Gabriel nodded and gestured to an empty chair. "Sit. What news do you have for us?"

Settling into the chair with a sigh, Jenkins looked at Gabriel as he spoke, "There has been an increased presence of Dark Fae in both Ellendyr and Avisten. We have been keeping track of one band in particular. They began moving around the time you left Hillwood, and they appear to be heading roughly parallel to you."

Silas sat up straighter in his chair. "What does that mean? You think they are following us?"

Jenkins shrugged. "Hard to know for sure, but it is a possibility."

"Seems a little convenient for a band of Dark Fae to be heading in a similar direction as us," Aeron said, looking at Silas. "The last thing we need is them following us to the Crown."

"What can we do about it?" Wren asked, looking between Gabriel and Silas.

"Not a lot we can do," Gabriel replied. "We'll have to monitor their movements. Jenkins, can you spare the men to do that?"

"Yes, sir. I have a few I can spare. I'll have them send reports with a falcon."

It had taken him years, but Gabriel had raised and trained ten falcons to deliver messages between outposts in Ellendyr. The result was worth it. He and his men could communicate important news quicker than a man on horse delivering a message. Wren had always been a little jealous. She loved animals, and falcons were beautiful creatures.

"Perfect," Gabriel replied and rose to walk with Jenkins out the door.

The rest of dinner passed in silence, everyone lost in their own thoughts. Jerricha yawned, causing a cascade of yawns to follow from everyone else. Wren Snd Silas bid the group goodnight and headed to their room.

"Do you think that band of Dark Fae will be a problem?" Wren asked as she got ready for bed.

Their room was small but pleasant. A bed big enough for both of them sat against a wall. Along the other wall was a dresser and washbasin, and below the window was a small desk. Silas had thrown his shirt over the chair and Wren eyed it. She undressed and pulled Silas's discarded shirt over her head. His scent lingered on the soft fabric and her heart did a happy little thump in her chest when she breathed it in.

"Honestly, it worries me a bit." Silas was already sprawled in bed, hands behind his head on the pillows and sheet tucked low around his waist. His eyes tracked her as she walked toward him, a dangerous glint sparking in the green depths. "But, like Gabriel said, there isn't much we can do about it right now." He snaked a hand out and wrapped it around Wren's wrist, pulling her down on top of him. "Do you know how much I love seeing you in nothing but my shirt?"

Wren's toes curled at the velvety softness of his voice. She ran her hand down his bare chest, fingers tracing the grooves of his muscles. She opened her mouth to respond, but yawned instead, jaw cracking wide. Tears sprang to the corners of her eyes at the intensity of the yawn.

Silas laughed and tucked her into his side. Kissing the top of her head, he said, "It's been a long day. Get some sleep, love."

She tried to argue but another yawn escaped. His hand moved in large circles on her back and she fought to keep her eyes open. The soothing strokes of Silas's hand pushed all thoughts out of her head and she was asleep before she knew it.

Silas woke to Wren thrashing in bed, murmuring incoherently in her sleep. He sat up and shook her gently. "Wren, wake up."

She came awake with a gasp, hand flying to her heart. Sweat dampened her brow and her breathing was heavy and uneven. He could feel her panic and fear through the bond as she looked around the room with wide eyes before her gaze landed on him. A sob broke free and she collapsed in a boneless heap on top of him.

"Shh, love. It was just a dream. I'm right here." He kissed her sweaty temple and ran his hand down her hair and back. Her tears landed warmly on his chest and he wrapped his arms around her, trying to hold her together as she fell apart.

Ever since the battle at Hillwood where he almost died, Wren had been having nightmares. It devastated him knowing he was the reason she thrashed awake so many nights and there was nothing he could do to make it stop. He wanted nothing more than to take her pain away, but all he could do was hold her when she woke scared and crying, and reassure her he was still with her.

Silas lay awake long after Wren had cried herself to sleep. His thoughts kept turning to the band of Dark Fae who were most likely following them. They were after the Crown and Wren. He knew this without a doubt and that worried him. This would be the perfect opportunity for them to get both, and he wouldn't allow them to take his mate. Looking at Wren, finally sleeping peacefully, he came to a decision.

Easing out of bed, Silas quickly dressed and headed for Gabriel's room. The man opened the door, hair mussed and eyes blurry with sleep.

"What is it?" Gabriel awoke instantly at the sight of Silas, alert for any sign of danger.

Silas pushed into the room. "I'm going after the Dark Fae."

Gabriel just stared at him, blinking owlishly.

"I'm going to find out what they are planning," Silas clarified. "I can't let them get close to Wren."

Gabriel sat on the edge of his bed, running his hand through his hair. "I'm assuming Wren doesn't know you plan on doing this?"

Silas didn't answer.

"No," Gabriel said finally. "This is a bad idea. I understand the need to know what they are doing, but sending you out there is not the way to do it. Especially if my sister doesn't know. Send Aeron instead."

"There is no one else who can go," Silas replied evenly. "If something goes wrong, I'm the strongest and I'll be able to get out."

Gabriel ran a hand down his face. "I don't like it. Wren will not handle it well."

"I know." Silas sighed, and he regretted making this decision. "But I can't risk this band of Dark Fae coming after us, after Wren. We need to know what their plan is."

Gabriel stared at him for a moment and Silas could have sworn he saw the thoughts flitting through his brain as he ran through different scenarios. "Fine," Gabriel at last relented with a sigh. "But leave the Sword here. We can't risk them getting their hands on that again." Gabriel stood to follow Silas down the hall to the stairs.

"I left it in our room," Silas replied at the top of the stairs before descending. "I'll meet you at Addler's Cove. I shouldn't be too far behind you." He stopped at the bottom of the stairs to look at Gabriel, his eyes serious. "Please keep Wren safe. Don't let anything happen to her."

"Always," Gabriel promised.

"And make sure she doesn't follow me."

"What about the bond? She'll be able to know exactly where you are."

Silas shook his head. "I can shield myself from the bond. She won't be able to sense me." He felt ill at the thought of doing that to her, but he had little choice. She would never let him do this alone, and they had to know what the Dark Fae were planning. There was no way he was going to let her get close enough to their enemy where they could take her again.

With a last look at Gabriel, Silas left, leaving Wren sleeping in the bed, unaware he was gone.

* * *

Wren woke the next morning and reached across the bed for Silas. Her hand met cool, empty sheets. She snuggled back under the covers and opened her mind to the bond. *Where are you?* she sent along the chain between them. Her words bounced back. She reached out with her mind and found a wall of swirling shadows she couldn't get through. There had never been a time when she couldn't feel Silas through the bond, but right now all she felt was emptiness. Her heart stopped, then started, then stopped again. It finally began beating so fast she felt it would erupt out of her chest.

Wren sat up quickly, blankets flying every which way as she scrambled from the bed. She looked around the room they were sharing—the Sword was lying by her bags, but Silas's bags were gone. Barely remembering to pull her pants on, Wren ran barefoot down the hall.

"Where is he?" she exclaimed as she pushed into Gabriel's room without knocking.

"Shit, Wren." Gabriel jumped, placing a hand on his chest. "Knock next time."

"Where is he, Gabriel?" She stopped directly in front of him, hands clenched into fists at her sides. He was so much taller than her she had to tilt her head up to glare into his eyes. Normally the height difference didn't bother her. Right now, she wished she were wearing heels, anything to put them on more even footing.

Gabriel looked around the room, refusing to meet her stare. "Why don't you sit down?" When Wren lifted one brow and didn't move, Gabriel sighed. "He left."

Wren's heart sank, as an icy feeling grew in her stomach inching outward through her limbs. "What do you mean *left*?" She placed her hands on Gabriel's chest and pushed.

He conceded a step and looked warily at his sister.

"Where did he go?" She could barely keep her voice under control.

Gabriel reached out as if to grab Wren's arm, but he hesitated. "He's looking into the band of Dark Fae. We need to know what their plan is."

Wren wasn't breathing. Her mind detached from her body, and she felt like the world was spinning around her. Silas had left, on his own, to scout out the Dark Fae? And he didn't tell her? She whirled around and ran out the door, stopping in her room to shove her feet into her boots before she hit the stairs at a dead run.

"Wren!" Gabriel shouted behind her, his feet pounding on the floor after her. "Aeron, a little help here!"

Wren was already halfway down the stairs, taking them two at a time. She was going so fast she didn't see Aeron until it was too late. It was like running into a brick wall. The impact was so hard she grunted and rebounded, arms flailing to find her balance. Unfazed, Aeron reached out and steadied her before she could fall.

"Move, Aeron." Balance regained, she reached up to push him out of the way, but he grabbed her hands and held tight.

"I can't let you go." He gave her an apologetic look. "I'm sorry, princess."

"I command you to move, as your princess."

He shook his head. "Silas would kill me if I let you leave."

"I need to find him, Aeron," she begged. "I can't feel him. There is nothing but vast emptiness in my head."

"I'm sorry, Wren."

Wren stared him down for a moment before screaming in

frustration. Breathing heavily, she turned around and pushed past Gabriel, who was standing on the stairs. It might have been childish, but she stomped on each step as she climbed. The need to expel her anger and fear overrode her common sense.

Once in her room behind the closed door, she eyed the window on the far side of the room. Gabriel's footsteps on the stairs behind her told her he had followed her. She knew he would camp out in front of her door to keep her from running after Silas. If she couldn't go out the front door, she would find another way. She let out a small, humorless laugh. Gabriel should know her better. A locked door wouldn't stop her from getting to her mate.

Wren unlatched the window and leaned out, assessing the best way down. The bricks were uneven, and she thought it would be fairly easy to descend the wall. Sitting on the ledge, she swung her legs out and grabbed the sill with her hands, twisting her body so she was facing the wall. With her heart in her throat, Wren stretched her leg until her foot touched an exposed brick.

Sucking in a deep breath, she let go of the window and grabbed on to another brick, the rough surface scraping her fingers. Slowly, she continued to lower herself from one brick to the next, focusing on one foot at a time. Before she knew it, both feet were on solid ground and she released a shaky breath, calming her trembling limbs.

She dashed toward the stables, already making plans in her head. The Dark Fae were north of them, which was about all she knew. She would head north and hope to cross Silas's path, or at least hope she would be able to sense him through the bond the closer she got to him. Wren skidded into the stables and halted.

"Not you, too?" she groaned, stomach sinking as she spied Jerricha leaning against her horse's stall.

Jerricha uncrossed her arms and linked her arm with Wren's. "I'm sorry." She did sound apologetic as she grimaced. "I promised Silas I wouldn't let you go after him."

"Jerricha, please." Wren dug her heels into the ground, not letting Jerricha lead her out of the stables. "Let me go." Wren blinked furiously, fighting back the tears that were threatening to fall.

"He'll be back before you know it." Jerricha pulled Wren out of the stables. "Silas is powerful, more powerful than you realize. He will be fine."

Wren knew how powerful he was. His strength had coursed through her veins when they merged their magic together and his was infinitely stronger than hers.

"He shut me out, Jerricha." Wren's voice cracked with her attempt to hold back emotion. She pressed a hand to her chest. "I can't feel him. There is just a black wall where he should be and I can't get past it."

"I know, and I know I can't say anything to make you feel better." Jerricha squeezed her arm. "But don't do to Silas what he did to you. If he returns and you aren't here, it will destroy him. Utterly and completely destroy him."

She was right, and Wren hated to admit that. It was awful for her not knowing where he was, but if she wasn't here when he returned, she couldn't imagine what he would do. He was so much more protective, so much more intense. If she was ready to burn the world to the ground to get to him, he would be so much worse. Wren sagged in Jerricha's grasp.

"I'll make a compromise," Wren said unwillingly. "I'll give him one day after we arrive at Addler's Cove. If he hasn't met up with us by then, I'm going to look for him."

Jerricha watched Wren out of the corner of her eye. "Fine," she agreed. "If he hasn't returned by then, I'll join you in the search."

Wren felt better, slightly. She was still a mess of worry and nerves, and she still felt like someone had removed something vital from her. The empty silence in her head crawled down her spine, an uncomfortable feeling settling over her shoulders. But at least she had a plan. It would take them four more days to reach Addler's Cove and a long four days it would be.

Jerricha led them through the open space between the stables and the inn, the soft early morning sun just starting to warm their skin. Wren entered the inn to the surprised looks of Aeron and Gabriel.

"The window," Gabriel growled. "You climbed out the fucking window." He shook his head and turned to Aeron. "This is going to be exhausting."

Aeron nodded in agreement. "I'll take the window if you take the door." At Gabriel's nod, Aeron left through the front door to keep watch below her window, muttering something about giving Silas a piece of his mind.

Wren stomped up the stairs and slammed her door shut without saying a word to them. Nothing pleasant would come from her mouth, so she kept it shut. She leaned against the door and sank to the floor, no longer able to keep her tears at bay. Silas's presence in her mind had become a comfort to her, like a warm blanket on a winter day. Now she felt cold and alone, missing a piece of her very soul. Alone in the privacy of her room, Wren let the tears fall and didn't try to stop them.

Chapter Three

The four-day journey to Addler's Cove was torture for Wren. She spent much of that time inside her own head, poking, prodding, and pounding on that wall Silas had built around the bond. Hawthorne said there was no way to break through without Silas letting her but that didn't stop her from trying.

The group traveled in silence. She was moody and cranky, and furious with them for letting Silas go and keeping her here. Her anger at her companions was on a short leash. After Aeron had tried to engage her conversation and received a tongue-lashing that left him gaping at her, her companions mostly left her alone. They kept a close watch on her at all times though, and she felt like a prisoner—she couldn't even go to the bathroom without Jerricha following.

To her relief, they at least traveled quickly, pushing the horses as fast as they could. On the fourth day, the scattered trees in open fields on either side of the road became fewer, replaced by random homes and farmland. In the distance, the wall surrounding Addler's Cove appeared, a dark gray line on the horizon.

Wren thought her anxiety would ease when they reached Addler's Cove but it only intensified. The city surrounded the large harbor with buildings made of graying wood and white-washed brick. The cobbled streets were winding and confusing, with no rhyme or reason to their pattern. It made Wren think of a drunk giant throwing buildings and streets around until he was happy. The smell of salt and fish permeated everything, and the squawking of gulls and shouts of shopkeepers crying their wares was almost overwhelming.

Wren entered the Wandering Voyager, the inn they had planned on staying at, and went straight to the bar, ignoring the rest of her surroundings. She had to fight back the fear that tried to take control of her when the innkeeper told her there was no one there with Silas's name. Gabriel placed a hand on her shoulder, which she promptly shook off and walked away. As she was leaving the inn, she overheard Gabriel asking after Captain Cassidy, but she didn't wait to hear the innkeeper's reply. Her fear and anxiety made her restless. She left the inn and headed toward the harbor, meandering through the winding streets with Jerricha following behind. Wren found an empty crate on the docks and sat, letting her mind wander.

She observed the sailors loading and unloading cargo from the many ships anchored in the harbor. There were so many vessels of different sizes and shapes. She had never been on a seafaring ship before and she was looking forward to this part of the journey—at least if Silas ever returned.

"What is Cassidy's ship like?" Wren asked Jerricha to distract herself.

Jerricha grinned. "His ship is his baby. Whatever you do, don't insult it. He sails a galleon." This meant nothing to Wren, who just nodded at Jerricha's description. "Cassidy is one of the most dangerous pirates of our time," the Viking-like woman continued. "He and his crew are well known on the seas. He is a very wealthy pirate, which means he is good at what he does. With his skills and ruthlessness, he is probably our best chance at making it through this magical barrier."

Wren shuddered at the thought of the barrier. That was one aspect of this journey she was not looking forward to. Another magical barrier intent on hurting them. Sighing, she stood from the crate and began the walk back to the inn. "Tomorrow morning," she said to Jerricha. "I'm leaving to find Silas. You guys won't be able to stop me."

"I won't try to stop you, but I will come with you. Silas will kill me if I let something happen to you." She jumped out of the way of a wagon trundling down the streets to the docks.

"Well, he should have thought about that before he left without a word." The irritation that flooded her at Jerricha's statement made her words sharper than she intended.

"True. I don't blame you for being mad. What he did was wrong." Jerricha returned to Wren's side and draped her arm over her shoulder. "I try not to pick sides, but this time, I'm with you."

Back at the inn there was still no sign of Silas. She sat in an empty chair at the table her companions had commandeered. The sounds of the inn didn't register with the worry front and center in her mind. Gabriel slid a plate of food in front of her and Wren picked at it distractedly. Her appetite had disappeared since Silas left—she was too full of worry to even think about food. What little she ate, she ate because Gabriel forced her to.

Not able to stomach any more, Wren pushed away from the table. "I'm going up. I'll see you in the morning." She looked at Jerricha when she said that. A silent command to be ready early. She was on the stairs when the door to the inn opened and the wall around the bond came down.

*   *   *

Silas had arrived at Addler's Cove later than he had wanted. Unfortunately, his horse had thrown a shoe, which delayed his journey back. As unmanly as it was, he was nervous about seeing Wren. He knew all too well the sharp blade of her tongue when she was angry, and he knew she would be livid with him for his disappearing act. The entire journey to Addler's Cove he had thought of and thrown out multiple ways to make it up to her. None of them seemed good enough for his mate.

He opened the door to the inn and dropped the wall around the bond. His gaze immediately fell on Wren. Her back was to him, but he could see her spine stiffen as she climbed the stairs. She paused, one foot on the next step, hand on the railing in a white-knuckled grip. She turned slowly, eyes alighting on him without fail. A breath rushed out of her and she placed her hand on her throat.

Silas didn't know what to do. Her emotions through the bond were a whirlwind. Relief, anger, hurt, love. He just stood in the door as she stalked down the steps and approached.

"You're okay?" she asked quietly, eyes full of emotion. "You're not hurt?"

He shook his head, unable to find his voice as he looked at his mate. Her blue eyes were like fire at the moment, her cheeks flushed in what he was guessing was anger. She was beautiful.

She nodded and drew her arm back before she punched him in the stomach so hard he doubled over, gasping for air. His breath came in wheezing pants as he looked up through watering eyes.

"Never do that again." Her voice was deadly quiet, her eyes shining with unshed tears.

He opened his mouth to respond, but she turned on her heel and stomped up the steps. Groaning, he wrapped his arm around his middle. Damn, she punched hard.

"Well, that's the least you deserve," Jerricha drawled from her seat at a table.

Chuckling, Gabriel looked at the empty spot on the stairs Wren had vacated. "You might want to let her calm down before trying to talk to her or you'll end up with a broken nose." He rubbed his own nose, remembering the time Wren had done just that to him. "Sit and tell us what you learned."

Sighing, Silas fought his instincts to go after Wren and collapsed in an empty chair at their table. "The Dark Fae aren't following us exactly, but they have heard the rumor of the Crown being on Edein Island," Silas explained. "However, they have no idea where the island is. They are hoping to get answers here, at Addler's Cove. So, we need to be on the seas before they get here." He leaned back in his chair, eyeing the steps. "Any news on Cassidy?"

Gabriel shook his head. "Apparently, he left three months ago for a mission. No one knows what it was or how long he planned to be gone."

Silas thought for a minute in the silence that followed Gabriel's statement. "His missions typically last three to four months. Let's hope it's closer to three this time. I give the Dark Fae a week until they arrive. They won't be traveling quickly." He gave his companions a feral grin. "I may have cut their horses leads, then spooked them. They will be traveling on foot to Addler's Cove."

Silas answered a few more questions, his gaze constantly straying to the stairs, before Aeron said, "Go on up and talk to Wren. There isn't much else we can discuss tonight."

Silas gave him a grateful look before heading upstairs. He hesitated in front of the door. The anger he felt pulsing through the bond set him on edge. This was not going to go well for him. Pushing open the door, he stepped inside. Wren was standing by the window looking out into the harbor through the dying evening light. She was only wearing one of his shirts and Silas's desire became a live wire inside him. Pushing those thoughts aside, he closed the door and cautiously approached.

"Wren," he began, but stopped with a flinch when she whirled around and pointed a finger at him.

"No, you listen," she said, digging her finger into his chest. "This?"—she waved her hand back and forth between them— "this won't work if you keep pulling stunts like that. We are a team, Silas. It's not just you anymore. Any decision you make involves me too."

His heart cracked at the pain he felt through the bond and the tears gathering on her lashes.

"Do you know what it felt like to wake up and find you gone? And not only gone but unreachable through the bond?" Her whispered words felt like a knife to his heart. "How would you have felt if I had done that to you?"

Gods, she was right. He would have lost all control. He would have left bodies and leveled buildings in his wake to get to her. She was so much stronger than him to have managed without losing it completely.

Silas closed his eyes and released a breath. "You're right. I shouldn't have left without talking to you first. And blocking the bond..." He shook his head and opened his eyes, looking deep into hers. "I'm sorry, Wren. I knew how much we needed that information, and the thought of you insisting on going with me terrified me." He reached out, tentatively running his fingers down her arm to her hand. "I made a mistake. I hurt you, and I hate that I'm the reason for your pain." He grasped her hand and tugged her gently. She allowed him to pull her closer, but her tears spilled over, tracking down her cheeks. Each one felt like a stain on his soul.

"Just talk to me next time, please." She rested her forehead against his chest, her words muffled by the fabric of his shirt. "Any decisions that need to be made, we make together. As a team. Don't leave me alone and in the dark again."

He pressed a kiss to the top of her head and wrapped his arms around her. "I promise. We'll talk everything through from here on out."

Her arms came around him, wrapping around his middle. She looked up at him through her lashes, chin resting on his chest. "I missed you," she whispered.

He marveled at how he could ever get so lucky to have Wren in his life. She deserved so much more than he could offer. He almost couldn't handle the fact she chose him. The urge to apologize again, to tell her how sorry he was for hurting her, was strong.

He wanted to tell her how much he loved her and what she meant to him, but words seemed inadequate at this moment. He would never be able to tell her all of that, so he decided to show her. With his mouth, his tongue, his body. He would worship her so she knew all the words he wanted to say.

He wrapped the length of her hair around his wrist, tugging gently on the silken strands to tilt her head back so he could better access her mouth. She opened for him and he slipped inside, loving the taste of her on his tongue. He reached a hand down to slide under the shirt she wore—his shirt, he remembered with satisfaction. The smooth expanse of her skin drove him crazy as he ran his hand up her thigh. He trailed his fingers up, over the flat plane of her belly, over her breast, pausing at her nipple. He pinched the peak between his fingers and she rewarded him with a breathy moan. Impatient, he tugged the shirt the rest of the way off and let it drop to the floor at their feet.

Wren reached up to unbutton his shirt and leaned forward to run her tongue from the exposed skin of his chest up the column of his throat. He closed his eyes at the feeling, grinding his hips against hers. He tore his shirt off and dropped it on top of his other shirt on the floor. Silas pressed Wren against the wall, wedging his leg between hers. Her body pressed tightly against his felt like home. He kissed her again until they were both breathless.

He tore his mouth from hers and rained kisses down her neck, chest, and belly. On his knees, he grasped one of her legs and placed it over his shoulder. With one hand on her hips to hold her in place, he lowered his mouth to her core and ran his tongue down her center. Wren bucked against the wall, gasping and pleading for more, as her fingers knotted in his hair. The taste of her almost undid him. He worked his tongue and added his fingers, keeping her pinned to the wall. The more she writhed against him, the more he worked her until she came on his tongue with a cry that was sure to be heard downstairs.

Wren leaned against the wall, breathing heavily as Silas slowly stood. Her hands went to his pants, unbuckling his belt and pushing them to the floor. He stepped out of them as he moved closer to her, molding his mouth to hers once again. Grabbing her hips, he lifted her and walked to the bed, all without breaking the kiss. He laid her gently on the bed and sat back on his heels, eyes traveling the length of her body.

"You are gorgeous," he said hoarsely. "Absolutely perfect."

As he leaned over her, she stopped him with her hands on his chest. Shaking her head, she grinned slyly, eyes twinkling with mischief. "Uh-uh, not this time." She pushed Silas to his back on the bed and straddled him.

Desire shot through him, fast and hot. He looked at her

through lowered lashes and gave her a half smirk, settling his hands behind his head. If this is what she wanted, this is what she would get. Wren rose on top of him and reached between them to position him at her entrance. His breath caught as she met his eyes and slowly lowered herself onto his arousal. Her eyes closed and her head tipped back, lips parting on a soft sigh. He brought his hands to her hips when she started moving on him. Slowly and deliciously. He groaned at the feeling of her around him, so tight and warm. She rode him, gaze locked on his until he couldn't take it anymore.

Lifting her off, he flipped her onto her stomach and grabbed her hips, angling them so he could enter her with one hard thrust. She gasped, grabbing the blankets and turning her head to look at him. The desire shining in her eyes had him growling as he moved one hand between her breasts and pulled her up against his chest. His hand slid up and lightly held her throat as the other slid lower, parting her folds. Her head fell back against his shoulder and she panted as he moved his hips.

He loved the noises she made as he pleasured her and he would wring every one of them out of her.

With a curse, he forced himself to slow down. This was about her tonight, not him. He circled the bundle of nerves at the apex of her thighs and she clenched around him.

"Silas," she begged, breathless. "Please, please, please."

"Please what?" he whispered in her ear, tugging her lobe with his teeth.

She moaned and grabbed his wrist, trying to move his hand where she wanted it. "Please, I need..." She stopped with a gasp as he bit her neck, then ran his tongue along the hurt.

"What do you need, Wren?" His finger danced around that bundle of nerves, but he didn't move them closer.

"Make me come, please, Silas." Her breathy moans and begging did it for him. He thrust into her, hard, while his finger finally pressed down on the bundle of nerves. Wren screamed as she came around him, clenching as he continued thrusting in and out. He found his own release at the same time. Groaning, he buried his face in her neck, inhaling her honeysuckle scent.

When he finally stopped moving, they collapsed to the bed on their stomachs. Wren opened her eyes slowly and gave him a satisfied smile.

"I..." She stopped and shook her head slowly. "I have nothing to say."

He brushed her hair away from her sweaty face. "You don't have to say anything." He gathered her in his arms and held her close to him.

He didn't fall asleep until Wren's body relaxed and her breathing slowed. Only then did he kiss her shoulder and close his eyes, content with his mate sleeping in his arms.

Chapter Four

Wren and Silas lounged in bed most of the next morning. She soaked up the feeling of his skin on hers and the way he lazily rubbed his hand over her body, eliciting shivers at his touch.

"What's the plan for today?" she asked as she ran her hand over the tight muscles ribbing his abdomen.

"Well, I was hoping to question a few more people about Cassidy's whereabouts." He tangled his legs with hers and pulled her closer. "Then I was going to continue trying to make up to you. What would you like to do today?"

"You don't have to do anything, Silas." She lifted her head from his chest to look into his eyes. "It's behind us. You made a mistake and I'm sure it won't be the last mistake either of us makes."

He kissed her forehead, eyes closing. "I don't deserve you," he murmured against her skin.

They eventually dressed and headed down for breakfast. When Wren reached the bottom of the stairs, her steps faltered. Gabriel and Jerricha were sitting at a table in the corner and both pairs of eyes locked on to Wren and Silas as they reached the bottom. Jerricha grinned deviously at them and actually waggled her eyebrows. Gabriel grimaced and refused to meet Wren's eyes. Her face flamed hot knowing there was no way they hadn't heard them last night. The whole inn had to have heard them.

Silas passed Wren on the steps and pinched her bottom while giving her a knowing smirk. She smacked his hand away and fortified herself, walking to the table for breakfast.

"What do you two plan on doing on this beautiful day?" Silas asked as he grabbed Jerricha's plate and dug into the meat and eggs on it.

Jerricha threw a piece of bread at him and snatched her plate back. "Get your own food," she growled.

"We were going to check out some other options to cross the ocean, in case Cassidy doesn't get back in time," Gabriel replied, sliding his plate and what was on it toward Jerricha.

"Good plan." Silas reached across and snagged another piece of bacon from Jerricha's plate. "We are going to see if we can find any more information on Cassidy's whereabouts."

Wren grabbed the bacon from Silas's hand and passed it back to Jerricha. "She is going to stab you if you keep eating her food." She rolled her eyes as Silas pouted at her, but he kept his hands to himself at least. "Where are Aeron and Hawthorne?"

"Stocking up on supplies for the trip," Gabriel replied. "That way we can be ready as soon as we are able to set sail."

Wren and Silas didn't linger long. They set off in search of information, leaving the inn to the sound of Jerricha's curses after Silas snagged the last piece of bacon from her plate on their way out.

Silas led Wren to the docks. They spent most of the afternoon stopping in various inns and taverns, each less reputable than the last, asking after Captain Cassidy. No one could give any more information than they already had.

Wren didn't let the disappointment or anxiety get to her. The weather was perfect and the breeze off the ocean was energizing. Being in another new city was an experience Wren refused to let go to waste. She enjoyed the time with Silas, hanging on to every moment, every touch, every laugh. He bought her a deep-fried pastry filled with chocolate and cream and if Wren hadn't already been in love with him, that alone would have sealed the deal.

They slowly made their way to the docks, and the flurry of people around them increased the closer they got.

"Well, well, well," Silas drawled. "Look what we have here."

Wren brushed the remaining crumbs from her fingers and followed Silas's gaze. A midsize ship had recently docked in the harbor, sails drawn in tight while sailors unloaded cargo and did whatever else sailors do after a voyage. Wren was woefully ignorant of ships and sailing.

"Is that...?" she began, but stopped as a large man walked down the gangplank. Her mouth dropped open as her gaze raked the man up and down.

He was wearing a large black tricorn hat adorned with red-and-black feathers and a golden skull. Shirtless, his tan skin and prominent muscles were on display for all to see under his open dark red leather jacket lined in black fur. Gold metal and black leather straps wrapped around the cuffs. Crisscrossing leather belts encircled his trim waist, clearly not holding up his low-slung black leather pants tucked into knee-high boots. The man was sex personified.

Silas rolled his eyes. "Yes, that is Captain Cassidy." He leaned down to her ear. "And you're drooling."

Wren snapped her mouth shut.

Captain Cassidy approached, his gait a slow prowl as his gaze landed on Silas. A grin split his face and Wren's breath caught. He was a beautiful man. She curled her hands into fists to keep from running her fingers through his shaggy brown hair.

"Isn't this a surprise?" Cassidy said as he clasped Silas's forearm. His voice was deep and melodic.

Was there nothing about this man that wasn't attractive? His gaze shifted to Wren and instantly his features became predatory. His dark brown eyes traveled down Wren's body slowly and as he raised them, a small satisfied smile graced his perfect lips. Wren suddenly grew hot and cold at the look he was giving her, as if he was slowly undressing her in his mind.

"Cassidy," Silas drawled, arm tightening around Wren's waist. "Meet Wren, my mate." He put enough emphasis on *mate* to make his point clear.

One brow raised, Cassidy reached for Wren's hand, bowing low and pressing a lingering kiss to the top. "It is truly a plea-sure to meet you, Wren."

Flushing even deeper, Wren stood there, completely at a loss for words.

"Okay," Silas sighed and grabbed Wren's hand from Cassidy's. "That's enough of your flirting."

Cassidy chuckled, a deep sound that caused Wren to shiver. "Apologies, Silas. You know I can't help myself around beautiful women. Why don't you join me for drinks tonight? We have a lot of catching up to do."

"Perfect," Silas replied, tightening his grip even more around Wren's waist. "I actually have a favor to ask you."

Cassidy groaned and walked away. Turning to face Silas while continuing to walk backward, Cassidy spread his arms wide. "It's always a pleasure to see you again, Silas. The Siren's Song. I'll see you there."

Wren tilted her head to the side and watched Cassidy walk away, his backside perfect in his leather pants.

"Really?" Silas was staring at her.

She cleared her throat. "Well, he was ... interesting."

"I'm sure that's the word you're looking for." Laughing, Silas led her away from the docks and back to their inn.

* * *

Wren sat at the table already occupied by her companions. Plopping into the chair next to her, Silas grabbed Jerricha's mug and took a swig. "Guess who we ran into today?"

"You're going to run into my knife repeatedly if you don't stop stealing my food," Jerricha growled and snatched her mug back.

Wren sighed at their antics and smacked the back of Silas's head. "Captain Cassidy has returned. We are meeting him tonight."

Aeron sat up straighter in his chair. "Did you tell him what we need? And where are we meeting him?"

"No, I didn't. I figured a few drinks will help make him more pliable." Silas pulled Wren's chair closer so their thighs were touching. He draped an arm around her shoulders and continued, "And we're meeting at The Siren's Song."

"I hate that place," Jerricha groaned.

Wren leaned forward, arms on the table. "Why do you hate it?" Having lived a sheltered life until recently, Wren had never visited a city like this. Jerricha's comment piqued her interest.

"It is the seediest place in the city." She shuddered. "Crowded, dirty, rowdy."

"Tavern fights, prostitution, drunken sailors. The list goes on," Aeron added with a grin.

"Sounds like the perfect place for a pirate." Wren placed her hand on Silas's thigh. "It also sounds dangerous."

"It is." Silas ran a finger up the back of Wren's hand, sending shivers through her. "That's why—"

"Don't you dare say Wren and I will be staying behind," Jerricha said, knuckles turning white on the knife she was gripping.

"I wasn't going to say that." Silas eyed the knife warily. "I was going to say that's why Gabriel and Aeron will be coming as well."

Jerricha gave him a look that said she doubted that is what he was going to say. Wren said as much through the bond. *Nice save, mate. You almost got stabbed.*

He squeezed her hand, still resting on his thigh. *You have no faith in me. I would never suggest you stay behind when we plan on doing something dangerous.* His eyes glittered with amusement as he looked at her.

Wren snorted and turned her attention back to her companions. Aeron was complaining about having to come along. "Why don't you want to go? Rowdy taverns not your style?"

"I don't mind the tavern. It's Captain Cassidy I prefer to avoid."

Wren's brow furrowed. "Why is that?"

"Have you met him, princess?"

Wren laughed and felt her face flush as she remembered his intense stare and the way his kiss lingered on her hand. "Yes, I have. He was quite interesting."

Silas growled and Jerricha laughed. "She's not wrong about that. You better watch him around her, Silas." Jerricha looked at Wren, then said, "Better yet, maybe you should watch *her* around *him*." She cracked a grin at the glower Silas gave her.

"Just watch yourselves tonight," he muttered before

pushing his chair back and standing. "I'll be back." He made his way to the stairs and climbed them without a backward glance.

* * *

The streets of Addler's Cove were busy at night, filled with people searching for drink and companionship after a long day of work. Drunken sailors stumbled in and out of taverns, light and sound spilling into the streets through the open doors. Scantily clad women lingered in doors and alleyways, luring men with batted lashes and shimmied hips. Even with the sun long gone, the night was warm and a balmy breeze blew in off the sea.

Wren walked behind Jerricha, Gabriel, and Aeron, with Silas's hand clasped in hers. Her head swiveled back and forth taking in all the sights, sounds, and smells. All of this was still so new and incredibly exciting to her. The streets and canals of Alynthi held a certain air of dignity even in the late hours of night. Addler's Cove had forgone class and dropped straight into depravity. She loved it.

Wren had been reading Silas's feelings through the bond all evening. His annoyance was plain as day, but there was another emotion woven in. Something tangy and sour. She didn't like it and she couldn't figure out what it was. It was something she had never felt from him before. Suddenly, realization dawned on her.

"Oh my Gods," she exclaimed and pulled him to a stop. "You're jealous."

Silas's brows pulled down. "Jealous? I am not." At her pointed look, he sighed. "I'm not jealous. I just don't like the way Cassidy looks at you."

"Or the way I looked at him?" Wren grinned at Silas. A fresh burst of tangy jealousy shot down the bond. The shadowed look in his eyes made Wren's heart ache. "Silas." She placed her hands on his cheeks, making sure he was looking at her. "You know I don't want anyone else but you, right?"

A muscle ticked in his jaw under her palms and he tried to pull his head away. She grabbed on harder.

"I chose you, Silas, and I have no regrets. I would choose you again. I choose you every day." She made sure he was looking at her before she continued, "I know you think you don't deserve me, but you are wrong. You deserve so much more than you give yourself credit for."

The tangy sensation faded slightly, replaced by tenderness and awe. Wren stood on her toes and wrapped her arms around Silas's neck. She didn't mean for the kiss to be more than a gentle peck, but when her lips touched his, she forgot they were standing in the middle of the street. The kiss was entirely inappropriate for public view and Silas pulling her tighter to his body, his hands cupping her bottom, made it even more so.

Someone groaned in front of them. "Please stop. I don't particularly enjoy watching my sister shove her tongue in some-one's mouth."

Wren pulled away from Silas. "Ew, Gabriel, don't be gross." Wren glared at him.

Silas chuckled and laced his fingers through Wren's. Leaning down, he whispered in her ear, "Tonight, I might need you to remind me why I'm not jealous."

Wren's toes curled, but the happiness shining through the bond was all she needed at the moment.

Hand in hand, they followed the others through the streets of Addler's Cove to the front door of The Siren's Song. The entrance was in an alley near the docks. The dim lighting from the open door reflected off puddles of unknown substances on the uneven cobblestones.

Silas tightened his grip on her hand and leaned down to her ear. "Do not leave my side."

As they entered the inn, Wren didn't bother to tell him that would not be a problem. She stepped closer to him as the raucous sound of a band washed over them. Women in corsets and layered petticoats meandered through the crowd, carrying drinks and food to the patrons. Men of varying degrees of wealth eyed the skin spilling over the tops of the corsets and pinched the bottoms through the petticoats.

Laughter, cursing, and the clanking of dice rose over the sound of music. Wren did her best not to listen to the words of the song after she caught a few describing certain parts of a male's anatomy. The smell of stale sweat and beer made her stomach rebel and she wrinkled her nose. Sweat beaded on her brow almost immediately from the press of bodies filling the establishment.

Silas led them through the crowded room to the dimly lit back corner. Sitting in a booth with a woman perched on his lap was Captain Cassidy, his hand buried under the woman's skirts. Silas cleared his throat and Cassidy looked up, lust clouding his dark eyes.

Cassidy smirked at Silas and motioned with his head for them to take a seat at the table. His eyes traveled through the group, stopping on Jerricha. He grinned. "Well, well, well." He pushed the woman off his lap and slapped her bottom, sending her away with a huff. "Why don't you take a seat here, Jerricha?" He patted his lap, and Wren averted her eyes from the obvious bulge trying to escape his leather pants.

Gabriel stepped closer to Jerricha as she said, "I have never accepted that invitation. What makes you think I have changed my mind?"

"Never hurts to ask." Cassidy eyed Gabriel as he pulled a chair out for Jerricha. Snorting, Cassidy turned to Aeron.

"You're looking good, Aeron." Cassidy's gaze traveled the length of Aeron's body before raising to his face again. "Can I convince *you* to sit on my lap?"

Wren choked on a laugh at Aeron's expression, something between embarrassment and incredulity.

Silas pulled a chair out for Wren, then sat next to her, so close their thighs and arms touched. "It is always a pleasure to see you, Cassidy."

Cassidy raised a finger to a barmaid, then pointed to the table. "How long has it been? Three years?"

"Four," Jerricha mumbled. "And not long enough."

Cassidy placed a hand on his heart. "You wound me, darling."

They passed banter back and forth until the barmaid returned and placed drinks in front of them. Silas leaned his forearms on the table and leveled a stare at Cassidy. "We actually came to Addler's Cove looking for you."

"Whatever you think I did, I didn't do it," Cassidy said immediately.

Wren smiled, and Cassidy's gaze strayed to her. She quickly wiped her smile away when Silas tensed next to her.

"We need your help," Silas said, drawing Cassidy's attention away from Wren. "We need a captain to take us across the sea."

Cassidy's eyes glittered with interest. "Why me? There are plenty of ships in the harbor."

"You are the only one who can get us to our destination." Silas brushed a curl out of his eyes. "It's a dangerous journey and you are the only captain I would trust to get us there safely."

"What's in it for me?" Cassidy leaned forward, eyes intent on Silas.

"Name your price."

Cassidy leaned back in his chair, crossing his arms over his bare chest. "You must be desperate. Either that or this is an incredibly dangerous journey, to let me name my price." He glanced around the group, eyes narrowing. "What's the location?"

"Edein Island."

Cassidy laughed, the sound loud and rich. "Edein is a myth." He paused at the looks on all their faces. "You're serious."

"Edein Island is not a myth," Silas countered. "And we need to get there. Fast."

Cassidy shook his head. "If the myth is true, then sirens and sea dragons surround the island. Not to mention powerful storms. No way will I risk my ship and my crew."

"You owe me," Silas said so quietly the tavern's din almost swallowed his words.

Cassidy's eyes widened in shock. "No, no, no." He shook his head. "What you did does not compare to sailing my ship through storms and mythical creatures."

"You would be in jail right now, better yet, hanging from the gallows, if it weren't for me."

"I could have gotten away without your help," Cassidy countered. "Besides, if I recall correctly, the twins you used to aid in the distraction weren't too uneasy on the eye."

Wren's ears perked up at that comment. She slowly turned her head to look at Silas with wide eyes. *Twins?* she asked down the bond.

Silas just smiled at Cassidy, a small smile that didn't reach his eyes. He did, however, squeeze Wren's thigh.

Cassidy sighed, running a hand down his face. "Gold," he finally said. "I want lots of gold for this."

Silas smiled. "Deal."

Wren sat back in her seat and removed Silas's hand from her thigh. *Where the hell are we going to get gold for him?*

I talked to your grandmother before we left. She said to offer him whatever he wants. She will give us what we need.

Wren startled. She had no idea Silas had talked to Queen Elowyn before they left, or that she had offered them anything.

"When can you be ready to sail?" Silas asked Cassidy.

Cassidy studied Silas before replying, "Two days. My crew needs time to rest before this voyage, and I'll need to get some supplies."

Silas smiled and held out a hand. Cassidy clasped his wrist and rolled his eyes.

"May the Gods save and protect us," he muttered, dismissing them.

Chapter Five

The *Ruby Maiden* bobbed in the harbor. Cassidy's ship was a midsize ship with its sails currently tied down. The figure head on the front of the ship was of a bare-chested woman with fire-red hair blowing in the sea breeze. It looked like a pirate ship, at least as far as Wren was concerned.

Cassidy glanced over to where Wren and Jerricha stood on the dock and smiled. He sauntered down the gangplank, his gait flowing with the rolling waves. He looked over their attire and his grin spread wider. "Well, don't you two beautiful ladies look ravishing in your pirate attire."

Wren smiled shyly and heat suffused her cheeks, while Jerricha crossed her arms over her chest and glared. They had gone shopping yesterday to buy clothes for their journey and both wore flowy white shirts tucked into tight black breeches. A corset over the top of the shirt accentuated their feminine curves. Knee-high black boots topped off the ensemble.

"Watch it," Silas grumbled behind Wren.

She jumped in surprise. Silas must have seen Cassidy

approaching them and quickly made his way across the docks, because the last time she had seen Silas, he was helping Gabriel bring their bags from the inn.

Wren laughed as she turned around, wrapping her arms around his waist. "I like it when you're jealous."

He glared at her before bending down and pressing a quick kiss to her mouth.

"Gross," Cassidy said as he turned away. "We'll be ready to set sail in a few minutes," he called over his shoulder.

Silas, carrying their bags, led Wren up the gangplank. "You do look ravishing," he whispered in her ear.

She slapped his chest and made her way to the bow. "You don't get to flirt with me until you tell me this story about the twins."

Silas's steps faltered but he relaxed when he saw the smile on Wren's face. He took their bags below deck and Wren leaned on the railing, taking in the view. She stood there until they were ready to sail, leaning into the salty breeze which blew her hair back from her face.

The ship made its way out of the harbor, Captain Cassidy at the helm. Wren watched the sailors man the rigging as the sails were raised and adjusted to catch the wind. The organized chaos was fascinating to Wren. Eventually, she turned back to the bow, watching the ship slice through the water.

Silas came up behind her and wrapped his arms around her middle. "I have always loved sailing."

"Really?" She rested her head against his shoulder, squinting in the glare cast on the swater.

"Mmm-hmm." His breath tickled her ear, making her toes curl. "There is nothing more freeing than being on the water with nothing around you but the wide-open ocean and sky."

Wren made a sound in her throat, then asked, "Did the twins join you on Captain Cassidy's ship?"

"You're not going to leave me alone until I tell you the story, are you?" He tightened his arms around her waist.

She grinned even though he couldn't see it. "You know better than to ask me that."

Silas sighed, then launched into the tale. "Cassidy and I have known each other for a while. I have sailed with him many times over the years on various missions for Torryn. Four years ago, I arrived in Addler's Cove looking for passage on his ship, only to find the city guard on the hunt for him. I still have no clue what he did to gain their interest, but I knew I needed him to complete my mission, so I launched into action.

"I knew a few of his hiding places and I found him hiding out in one. He needed me to help create a distraction so he could escape to his ship and set sail. I actually led the guards to him, and he set off and led them on a merry little chase. I had these twins ready at an intersection where I knew Cassidy would run past. When the guards appeared, I..." He cut off and cleared his throat. "I may have helped divest them of their clothing."

Wren gasped and spun around, her eyes wide with shock.

Silas held up his hands and rushed to say, "They were willing participants. I didn't force them into anything."

"And a pair of naked twins was enough to distract the guards?" She placed her hands on her hips and stared at her mate.

"Well, that probably would have been enough, but of course I just had to take it one step further. I needed to make sure Cassidy got away safely."

When he didn't expand on that statement, she raised one brow and tapped her foot.

Heat crept into his cheeks and he rubbed the back of his neck with his hand. "Believe it or not, as unlawful as Addler's Cove is, public displays of a certain sort are frowned upon. I may have engaged in some public display with them to distract the guards further..." He trailed off at Wren's open mouth and wide eyes.

She shook her head. "I don't even know what to say right now."

"Well, if it makes you feel any better, after a firm talking-to from the guards, I couldn't get the twins to leave me alone. I had to lock myself in my room at the inn I was staying at. I was stuck there for three days before they finally gave up and left. By that time Cassidy had long since sailed and I had completely failed my mission for Torryn."

Wren tried to fight a smile and put on a stern face, but she failed. "I hope you learned your lesson."

"Oh yes, never offer to help Cassidy with anything. It will undoubtedly backfire."

Wren was opening her mouth to reply when she heard somebody retching over the side of the ship. She turned her head and found Aeron leaning over the rail, white-knuckled grip on the railing.

"Oh no." She turned to Silas. "Please don't tell me he gets seasick."

Silas chuckled. "He most certainly does. Lucky for him, it lasts only a couple of days before he adjusts."

Wren walked across the deck and stopped next to Aeron.

Wiping his mouth on the back of his hand, Aeron sank to the deck, leaning against the side of the ship. "I hate my life." He closed his eyes and thumped his head backward.

Jerricha approached and sat next to him, handing him a piece of candy. "Peppermint. It will help settle your stomach."

Aeron put the candy in his mouth. "How did I forget about this part?"

"You probably blocked it from your memory," Silas supplied, striding for Aeron.

Aeron surged up, leaned over the rail again, heaving up his insides.

"Okay," Jerricha said, standing and walking away. "That is too gross for me."

"Oh sure," Aeron called, hanging halfway over the ship. "Leave me in my hour of need."

Wren wrinkled her nose. "I think I'm with Jerricha on this one." She patted Aeron on the back before following Jerricha below-decks. "Feel better," she called over her shoulder.

Silas stayed with Aeron, while Wren and Jerricha went in search of Hawthorne and Gabriel. They found them in a small cabin, leaning over a map.

"What's this?" Wren asked, peeking around Gabriel's shoulder.

He scooted to the side so she and Jerricha could have a better view. "A map we found of Edein Island."

Jerricha looked up sharply. "Is it accurate?"

"As far as we can guess." Hawthorne shrugged and pointed a finger at the map. "This is where we are aiming to land." It appeared to be a cove or a bay. He moved his finger slightly to the right. "This is the capital."

Wren squinted at the words, but she couldn't read whatever language it was in. "And we know that how?"

"The texts we found detailing the island," Gabriel answered. "We believe that is where we will find more information on the Crown."

"If the Elementals are still alive." Jerricha frowned.

Hawthorne crossed his arms over his chest. "Even if they aren't, I'm hoping there will be ruins we can search. Maybe we can find something, a text or map or clue, something that can lead us to the Crown."

Wren chewed the inside of her cheek, thinking of another

problem they had to deal with. "We also have to beat the Dark Fae who are trying to find the Crown as well."

Gabriel sighed. "All we can do is take it one step at a time."

"Where exactly will we run into this magical barrier?" Jerricha looked up from the map. Concern shone in her eyes as she stared at Gabriel.

"Around here." He pointed to a slice of the ocean about fifty miles off the coast of the island. "If all goes according to plan, about a week and a half into our journey."

They were all silent as they stared at the map, each lost in their own thoughts. Wren surveyed the island, forcing her mind from the dangers that awaited them in the magical barrier. The island looked like a lush tropical forest interspersed with cities and small towns. In the center of the island was a massive mountain with a smaller range reaching from the center peak across to the eastern shore.

"Did any of the texts you found have any information on the Elementals? Their hierarchy? Their beliefs? Will they be friendly?" Wren looked to Hawthorne.

"The emperor of the Elementals rules them. As far as I'm aware, they are immortal. The last emperor mentioned in the texts was Emperor Verellis, the same emperor who helped the kings create the Obsidian Artifacts."

Gabriel picked up the rest of the explanation. "They were primarily a peaceful race, however when needed, they could rise to the occasion with a deadly army. Not only are they impossibly powerful with their raw magic, but they are incredible warriors." He released a breath. "Everything we read led us to believe they would accept us. However, after King Bhardyl defied their orders and stole the Sword and Eyeglass, I'm not sure what kind of reception we will receive. Especially since we are traveling with three Dark Fae."

"If they are still alive," Jerricha repeated.

Gabriel shot a look at Jerricha. "We could do without your negative thoughts."

"Just keeping it real." She shrugged, then added a wink for good measure.

"Where is Aeron?" Gabriel asked.

"Puking up his guts on deck," Wren said sweetly. "I believe my mate is the only one willing to keep him company."

Gabriel chuckled. "Might as well go join them. Maybe we can get some planning done."

"You boys have at it." Jerricha waved her hand in the direction of the door. "I'm not going up there with him."

Gabriel and Hawthorne left the girls in the cabin.

Wren looked at Jerricha. "Do you think this is a pointless mission?"

"No." She shook her head, blond braids swaying with the movement. "As much as I like to give Gabriel a hard time, I think Hawthorne is right. Even if the island is deserted and the Elementals gone, it's worth looking through any ruins for the Crown."

"And the magical barrier?" Wren didn't want to admit it, but she was terrified to pass through that barrier. The one she and Silas had walked through in the pass to Valasia had been bad enough, and they had been on solid ground, not a ship in the middle of the sea surrounded by sirens and sea monsters.

Jerricha sighed. "We'll just have to wait and see, I guess."

* * *

Hours later, Wren was asleep in the small bed in her and Silas's cabin. It was a decent-sized room considering they were on a ship. There was a bed, desk and chair, dresser, and washbasin. All furniture was anchored to the wall to make sure it stayed in place when the ship sailed through rough seas.

Wren had waited for Silas to come down, but he remained above deck with Aeron and the others. Eventually, the motion of the ship and the sound of the waves against the hull, combined with the soft mattress and warm blanket, and Wren hadn't been able to stay awake.

She awoke to gentle kisses along her neck and shoulder. She angled her head to give Silas better access, and he chuckled against her skin.

"Sorry to wake you."

"No you're not." She stretched under him, reveling in the feeling of his body on top of hers.

"You're right," he said in between kisses. "I'm not sorry at all." His voice washed over her, sinking deep into her bones.

She tangled her fingers in his curls and tried to push his head lower, arching her back in a silent demand for more.

"You're greedy tonight," he mumbled as he obliged her, kissing the slope of her breast, slowly, so slowly, making his way to her nipple. "You know, these walls provide little privacy."

He traced her nipple with his tongue and Wren moaned, urging him on. "Wouldn't be the first time everyone heard us."

He didn't answer, instead he wrapped his lips around her nipple and sucked it into his mouth, teeth scraping lightly. Lightning flashed through her veins and she clawed Silas's back, begging for more.

He continued trailing kisses down her body. Her stomach clenched as heat pooled in her core at the feeling of his lips and tongue on her, his fingers along her skin. He slid his hands under her and lifted her to his mouth.

At the first stroke of his tongue, Wren gasped and fisted the sheets in her hands. Silas looked up, keeping his mouth on her, his beautiful green eyes shaded by his thick lashes. The sight almost undid her.

Silas worked her into a frenzy, bringing her to the edge,

then backing away, over and over again. She wasn't sure she could take much more. Just as she was about to beg him, he sucked the bundle of nerves into his mouth and Wren shattered.

Her magic ripped away from her, lighting the dark space with the glow of dozens of fireflies. Silas's shadows, her shadows now, wove between the fireflies, curling and twining with them.

Silas brought her through it, then gently lowered her to the bed. Lust and desire glazed his eyes as he licked his lips and crawled back up the bed, leaning over Wren. He kissed her deeply, and she could taste herself on his tongue.

She reached for him, but he stopped her, tucking her close to his body.

"Silas," she began.

He placed his hand on her cheek and kissed her gently on the forehead. "Not tonight," he whispered against her forehead. "Tonight was about you."

She buried her face against his chest and smiled. How had she ever gotten so lucky? When she pulled away, she saw Silas reach out his hand, and the shadows swirled around his fingers as fireflies alighted on his palm.

"I love you," he whispered, looking down at her.

She didn't need his words to know that, the bond practically vibrated with his feelings. She laid her head on his chest and his arm tightened around her.

"I love you too."

* * *

Silas woke to the violent tossing of the ship. Lightning flared outside the porthole, illuminating the darkness briefly before thunder crashed. The ship lurched and Silas had to grab the side of the bed to keep from falling to the floor. Only his weight on top of Wren kept her from rolling out.

"Wren." He nudged her with his knee, trying to maintain his balance so he didn't completely crush her.

Wren's eyes slowly opened and she looked around sleepily, confused.

"How the hell are you sleeping through this?" he asked through gritted teeth.

"Through what?"

The ship lurched again. This time the motion threw Silas from the bed, and he landed on the floor with a thud. "Through that," he said as he knelt next to the bed.

"Is it storming?" She was trying not to laugh. Silas could hear the tremor in her voice as she held it back.

"Glad you find this amusing," he muttered as he used the bed to help himself stand.

He pulled on his clothes. The simple task took far longer than it should have with the waves tossing him around their cabin like a rag doll. He wasn't sure he had ever cursed so much in his life. Wren sat on the bed through the whole thing, a smile on her face.

"Where are you going?" she finally asked as he headed for the door.

"To see if I can do anything to help. Stay here."

"You don't have to tell me twice." She snuggled back down under the covers, one hand gripping the side of the bed to keep from rolling out.

Silas opened the door at the same time Gabriel left his room. Without speaking to each other, they climbed the ladder to the upper deck, holding on to the rungs for dear life. Lifting the hatch with his shoulder, Silas climbed out into the fray.

The rain pelted him and immediately soaked through his clothes, chilling his skin and plastering his hair to his head. The sound above deck was deafening. Waves crashed, thunder boomed, and wood groaned. Over it all, Cassidy shouted orders to the crew.

Holding on to the railing with white-knuckled grips, Silas and Gabriel made their way to the quarterdeck. Cassidy spied them and grinned. He looked like a madman standing behind the wheel wearing nothing but breeches, with the wind blowing his wet hair around his face.

"Beautiful storm, isn't it?" he shouted over the cacophony.

Lightning forked through the sky, punctuating his statement. Momentarily blinded, Silas spread his feet wider and fought for his balance as the ship lurched, throwing him into Gabriel.

"*Beautiful* is not the word I would use to describe this," Silas shouted back. "What can we do to help?"

Cassidy glanced behind Silas and frowned when he saw Gabriel. "Where is Aeron? He could help with the wind."

"I imagine Aeron is currently curled up in a corner, slowly dying," Silas answered.

"That's a shame." Cassidy shook his head, eyeing the sails tied down to the masts. "You two will probably be more of a hindrance than anything. Go back to bed. We'll be fine. Been through worse." He looked at Silas pointedly. "And we'll go through worse before we get to the island. Better get used to it."

Silas barely heard Gabriel groan behind him. "That is not a pleasant thought."

Carefully, they made their way back down the ladder and below-decks. It was quieter without the wind and crashing waves. However, the ship continued to toss back and forth in the swell. Silas felt like a drunk as he lurched this way and that, bumping into one wall, then the other. When they reached Gabriel's door, it opened and Silas stared, unable to process what he was seeing. Jerricha stood in the doorway, silhouetted by the light of the swaying lanterns behind her.

His eyes widened as he took in the blanket wrapped around her, sliding down her bare shoulder. Her braids were in disarray, some completely unbraided and tangled. Silas slowly grinned, gaze traveling between his cousin and Gabriel.

Gabriel's cheeks flushed and he stared at Silas. "It's not... I... We..."

Silas laughed at Gabriel's stammering and turned his gaze to his cousin.

Jerricha shoved her finger under his nose. "Not. One. Word." She reached out and grabbed Gabriel, pulling him into the room and slamming the door.

Silas was still laughing when he lurched into the cabin he was sharing with Wren. She looked him over, with his soaking clothes and hair, and raised one eyebrow.

"Something funny?"

Silas stripped off his wet clothes, as the chill in the cabin pebbled his skin. He grabbed a dry shirt from the floor and used it to dry his hair as much as he could. Climbing under the covers with Wren, he groaned in delight. She was so warm against his chilled skin and he couldn't resist wrapping himself around her to soak it in.

Wren squealed. "You are freezing!" She tried to scooch away, but he grabbed her tight, pulling her against him.

"Mmm, and you feel so warm," he mumbled.

She squirmed, trying to get out of his hold, but eventually gave up and turned in his arms to face him. "Why were you laughing before?"

"Guess who is sharing your brother's room?"

Wren's brows furrowed for a second before raising to her hairline. "Not Jerricha."

Silas smiled. "Yes, Jerricha. She opened the door wearing nothing but a blanket."

"I wondered when that would happen," she mused.

Silas kissed her nose and snuggled down in the bed. "I can't wait to give her hell tomorrow."

Wren elbowed him. "Don't you dare. Be nice, for once in your life."

"For once in my life?" he asked, affronted. "Excuse me, I am plenty nice." He paused before adding, "To you."

Wren's eyes danced with amusement, but she said, "What's going on out there?"

"Just a storm. Cassidy said it will be fine. We just have to ride it out."

Already the sea had calmed somewhat, the flashes of lightning were fewer, and the sound of thunder was more distant.

The warmth of his mate against his chilled skin and the rocking of the ship tugged at his consciousness. Silas sighed and his muscles slowly relaxed. It didn't take long for him to fall asleep.

Chapter Six

The next week passed without incident. No storms crossed their path and sailing was smooth. Wren spent most of her time at the bow of the ship, enjoying the sun on her face, the wind in her hair, and the scent of salt on the breeze.

Aeron finally got his sea legs and no longer spent his time heaving over the side of the railing. Gabriel and Jerricha spent most of their time together, huddled close on the stern of the ship, away from prying eyes. Silas and Hawthorne trained every day with the Sword on the main deck, providing a show for everyone on board.

That is where Wren sat one afternoon, watching Silas practice blending his magic with the Sword. His shirt had long since been discarded, and the afternoon sun gilded his muscles while sweat ran down his chest. It was a sight she was thoroughly enjoying.

Shaking his hair out of his eyes, Silas turned to Hawthorne. "It still feels off, as if the Sword is fighting me but not." He shook his head. "I don't know how to explain it."

Hawthorne's eyes creased in thought. "King Bhardyl infused the blade with his magic. He was a Shadow Caster, so you, being a Shadow Caster, should account for that." Rubbing his chin, his eyes suddenly widened. "But the Elementals helped to create the blade while Bhardyl worked his magic. Have you tried using a bit of Wren's Light magic? She isn't an Elemental, but the Light Fae are descended from them."

Silas blinked at Hawthorne. "Why hadn't I thought of that? It's worth a shot." He hefted the Sword, taking up his fighting stance. He began working through his warm-up routine, muscles in his abdomen bunching as he moved through the steps. As always, Wren admired how he made it look like a dance, ornate but simple.

Silas closed his eyes as he sent his Dark magic into the Sword. The obsidian swirled, as if Silas's shadows were indeed inside the blade. As Wren watched, the Sword started glowing, shadows and light building inside, the emerald in the pommel shining brightly. Silas brought the Sword down in a maneuver and magic shot out of the tip.

Hawthorne jumped to the side as a beam of glowing shadows hit the deck where he had been standing. He looked wide-eyed at Silas.

"Shit." Silas lowered the Sword, shadows and light leaking out like water. Then he smiled. "That's it. That's what we've been missing." He ran a hand down the now-normal obsidian. "Using Wren's Light magic tied it all together. That was the easiest it has ever been to wield."

"Clearly," Hawthorne replied dryly. "It will take some practice to learn how to use it appropriately and not incinerate everything in your path."

"Probably best to not do that on a ship in the middle of the ocean," Wren supplied from her position sitting on the deck. She eyed Silas's muscled form as he turned toward her.

"Enjoying the show?" He raised one brow, his signature half smile playing about his lips.

"Immensely." She smiled back.

"Um, you guys?" Aeron appeared, leaning over the railing of the forecastle. He used his thumb to indicate behind him. "You might want to come see this."

Silas sheathed the Sword at his waist and grabbed his shirt. He helped Wren to her feet and they climbed the ladder. What they saw stopped them both in their tracks.

The horizon was black, as if a massive storm was gathering. Everything before that storm was bright, clear skies. Then, as if an artist had taken a brush and drew a line, black clouds churned. Lightning forked through them illuminating the darkness in bright flashes. The waves under those clouds were massive, ship-sinking waves.

Wren approached the railing, heart thundering in her chest. "Is that..."

"The barrier," Silas finished, stopping at her side.

Wren tore her gaze away from the magical barrier and the raging storm inside it and looked at Silas. His face was white and uncharacteristically solemn as he swallowed thickly and met her eyes. They didn't need words or the bond to convey what they were thinking. They would never survive that.

* * *

The deck was a flurry of activity as Cassidy shouted commands and the crew readied the ship for the storm ahead. Wren tried not to look at Cassidy's face. The severity and fear lining his features did nothing to calm her nerves.

Silas and Gabriel met with Cassidy to get their orders for what everyone else was supposed to do during the storm. Cassidy ordered everyone to remain above deck. If the ship went down, you didn't want to be stuck inside. He provided a thick rope to tie everyone to the mast so no one would get washed overboard by the waves. When Silas relayed this information to Wren, she almost whimpered with panic.

Now she and Jerricha sat on upturned barrels near the bow, watching the dividing line between light and dark draw closer and closer. Neither spoke, but Wren reached out and clasped Jerricha's hand, squeezing tightly. Jerricha squeezed back, just as hard.

The ocean began to churn more and more, the ship bobbing in the rough waters. Stray clouds drifted across the sky, occasionally blocking out the sun and casting the ship into darkness. The distant sound of thunder could be heard echoing across the water. When the first few drops of rain began to fall, Silas pulled Wren aside.

His green eyes were churning as much as the sea below them. He placed his hands on either side of her face and swallowed. "Wren—" he began.

Shaking her head, she interrupted him. "Don't." Her voice came out raspy and wobbly. "Don't do that. It's too much like goodbye."

"We might not survive this." His thumbs brushed raindrops from her cheeks.

She closed her eyes and her heart squeezed painfully. Silas leaned down and kissed her. It was a sweet kiss, slow and loving. Tears burned the back of her throat and she grasped the back of Silas's head, pulling him to her.

I love you, Wren, he said through the bond. *You are the best thing that has ever happened to me. You are the light in the darkest of my nights and I will forever be thankful for you.*

Wren's eyes blurred with tears. *I love you, Silas.* She didn't know how to say everything she felt, so she sent her feelings down the bond. All of her light and joy and pure, unrelenting love. She wrapped it around the chain connecting them and kissed him. They lost themselves in that kiss for a time, using their bodies to show each other the truth of what they felt.

When they finally pulled away, rain mingled with the tears on her cheeks. Silas kissed her forehead once before turning away, lacing his fingers through hers.

Wren saw Gabriel and Jerricha wrapped in each other's arms, silent conversation passing between them, and her heart thumped at the sight. She tried to tell herself it wasn't goodbye, but it sure felt like one to her.

The rain began coming down earnestly. Cold fat drops that pelted their skin painfully. The afternoon turned to midnight as the clouds darkened until they completely hid the sun. Lightning forked across the sky continuously, flashes lighting the ship in stark relief. Thunder boomed and the sound was deafening. The ship creaked in the wind that lashed about them, the masts empty, ropes swaying from where the sails should be hanging. The smell of ozone and salt permeated the air.

Cassidy stood at the helm, wrestling the wheel to keep the ship sailing through the storm at an angle. The waves grew bigger by the second, tossing the boat and soaking everyone on board as they crashed over the deck.

Wren stood next to Silas with her teeth chattering from cold and fear. He kept one arm around her waist and the other held the railing to keep them steady. The sudden disappearance of her magic made her stumble. One second it was there, the next it was gone. She tried to reach for it, but it was like grasping at air. Similarly, the silence in her head told her the bond was no longer accessible. She shivered, and not just from the cold.

"How long do you think it will take to get through the barrier?" Wren had to shout to be heard over the noise. She was fighting back her panic at the feeling of emptiness she felt at that loss of the two most important things in her life.

Silas shook his head, water spraying from his dripping wet hair. "I have no clue. Hawthorne estimated a of couple days, but it all depends on how fast the ship can make it through."

Wren's stomach dropped as a wave fell out from below the ship, sending them plunging down, water crashing over the railing trying to rip her out of Silas's arms.

That began happening more often, the ship rising on a wave only to plunge straight down as the wave ebbed. The waves were getting bigger, the drop longer and more terrifying. Sea-water was constantly crashing over the railings, tugging and pulling at the people on deck, eager to take them down into the murky depths below.

Cassidy shouted over the din, an order to tie themselves to the mainmast. They made their way there, slipping and stumbling under the rocking ship. Silas pressed Wren's back into the wood, blocking her body with his, adding an extra layer of protection.

Jerricha was in the same position with Gabriel pressed against her. Aeron and Hawthorne followed, then the rest of the crew. The rope was passed around them, looped and tied tightly to keep them all secure. Cassidy tied himself to the wheel while continuing to fight the current to keep the ship on course.

Wren pressed her face against Silas's chest and fisted her hands in the fabric of his shirt. She squeezed her eyes shut and tried to keep her mind from what was happening around them. She focused on Silas's powerful arms, banded around her, keeping her steady. The sound was deafening. Pouring rain, crashing waves, roaring wind, thunder, and the creaking of the ship. It all pressed in on Wren until she wanted to curl into a ball and cover her head.

She lost track of how long they stayed like that, tied to the mast, rocking with the ship. Time was a concept she couldn't grasp in constant lurching movement and flashes of lightning. The cold seeping into her bones made her teeth chatter. Her legs were wobbly and she was struggling to remain upright, even with the rope tied around her. Fatigue was coursing through her and made her body feel as if it weighed a thousand pounds. Her throat was dry, burning from the salt water that forced its way down her throat on crashing waves.

Those waves were getting even stronger, the force of them almost impossible to fight against as they battered them. She was pressed against the mast with Silas before her, his arms around her waist. Then a wave crashed over them, prying her from Silas's arms. The rush of water tugged her under the rope and the next thing she knew, she was sliding across the deck, grappling for anything to hold on to as the wave pulled her farther away from Silas.

"Wren!" The wind and waves almost drowned out Silas's howl.

She slammed into the railing, her side screaming in agony at the impact. She gasped and grabbed the railing, holding on to it with all of her remaining strength. Rain and seawater plastered her hair to her head and ran into her eyes. Unable to see clearly, Wren squinted and tried to find Silas.

A wave crashed over her, flattening her to the deck while it tried to drag her into the ocean. She screamed and choked, her hold on the railing slipping.

A thud sounded next to her and strong arms wrapped around her. "Hold on, princess, I have you." Aeron began wrapping a rope around them, tying it to the rail.

She turned to him and wrapped her arms around his middle. She clung to him as waves crashed over them, drowning them in a constant torrent of water. All they could do was hold on.

A loud crack tore their attention from the turbulent sea to the mast looming over their heads. Wren squinted through the pelting rain, unable to see through the falling curtain to her friends tied to the mast. The mast that was now creaking and tilting. Tilting so slowly, toward Wren and Aeron.

"Fuck." Aeron grabbed his dagger and began sawing through the rope he had just tied around them.

"Aeron." Wren's heart pounded as she watched the mast fall. It was as if time had slowed to a crawl. Each second, the falling mast loomed closer and closer.

The rope holding them snapped and Aeron pushed Wren down to the deck, covering her with his body. All Wren knew was the sound of cracking of wood and then cold water rushed over her as she was thrown into the ocean.

Silence, almost unbearable after the noise of the storm, met her ears as the crashing waves shoved her head under the surface. She thrashed, trying to find her way up, but the water was pulling her under, farther away from the surface.

Pieces of wood and debris littered the water and blocked her view. She couldn't tell which way was up. Her lungs burned, begging for oxygen. She struggled against the pull and the need to draw in a breath. She fought the panic back until a hand grabbed her under her arm and hauled her up. Her head breached the surface and she gasped for air, choking and spitting seawater.

She found Aeron pulling her toward a piece of wood, and she kicked uselessly trying to help him. Her muscles were so tired they didn't want to obey her commands.

They reached the wood and Aeron hauled her up onto it. Her upper body fit, but her lower body still dangled in the icy water. Aeron hauled himself up next. They lay there, panting and coughing, until Wren's breathing finally steadied.

She looked around. All she saw was wood and rope floating in the heaving waters. She turned to Aeron. "Where is the ship? What happened?" Her voice was raspy, painful from the salt water.

Aeron shook his head. "It's gone. The mast broke off and punched a hole right through the hull. It didn't take long for the ocean to claim it. It tore the ship apart in seconds."

"Silas." She looked around, thrashing on the piece of wood and threatening to overturn it with her movements. "Where is Silas?"

"I don't know what happened to anyone else." His voice was quiet, almost too low to hear in the storm.

"No," she whispered. "No, no, no. Silas!" Her scream tore out of her, ripping her throat until she thought it would bleed. "Silas!"

Aeron grabbed her chin and forced her to look at him. "You need to calm down, Wren." He looked into her eyes, pleading. "Calm down! You are going to sink the wood."

Wren stilled, but her eyes were wild, her breathing uncontrolled. She was breathing in more than she was breathing out. What if he was hurt? What if he was drowning? She couldn't even bring herself to think about the worst possible scenario. She knew it was fruitless, but instinct had her reaching down the bond, desperate to feel him at the other end. Nothing but fog met her.

"Wren, look at me!" Aeron grabbed her chin again. "Breathe. Breathe, Wren. There is nothing we can do right now but survive."

His words hit her at the same time she noticed the cold. She thought she had been cold on the deck of the ship. That was nothing compared to the water she was in. Icy fingers pierced her flesh, burrowed deep in her bones, splintering them with hoarfrost. She shivered uncontrollably.

The waves kept slamming into them, drenching and choking them. Their little raft was tossed around, and they held on with every bit of strength they had left.

Movement under the water, highlighted by the flash of lightning in the sky, caught Wren's eye. "Aeron..."

"I see it," he said hoarsely, head tracking the movement.

It circled below them. A predator with its prey in sight. It rose to the surface slowly, breaching the water a few feet away. A long scaly body, only visible in sections as it undulated in the waves, swimming closer and closer.

"Is that a sea dragon?" she breathed. Afraid to make any noise or movement.

Aeron's eyes were wide as he stared at the massive head surfacing in front of them. Large yellow eyes trained on them, floating helplessly on their makeshift raft. The long snout rose from the water, with two large holes for nostrils. Teeth the size of Wren's hand glistened in the lightning flashes. Blue-green scales shimmered along its massive sleek body, and a single fin ran the length of its serpentine back. The large curving horns that protruded from its skull and pierced the water were deadly sharp.

Wren didn't dare breathe as the creature swam within arm's length of them. Its nostrils flared, scenting them. The creature looked at Wren with its yellow eyes and tilted its head as if it were studying her. Lightning reflected off Aeron's dagger as he brought it out of the water.

The creature growled and shifted its gaze to Aeron. Something made Wren grab Aeron's hand. She stared at the creature and its gaze returned to her—she could have sworn ancient intelligence swam in their depths.

It floated closer, gaze never leaving Wren. Slowly, she

reached out a hand, ignoring Aeron's hiss. Time stopped. The waves ceased crashing around them and the ocean stilled. The rain that had been mercilessly pelting them relented.

The sea dragon's head bumped Wren's hand. The scales were slick and cool beneath her fingers. It huffed a warm breath into her palm like a horse. Wren smiled tentatively. The creature blinked and dove under the water, its serpentine body following in waves.

Time resumed, the ocean crashed, and the rain fell.

Aeron was staring at Wren with his mouth hanging open. "What just happened?"

Wren shook herself. "I have no clue," she breathed.

Chapter Seven

It felt like hours after the sea dragon left before the seas calmed, the storm lessened, and then disappeared entirely. The gray clouds that had taken up residence in the sky broke apart and blew away, leaving nothing but blue skies and bright sunshine in their wake.

Wren and Aeron floated. Even after the storm broke, they shivered in the still icy water. Wren was drifting. Her eyes kept closing, no matter how hard she tried to stay awake.

"Don't close your eyes." Aeron shook her. He looked as cold as she felt with chattering teeth, pale skin, and lips as blue as the ocean.

"I'm so tired," she mumbled. She could barely form the words.

"You can't fall asleep. You have to fight it."

A violent shiver racked her body, almost throwing her from their little raft. Warmth. They needed warmth. Even the sun above them wasn't enough. Wren lifted her head.

"The sun," she muttered to herself.

She held her hand out, palm up. Hoping the lack of storms

meant they were past the barrier, Wren dug deep within herself and felt her magic stirring. She coaxed it forth and a little ball of light appeared, hovering above her palm. It was the most she could manage at the moment, but the heat it emanated washed over them.

They both groaned in relief, scooting as close as they could get to the ball of warmth.

They floated, unaware of their surroundings or the direction in which their little raft bobbed, completely at the mercy of the current. They drifted in and out of consciousness, unable to fight it any longer. When one of them would slip from the raft, the other would grab them and haul them back up. They did this until their little wooden raft bumped into dry land.

"Wren." Aeron shook her awake.

She opened her eyes. They burned from the seawater, along with her throat. Thirsty. She was so thirsty. Lifting her head was a struggle, but she managed to look around.

They landed on a beach with soft white sand and palm trees swaying in a warm ocean breeze. Beyond the beach a dense forest blocked the view of whatever else inhabited this island. Together they crawled their way onto the beach, sand sticking to their wet bodies, and collapsed.

"What now?" she asked through her scratchy throat.

"Now we rest." He sounded as bad as she did. "Then we find the others."

Darkness was creeping into her vision, unconsciousness swiftly rising to claim her. She tried to fight it long enough to reach down the bond, but the darkness was quicker. It slammed into her and she collapsed, unable to hold out any longer.

* * *

A hand on her shoulder woke Wren a couple of hours later. The sun was high in the cloudless sky, and a warm breeze blew in off the ocean, carrying with it the scent of salt.

Wren sat, brushing sand off her as she stretched her arms over her head. She ached all over, her muscles protested every movement, and her eyes and throat were dry and scratchy. It took her mind a few seconds to recall where she was and what had happened. Even after having slept for a bit, she was still exhausted to her core.

"Wren." Aeron's raspy voice jolted her. He gently turned her head to the left.

Her gaze caught the movement and she squinted in the bright sunshine trying to make out what it was. Her hand flew to her mouth and she let out a noise, something between a sob and squeak. She tapped into a hidden well of strength, ignored her aching muscles, and took off across the sand, running as fast as she could.

Her body crashed into Silas so hard he rocked backward. When his arms came around her and pulled her to his chest, something broke open inside her. Tears welled in her eyes and flowed over, and she wouldn't have been able to stop them had she wanted to.

"You're okay," she cried into his chest. Her body was shaking, fine tremors running through her limbs as relief swept through her.

He pressed his face into the crook of her neck and inhaled deeply. "I'm fine. Are you okay?" He pushed her back and ran his eyes over her. She assumed she passed inspection when he pulled her back against his chest, rubbing a hand soothingly over her back.

She stood in his arms and soaked in his steady strength. If she could have stood there forever she would have, but Silas slowly pulled away, interlacing their fingers and leading them toward Aeron.

"Thank you for keeping her safe," he said gravely.

Aeron placed a hand on his heart and bowed his head. "It's an honor." The gravity of the moment was lost as Aeron turned to Wren and winked.

She rolled her eyes and turned to Silas. With his torn shirt, scratches on his face and arms, and his curls a wild mess, he looked awful—although she probably didn't look any better. He was okay though, and that was all that mattered. She wrapped her arms around his middle again and squeezed him tightly, just to reassure herself.

"How did you find us?" Aeron asked as he sat in the shade under a palm tree.

"I followed the bond." He tilted his head toward Wren.

She reached out and indeed found the bond was again flowing freely between them. The relief she felt at the feeling of Silas in her head again almost buckled her knees.

Silas continued, "I didn't know if you were hurt, but I knew you were alive. Either asleep or unconscious."

"A little of both," Wren replied. "I haven't felt that kind of exhaustion ever."

Silas sat next to Aeron and pulled Wren down with him.

"What next?" Aeron looked up and down the coast.

There was nothing to see for miles in either direction. White sand, palm trees, forests, and the occasional washed-up piece of wood or rope from the shipwreck.

"Our priority needs to be food and water." Silas looked around, mouth pulled down into a frown.

At the mention of water, Wren whimpered. Water. She desperately wanted water.

Silas stood and strode to a palm tree. His shadows swirled around the trunk, climbing into the leafy branches. Several coconuts fell to the sand with thuds, shaken free from their branches by Silas's magic. He gathered them in his arms and returned to Wren and Aeron. Using his magic again, he cracked them open.

"Coconut milk." He handed one to Wren and grinned at the disgusted look on her face. "It's better than nothing."

He was right. Wren took the coconut and tipped it toward her mouth. As much as she hated coconuts, the liquid sliding down her throat was divine. She moaned and licked her lips. Silas's eyes darkened as he watched her.

Seriously? she asked through the bond, even though butterflies took flight in her stomach at the look he was giving her.

Oh, I'm always serious. His purr sent shivers down her spine.

"Okay," Aeron grumbled. "That's enough, you two."

Wren quickly looked away and felt her cheeks heat but gladly accepted another coconut from Silas. The three of them sat under the tree and finished the coconut milk.

"Now what?" Wren threw the last empty coconut into the ocean.

"Now we walk." Silas stood and helped Wren to her feet.

He looked both directions before shrugging and choosing one. Silas and Wren walked hand in hand along the beach in silence with Aeron trailing behind. Now that Wren knew Silas was okay, her worry had turned to Gabriel and the rest of her friends.

"What happens if..." she trailed off, unable to finish that thought. If something had happened to Gabriel, it would destroy her.

Silas squeezed her hand. "Don't do that yet. You can't go down that road or it will consume you."

The dense forest to their left remained unchanged. Dark and uninviting. The white sandy beach continued as far as

Wren could see, with nothing but blue ocean to their right. Eventually, more debris from the shipwreck washed ashore— wooden planks and barrels, ropes, and pieces of sail.

Silas's shoulders relaxed and Wren looked forward, her own body collapsing against his in relief. Gabriel and Jerricha sat on the beach. Hawthorne stood next to them and Captain Cassidy and most of his crew crowded under the few palm trees nearby. Wren would have rushed forward, but along with the relief sweeping through her, exhaustion did as well.

Gabriel met them halfway and embraced his sister. "Thank the Gods you're okay."

Wren pulled away and looked her brother over. "Are you okay?"

He nodded. "I'm fine, as is Hawthorne. Jerricha's ankle is most likely broken, but other than that, she is fine." He glanced over his shoulder at Cassidy, who was staring at Silas with murder in his eyes. "Cassidy lost a few crew members, and he is not happy about his ship."

Silas sighed. "I'm sure he isn't." He squeezed Wren's hand and walked toward the group. "Well, let's get this over with."

Cassidy stomped forward, all of his sexy swagger gone. His brown eyes were practically glowing with rage and his voice was deadly quiet when he spoke. "That ship was my livelihood, as well as that of my crew. Not to mention, we lost three. That falls solely at your feet, Silas."

Silas bowed his head. "I'm sorry about your crew and your ship. Truly, I am. I will ensure your ship is replaced when we return to Ellendyr. You have my word."

Cassidy stared Silas down and no one spoke or even dared to breathe too loudly. Then Cassidy stuck out his hand and said, "It had better be a bigger ship."

Silas clasped Cassidy's wrist. "It will be the biggest ship in the ocean."

Wren gaped at Silas. *Where the hell are you going to get a bigger ship?*

Silas shrugged and grinned at Wren. *Your grandmother?*

Wren snorted softly and sat down by Jerricha. "How are you?"

"I'm fine. Glad it's just my ankle." She grimaced in pain as she adjusted her position.

"I wish I had some healing powers," Wren mumbled. She looked around for any plants that might ease Jerricha's pain, but she found nothing that looked familiar.

Jerricha waved her hand. "I've had worse. I'll survive."

Wren looked to Gabriel, who sat on Jerricha's other side. "What will we do next?"

"We have already scouted the other direction and found nothing but more beach. Hawthorne believes there should be a path somewhere in the forest along the coast that leads to a city. Our best bet is to find that path."

"Any idea where that is? Or better yet, where we are?" Wren asked Hawthorne.

"Along the northern coast of Edein Island. I believe if we keep heading west, we'll find that path."

Gabriel looked at the sky, at the sun already moving past its zenith. "We should probably camp here on the beach tonight. I don't want to be traipsing through an unknown forest at night."

"What about food and water?" Wren's stomach was cramping painfully. She had never gone so long without either.

"Cassidy sent some men into the forest to hunt. Hopefully, they will bring some food back. As for water"—he shrugged—"we'll just have to deal with coconut milk for the time being."

Cassidy's men brought back a few small pieces of game. Wren didn't question what it was, she just ate it as quickly as she could once it was cooked over the fire they built on the beach.

That night, she cuddled up with Silas under a palm tree. The stars were unimaginably bright in the night sky.

"You know," Silas said quietly, "This could be an incredibly romantic moment if it weren't for everything going on."

She laughed. "Yeah, it could be."

Silas looked at her and gave her a lingering kiss, his green eyes dark in the night. Wren laid her head on his shoulder and closed her eyes. It didn't take long for her to fall asleep.

* * *

"Ahh! Get it off me!" Wren frantically danced around, brushing her hands down her body. They had been traipsing through the dense forest for an hour when Wren walked into a spiderweb, and not a normal spiderweb, but a thick, gooey spiderweb.

Silas made a face but helped Wren pull the sticky, ropelike strands from her body. "That is disgusting."

Wren shivered. "Not helping, Silas."

He grinned at her before continuing on. They were following Hawthorne on a narrow trail they had found along the beach, hoping it was the right one. The forest was dense and dark. Dappled sunlight occasionally filtered through the overhead branches. Trees, as wide as any she had ever seen, reached high into the sky and she didn't recognize any of them. Thick foliage, roots, and fallen branches covered the ground, often creating obstacles they had to climb over.

The silence was heavy, broken by the sound of creaking branches and unfamiliar bird calls. Altogether, the place gave Wren the creeps. She felt like there was always something watching them. She couldn't quite explain why it bothered her, except it didn't feel like a normal forest found in Ellendyr or even Valasia.

Exhaustion already dragged down the entire party, thirst and hunger weighing heavily on them. The air was heavy and sticky, with no breezes to alleviate the heat. Wren was rapidly wilting, and a quick look behind her showed most of the party doing the same.

Jerricha was leaning heavily on Gabriel as he helped her navigate the path on one foot. Jerricha wouldn't make it much farther without needing to stop.

How long do you think we'll be in here? Wren fired across the bond.

She watched Silas's shoulders rise and fall with a sigh. *A few hours?*

I'm not sure Jerricha can handle that. Do you think it's safe to rest in here?

I'd rather not. There are too many unknowns lurking in this forest.

Wren bit her lip but continued trudging along, focusing on the forest floor before her. She was so focused on her task she didn't see the man appear from the trees in front of them until Silas reached his hand back to stop her.

The most intriguing person Wren had ever seen stood before them. He was tall and lithe, with long black hair that fell in a smooth curtain to his waist. His unbuttoned leather vest showcased his dark skin, and he wore leather pants that clung to his legs. His clothing was all browns and greens, making him almost invisible in the forest. He held a longbow in one hand with a full quiver at his waist, along with a curved hunting dagger.

His deep brown eyes traveled over their party, stopping on Wren. He blinked, and when his eyes opened again, they were glowing.

Chapter Eight

Wren gasped, taking a step back. The stranger's eyes stayed on her even though the glow had subsided. She felt laid bare beneath his intense gaze and tried to make herself smaller.

Silas stepped in front of Wren, blocking her from the man's view. His hand rested on the hilt of the Sword, and Wren could feel his magic building around him.

As if Silas's motions caught his attention, the strange man's gaze drifted to Silas and his eyes narrowed.

Hawthorne raised his hands, trying to keep the peace. "We are sorry for intruding in the forest. Our ship wrecked off the coast and we are trying to make our way to Isperiline. Would you be able to help us?"

The man's eyes once again traveled over their party, lingering on Wren a second longer. "Follow me." His voice was deep with a beautiful lilting accent.

No one moved.

His eyes narrowed again, this time in frustration. "I will take you to Isperiline."

Silas and Hawthorne exchanged a glance before Silas nodded grudgingly. He looked back at Wren. "Stay near me."

She could hear Gabriel saying the same to Jerricha, not that Jerricha could go anywhere without help.

They traveled through the forest for another hour, following in this strange man's footsteps. Wren was about to collapse when the forest suddenly opened before them. Her mouth fell open, and all thoughts of exhaustion and hunger were forgotten.

They were standing on a cliff, looking down into the most beautiful view she had ever seen. The entire city was crafted from different colored glass. Buildings, bridges, fountains. All of it was glass. The sun's reflection would create a prism of colors at all hours of the day. It was breathtaking, and Wren couldn't move her eyes fast enough to take it all in.

Isperiline. The City of Colored Glass.

Their guide didn't pause at the cliff. He kept walking, heading for a steep path that meandered down the cliff side. Wren took one look at the path and the rocky terrain and wanted to cry. It would not be easy going. She looked back at Jerricha, who was eyeing the path with uncertainty.

"I'm not sure I'll be able to do that," Jerricha said quietly to no one in particular.

Aeron came up to her other side and looped her arm around his neck. "Between Gabriel and me, we can get you down."

Jerricha did not look pleased to have to rely on them, but she didn't have any other choice.

Wren sighed and began the trek down the cliff. At the bottom of each switchback, she paused to catch her breath and check on Jerricha. At one point, a rock slipped out from under her foot and only Silas kept her from sliding all the way down. But, to Wren's relief, they eventually made it to the bottom.

Wren's legs were shaking, and her stomach was once again cramping painfully. She fought back the tears that wanted to escape. She desperately wanted to sit down and eat a meal and drink as much water as her stomach could handle.

The trail let them out near the palace and the guide led them through the front gates. Wren momentarily forgot her discomfort as her eyes took in the grandeur of the Crystal Palace. Pale blue glass gates loomed on either side of the main entryway. The palace itself was clear glass, frosted enough to make it impossible to see inside. Spires and towers rose high into the air, blending in with the blue sky to the point it looked like they disappeared. The sun reflected off the glass, almost blinding Wren.

Guards on either side of the gates watched from under their helms but said nothing. A woman opened the massive glass doors in front of the palace and led them inside. The floor was polished glass, so shiny Wren could see her reflection on it. Her torn and stained clothing made her cringe. Her braid had long since fallen out and her curls were a wild riot around her face. She looked at her hands and the grime coating them. She desperately needed a bath. Looking at her companions, they didn't fare any better.

Their guide led them through the palace to a set of ornate, golden glass doors. They opened on a whisper-soft wind and Wren blinked at what she saw inside. Glass everywhere. Twisting, spiraling columns raised so high to the ceiling, Wren couldn't see the top. The floor was a mosaic of colors, swirling in beautiful glass patterns. A raised dais with a crystal-clear glass throne sat in the middle of the room.

Sitting on the dais, the emperor of the Elementals stared at them with impassive eyes. His skin was beautifully dark and his hair fell in a snow-white cascade to his waist. He was wearing a white cloth wrapped around his body, leaving his upper arms bare. Golden bands adorned his arms and ankles, and a golden circlet sat atop his brow. His eyes were pure molten gold.

They approached the dais and their guide halted, bowing deeply. "Imperial Majesty, I found them in the forest. I thought it best to bring them straight here."

The emperor's golden eyes roved over the group, flaring slightly when they landed on Wren. He turned to their guide. "And our suspicion?"

Their guide turned to Wren and pointed. "This one, Imperial Majesty."

Silas tensed and took a step closer to Wren. Aeron did the same on her other side. Wren stared wide-eyed, unsure what to do or say.

"Step forward," the emperor commanded her.

Wren hesitated for just a second. Their guide reached out and grabbed her arm, roughly pulling her forward. Silas reacted immediately. He drew the Sword and leveled it at the guide, eyes blazing with fury. Shadows rose from the floor as his magic swirled around him. Before he could take a step, guards surrounded him with arrows trained on his heart. Aeron and Hawthorne drew their blades while Gabriel did his best to shield Jerricha while keeping her supported.

Cassidy and his crew, separated from Wren's group by a few feet, took steps backward to put even more space between them. They kept their hands from their weapons at Cassidy's quiet command.

Fear flared in Wren's chest at the sight of the arrows aimed at her mate. "Silas, no!" Wren wrenched her arm out of the guide's grasp and took a step toward Silas.

"Cease!" The emperor's voice flooded the throne room. He stood slowly from his throne and tilted his head to the side as he looked between Wren and Silas. He nodded to the guards surrounding Silas and they retreated.

Silas rushed to Wren's side, his hand still gripping the Sword tightly.

"Interesting," the emperor murmured. He returned to the throne and leveled a stare at Wren and Silas. "We have much to discuss, but I wouldn't be a very good host if I didn't let you rest and clean up first. My guards will show you to your rooms. I'll have food sent up shortly. Tomorrow we will talk."

* * *

Tomorrow dawned, and Wren felt better than she had in a long time. The night before, Wren and her companions had gathered in her room to eat and discuss their plans. Cassidy and his crew were given leave to find lodging in the town outside the palace.

Silas had a feeling the Elementals already knew what Wren was, which raised her anxiety a notch higher. Even though the Elementals most likely knew who the magic wielders of the group were, they decided to keep their magic under wraps, just in case.

Wren stretched in bed, her muscles protesting at the movement. Groaning, she rolled over and was rewarded with a sleepy smile from Silas.

"Good morning, love." He propped himself up on one elbow and tucked a strand of hair behind her ear.

Wren winced and pulled the strand into her line of vision, glaring at it. "I am so disgusting." She looked Silas over and grimaced. "And so are you."

"Excuse me? I take great offense to that."

"Mmm-hmm." Wren stood and padded to the bathing room. She paused in the doorway. "Umm..."

Silas stepped up behind her. "Well, this will be fun." He stepped around her into the bathing room.

The space was made of pale green glass, but what caught Wren's eye was the lack of a bathtub. Instead, a shallow, sunken pit took up the back corner of the room. A gauzy curtain hung around the pit, creating a semblance of privacy.

Silas walked to the pit and turned a knob along the wall. Water poured from the ceiling, a gentle rain shower. He grinned at Wren and stripped off his pants.

"Care to join?" he purred and Wren's toes curled at the promise in that sound.

Shedding her filthy clothes, Wren stepped under the fall of water. Silas followed her in and pulled the curtain closed.

She closed her eyes and moaned as the water hit her, washing away the dirt and grime from their journey. When she opened her eyes, her breath caught in her throat. Silas was staring at her with an intensity that burned her to her core. He grabbed a bottle of soap off the ledge and motioned her to turn around.

Silas lathered the soap and slowly began washing Wren's body. The scent of citrus filled the steamy space, tingling along her skin, which was further awakened by Silas's touch. When he finished with her body, he moved to her hair and Wren almost melted to a puddle at the feel of his hands massaging her scalp. With her hair and body washed, she turned to face him.

He handed her the soap and she helped him wash. Her hands glided over his shoulders and Wren watched water droplets run down his chest to his abdomen and lower. She traced the path of a droplet with a finger. She glanced at him from under her lashes and wrapped her hand around the length of him. He made a sound low in his throat and his head fell back.

These moments with Silas were what Wren lived for. Just the two of them, enjoying each other, showing each other their love. No need for words. The golden chain threaded between them was all they needed.

Silas braced his hands on the wall behind Wren and captured her mouth in a kiss. She melted under him, savoring his taste and feel. He pressed her against the wall, the cold surface on her back making her gasp. Silas's muscles bunched under her hands as he lifted her, and she wrapped her legs around his waist. He teased her entrance, and Wren could barely control her shaking as need coursed through her.

She bit back a cry as he slowly slid into her. Once she was seated to the hilt, he pulled back and looked into her eyes. He didn't break her stare as he began moving his hips, sliding in and out. Despite how many times they had done this, despite the bond between them, Wren had never felt more than she did in this moment. She could tell by the gleam in Silas's green eyes that he felt the same. Their actions washed away the heaviness of what was to come later that day. The bond between them strengthened, the tether sinking deeper into them. Unbreakable. Unshakeable. Infallible. Just like their love for each other.

* * *

Wren and Silas stepped out of the shower and heard a knock on the bedroom door. Silas slung a towel around his hips and went to answer while Wren dried off and stared at her dirty clothes.

They had nothing else to wear. They had lost everything on the ship, including her bow, which she felt a stab of regret over. She sighed and picked up her shirt, ready to put it on when Silas came back with a pile of fabric in his hands.

"This was outside our door, along with Gabriel and Jerricha." He handed her a piece of white fabric.

She held it up and raised her brows, looking at Silas over the garment. "And how, exactly, do I wear this?"

Silas smirked. "I think you wrap it around yourself?" He took the garment back and helped wrap it around her body.

She stared in the mirror with a frown. It hung over one shoulder and wrapped around her body, falling to her knees. "It's a little short," she muttered, tugging the dress down. She ignored Silas's grin and grabbed her black leather leggings, sliding them on under the dress. "Much better." She smiled as she buckled a golden belt around her waist.

Silas dressed quickly in brown leather pants and a dark green sleeveless tunic. The color made his eyes appear to glow.

Together, they left the bathing room and found everyone already waiting. Gabriel, Aeron, Hawthorne, and Cassidy were wearing similar clothing to Silas. Wren grinned when she saw Jerricha wearing a similar dress as herself, also with leggings underneath.

"Dress a little short for you too?" Wren laughed.

Jerricha snorted. "And completely impractical if we have to fight."

That was also true. Wren's nerves finally made themselves known as she thought about what could happen today. The emperor seemed very interested in her and it set her on edge. He could want anything from her. Swallowing, Wren sat on the couch next to her brother.

Gabriel slung his arm around Wren's shoulders. "On a positive note, they sent a healer this morning for Jerricha."

Wren leaned over Gabriel, nerves completely forgotten again. "They did? Is it better? How did it feel?"

"Completely healed." Jerricha wiggled her ankle to prove it. "It felt strange. Like a deep pressure and warmth, kind of tingly."

"What did it look like?" The Elementals' use of raw magic completely fascinated Wren. She wanted to know everything about it.

"It was like a smoky, bluish light surrounded my foot. It was strange to think raw magic was being used on me." She shivered slightly, rubbing her hands down her arms.

"Well, I'm glad they sent a healer." Wren glanced at Silas. "That has to be a good sign, right?"

Silas shrugged. "I hope so." His gaze traveled around the party before he asked, "What is the plan for today?"

They discussed what they planned on doing when they met with the emperor, the questions they wanted to ask, and how they wanted to ask them. In the end, despite Wren's and Jerricha's protests, they all agreed the women were to be protected at all costs.

"You know we can take care of ourselves," Jerricha grumbled.

"We know." Gabriel brushed a braid behind her ear. "But these people are also completely unknown to us, their magic a different entity from what we are used to."

"He's right," Silas agreed. "In fact, we all need to look out for each other."

It wasn't long after that a servant knocked on their door, ready to take them to meet the emperor.

Wren's heart was in her throat the entire walk through the palace. She couldn't even marvel at the beauty of the place, all colorful glass and ornate decorations. Her thoughts kept wandering to what the emperor would say, each more disturbing and terrifying than the last.

Silas finally pulled Wren to the side when they stopped in front of a surprisingly simple glass door. He framed her face with his hands and looked into her eyes. "Stop with those thoughts. No matter what happens, I will be right there with you." He gently squeezed her face for emphasis. "I will let nothing happen to you."

Her racing heart calmed a bit. She reminded herself she

wasn't alone. Her friends and family were here. They were all in this together.

She nodded and gave Silas a wavering smile. He laced his fingers with hers before rejoining the group.

The servant made sure they were ready, then knocked on the door once and opened it. It swung away without a sound and the group entered a large room with pale blue glass walls full of overstuffed couches and chairs. Mounds of pillows dotted the floor around a low table. Floor-to-ceiling windows let in bright morning sunlight that cast the entire room in glittering rainbows.

The emperor lounged on a chair while a woman, who Wren assumed was his wife, sat on a pillow mound next to him. They both wore white dresses similar to Wren's and Jerricha's, although their gold belts matched the many necklaces and bracelets adorning them.

"Welcome," the woman said with a voice that was low and melodic. She was beautiful with dark skin and dark hair that fell to her waist in locs. "Please, have a seat." She gestured toward the seating options, the bracelets on her wrist tinkling in the silence.

Silas, still grasping Wren's hand, led her to a chair while he perched on the armrest. Their companions settled in around the low-lying table bearing glass pitchers containing various drinks and platters of fruit.

A servant appeared and began filling glasses, passing them out to the guests. Once he was done, he left the room, leaving the emperor and empress alone without guards. Although, Wren supposed, they didn't need any with the magic they possessed.

"I would like to welcome you to our island," the emperor began. "It has been awhile since we had visitors." He smiled kindly at them. Wrinkles crinkled the corners of his eyes.

Wren exchanged glances with Silas. This man seemed completely different from the one they met yesterday.

Seeming to read their expressions, the emperor grimaced. "I would also like to apologize for my actions yesterday. I have to keep up appearances in my court. You never know who is watching."

"Thank you for the welcome," Wren said tentatively.

Introductions were made, and the woman was indeed his wife, Empress Cista.

"I assume you had a purpose for visiting before your ship sank in our barrier." The emperor's gaze traveled through the group.

"We did, Imperial Majesty—"

The emperor interrupted, "Please, just call me Verellis. Titles are too formal and time-consuming."

"Verellis, we have a reason for braving your barrier." She swallowed. "We would like information on the Obsidian Artifacts, specifically the Obsidian Crown."

Emperor Verellis sat back in his chair, rubbing his chin thoughtfully. "The Obsidian Artifacts," he mused. "I assume you are wondering where the Crown is."

It wasn't a question, but Wren nodded anyway. "Yes. I don't know how much you know about what is happening in Sorentiv, but the Dark Fae are gathering power once again. They are searching for the Artifacts. We have possession of the Sword"—a nod at Silas—"and the Eyeglass, sort of. But we need to get the Crown before the Dark Fae do."

"You are Light Fae, no? Along with Hawthorne?" His stare seemed to dissect them, looking inside their skin, their bodies, to see what they were made of.

Wren shivered. "Yes, we are."

"Are you aware that three of your companions are Dark Fae? Including the man in possession of the Sword?"

Wren smiled. "Yes, we are well aware."

The emperor appeared to think this through, eyes traveling between Silas, Jerricha, and Aeron. Finally, he looked at Silas. "Have you figured out how to use the Sword?"

"I have, with Hawthorne's help. I was finally able to use it on the journey here."

The emperor jerked back, surprised. "Use it? You mean just as a weapon, a normal sword, correct?"

Silas shook his head. "As both a sword and a conduit for my magic."

"That's impossible," the emperor breathed. His grip on the arms of his chair turned his knuckles white. "The Sword can only be used by someone who possesses Light and Dark magic."

Wren smiled again, looking at Silas. "We are mates. We both can use Light and Dark magic."

At this statement, the emperor looked about to fall out of his chair. He exchanged glances with his wife. Wren wasn't able to read the meaning behind the look, but it had her on guard once again.

The emperor gathered himself. "What do you know about the Obsidian Artifacts?"

As one, Wren and her companions all looked to Hawthorne. He preened under their attention. This was the area he shone in.

"We don't know a lot. King Adriel of the Light Fae and King Bhardyl of the Dark Fae traveled to Edein Island to create the Obsidian Artifacts. Adriel assisted with the Crown, and Bhardyl assisted with the Sword. When they left, Bhardyl stole the Sword and Eyeglass." Hawthorne sat back on his pillow mound. "At some point, the Light Fae got the Eyeglass back in their possession. They put it under tight security, keyed to King Adriel's blood. Only a descendant of King

Adriel can unlock the Eyeglass." He looked at Wren as he finished.

The emperor's eyes widened once again, and his gaze traveled to Wren. "You are a descendant of King Adriel?"

"I am," Wren said quietly.

He stared at her thoughtfully before nodding. "We created the Obsidian Artifacts to fight a force of evil we had not yet known about. Years and years ago, a seer foretold a time when evil would arise. She said the only way to fight it was using weapons created of all powers; raw, Light, and Dark. To wield these weapons, a person must be able to use both Light and Dark magic." He again peered at Wren and Silas in awe. "We thought little of her foretelling. The ability to wield both Light and Dark magic was impossible, or so we thought. Still, we heeded her warning and created the Obsidian Artifacts as a precaution."

"Why did you think it was impossible to wield both magics?" Wren asked curiously. It didn't seem impossible at all to her.

"Light and Dark Fae were already divided. Their hate for each other ran deep. Bondings were becoming rare, let alone mates. That a Light and Dark Fae could mate and combine their magics seemed impossible." He leaned forward. "You two have proven us all wrong."

Silas leaned closer to Wren. "What kind of evil did the seer think was going to rise?"

The emperor shook his head. "She never said. I'm not sure she knew. She just told us when the one who carries the blood of night and day walks the earth, darkness will rise."

Wren and Silas exchanged startled glances.

It can't be, Wren said down the bond.

The blood of night and day, Wren. Your mother was Light

Fae and your father is Dark Fae. What else could it be? The Dark Fae are strengthening. It fits.

"You two just realized something," the emperor murmured with narrowed eyes.

"My mother was Light Fae," Wren said slowly. "My father is Dark Fae."

Chapter Nine

I f Wren thought the emperor had looked surprised before, it was nothing compared to his expression now. His mouth dropped open and his eyes popped. He turned to his wife, who had a similar expression on her face.

"That explains so much," he muttered to the empress.

"Explains what, exactly?" Silas asked sharply, eyes narrowed on the pair.

The emperor sighed. "I rarely allow strangers to our island. The barrier is up to prevent people from getting through. Your group would not have made it if I had not allowed the barrier to drop."

"Why did you let it drop?" Wren asked.

"My sea dragon told me to let you through."

Memory crashed into Wren, and she looked at Aeron. "I forgot all about that in the chaos that followed."

"I did too," he said.

Silas was looking between Wren and Aeron, one brow raised. "Care to fill the rest of us in?"

"While we were floating on the piece of wood," Wren

began, "a sea dragon appeared. I thought we were going to die, but it slowly approached us. It sniffed me and quickly swam away."

"Don't forget to mention you pet the thing," Aeron muttered.

Silas whipped his head toward Wren. "You pet a sea dragon? Are you crazy?"

"I don't know what happened," she explained. "It was as if I was called to do it. I can't explain, but I knew it wouldn't hurt me."

The emperor chimed in, "Falkor came to me and told me to drop the barrier. I trust his judgment, probably more than anyone else's, so I did. He must have sensed your blood, Wren."

"You really have a pet sea dragon?" The look Silas gave the emperor said he thought the man was crazy.

Wren elbowed her mate in the side.

The emperor chuckled. "Falkor is not so much a pet as a companion. We have been together for most of our lives and have developed a bond. Not too different from your bond with Wren."

The emperor's statement made Wren wonder if, given time, she and Winston would develop a similar bond. The emperor's next statement interrupted her thoughts.

"While you're here, you should meet him. I'm sure he would love to be introduced to you."

Wren smiled. "I would love that, actually."

"It will be done. But before that, and before we discuss the Crown, have you two been formally mated?"

Wren and Silas exchanged a confused glance. "What do you mean by that?" Silas asked.

"Have you taken part in a tethering ceremony? Have you been marked?"

"We have had no ceremony," Wren said. "Or been marked."

The emperor sat back in his chair and crossed one leg over the other, displaying his powerful muscles. "In order to use the Obsidian Artifacts fully, you will need to be formally mated. You could use the Artifacts without that, as you have discovered, Silas. But formally mating will make it easier for your magic to work with the Artifacts." He looked at Silas. "When you used the Sword, did it seem to fight you? Even after you added Wren's Light magic?"

Silas nodded. "Yeah, it did, but I thought little of it. It was much easier than when I tried to use it without her magic."

The emperor nodded. "Without formally mating, the Artifacts will fight you. The longer you try to use them, the harder it will become."

"So, we need to be formally mated." Wren looked at Silas, then back at the emperor. "How do we do that?"

The emperor waved a hand at his wife. "Cista will arrange a ceremony within the next two days. I'm sure she will love it." He smiled fondly at his wife. "It has been too long since we have had a mating ceremony."

Cista smiled back. "Oh, I certainly will enjoy planning this."

"What exactly happens during a mating ceremony?" Silas placed his arm on the back of Wren's chair, idly toying with a stand of her hair.

"You say some vows and exchange blood," the emperor answered. "The blood exchange is usually the first time a couple merges their magic. For you, the exchange will be symbolic, as well as to create the marking."

"The marking?" Wren tried not to sound hesitant, but she wasn't sure she succeeded. Being marked sounded slightly ominous to her.

Cista answered, holding out her wrist. "It's a tattoo. It will appear on both of you after the blood exchange." On her wrist were two wavy lines that looked like ocean waves. "Verellis has the same mark, his is across his upper back."

"Your marking will be symbolic to both of you," the emperor added. "It isn't painful, but by marking each other, your bond can never be broken, except in death. Right now your bond is permanent," he explained to them. "But if you wanted to, you could break it. It would be a lengthy and painful process, but it can be done. With the marking, the bond can never be broken."

Wren looked at Silas, already knowing what her answer would be. His voice rumbled across the bond, silky and loving. *You know I never want to be parted from you, but the choice is always yours.*

Wren smiled and placed her hand on his thigh. She turned to the emperor and his wife. "We'll do it."

* * *

The two days Cista needed to plan the tethering ceremony were a blur. Wren and her companions spent the time exploring the glass city and meeting Falkor, the sea dragon. Hawthorne spent his time in the library, reading as much as he could, learning about the Artifacts and storing the knowledge for when it would be useful.

Two hours before the ceremony, Cista knocked on Wren's door, a dress thrown over her arm and a trail of servants behind her. She shooed Gabriel and Silas out of the room, leaving Wren and Jerricha standing in the wake of the whirlwind Cista created as she arranged everything the servants brought.

"Sit," Cista commanded with a smile and a wave to the chair in front of the dressing table.

Wren sat, and the empress began brushing and sectioning Wren's hair. "This brings back memories of my own tethering ceremony." Her smile was wistful, her gaze going distant. "I'll never forget that night and how handsome Verellis looked, how it felt to have our magic merged." She looked at Wren, eyes sharpening. "What you have is so very special and rare these days. Treasure it—don't take it for granted."

"I won't." It was the easiest promise she had ever made. She had no doubts, no fears, when it came to binding herself to Silas for the rest of her life. Nothing had ever felt more right.

The three women chatted while the empress fixed Wren's hair and applied her makeup. When she was done, Cista stepped back with a smile.

Wren stared at her reflection. Her auburn hair fell in loose curls down her back. Cista had pulled the sides back, and it almost looked like she had woven them together in the back. The empress added a pale green clip that looked like delicate vines. Her makeup was subtle yet beautiful. Pale pink lip stain and blush, with gold dusting her eyelids. Kohl lining her lashes made them appear impossibly long.

"You look beautiful, Wren." Jerricha smiled at her in the mirror.

The empress motioned Wren to stand and take off her robe, and Jerricha and Cista helped her into the gown. Wren's mouth dropped open when she looked in the mirror once again.

Cista had brought a cream-colored gown that set off her auburn hair. The under layer was a beaded sheath dress that glittered with every move Wren made. The thin straps were simple and attached to the deep, narrow V of the gown. An overskirt of cream silk attached to either side of her hips and wrapped around the back, leaving the front open to show off the beaded underdress.

"It's beautiful," Wren breathed, running a hand down the silken skirt.

The empress smiled and placed a simple golden necklace around Wren's neck and a matching bracelet on her wrist.

"Where did you find such a beautiful dress to fit me?" Wren turned to face the empress.

Cista's smile faded a bit and her eyes filled with unshed tears. "It was supposed to be my daughter's tethering gown. I thought you were a similar size, and I was correct."

Wren reached a hand out and placed it on the empress's arm. "Supposed to be? What happened?"

Cista swallowed and brushed her locs behind her shoulder. "She was involved in an accident. Despite all of our magic, she succumbed to her injuries." Cista forced a laugh and waved her hand. "That was years and years ago. I'm just glad someone can enjoy her dress."

Wren turned back to the mirror. "Thank you for letting me wear her dress," she whispered. "I'm honored."

Cista left when Gabriel knocked on Wren's door. He entered and smiled at the sight of Wren.

"You look beautiful, Wren." He pulled her into a hug. When he stepped back, his eyes were glistening.

"Thank you, Gabe. I'm so glad you are here for this."

"Me too. I couldn't be happier for you. If anyone deserves this happiness, it's you."

Wren smiled. "So, you approve?"

"How could I not? I have seen how happy you are with Silas. And he's a good guy. I know he'll treat you right. I honestly couldn't have chosen anyone better for you."

As tears threatened to fall, she waved her hands at her face. "Stop it, you'll make me ruin my makeup."

He held out his arm and escorted Wren through the halls, Jerricha a step behind. He led her to a small garden filled with tropical flowers, whose scent drifted by on a warm breeze. The sound of birds in the potted fruit trees was melodic and calming to her fluttering nerves. Gabriel kissed her cheek and took Jerricha's hand, leaving Wren standing alone in front of a fountain.

Gravel crunched behind her and she turned. Her heart stopped at the sight of Silas in his usual all black. Except this time, he wore a fancy black jacket that buttoned to the waist and flared slightly at his hips, falling to his knee-high boots. His black curls blew in the gentle breeze. The sight of him took her breath away. He was beautiful.

His green eyes sparkled as he approached. He took her hands in his and looked her up and down. "Wren," he breathed. "You are stunning."

She ducked her head to hide her blush. "Thank you."

He lifted her chin with his fingers. "This is where you say 'You look stunning too, Silas.'" He flashed his half smirk.

Wren laughed. "You do look beautiful, and arrogant as always."

He rolled his shoulders and tugged at the neckline of the coat. "This thing is choking me to death." He unbuttoned the top few buttons.

Wren laughed and shook her head. She leaned forward and placed a kiss on the bit of tan skin of his chest now on display.

His smile faded as he looked at her. His eyes were shining so bright. "Are you sure you want to do this? You really want to be stuck with me for the rest of your life?"

She stood on her toes and placed a gentle kiss on his lips. "I'm positive. I have never been more sure of anything in my life. It has been a long time since I ever felt like I belonged somewhere." She placed a hand on his chest, feeling the steady thump of his heart under her palm. "I'm home when I'm with you. I finally belong somewhere." Tears threatened to fall again and Wren blinked them back furiously.

Silas cupped her cheeks and kissed her. It was a long, slow kiss. Sweet and loving. When he pulled away, he held out his arm for her. "Shall we?"

Wren linked her arm through his and let her mate lead her through the garden.

* * *

The tethering ceremony was to take place on a hilltop outside the city. The view from the top was breathtaking. Deep oranges, pinks, and purples from the setting sun reflected off the glass buildings in the city, making them sparkle. White Queen of the Night flowers, just unfurling their petals, decorated an arch on top of the hill. The fragrant scent of the flowers wound its way around the crowd gathered for the ceremony.

Wren and Silas stepped up to the trellis, hand in hand. The emperor was waiting for them with a wide smile. Behind them stood the empress and the rest of their companions. Gabriel smiled at Wren, pure joy etched across his face.

Verellis stepped forward and began the ceremony without further ado. "Clasp hands," he said simply. He wrapped their hands in a golden rope that shimmered in the setting sun. "Wren, repeat after me."

The emperor spoke words in a language Wren didn't understand, but somehow she felt she understood in her soul. As she repeated them, they sank into her skin, forging to her bones. She felt the words floating before her, waiting.

Silas repeated the words next, the same wonder and understanding showing on his face. His words collided with hers, twisting and twirling together, settling over them and sinking deep, creating an even stronger chain between them. They stared at each other, lost in the moment.

The emperor held a glass chalice filled with white wine in one hand and a glass dagger in the other. He pricked a finger on each of their hands and they let their blood drip into the wine. Wren watched as the red swirled and eddied with the wine.

Wren took the glass first, drinking deeply. She handed it to Silas, who did the same. Immediately, Wren felt their magic surge forth, dancing and twining around them. Shadows and fireflies. Wren gasped when she noticed flickering stars shimmering in the shadows as well. That was new.

Their eyes met, and across her skin she felt a tingling sensation. It traveled over her body until it settled on her right forearm before disappearing. She looked down and saw a tattoo of swirling smoke and twinkling stars. Silas placed his hand on his chest, and peeking through his unbuttoned shirt and jacket was a matching tattoo, sprawled across his tan skin.

They didn't have words as they stared into each other's eyes, the chain between them glowing fiercely. Each link a tether to the other, forged in love and trust and loyalty. Silas stepped forward and lowered his mouth to hers. Wren met him halfway and poured every ounce of what she was feeling into the kiss.

When they finally parted, the emperor unwound the golden rope. He smiled at them. "Congratulations. May your mating be long and prosperous." At his words, music filled the air, and a banquet appeared. "Now we celebrate."

* * *

Wren and Silas danced long into the night, celebrating with their friends and family. When they finally made their way back to the palace and their room, the sun had long since set.

Silas closed the door behind them and slowly approached Wren. He stared into her eyes, one hand on her hip, the other on her cheek. "Even with everything that has happened and everything still to come, I have never been happier since you came into my life."

Wren felt tears build in her eyes. She blinked furiously to clear her blurry vision.

"You are the best thing that has happened to me."

He brushed his thumb over her bottom lip. His eyes had never shone so bright as they did in this moment.

Wren pressed her lips together, trying to hide their wobbling. A single tear escaped, tracking down her cheek. Silas leaned forward and kissed it away.

"You are my world, Wren. The light that shines in my darkness. I love you."

Wren brushed a curl off his forehead. This man, her mate. She had never dreamed she would have something as amazing as this. She stood on her toes and kissed him. It was a slow, sweet kiss. She wrapped her arms around his neck, never breaking the kiss.

Silas threaded his fingers through her hair, tilting her head back. She opened for him and his tongue slid inside. She moaned at the taste and feel of him.

At the sound of her moan, Silas slid his hands over her shoulders, slipping the dress from her arms. It slid down her body, silk whispering in the quiet. It puddled at her feet, leaving her completely bare for him.

He broke the kiss, both of them breathing deeply. He stepped back and ran his hooded gaze over her body.

"So fucking beautiful," his voice was hushed, awed.

Wren felt her face heat. Even after all this time, she still blushed when he complimented her. Wren slipped her hands over his shoulders, removing his coat. She tossed it on the chair while Silas began unbuttoning his shirt.

Every inch of skin he displayed with each button had Wren's fingers itching to touch him. To feel his skin beneath her hands.

Silas pulled his shirt off and Wren ran her fingers over his chest, over the tattoo now inked onto his skin, a permanent reminder of what they shared. She moved her hands lower to his abdomen. His skin was warm and smooth. The muscle beneath was hard and unforgiving.

She reached the waistband of his pants and popped the button, helping them slide to the floor. Her mouth went dry at the sight of his arousal. Heat pooled low in her belly, anticipation growing.

She ran a finger down the long, hard length of him, smiling as he jerked at her touch. She reached the tip and ran her finger through the bead of moisture collecting there and brought it to her mouth, the taste musky and salty.

Silas's eyes flared, and he grabbed her hips, lifting her off the floor. She wrapped her legs around him and their mouths collided. All sense of taking their time was replaced by the urgent need coursing through their veins.

Her back thumped against the wall as Silas pressed her against it. The chill from the wall contrasted with the burning heat of Silas at her front.

He ran a finger through her core, growling his approval at her wetness. Wren gasped and ground against him. Anything to ease the ache building between her legs.

Silas hissed at the contact and gripped her hips harder. He lifted her with one smooth motion before slamming into her.

Wren screamed and threw her head back against the wall. Her nails dug into his shoulders as he pulled out and thrusted in. Again and again.

The feel of him inside her, of his skin rubbing against hers, was pure ecstasy.

He leaned his head down and ran his tongue over her nipple before grazing it with his teeth. Wren cried out again, the pressure in her building higher and higher.

"Silas," she breathed. She begged him with that one word.

He covered her mouth with his own at the same time he thrust so deep Wren came apart around him.

Her vision fractured as she clung to him, moving her hips while Silas continued pounding into her. When he had wrung every bit of pleasure from her, he carried her to the bed and laid her down gently.

He settled over her, brushing her hair away from her face. Wren felt like her heart was breaking looking at her mate. He was so beautiful, and nothing in the world could make her happier. The feeling was almost painful.

Silas slid into her again, molding his mouth to hers. This time they savored the feel of each other, slowly building the ache between them, mapping each other's body with their hands and mouths. When the pressure built to its peak, they came together, clinging to each other. Neither wanting to let go, they curled together on the bed and slept deeply.

Chapter Ten

"The Dark Fae tried to cross the barrier," the emperor stated early the next morning.

They were all seated in the same room they had met in a few days ago. This time, Wren sat next to Silas on a couch. She sleepily rested her head on his shoulder. She tried to focus on the emperor's words, but her thoughts kept drifting to what had happened the night before. The tethering ceremony, the night spent in bed with Silas, and waking up in his arms. All of that amounted to the happiest moments of her life.

She forced herself to pay attention to what the emperor was saying.

"They didn't get through the barrier, of course, nor will they ever. But I think it's time you set off for the Crown, before things move too far along on Sorentiv."

"You mean the Crown isn't here?" Gabriel sat next to Jerricha on a pile of cushions, looking entirely too comfortable snuggled together.

"No, it's not." The emperor sighed, crossing his arms and leaning back in his chair. "Someone stole the Crown from the palace many years ago. We caught the thief and questioned him before he took his own life. We have the location narrowed down to one of three mountains along the Silvaquen Mountain Range. The idea that the Crown would ever be used was so far-fetched, we never thought it worth our while to find it."

Gabriel and Silas exchanged a look. They had clearly been hoping this would be an easy quest. It did not appear this was to be the case.

Verellis stood and took a map from a servant. Kneeling at the low table, he spread the map with scar-flecked hands. He drew a finger along a mountain range. "These are the Silvaquens. They are brutal and not easily traversed." He pointed to three separate peaks. "Mount Caligo, Mount Aquila, and Mount Ventus. We believe the Crown is on one of those peaks."

Silas ran his eyes over the map. "How, exactly, are the mountains not easily traversed?"

"The path is steep, where there is one. When there isn't a path, you will have to climb rock walls and scale narrow ledges. Sometimes you'll have to either jump ravines or find trees to walk across. It is windy and cold, the only place on the island that sees snow."

Wren groaned when he mentioned snow. Silas glanced at her and grinned, clearly remembering their time crossing the mountains to Valasia as well.

The emperor paused, looking each of them in the eye. "And you cannot access your magic on the mountains."

"I don't think we have much of a choice," Gabriel murmured, scanning the map as well. He looked at Wren and Jerricha. "I suppose we can't convince you two to stay behind?"

Wren raised a brow and Jerricha crossed her arms. Neither woman deigned to respond.

"Didn't think so." Gabriel sighed.

"I will stay behind," Hawthorne said. "I'm not one for big adventures, and the library here is calling my name."

After more discussion, much of which Wren struggled to pay attention to, the group broke for lunch. Jerricha and Wren ate in the garden, and the men ate while continuing to pore over maps with the emperor.

The day was beautiful with a warm balmy breeze. The potted citrus plants in the garden perfumed the air, along with the many tropical flowers. Wren and Jerricha sat on a blanket, chatting about the night before and how wonderful it had been.

"I have never seen my cousin so happy," Jerricha said between bites of cucumber sandwich. "He has been through a lot, experienced a lot of dark things. He could never convince me he was okay, despite how hard he tried. That all changed when he met you."

Wren's heart warmed at her words. "I'm glad I could help pull him from that darkness." Wren took a sip of lemonade. "Speaking of seeing someone happy, you and Gabriel have been looking awfully happy together."

Jerricha blushed. The strong Viking woman, who wasn't afraid to take on anything, actually blushed at her words. "It's nothing," she said quickly.

Wren grinned. "Mmm-hmm. Sure doesn't seem like nothing. For what it's worth, Gabriel is a good man. I couldn't pick anyone more perfect for my brother."

As Wren said it, she realized how true that was. Gabriel's need to protect and defend was something Dark Fae admired. While Jerricha didn't need the protection, it was something she appreciated. Gabriel's outgoing personality was a perfect match for Jerricha's tendency to be more reserved. They would balance each other wonderfully.

"I appreciate you saying that." Jerricha set her sandwich on the plate. "But I'm Fae and he is human. There is nothing but heartbreak in our future. He will die and I will have to live on without him."

The words hit Wren in the chest like a physical force. Her heart squeezed painfully as she realized the same would happen with her. She would have to watch her brother grow old and die. There would be a time in her life when his steady presence would be gone. She forced the thought from her mind. She would discuss it with Silas later. Right now, she could practically feel the despair radiating from her friend.

"While that's true, isn't it better to enjoy it while you can? Make memories you can look back on?" She bit her lip. "Besides, isn't it too late at this point? No matter what happens, you are going to get hurt, whether it's now or years from now. We should live our lives for the now, so we have the memories to help us through the times of heartache."

Jerricha said nothing. She sat back on her hands and peered off into the distance.

Wren left her to her thoughts as Wren's own thoughts became a whirlwind of fear and sadness.

Are you okay? Silas's voice penetrated her thoughts. She must be sending all her feelings across the chain of their bond.

I just realized I will outlive Gabriel. Just sending that down the bond made her nauseous, as if admitting it made it real.

Ah, I wondered when this would come up.

I don't know what I will do without him. He has always been there, a force in my life I could never ignore.

You can't think of the future, Wren. Silas's voice was a cool balm to her agonized thoughts. *Enjoy the time you have with Gabe. If you let your fear of the future rule your life, you will miss out on all the amazing memories you can make with him.*

Wren smiled ruefully. *I pretty much just said the same thing to Jerricha.*

Silas's chuckle rumbled in her mind. *Sounds like you*

already know what to do. You just have to follow through on your own advice.

The bond fell silent, and Wren thought about what Silas said. She knew he was right. She had just told Jerricha the same thing. It didn't make it any easier to think of losing Gabriel.

The appearance of the empress interrupted her thoughts.

"Hello, ladies," she chimed as she breezed into the garden. "I've heard about your upcoming journey and I think we ladies need to go shopping."

The rest of the day was chaos as everyone prepared for the upcoming adventure. Silas and Gabriel planned with the emperor, learning everything they could about the land and what they might expect. Aeron spent the time with the emperor's advisor, gathering supplies and weapons. Wren and Jerricha found themselves in the city with the empress, shopping for clothing—fur-lined coats, mittens, scarves, fleece-lined leggings, and socks.

By the end of the day, Wren was exhausted. She collapsed into bed and was asleep before Silas came up for the night.

They started early, before the sun had risen. Their plan was to ride to the base of the mountains, then continue on foot, as the terrain was too steep and rocky for the horses. The boys had decided on starting with Mount Caligo. It was the most likely location of the Crown, according to the emperor.

Mount Caligo was a magical mountain covered in mist, similar to the barrier around Valasia. The emperor said the magic was old and predated the Elementals by thousands of years. He also stated it was a finicky magic. Only two people could ascend to the top and they couldn't have any kind of bond.

Wren could feel through the bond how uneasy that made Silas. He would have to let his mate ascend the mountain without him. And, if Wren was being honest, she wasn't particularly thrilled to be traipsing through a magical mist without him. They debated on whether Gabriel or Aeron would go with her. In the end, Aeron was the lucky chosen one. They weren't sure how the magic would react to the bond she had with Gabriel, even if it wasn't a physical one.

It took half a day for them to make it to a plateau where the mist began. The view of the glass city below was breathtaking, but Wren only had eyes for the wall of swirling gray mist. She donned her fur-lined coat, trying not to think about what could happen in that mist. Silas approached, and the others backed away, giving them privacy.

He kissed her hard, holding her gaze through the kiss. "Remember, don't listen to anything you hear in the mist. Believe nothing you see or hear."

She nodded, heart pounding.

"Don't let go of Aeron's hand for any reason. Focus on your task and nothing else."

She nodded again, swallowing thickly.

"You can do this, Wren. You are strong and brave. I'll be here waiting for you when you get back." He kissed her one last time before turning to Aeron.

"I will protect her with my life." Aeron bowed his head to Silas, hand on his heart.

Satisfied, Silas stepped away. Wren almost reached out for him, not ready to let go yet, but Aeron approached and took her hand.

"Ready, princess?" He gave her a cocky grin, eyes twinkling.

Wren sighed, gathering her courage. "Let's get this over with."

"That's the spirit." Aeron laughed.

Together, they stepped into the mist.

Immediately, it felt like someone had cut the chain between her and Silas. She knew they wouldn't be able to communicate, but the feeling left her reeling and clutching her chest. At the same moment, her magic turned to vapor in her veins. No bonds, no magic inside the mist. A chill skittered down her spine.

It was as if they had entered another world. The mist dampened all sounds. She could hear their breathing, but all noises from outside disappeared. The mist was cool on her exposed skin, the damp already seeping in like an unnatural blanket wrapped around her. The light filtering through was dim, casting everything in shades of white and gray. Wren tightened her grip on Aeron's hand.

Neither spoke. The quiet was so unnatural it felt like an invitation to bring something evil down upon their heads by breaking it. They steadily climbed, stopping only for brief drinks of water and a bite or two of food. Both were eager to reach the top as quickly as possible. Aeron carried a small tent on his back—they would have to spend at least one night in this mist.

Toward what Wren assumed was evening, a memory assaulted her. It was dragged forth from her, a force prying into her mind and replaying the scene in her head. It was the evening the general had declared she would marry Crown Prince Castain. The feelings from that night surged forth— anger, hurt, and betrayal. Wren gasped at the same time Aeron grunted.

She looked at him and found his eyes glazed, lost in his own memories. Was this the magic of the mist? Making them relive their memories? Wren shook her head to dispel the remnants of the images in her mind, but the feelings lingered. Neither

Wren nor Aeron mentioned what happened, but they continued on, holding tighter to each other's hand.

When it was too dark to continue on, Aeron set up the tent. Wren stayed near him, keeping him in her sights at all times. She dug through her bag for food and water. Inside the tent, they ate their meager meal in silence and darkness.

As Wren was lying down, another memory surfaced, crashing its way into her consciousness—Gabriel telling her he had known all about her past, that she wasn't his sister, that her mother was Fae. The feelings from that night came with it, and Wren felt lost all over again. She shook herself, balling her hands into fists. She told herself it was just a memory. It was the magic using her worst fears and nightmares against her.

She lay in the dark, listening to Aeron's unsteady breathing as he also worked through whatever the magic was showing him. It was a long while before she fell asleep.

* * *

Time had no meaning as they continued climbing the next day. Everything was the same—the same gray landscape, the same unending silence, and the same damp chill on their skin. The same swirling gray mist. Wren's legs and lungs burned as the ground sloped higher. Aeron had whispered earlier he believed they would reach the summit that night.

Wren couldn't wait. Memories were constantly replaying in her mind. Some were true, some were not, and some were a mixture of both. It was those memories, the ones that were partly true, that left Wren feeling shaky and unsteady. It didn't take long for her to forget what was real and what was not. Each memory left her questioning the truth. She tried to remind herself it was the magic, none of it was real, but some of it was and it was getting harder and harder to tell the truth from the lies.

When she would glance at Aeron, she could see the same battle raging on his face. At times, his hand would tighten on hers almost painfully. She didn't mind, because she was sure she was doing the same thing to him.

She was getting ready to ask Aeron if they could stop for a quick break. She opened her mouth, but paused as a memory of Silas crashed through her. It was when the Dark Fae had taken her hostage the first time.

She was sitting on the throne, subjected to the depravity of the Keep. Silas entered and hope flared in her chest. He was going to rescue her. He looked at her and a cruel smile curled his lips. His eyes were cold and unfeeling as they traveled over her body, their usual warmth absent. He sauntered over to her and laughed at the expression on her face. Her heart crumpled, and she fought the tears that burned her eyes. He gripped her chin painfully and tilted his head to the side.

"Did you honestly believe I cared for you? So naive." He clucked his tongue and walked away.

Shame made her cheeks heat. She had believed he cared about her. How terribly wrong she had been. She watched as he pinned another woman to the wall, her blond ponytail swaying as her bright red lips spread in a smile.

Wren tried to look away as he kissed her, hands roving over her body and under her skirts. She couldn't. It was as if some force made her watch. The woman writhed against Silas's hand and she dug her hands into his curls. They left the hall, Silas never sparing a glance behind him.

Wren fell to the ground with a sharp cry. She didn't feel the sting in her hands or knees, only her tears, warm against her cool flesh. That couldn't be true, could it? She racked her brain, trying to discern the truth from the lie, but it was all a muddled mess of confusion and uncertainty. Had Silas really betrayed her like that? She could vaguely remember feeling betrayal caused by him. Her chest ached and she sobbed, unable to keep the pain at bay.

Aeron knelt down in front of her and wrapped his arms around her. He said nothing, just held her as she cried onto his shoulder. When she finally got her emotions under control, she pushed away. Aeron's face was haunted and pale. Whatever memories he was fighting were not pleasant either.

"Almost there, princess," he murmured.

He helped her to her feet and they continued on, battling memories the whole way, until they came upon a cave. They peered inside.

"Is this it?" Wren whispered.

"I don't know," Aeron whispered back. "We're at the top of the mountain though. There is nowhere else to go."

Aeron took a torch out of his pack and lit it with a flint. Wren squinted in the sudden brightness. Both drew their weapons and took one step inside. Nothing happened. They took another step. Then another. They reached the back of the cave in minutes. There was nothing there but darkness and scurrying insects.

Feeling defeated, Wren and Aeron settled at the mouth of the cave for the night. Wren sat with her knees drawn to her chest. She didn't sleep—she just stared out into the mist, unblinking. Aeron lay next to her, but his eyes also remained open, trained on the ceiling above them.

Despair washed through Wren. They had traveled all this way and relived their worst memories for nothing. She stubbornly brushed away a tear that escaped. It was going to be a long night.

Chapter Eleven

They didn't make it to the plateau by nightfall the next day, despite how fast they traveled. They had to camp one more night in the magical mist. One more night of torture. Both she and Aeron were quiet and withdrawn, haunted by what they were seeing in their own heads.

The last leg of the journey was the worst. The magic showed her memories that made her want to cry and scream and curl up on the ground, never to get up again. It showed her all of her friends and family hurting her in some way. She had no idea what to believe anymore. The worst were the memories of Silas.

The last memory the mist showed her was after she and Aeron had escaped the Keep with the Sword.

Wren walked numbly to Silas and asked him about Inara. He smiled a small, hateful smile.

"Yes, I am engaged to Inara. We are to be married next year. What? Did you think you actually meant something to me?"

"What about the bond?" she whispered.

Silas laughed. "It's nothing. We'll use it to get the Artifacts

116

and stop your father. I had no intention of staying with you after this is done."

Wren felt herself breaking. "You said you wanted it. You said you wanted me."

"And you were so desperate for anyone to love you, it wasn't hard for me to convince you. I needed you to accept the bond so we could use the Artifacts. Nothing more." A cruel smile graced his lips. "Inara is my true love, my only true love. And I will return to her side when this is through."

Wren stumbled a step and Aeron caught her. She thought the memories of Silas would get easier to bear, but they only got harder. Had he really only gone through with the tethering ceremony for those reasons? She looked at her forearm, the tattoo was proof the ceremony had happened. She hated the sight of the shadows and stars, hated the reminder of him that broke her a little more each time he entered her thoughts.

She forced herself onward. Aeron's presence at her side had become a comfort in the nightmares of her memories. She had a feeling he felt the same way.

One step they were in the mist, and the next they were squinting in the afternoon sun. Their companions were sitting around a fire waiting for them. Wren felt the bond snap into place, and she immediately blocked Silas from her thoughts and feelings.

He stood and took one step toward her. She felt a sob rising in her chest and pushed it back. She rushed to Gabriel and threw herself into his arms.

"Wren?" Silas's voice, obie concern and worry, made her tense in Gabriel's embrace.

"Please," she whispered to her brother, the word catching in her throat as the first few tears fell.

She felt him look to Silas before leading her away from the group. She knew some of the memories the mist showed her of

Gabriel were true. She knew he had hurt, but he was still her brother and she needed him right now.

He sat her down on a rock and knelt in front of her. He took her head in his hands and looked into her eyes. "Talk to me, Wren. What's wrong? Are you okay?"

Once her tears started, she couldn't stop them. She felt raw and exposed. Confused about what was real and what wasn't. Her heart hurt. She physically ached at the thought of Silas.

She looked at her brother through her tears. "The mist..." She stopped to swallow. "It showed us memories. Real and fake. There were so many, it was constant. It became impossible to tell what really happened." Her breathing hitched and she forced a deep breath. "I don't know what memories are real anymore."

She finally broke down, falling forward into Gabriel. He caught her and held her through her tears, rubbing gentle circles on her back.

"What can I do? How can I help you?" He sounded pained, as if the idea of what Wren went through actually hurt him.

"Silas," she whispered, voice thick with emotion. "Is he engaged? Does he love her?"

"Oh, Wren," Gabriel began. "Whatever the mist showed you about Silas was not true. He loves you more than anyone else in this world. I can promise you that."

"He chose to be mated with me because he wants me? Not just for the Artifacts?"

Gabriel pulled away and looked Wren in the eyes. "I swear to you, Wren, there is no one else he would rather be with. He chose you because he loves you and he wants to spend the rest of your lives together."

Wren was quiet for a moment, thinking through what

Gabriel said and trying to work it into the images that had assaulted her nonstop for the past three nights.

"You should talk to him, explain what happened, and hear what he has to say," Gabriel finally said.

Wren nodded. "Not right now though. I think I need some time."

"I understand." Gabriel stood and pulled her to her feet. "I'll go tell him to give you some space."

Wren stood by herself, staring at nothing, feeling nothing. She was numb. Aeron was similarly standing apart from the group. She approached him and grabbed his hand. He looked at her, his expression mirroring her own.

"How do we get past this?" he asked quietly. The pain in his eyes made Wren want to cry all over again.

"I don't know," she replied honestly.

He pulled her in for a hug, his arm a comforting weight around her. They stood like that until the sun began its descent.

* * *

When Wren and Aeron finally told the group they hadn't found the Crown, Gabriel and Silas began making plans to go to the next peak. Mount Ventus was the highest peak of the Silvaquen Mountain Range. The emperor had warned them the wind and cold would be brutal, as would be the terrain. Crevasses covered Mount Ventus and rockslides were frequent.

Throughout the planning, Aeron and Wren sat quietly, both lost in their own thoughts, trying to reel themselves back in from what they had just endured. Wren felt Silas's eyes on her frequently, but she ignored him. She wasn't ready to talk— she needed more time to sift through her feelings.

She shared a tent with Jerricha that night but didn't confide in her. The presence of the mist just outside the tent made her weary. Recollections of her venture into the magical barrier wouldn't be leaving her anytime soon. She laid down early, but sleep was a long time coming. She sifted through the memories that had plagued her in the mist, trying to sort through them to find the truth. It left her head confused and her heart aching.

When the sun finally began peeking over the horizon, Wren wasn't sure she had slept at all. Her steps dragged as they began their trek to Mount Ventus. She kept close to Aeron. His presence was comforting for the fact only he understood what she was going through.

The magic of the mist dissipated the farther they got from Mount Caligo. She was finally able to sift through the memories, finding what was real. It was a relief to know what Gabriel had said was true. None of what the mist showed her of Silas was accurate. Despite this knowledge, she still wasn't ready to talk. The pain she felt was too real, and she needed a little more time to pull herself together.

The terrain got rockier the higher they climbed. No one spoke, and the silence was heavy. It took all of their focus not to trip and fall. Wren and Jerricha frequently needed help from one of the boys to lift them over boulders that were too high for them to climb. By midday, they had to pull up hoods and dig gloves out of bags. The wind whipped around them, its icy fingers penetrating even the warmest clothing.

Twice they had to stop and wait for a rockslide to settle before continuing on. The rumble of the mountain under her feet was terrifying. The sound was deafening as rocks clambered down the mountainside. Each time, Silas began to make his way to Wren, but each time he stopped, honoring her request for space.

The day was never-ending, and Wren's sleepless night was catching up with her. Aeron had to help her maneuver around more and more boulders as her strength and endurance flagged. When they finally stopped for the night, Wren collapsed on the ground, staring up at the darkening sky. The few stars that winked into existence made her think of her tattoo and the tethering ceremony with Silas.

"Your tent is ready." Aeron stood over her, blocking her view of the sky. He helped her to feet. "I'll bring you some food."

She barely remained awake long enough to eat before she and Jerricha were sound asleep.

* * *

Everyone gathered around the precipice. The ravine before them was deep, the bottom shrouded in darkness. Across the way was more rocky terrain, the boulders even larger. Wren wasn't sure how she would get over them.

But first, they had to find a way across the ravine. It was too wide to jump and to risk it would certainly mean falling to their deaths.

"We have rope." Gabriel pulled the length of rope from his bag. "But no way to secure it to the other side."

"What about that tree over there?" Silas pointed to a stunted tree that looked about to blow over in the wind. "We could knock it down and span the width of the ravine."

Wren swallowed. She wasn't afraid of heights, but crossing a ravine on a pitiful-looking tree with the wind blowing around her wasn't her idea of a good time.

Silas pulled a hatchet out of his belt and began chopping the tree down. Jerricha sidled closer to Wren.

"This is a horrible idea," she muttered.

Wren nodded. "I don't see another way though, do you?"

Jerricha didn't answer.

The tree crashed down after only a few hits with the hatchet. It looked splintered and weak, which didn't bode well for being able to bear their weight as they crossed.

The boys stretched it across the ravine and stood back to examine their work.

"It will have to do," Gabriel said. He wrapped one end of the rope around his waist and handed Silas the other end.

Once Silas had the rope secured around his middle, Gabriel took a step on the tree. Wren held her breath, hand clutched in Jerricha's. Gabriel tentatively took another step, then another. The tree was holding. He slowly inched his way across, arms out to either side for balance. He jumped the last few feet to solid ground and turned to grin at everyone.

"Just like old times, Wren," he called across the ravine.

Wren shook her head. This was nothing like the times they jumped from tower to tower at home. That fall would have merely broken a leg. This one would kill them.

He untied the rope, and Silas pulled it back to their side. Jerricha went next without incident. Wren decided it was time for her to go before she lost her nerve.

She tied the rope around her middle and stepped up to the ledge. Her stomach was a mass of writhing nerves and she felt like she was going to vomit. She sensed Silas move toward her, wanting to say something, but she stepped on the tree before he could.

The wind battered her, threatening to knock her off the bridge. The tree wobbled, and Wren gritted her teeth as she inched her way forward. She kept her eyes straight ahead, her focus anywhere but on the unending drop below her. Before she knew it, Gabriel was pulling her to safety. She released the breath she was holding and collapsed on the ground in a shaky puddle.

Aeron crossed next. The wind picked up and he struggled

to maintain his balance. He had to drop to his knees and crawl across to avoid being tossed over the side. He crawled onto the ledge and lay there, panting.

"I never want to do that again." He slowly stood and motioned for Silas.

Wren stood, hands pressed to her stomach as Silas took his first step onto the makeshift bridge. Three steps in and a gust of wind blew his hood off, sending him rocking backward a step.

Wren stifled a gasp with her hand. She almost dropped the wall around the bond but didn't want to distract him.

Halfway across, the tree cracked, the sound snapping through the silence like a firecracker. Silas's wide eyes shot to Wren. Another crack, this time the tree buckled.

"No," she breathed. She took a step forward. Not like this. It couldn't end like this. Not with the words unsaid between them. Not after all the horrible memories the mist had forced on her.

Silas took another step, another crack. Wren could see it snaking through the tree. One more step and it would break.

Silas held her gaze, eyes softening. She shook her head and her breathing hitched.

Dropping the wall around the bond, she said, *Don't you dare.* Tears fell freely down her cheeks now, freezing in the icy wind.

He said nothing, just took that last, irrevocable step that broke the tree. Wren felt the crack in her bones as Silas plunged down into the darkness.

She screamed and rushed forward, but Jerricha grabbed her around the waist and held her back.

"Silas!" she screamed his name until her voice was hoarse. She fell on her knees and screamed to the heavens. It echoed around them, bouncing off the side of the mountain and causing a few pebbles to tumble down the mountainside.

Aeron jerked as the rope connecting him to Silas went taut. Gabriel grabbed Aeron and the rope, and together, they pulled. They pulled and pulled until a hand reached up and grabbed the ledge.

Silas hauled himself up, collapsing on the ground and rolling onto his back. Blood streamed from a cut on his forehead. His chest rose and fell in heaving pants. Wren cried out and ran to him, landing on top of him so hard he grunted. In that moment, Wren didn't care if he had bruises or broken ribs. She just needed to feel him.

She sobbed into his chest, her body shaking so hard she thought she would fall apart. His arms came around her and she cried even harder.

"I'm sorry. I'm so sorry, Silas."

"Why are you sorry, Wren? You have nothing to be sorry for." He tightened his hold on her.

"I shut you out. I shouldn't have shut you out." She pushed up far enough to look at him. His curls were windblown and his cheeks and nose were red from the cold. "I had so much to process after the mist, but I should have talked to you."

He sat up, grimacing slightly in pain, but his arms remained around her, and he kissed her forehead. "Don't apologize. You needed time, and I understand that."

"I thought I had lost you," she whispered. "I thought you were gone and I would never be able to explain, never be able to tell you I loved you."

He smiled softly. "I know you love me, Wren. It will take more than a bit of magical mist to change that."

She laid her head on his shoulder and memorized the feel of his chest rising and falling.

"We need to keep moving," Gabriel interrupted. "We need to get to the next waypoint before it gets dark."

Wren reluctantly removed herself from Silas's arms. She

wiped her tears. Already they felt like they were beginning to freeze on her cheeks. Jerricha handed Wren a clean cloth and Wren quickly wiped the blood from Silas's face. She pulled his hood back up, tucking his curls underneath. He pressed a quick kiss to her lips before they set off again.

By the afternoon, snow began falling. Wren glared at it as it accumulated on the ground beneath their feet. The snow made it more treacherous and they had to focus on each step to keep from slipping.

As before, on their journey to Valasia, Silas appeared unaffected by the snow or cold. In fact, he seemed to enjoy it. A smile graced his lips, and he frequently chuckled at Wren as she stumbled and cursed her way along the mountainside.

"Keep laughing and I'll push you over the edge," she threatened him at one point, instantly regretting it as she remembered that had just almost happened.

He only laughed harder.

By the time evening fell, the snow was past their ankles. They set up the tents and lit a fire to help warm them through the night, although the wind blowing around the camp negated the effects of the fire pretty quickly. Wren gladly shared her tent with Silas that night, and although Jerricha didn't say it, Wren knew she was glad to share her tent with Gabriel.

Wren laid on the ground, the wind howling through the mountains, rippling the walls of the tent. She silently cursed the cold and the need for so many layers of clothing. Silas must have read her expression or her emotions through the bond. He gave her his half smile and laid down next to her.

"Clothing never stopped me before," he whispered in her ear.

Her back arched and she closed her eyes. He bent his head and kissed her deeply. She needed this, needed the reminder he was alive and he loved her. She needed to erase the horrible memories the mist had planted in her mind.

Silas's hand found its way under her coat. She yelped at the coldness of his skin but quickly forgot about it as his hand worked its way under the waistband of her leggings. She lifted her hips, urging him on, and he complied.

The wind drowned out her moans of pleasure as Silas worked her into a frenzy until release barreled through her. When she lay panting, eyes closed with a smile on her face, he gathered her close to him and laid down. She slept deeply for the first time in days.

Chapter Twelve

W ren felt refreshed the next day. A full night's sleep next to her mate was all she needed.

They continued their trek across the mountain. The snow had fallen most of the night and was up to her waist in some areas. Progress was slow, and Wren wished she had her magic to melt a path for them.

During one break, Wren noticed the glazed look in Aeron's eyes. She bit her lip and made her way to him.

"Are you okay, Aeron?" She kept her voice quiet. No one needed to know what he went through in the mist.

At first, Wren thought he wouldn't respond, but then he said, "When I was younger, I told my mother something, thinking she would support me. I was wrong. She told my father, and it outraged him. He beat me every day because of it." He looked down at his hands fisted in his lap. "I went with Silas on one of his first missions. When I returned, my father was dead. I suspected Torryn had something to do with it, but he would never admit it. My mother never spoke to me again after that."

Wren shifted to face Aeron fully, heart aching at his story.

"The mist showed me memories of my parents accepting me, loving me for who I am, instead of hating and beating me. The hope it gave me that maybe those were genuine memories almost destroyed me."

"Oh, Aeron," Wren breathed. She couldn't imagine how painful it would be to have been given hope for something you so desperately wanted, only for it to be ripped away. She thought it would be worse than the false memories she had experienced.

"I thought I was over it, over wanting them to accept me, but the mist showed me otherwise." He sighed and looked out toward the group resting and eating. "I always told myself it was okay because I had a group of friends who accepted me, but in all honesty, they haven't."

Wren tried to protest, but Aeron cut her off.

"I have never told them what I told my parents all those years ago. My friends really don't know the real me, so how can they truly accept me?"

The pain etched across his features had tears blurring Wren's vision.

"The one thing the mist made me realize," Aeron continued, meeting Wren's gaze, "is that I want to be accepted by my friends."

"Aeron, you don't have to tell us anything you don't want to." Wren clasped his gloved hand in hers.

"No, I think I need to." He took a deep breath, steeling himself and looked away, unable to meet Wren's gaze any longer. "I like men. I prefer men over women."

Oh. Wren sat in silence for a moment, thinking of what to say. What Aeron had just told her was the ultimate taboo in most of Sorentiv. If people knew, he would be shunned and publicly shamed. And being Dark Fae, it would probably be so much worse for him.

"When I first arrived in Valasia," Wren said slowly, "I saw couples that were both male or both female. At first, it shocked me. I had never seen that before in Ellendyr. I had heard about it, I had heard what people said, all the awful things. But it was the first time I saw it with my own eyes." She looked up at the sky, squinting her eyes at the brightness. "After seeing it a few times, I questioned why it was so upsetting to other people. I saw nothing wrong with it. They looked at each other the same way I look at Silas. It was beautiful." She turned to Aeron. "Love is something to be cherished and protected, no matter who you love. If a person can be lucky enough to find that unconditional acceptance and understanding, why does it matter who it is with?"

Aeron looked at Wren, and she could see the weight lifting off his shoulders at her words. Tears built in his eyes, and Wren wrapped her arms around him.

"It doesn't matter who you love, Aeron, as long as they love and respect you." She pulled away. "I won't tell anyone what you told me, but I know none of them will care who you love."

Aeron swallowed thickly. "Thank you, Wren. You know, if you ever decide to take up your title, you will make a great princess."

She shuddered. "Bite your tongue."

The sun was low on the horizon when they came to another ravine. This one at least had a narrow ledge along the wall of the mountain they could make their way across. The ledge was half a foot wide and covered in snow.

"I'll cross first and knock the snow off as I go," Silas said as he began tying the rope around his waist.

Wren whipped her head in his direction. "No."

He wrapped her in a hug. "I'll be fine." He kissed her cheek and began shuffling his feet along the ledge, facing the mountainside. As he went, he used his boot to knock the snow off, leaving a glittery trail of ice in its wake. "It's really slippery, guys. Be careful."

Wren fisted her hands against her stomach and held her breath. She didn't dare blink as he slowly reached the other side. Once he was finally on solid ground, he untied the rope and let Gabriel reel it back to the other side.

Wren went next, followed by Aeron. Neither had any problems crossing. Jerricha slipped once, her boot glancing off the ledge, but she was able to get her balance and continue. Gabriel was the last to cross.

Once they were all on solid ground, Wren looked around. Her gaze caught on a dark patch on the mountain wall behind them. She approached and found a narrow crevice gouged into the rock wall. The opening was so narrow she wouldn't be able to make it through with her bag. Without thinking, she dropped the bag and turned sideways, sucking her stomach in as she started sliding through.

"Whoa, Wren." Silas rushed up and grabbed her arm. "What are you doing?"

"I need to go this way." She felt something pulling her, tugging on her middle. It was an incessant tug, drawing her deeper into the crevice. She pulled her arm out of Silas's grasp and continued on.

He cursed, dropping his bag and squeezing in behind her. "You are going to be the death of me, Wren," he muttered.

Wren barely heard him. The pull on her middle was getting stronger. Her breath came in rapid pants as she pushed herself through the crevice faster and faster.

The walls suddenly opened up and Wren tumbled out, staring straight ahead at another cave. Silas stumbled into her as he fell out of the crevice. He stood behind her, hands on her hips as he too stared at the cave.

It was massive, the entrance almost as tall as the palace in the glass city. The inky darkness leaking out seemed to call Wren further, invisible fingers beckoning her inside. Even with her magic dampened by the magic in the mountains, she felt it stirring in her veins, the telltale flutter of firefly wings waking up.

"It's in there," she breathed. She took a step forward, but Silas's hand on her hip stopped her.

"Slow down." He stepped around her and drew the Sword and his dagger. They didn't have a torch since they had left their bags behind. They were going in blind.

Wren kept her hand on Silas's shoulder as they stepped into the darkness. It completely enveloped them. She held her hand in front of her face and the darkness was so complete she couldn't see it. Silas took small, slow steps, testing the ground in front of him with his foot and the surrounding space with the Sword.

They walked for what felt like hours. In reality, it was probably only minutes, when the Sword hit something in front of Silas. The sound of rock hitting rock was loud to her ears after the silence of their journey.

Keeping her hand on Silas, she stepped around him, arm out. Her hand brushed a rough, rocky surface. She trailed her fingers up over a ledge until they met something that sent a shudder through her body.

Silas grabbed her tighter. "Wren!"

"I'm okay," she breathed. She wrapped her hand around the object and instinctively knew what it was. "It's the Crown."

She lifted it from where it was sitting and both she and Silas froze. A tremor rocked the ground beneath them. Wren grabbed tighter to Silas, eyes wide in the dark.

"What was that?" she whispered.

Before Silas could respond, another tremor rocked the earth, this one almost knocking her off her feet. Dust and small pebbles rained down from above.

Silas sheathed the Sword and grabbed Wren's arm. "Let's go now!"

He pulled her back in the direction they had come, both stumbling as the earth rocked beneath them. The sound of heavier rocks falling raced toward them, the cloud of dust quickly catching them and taking over.

Wren pushed her legs faster, her grip on Silas's hand almost painful. The dust in the air choked her as she gasped for breath.

Light pierced the darkness ahead of them and Wren almost cried out with relief, but the sound of crashing rocks grew closer and louder. Silas cursed and pushed Wren ahead of him, toward the light. She didn't let go of his hand, only held on even tighter.

As they ran through the entrance of the cave, the whole thing crashed down behind them, sending dust and rocks flying. Silas pushed Wren to the ground, covering her body with his own as the surrounding mountainside crumbled.

When the ground finally stopped shaking and the sound of falling rocks faded, Silas slowly sat up, pulling Wren with him. The entire cave had been reduced to rubble. The narrow crevice they had passed through was gone. Debris had rained down around them but they had been spared. A circle free of rock surrounded them, as if an invisible shield had protected them.

Wren looked at the Crown in her hands. It was surprisingly light. A solid piece of obsidian carved with alternating tall and short spikes. It glinted dully in the dusty evening light.

Silas stood and walked to the collapsed crevice. Their

bags were on the other side, as were their companions. He cupped his hands around his mouth. "Hello! Are you three okay?"

Wren held her breath until she heard Gabriel's muffled voice through the fallen stone.

"We're fine. What about you?"

"We're both good. We got the Crown, but we're trapped in here." Silas looked around. There was no way out for them, except over the rock. There was a smaller plateau to their right they might be able to climb to. "I think we will have to climb our way out. Can you get back to the palace?"

"Yeah, our path is clear. We'll head back and meet you two there. Be careful!"

Silas turned and looked at Wren. "Guess we're climbing." He gave her a crooked grin, the familiar sight settling some of her nerves.

They didn't have any supplies. Both of them had dropped their bags at the entrance to the crevice. Silas had a dagger and the Sword, and luckily, he still had his waterskin slung over his shoulder. Wren swallowed the nerves that fluttered to life inside her. They were going to have to climb down the mountain with no supplies. Even their magic was gone.

Silas sensed the unease skittering through her and wrapped his arms around her. "We'll be fine. I promise I won't let anything happen to you."

Wren sighed. She knew there was only so much he could do, but she knew he would do everything possible to get them down the mountain safely.

They slept where they were for the night. The collapse had created a little pit that provided enough shelter from the elements for the night. Silas sat with his back resting on a wall and Wren snuggled in next to him.

She didn't think she would sleep, but the warmth of Silas's

body next to hers and the slow circles his hand rubbed on her back had her eyes closing before she knew it.

* * *

Silas woke Wren before the first rays of the sun penetrated their little pit. They didn't have any food, and Wren's stomach was already growling. She took a swig from Silas's waterskin, hoping the water would pass a worthy substitute. The rumble her stomach emitted said otherwise.

Silas headed for the plateau, reaching to grip the edge with his hands. He hauled himself up and leaned over, hand down to help Wren. She rolled her eyes before jumping up, grabbing the ledge, and pulling herself over. She gave him a look and he chuckled.

They continued this way, climbing up the mountain to get out of the pit they had been stranded in. When they finally reached the top, Wren glanced around. Snow covered everything. The morning sun was blinding as it reflected off the white landscape. She looked to Silas for direction.

"We head down." He pointed to an area that looked relatively smooth compared to other areas around them. "We're on Mount Ventus." He bent and drew a rudimentary map in the snow. "I'm guessing we're around here. If we head down this way, we will come out near a small town where we can get supplies and horses to make our journey back to the glass city."

He stood from the map and held out his hand. Wren grasped it, savoring the warmth from his skin. She wished she had some gloves. Together they slowly trekked down the mountain. Silas kept them to the flattest parts of the terrain, avoiding large boulders that would require climbing over.

The snow was almost to Wren's knees, and she was quickly tiring from trudging through the deep white stuff. She grumbled to herself the entire way, her stomach rumbling in tandem. She occasionally caught Silas's grin when a particularly vulgar curse would escape her mouth and she was tempted to throw a snowball at him to make him stop.

"Where are we going to sleep tonight?" Wren finally asked through gasping breaths. "There is no way we are making it down this mountain before nightfall."

Silas bit his lip and looked around. He shook his head and said nothing. His uncertainty wormed through her. If Silas was worried, she should be extremely worried. As it was, she was too tired to worry. With each step, she felt like her muscles would give out. She gritted her teeth and continued on, determination steeling her spine.

When Wren could no longer convince her legs to keep walking, she collapsed to the ground. Hunger and fatigue were wearing her down quickly. She looked up at Silas in desperation.

He pursed his lips and looked around. Finally, he reached down and hauled her to her feet. "That tree over there"—he pointed to a stunted evergreen—"I think it will be our best option for shelter tonight."

She numbly trudged to the tree and fell against the trunk. She slid to the ground and thumped her head against the bark. A shower of dead needles rained down around them.

The tree provided little shelter. Its branches were wind-blown and mostly brown. It was barely enough cover to block the wind. At that moment, Wren didn't care. She was sitting down and her quivering muscles were finally getting some much-needed rest.

Silas looked around before sitting next to her, offering as much warmth as he could. "I had hoped to start a fire, but the snow is making all the wood too wet." He looked at Wren, worry pinching his brows. "You okay?"

She swallowed and was able to find words, well, a word. "Fine," was all she could manage at the moment.

Silas's brow drew down in worry, but she knew there wasn't much he could do. He handed her the waterskin. At least all the snow provided them with plenty of water. She drank deeply, filling her belly with water. It wasn't food, but it eased a bit of her hunger.

Silas wrapped her in his arms, pulling her tight against him. It was going to be a long cold night.

* * *

Wren slept fitfully. When they finally rose from the shelter, they were almost buried in snow. She was shivering so violently she could hardly walk. Silas wasn't doing much better. He was hunched over, shivering and hungry, but he kept on walking. So, Wren did too.

The walk was uneventful, besides the myriad of times Wren fell and struggled to keep going. Only Silas's presence kept her putting one foot in front of the other. By evening, the snow was gone and the slope of the mountain got smaller. Eventually, they had to take off their coats as the temperature steadily rose.

Rocky ground became fields of wild grasses that waved in the warm island breeze. Silas's pace picked up as the terrain became easier to traverse, but Wren still stumbled and tripped as her exhaustion and hunger weakened her.

"There." Silas finally pointed. In the distance Wren could just make out a small town, firelight flickering in the oncoming darkness. "We'll find a place to eat and sleep for the night."

The town was small but well-kept. Whitewashed buildings with dark wood shingles lined the gravel street. Plots of gardens, growing everything from flowers to herbs to fruits and vegetables, stood in front of every house they passed. Firelight lit the gravel road, shadows dancing in the wavering light.

Both Wren and Silas had been too exhausted to notice their magic returning, however at the sight of the light and dark flickering by the torches, Wren felt her magic stirring in her veins. It gave her a bit more strength to continue the short distance to the tavern.

A sign hanging above the door depicted an overflowing basket of fruits and vegetables, the name written in a language Wren couldn't read. Silas opened the door and walked to the bar, and Wren followed closely behind him. The room was large, with round tables scattered throughout. Many of the tables were filled, and barmaids bustled back and forth from the kitchen, taking orders and filling mugs.

"Can I help you?" An older woman with gray-streaked black hair smiled at them from behind the counter. "You look like you have had quite a journey." She looked them over, curiosity painting her features.

"We are guests of the emperor," Silas began.

The woman's eyebrows rose. Clearly that was something she wasn't used to hearing. Wren assumed most visitors didn't make it through the barrier around the island.

Silas continued, "We were in the mountains when we experienced a quake. We were separated from our group and our supplies. Would you know of a place we could sleep for the night?"

"We felt that quake all the way here. Thought the mountain would tumble down around us." She appraised them again. "There are a few rooms upstairs. You can use one for the night."

"Food," Wren blurted, staring at a plate a barmaid carried past. The smells that wafted from the plate made her stomach cramp painfully.

The woman smiled. "Of course. Take a seat. I'll get food right out to you."

Wren and Silas had just sat down when a barmaid placed plates and mugs in front of them. Wren closed her eyes and inhaled. Chicken on a bed of rice with some kind of gravy and vegetables Wren had never seen before. Not letting it cool down, Wren dug in and began stuffing food in her mouth, ignoring how it burned her tongue.

Silas chuckled. "Slow down, love. You'll make yourself sick." For all his words of slowing down, he ate his food just as fast as she did.

"I have never eaten anything so delicious." She was looking at her empty plate, contemplating licking it clean. The warm food in her stomach had her eyelids growing heavier.

Silas watched her yawn and got the key from the woman at the counter. He motioned Wren to follow him. Each step felt like climbing a single mountain. She had to use the handrail to pull herself up. Silas stopped at the third door down the hall and unlocked it.

Wren didn't even look around the room before collapsing into the bed, Silas not far behind her.

Chapter Thirteen

Silas woke the next day before Wren. He sat in bed and watched his mate sleep. She looked so peaceful, with none of the worries or stresses of their lives weighing her down. He couldn't wait until all this was over and they could enjoy each other without the threat of battle looming over them.

Sighing, he stood and walked to the attached bathing room. It was much smaller than the one in the palace, but still contained a rain shower. He stripped off his dirty clothes and turned the knobs. Soon the room was warm and steamy from the hot water falling from the ceiling.

He stepped in and almost groaned at the delicious heat that fell over his aching muscles. Trudging through the mountains had not been easy. Almost dying on that broken tree had shaken him more than he was willing to admit. Almost dying and Wren not speaking with him had been even worse.

He understood why she had distanced herself after the mist of Mount Caligo, but he hated that something had driven a wedge between them. He hated she had felt those doubts and fears and he had been able to do nothing about it. What was worse, he knew it wouldn't be the last time. They still had so much to face ahead of them, and even with all his magic, he was powerless to stop it.

A sudden blast of cold air on his skin had him turning toward the curtain, but he stopped when Wren's arm came around his waist. She rested her head on his back, and he wrapped his hands around her wrists.

"I really need one of these back home," she murmured onto his skin.

He chuckled. "I'll make sure you get one."

Her hands began roving south and Silas felt heat pool in his stomach and lower. He hardened as she teased him, moving her hands back up his stomach. Her name left his lips on a growl and he tried to turn around, but she stopped him by wrapping her hand around him. He hissed through his teeth at the contact, placing both hands on the wall in front of him.

He watched as she began working him from base to tip, pausing to swirl her thumb around the head. His hips jerked and her throaty laugh almost had him coming right then. He let her work him until he decided it was her turn.

He grabbed her hands and pulled her around, pressing her back to the wall. She gasped, and Silas took advantage, sweeping his tongue into her mouth. She melted against him, her soft curves clinging to him. His arousal pressed against her stomach and she tried to move against him, but he held her in place.

He lowered his hand between them, parting her flesh. Her head fell back as he ran a finger down her core. Pressing biting kisses to her neck, he slid a finger inside. She moaned and dug her nails into his shoulders, trying to move on his hand. He held her still, and he pumped in and out, slowly working her into a frenzy.

He added a second a finger and Wren pleaded with him breathlessly. Loving the way his name sounded on her lips, he smiled. He pressed his thumb to the bundle of nerves between her thighs and she cried out, clenching around his fingers.

He watched her, heat building in him as his mate found her release. She looked beautiful with her skin rosy and flushed from her pleasure and the heat of the shower. He removed his hand and met her eyes as he licked his fingers clean, the taste of her like some kind of exquisite fruit. Her eyes darkened at the sight and he grasped her hips, lifting her until he teased her entrance.

"Should I continue?" His voice was low and smoky.

She only nodded and swallowed, trying to push herself down onto him. He chuckled and watched as he slowly lowered her onto his arousal. He gritted his teeth at the warmth and tightness that surrounded him. It was like coming home. He knew this was where he belonged, with Wren, his mate.

"I will never tire of this," he said as he gently placed a kiss on her lips and began moving in and out slowly.

They both needed a reminder after what they went through on the mountain. A physical reminder of their love for each other. He was alive, she was alive. They had survived another hurdle. They would continue to survive no matter what was thrown their way.

When they had both found their release, he lowered Wren to the floor. They finished their shower in a comfortable silence. When they stepped out and wrapped towels around themselves, Silas looked at their clothing.

He wrinkled his nose, picking up his shirt. "I really don't want to put this back on."

Wren grabbed the shirt from his hand, as well as the rest of their garments. She washed them in the shower, cleaning them as best she could. When she was done, she used her magic to create a fiery ball of light that quickly dried them.

"That's a handy trick," he muttered as he took his clothes from her.

"Too bad I couldn't use it to keep us warm in the mountains."

They dressed quickly and went down to the tavern, where they ate a small breakfast and prepared to head back to the palace. Silas approached the lady behind the counter who let them use the room.

"Thank you for letting us stay the night. How much do we owe you for the room?" He reached into his pocket, hoping he had something to pay with.

The lady smiled brightly. "You owe nothing. I'm just glad you both look more rested. A friend of the emperor is a friend of mine." She placed her hand on her heart and bowed her head.

Silas repeated the gesture and said, "Thank you. We will not forget your kindness."

She reached under the counter and pulled out two bags. She handed them over to Silas and said, "Some food for your journey. Safe travels."

Silas thanked the woman again and headed out of the tavern. Wren was waiting for him outside, and Silas looked her over with a critical eye. She looked more rested. Her face had some color and the circles under her eyes were gone. She turned and smiled at him. His heart pounded in his chest at the sight, muscles he wasn't aware of being tight relaxed. The worry of her health melting away.

"Are you feeling okay enough to travel?" He couldn't resist asking, just to make sure. "We can stay another night if you need to rest some more."

"I'm fine. With my magic returned and the food and sleep last night, I feel more like myself."

"Good. Then we can head on out." He swung the bags of food onto his shoulder along with the waterskin. He grabbed Wren's hand in his own and they headed down the street toward the outskirts of town.

"How long will it take us to get back to the Crystal Palace?" Wren asked as they walked.

"I'm guessing about two days. Luckily, it will be warm enough to sleep out in the open without a tent." He looked at Wren and smiled. His heart felt the lightest it had in a while. He lifted her arm and placed a kiss on the tattoo marking her as his. "There is no one else I would rather be on this crazy adventure with."

Wren's beautiful blue eyes sparkled as she smiled. "I couldn't agree more."

* * *

Wren actually enjoyed this part of their journey. Despite the need to get back to Sorentiv quickly, they took their time traveling back to the Crystal Palace. The landscape was beautiful and easy to navigate. They crossed fields of tall sprawling grasses with random trees growing in their midst. They waded through streams meandering lazily through the fields. Silas caught rabbits for dinner and they cooked them over a fire near a stream.

Conversation flowed easily between them, as it always had. They talked about anything and everything, but neither brought up the war nor what they would face when they returned to reality. They slept under a tree, wrapped in each other's arms, the stars a blanket above them.

When the city finally appeared on the horizon, the Crystal

Palace rising above it all, disappointment flooded Wren. Reality crept back in, stealing the quiet peace she and Silas had found the past two days. She didn't want this time with him to end. She didn't want to return to Sorentiv, to the war and all the uncertainties that came with it. Here, on this distant island with no Dark Fae threat looming over them, Wren had gotten a glimpse into what the future could be like for her and Silas. It solidified the risk of everything they had to lose, of everything that could be destroyed and taken away from them.

Sensing her quickly spiraling emotions, Silas pulled her against his side and kissed the top of her head. He said nothing. There wasn't much he could say. It was the reality of what they faced and what they fought for. One thing was for certain though. Wren would use these quiet, happy memories she had made. She would remember that this is what she was fighting for. This waited for her on the other side, and she would be damned if she let anyone take it away from her.

Word spread quickly after they entered the City of Rainbows and, by the time they reached the palace, Gabriel and Jerricha were waiting for them in front of the grand doors.

"Are you guys okay?" Gabriel asked as he pulled Wren in for a hug.

"Yes, we're fine." Wren squeezed Gabriel back before giving Jerricha a quick hug. "And we got the Crown." She indicated the bag Silas carried. A telltale bulge showed through the thick material.

"So, we have all three," Jerricha breathed.

"Kind of." Wren shrugged. "Don't forget the Eyeglass is in Valasia under siege. I have no clue how we are going to get it."

"Don't worry about that right now." Silas led Wren through the doors into the fancy glass foyer. "Let's just focus on figuring out the Crown and getting back home safely."

"Agreed," Gabriel said quietly, brow drawn in thought.

Wren studied her brother's furrowed brow with a frown of her own. "What worries you, brother?"

Gabriel laughed without humor. "What doesn't worry me?" He shook his head to dismiss Wren's further questions. He grabbed Jerricha's hand and led her away. "We'll let the emperor know you have returned. Go clean up and get some food. You both stink."

"That's rude," Silas murmured as they walked to their suite. He lifted his arm and sniffed, recoiling with a grimace. "Then again, he speaks the truth."

Wren laughed before falling quiet. Silas always seemed to make her smile when it was the last thing she wanted to do. The world could be falling apart around her —in fact, it kind of was—and still, Silas was able to bring joy to her life. The thought struck her so fast and violently, she had to blink rapidly to keep tears from falling.

"What's on your mind, love?"

"Thank you," she blurted.

"For what?"

She looked up into his face. His shining green eyes, his perfectly kissable lips, his black curls falling in disarray around his head. Her heart skipped a beat, and she squeezed his hand tightly. "Just ... thank you."

The next morning, Wren and Silas met with the emperor and his wife. Gabriel, Jerricha, Aeron, and Hawthorne were also in the emperor's sitting room. Wren felt rested after a good night's sleep in a comfortable bed next to her mate, and she was ready to tackle the issues at hand. Namely, how to use the Crown and Eyeglass.

Wren set the Crown on a low table in the middle of the circle of chairs and cushions. The black shards of obsidian reflected in the pale glass it rested on, while the sun streaming through the windows appeared to be swallowed up by the dark stone.

The emperor released a breath as he stared at the Crown. "I haven't seen that in many years." He turned his gaze on Wren. "Can you feel it?"

Now that she had the time and energy to properly focus on the Crown, she could feel the pull on her magic. As if the Crown were trying to suck her magic into itself. She shuddered.

The emperor chuckled at her reaction and took that for her answer. "Yeah, it's not very pleasant, is it?"

Everyone else glanced between Wren and the emperor, feeling nothing of the devouring sensation. Even Hawthorne looked bewildered by their reactions.

"The Sword, as we said before, is a conduit," the emperor explained. "You send your magic into it, and the Sword sharpens it—strengthens it while you use less. The Crown is an amplifier. You feed it magic and it will store it until you are ready to use it, in which case the Crown will amplify the magic being released from it."

"I'm assuming only Light magic will work with the Crown?" Wren asked, not taking her eyes off the Artifact.

"Correct, and only the Light magic from a Sun Caster who is bonded to a Shadow Caster. Just like the Sword, you will need to use a bit of Silas's Dark magic to get your magic into the Crown."

"So, I just give it my magic and it will hold it until I need to use it? How do I do that? And how much does it hold?"

"It can hold more than you can give it in one sitting. I would imbue a little every day until you need to use it. As for feeding it your magic, just imagine your magic as a thin thread and the Crown as a needle. Thread your magic through the eye of the needle. Once you try it, it will come naturally. Same with using it."

Wren reached out and grabbed the Crown from the table. Closing her eyes, she did as the emperor instructed. She imagined her magic as the fireflies fluttering around her. She lined them up and sent them off to the Crown, one after another. A gasp in the room had Wren opening her eyes. The black shards of obsidian were glowing with an inner light, a faint pulsing of her fireflies. She smiled and glanced at the emperor.

"See? Pretty easy," he said.

Wren set the Crown back on the glass table and looked at Silas.

"What about the Eyeglass?" Silas asked the emperor.

The emperor sighed heavily, settling back in his chair. "The Eyeglass is nastier to use, I'm afraid. It destroys magical barriers and shields. Any wards placed on an object or city, or shields placed on persons or armies, can be destroyed by the Eyeglass. Thus allowing the Crown and Sword to be used to their fullest potential—without having to take down anything in their way."

"Why is it nastier to use?" Silas leaned forward, unease passing through the bond to Wren.

"While the Crown and Sword were infused with magic and can only be used by magic wielders, the Eyeglass was not infused with magic. Only a human can use the Eyeglass—at the cost of their mortal life."

Chapter Fourteen

"No!" Wren's gaze shot to Gabriel, already knowing what was going to happen. "You are not using the Eyeglass."

Gabriel looked resigned as he stared at his sister. "It's the only option, Wren."

"No, it's not! Someone else can use it. It doesn't have to be you." Wren's heart began beating faster, the rhythm stuttering in her chest as her breathing grew quicker and quicker.

"Would you trust anyone else with it?" Gabriel shook his head sadly before continuing, "besides, I won't allow one of my men to die for this. You know it has to be me."

Wren thought back to her and Silas's return to the Crystal Palace and the worry she saw on Gabriel's face. "You knew," she breathed, blinking back tears. "You knew it was going to come to this."

"Suspected," Gabriel clarified. "Hawthorne found some information on the Eyeglass in one of the scrolls we found in Sorentiv."

Wren turned her gaze on Jerricha. The Viking woman was

quiet, eyes focused on her lap. Her arms were wrapped tightly around her middle and she appeared to be barely breathing. Looking back to Gabriel, Wren stood. "I won't allow you to do this. End of discussion."

"You can't stop me, Wren."

"The hell I can't." Wren stormed out of the room, the glass door closing quietly behind her. She wanted it to slam. She wanted the glass to shatter into thousands of pieces, a representation of how she felt at the moment.

She couldn't lose Gabriel. He was her only family besides Silas. He was the only person who knew her as a child, her one link to her innocence. Gabriel was such an ingrained part of her that she couldn't imagine living life without him. She refused to let him kill himself using the Eyeglass. They would find another way. They had to.

Wren wasn't paying attention to where she was going. She just knew she had to get away. Her heart was breaking in her chest and her breaths were coming in ragged pants. She fisted her shaking hands and wrapped her arms tightly around her middle, trying to quell the nausea she felt at the thought of Gabriel dying.

Before she knew it, Wren found herself on the dock behind the palace. The sun was warm on her face and the breeze blowing in off the ocean was chilly and scented with salt. She breathed deeply, drawing in the calming scent, trying to slow her heart rate. The wooden dock creaked under her boots as she approached the edge and sat, legs dangling over the crystal waters.

She didn't know how long she sat with the rough wood digging into her palms and the sea breeze blowing her hair around her face. A shadow appeared in the water below her, growing bigger as it approached the surface.

Not a shadow. Falkor, the sea dragon.

His broad head breached the surface, nostrils blowing water in a spray of droplets. His amber eyes glowed with unfathomable, ancient knowledge as he looked at Wren. He raised his head on his serpentine neck until it was level with her then slowly he lowered it in Wren's lap.

The heavy weight of his head was a comfort. The warmth of his massive body seeped into her pants, along with the water dripping off his scales in rivulets. He exhaled in a rush of warm air, causing Wren's hair to flutter around her face. She placed her hand on top of his head and ran her fingers down the smooth, hard scales. Falkor's eyes closed, and he made a sound deep in the back of his throat that reminded Wren of a large purring cat.

The distraction the sea dragon provided was welcome. She watched the way the sun reflected off his blue-green scales and made the iridescent colors shimmer. She watched his lower body float lazily in the ocean, the occasional swish of his massive tail keeping him afloat. He was a beautiful creature, terrifying and kind. His presence was doing more to calm her nerves than anything else could have.

"I wish I could take you back with me," she whispered to the sea dragon.

Falkor chuffed, a sound that made Wren think he was laughing.

The sound of boots thudding on the dock distracted Wren from the sea dragon. She glanced over her shoulder and saw Silas prowling toward her. Falkor lifted his head and sank below the waters before Silas sat next to Wren.

"I wish I had a pet sea dragon." Silas settled back on his hands, tilting his face toward the sun.

Wren didn't bother to reply. She braced her palms on the edge of the dock and leaned forward, watching the shadow of Falkor slowly disappear into the depths. She remained in that position long after the sea dragon had disappeared, staring into the crystal blue waters eddying around the dock.

Silas sighed and turned his gaze on Wren. "We don't have to talk about it now. Let's get back across the ocean and get the Eyeglass in our possession before we worry about it."

"I can't let him do it. I can't let him kill himself for this war. Maybe it's selfish of me to risk everything, to risk all those lives just so he can live, but I'm okay with that. I'm not okay with losing my brother."

Silas pulled her against his chest as her voice caught on the last word. She kept her tears from falling, but she shuddered in his arms. His palm was warm as it drew gentle circles on her back.

"We'll talk about it later. Don't worry about it right now. Just try to keep an open mind and think about it from all angles."

Wren shook her head, her cheek rubbing against the soft fabric of Silas's shirt. She couldn't ever imagine a world where she would agree to letting Gabriel use the Eyeglass.

Silas sighed again and stood, reaching a hand down to help Wren to her feet. He placed his palm on her cheek, his thumb rubbing gently back and forth. He looked into her eyes and she had to fight back a sudden surge of fear at the sadness swirling in those green depths. She suddenly felt the need to be closer to him, to feel his body against hers.

She speared her hands into his hair, gripping tightly as she pulled his head down to hers. Their lips met, and Silas matched her intensity with his own. He pulled her tight against him and she felt the hard ridges of his muscles through his clothing. She felt the barely contained power in his body as he surrounded her.

When they broke apart, Silas rested his forehead against Wren's while he ran his fingers through her hair. His breath fanned across her lips as he whispered, "Let's go eat some lunch. The emperor wants to make plans this afternoon for our journey home."

Wren nodded and laced their fingers together before turning back toward the palace.

After a mostly silent lunch where Wren remained lost in her own thoughts, everyone met back in the emperor's sitting room. The Crown was still sitting on the low glass table, sucking up the afternoon sunlight streaming through the windows.

Wren grabbed the Crown and sat in a chair off to the side, hoping no one would sit around her. She wasn't sure she could fake being civil to anyone right now. Sensing her mood, Silas sat on the couch next to Aeron but kept one eye on Wren. He was tense, his muscles coiled tightly as if he was prepared to jump to Wren's side at a moment's notice.

Jerricha was sitting next to Gabriel, but she appeared as lost in her own world as Wren was. Gabriel's gaze kept bouncing between Wren and Jerricha, his lips tightly pressed in a flat line. His knee was bouncing up and down uncharacteristically, his nerves getting the best of him.

They were quite the group today.

Keeping her focus pinned on the Crown, Wren spun the Artifact in her hands. She couldn't keep her thoughts from the war and what was waiting for them when they returned home. There was no way she was going to let Gabriel use the Eyeglass.

Without the Eyeglass though, she imagined their fight would be a lot harder. They would have to use everything in their power to win against the Dark Fae. Wren called up her magic, ignoring the voices around her making plans for their journey home. She sent a thread of her magic into the Crown. If they were going to need as much help as they could get to win this war, Wren would fill the Crown to bursting with her magic to give them an edge.

* * *

Silas rolled his shoulders as discussion continued on what supplies would be needed for their return trip home. Wren had blocked him from the bond and it left him feeling uneasy, as if someone was staring at him from the shadows. He glanced in her direction again and found her in the same position she had been in since she had sat in that chair. Legs curled under her, shoulders slumped, head bent over the Crown she was twirling in her palms. Her eyes were unfocused, unseeing of the world around her. And the bond was silent. No, not just silent, but walled off like a dam in a river.

He was worried about her, but there wasn't much he could do right now. He would have to get her to talk to him later. Get her to open up and let her feelings out. Bottling that shit up was never a good idea.

He refocused on the conversation as he heard the emperor mention Captain Cassidy.

"What did you say?"

"Captain Cassidy and his crew sailed home already," the emperor repeated. "They wished to return home, and I sent them on one of my ships while you were retrieving the Crown."

Another thing Silas had to add to his list of things to do. Repay Cassidy for his wrecked ship. He also planned on sending money to the families of the sailors lost at sea. Silas ran a hand down his face, feeling like he had aged twenty years in the past few days.

"Do we know what the current situation is in Sorentiv?" he asked.

"I've heard a bit, but news is slow in getting here. By the

153

time you leave and arrive home, things will have changed." The emperor shook his head before continuing, "But what I have heard is not good. The Dark Fae have laid siege on Tethoris."

"Shit," Silas muttered under his breath. It truly didn't surprise him, but it was definitely something they could do without. "What about the Avisten army? Were they able to get out in time, or are they stuck behind the walls?"

"That I haven't heard. I hope for your sake they can join with Ellendyr's army or I'm not sure you will win this one."

"Shit," he muttered again, darkly. A war at two fronts, Valasia and Avisten. This was definitely not what they needed. Silas took a deep breath, bracing himself for the question he was preparing to ask. "What about the Elementals? Are you able to provide us with any kind of help?"

The emperor glanced around the group gathered before him. A muscle feathered in his jaw as the wheels turned in that ancient brain of his.

Silas held his breath, not daring to move in the slightest. He could see how this would play out. If the emperor said no, they were done for. Even if they got the Eyeglass, they didn't have the forces or power needed to fight the Dark Fae on two sides. Even with both human armies, the Light Fae, and all three Artifacts, the Dark Fae had tremendous power and their numbers were far greater than the Light Fae. It would be a bloodbath.

The emperor nodded his head. "It goes against everything we have done to create this life for us here, but I will send a small force with you."

Silas sagged on the couch. A small force of Elementals may very well change the tide if everything played in their favor. He was opening his mouth to give his thanks when a light suddenly flared to his left where Wren was sitting. He turned his head and watched as if the world slowed down as Wren gasped and collapsed in a heap, falling forward from the chair. She landed on the floor with a thud, her auburn hair splayed around her.

He lunged toward Wren with a wordless cry, scooping her up in his arms. Her skin was paler than normal, her brows drawn down over her eyes, and her breath came out in small pants. He placed his hand on her cheek and her skin was ice-cold, as if all the warmth had seeped out of her.

"Wren," he said out loud and down the bond. "Wren, wake up!" He looked up at the emperor as he knelt next to Silas. "What's wrong? What's happening?"

The emperor looked at Wren, his gaze roaming up and down her body. A slight crease formed between his brows.

"Help her," Silas growled when the emperor said nothing. "Why are you just sitting there? Do something!" His heart was beating frantically in his chest. His mate was laying in his arms, unmoving and cold, and he didn't know what to do. There was no obvious threat to protect her against.

He was opening his mouth to yell at the emperor some more when the man finally reached a hand out and pried the Crown from Wren's fingers. Silas hadn't even noticed she was still clutching the thing in her fist. As soon as her skin was free of the touch of the Crown, Wren released a gasping sigh. Silas stopped breathing himself as he watched Wren's chest fall. He stared and stared, silently begging anyone who was listening to save his mate.

He watched as her chest rose again, her lungs inflating, breathing life back into her skin. Her color improved and her skin warmed to normal. Her face relaxed, smoothing out until it looked like she was sleeping peacefully. Silas brushed his hand down her face, watching her chest rise and fall normally. He looked to the emperor, the question in his eyes so he didn't need to speak it aloud.

The emperor twisted the Crown this way and that so the

glow within the obsidian shards showed, pulsing brightly now. "She was feeding the Crown and she gave it too much. The Crown took over. She needs to be careful or it will take until there is nothing left of her."

Fear spread through Silas, a frozen blast that unfurled from his middle and gained speed until it took over. He looked at the face of his mate with her long auburn eyelashes fanned against her cheeks. "Will she be okay?" he breathed.

"Yes, this time she will be. She needs to rest and let her magic replenish. She can't do that again. Next time, she might not be so lucky."

Silas stood, holding Wren close to his chest. He didn't say a word as he departed and ignored everyone's worried stares. He kept looking at Wren's face as he took her back to their room. That was too close. He knew what they were facing was going to be dangerous. He knew all of them might not make it through to the other side safely.

What he had never let himself imagine was losing Wren. It was something his mind and body couldn't physically handle. This scare with the Crown just reinforced how much she meant to him and how much he took for granted her presence in his life.

He laid her on their bed, brought the covers up, and brushed her hair back. He leaned over and kissed her forehead. "I can't lose you, Wren," he whispered. "I love you too much."

He pulled a chair close to the bed and settled in to watch over his mate.

Chapter Fifteen

Wren had learned her lesson. Don't give the Crown too much of her magic. After waking in their bed, Silas had explained what happened. Since then, Wren had been very careful about how much she fed the Crown.

Now, on the deck of the emperor's personal ship, Wren held the Crown loosely in her hand while looking out over the crystal-blue waters. Falkor had kept pace with the ship for the first two days, however, he had departed with a splash a day ago and Wren found herself curiously lonely without his presence.

Silas spent most of his time with Gabriel, Aeron, and Hawthorne, making plans for when they landed in Alynthi. He was giving Wren the space she needed to sort through her thoughts about the Eyeglass and Gabriel. Jerricha was likewise spending her time alone, and Wren had a feeling she was doing the same thing.

After the incident with the Crown in the emperor's sitting room, Wren thought back to the moment she had collapsed and lost consciousness. Much of that moment was a blur, but what she clearly remembered was a tugging sensation along her spine. As if her very life essence was being sucked away. She assumed that feeling was her body telling her she was using too much magic.

During the three days at sea, Wren had tested that theory and found it to be correct. So, she spent her time filling the Crown and paying attention to her body. When she felt that tugging along her spine, she stopped and rested. Never for long though. She couldn't stand the thought of Gabriel sacrificing his life to use the Eyeglass.

As a result of the constant drain on her magic, Wren was listless and fatigued. She could hardly walk from one end of the ship to the other without getting winded and requiring a break. The sacrifice was worth it though. To save her brother, she would sacrifice anything and everything.

While he gave her the space she needed, Silas frequently checked in with Wren through the bond. Nothing more than a tug on the chain between them, making sure she was okay. Wren would tug back, letting him know she was. Well, as okay as could be expected. Unfortunately, as one of those tugs came through, Wren was too engrossed in what she was doing to reply. Instead of tugging back, she stared out across the rolling waves, the sun glinting atop the peaks of the swells.

The next thing Wren knew, Silas was beside her, his broad hand warm on her low back.

"Are you okay?"

She turned her head to look at him and the world kept right on spinning even though her head had stopped moving. Silas grabbed her upper arms and steadied her.

"Whoa. Wren, you need to take a break from the Crown and let your magic fully replenish. You are wearing yourself to the bone."

She looked into his sparkling green eyes and saw the

concern in them. The same concern she felt flowing through the bond. She knew he was right, but it felt wrong to stop. She felt a compelling need to do whatever she could to give them an edge. Frustrated, scared, and utterly exhausted, Wren couldn't fight the tears that pooled in her eyes.

Silas pulled her against his chest, tucking her head under his chin. "I wish you didn't have to deal with any of this. If there was something I could do to make this easier on you, I would do it in a heartbeat. I am so sorry, Wren."

Unable to keep the tight hold on her emotions any longer, she buried her face in Silas's chest and wept. He said nothing. He just held her tightly, supporting her without words. When she finally calmed, she took a deep breath and looked into his eyes again.

"Promise me," she whispered. "Promise me, if we get the Eyeglass, you won't let Gabriel use it."

Silas wiped her cheeks with his thumbs, staring deeply into her eyes. "Are you sure? You are willing to risk the outcome of the war to save his life?"

There was no judgment in his voice. He wasn't condemning her for her choice. He just wanted to make sure she understood and accepted the consequences of this decision. She nodded, fully aware of the implications.

"Okay, I promise."

Wren fell in his arms at his words, relief rushing through her body, causing her muscles to go lax. With that reassurance, not only Wren's body sagged in relief, but her mind did as well. Suddenly, without having the constant worry of Gabriel's life suspended over her head, Wren's consciousness shut down. Her thoughts slowed until all she could focus on was the warmth of Silas's body surrounding her. Her eyelids grew heavy and her breathing slowed. Before she knew what was happening, she was collapsing to the deck in an unconscious heap.

* * *

Silas lounged in a chair next to Wren's bed as she began returning to consciousness. He tried to control his emotions. The last thing he wanted was for her to wake up to his emotions thundering down the bond. Anger and frustration and fear all warred within him.

When he began the task of freeing the Dark Fae from King Deimos, Balor, and his uncle, he never expected it to be quite this hard. Wishful thinking on his part to assume he was strong enough to handle those three men while keeping casualties to a minimum. The group he was part of, the rebel Dark Fae, was a joke. They would never have survived what had happened so far. Never in his life had he imagined this route becoming so serious. With the Artifacts in play, the entire game had changed.

He glanced at Wren. When he started this journey, he never had imagined himself falling in love. The stakes were so much higher now. Wren's life, the future they could have, the lives of his family and friends, all of it weighed on him. All of it was at risk of being lost. He broke out in a cold sweat at the thought and he rubbed his chest as if he could ease the ache that had taken up residence in his sternum.

"You're angry," Wren mumbled as her eyes fluttered open.

Silas took a deep breath to calm himself before speaking. "I'm not angry—"

"Yes, you are. You can't lie to me about your feelings."

He rubbed his hands down his face and collected his thoughts. "I know what you're doing and I don't blame you for it, but I need you to take care of yourself."

Wren shifted her eyes from his gaze and fiddled with the sheet covering her chest. "And what exactly am I doing?"

"You are trying to carry as much of the weight as possible. You don't want to see your friends and family get hurt, so you are doing everything you can to make sure they are safe." When she didn't respond, Silas continued, "Like I said, I don't blame you for doing that. Hell, I'm trying to keep myself from doing the same thing. The thing is, if you don't slow down, if you don't let other people do what they need to do, you won't live long enough to see them safe at the end of the road. You need to take care of yourself first. *I* need you to take care of yourself. If you don't make it through this, Wren, I won't make it through either."

Wren swallowed thickly. "You promised Gabriel wouldn't use the Eyeglass. Are you going back on that?"

"No, I won't take that back. I understand, I truly do. If the roles were reversed, I can't say I wouldn't be getting the same promises from you. But, because of that promise, because Gabe won't be using the Eyeglass, you are running yourself into an early grave. I need you to promise me you will slow down. Give your body and magic time to heal and recover."

Wren struggled to sit up in bed. Silas let her, hoping she would realize how weak she had become, even though watching her struggle and doing nothing to help her went against every instinct screaming in his body. When she got herself settled against the headboard, she looked at him. The pain in her eyes magnified the despair coming through the bond.

"I am so scared," she whispered. "When I left the manor, I thought I was just traveling to Valasia. I thought I was going to find out who my mother was, learn my magic, and return home. I never thought I would be thrust into the middle of war fighting for not just my life but all of Sorentiv." Tears shimmered in her blue eyes and gathered on her lashes. "I don't know how to do this."

Her whispered words cut through him more painfully than any knife or sword ever could. He slipped off the chair and gathered her up in his arms. There was nothing he could do or say to ease her fears. There were no instructions to give her about fighting a war. It was all uncharted territory for himself as well. He felt completely helpless as he held his mate while she cried in his arms, every instinct in him roaring to take away her pain and remove all threats. If only he could do that for her.

When her tears finally slowed and she could breathe deeply, Silas shifted her so she was straddling his hips. He fanned his hands on her face, rubbing away the last few tears that fell.

"I wish I had something to say to make this all okay. Better yet, I wish there was something I could do to make it all go away. I can't guarantee anything except my love for you. I will be here with you, supporting you, loving you. Lean on me as much as you need to. That's what I'm here for." He pressed a gentle kiss to her lips. "You're not alone, Wren."

She nodded and kissed him back. "Thank you."

Trying to lighten the mood, Silas gave her one of his crooked grins. "Feel up for taking a walk?"

Hand in hand, they walked the length of the ship twice, taking their time to look out over the railing to the crystal-blue waters below.

"Oh look," Wren exclaimed, the top half of her body leaning precariously over the railing.

Silas grabbed her arm, his heart in his throat, and yanked her back. "Do you have to throw yourself over the side of the ship?"

She rolled her eyes. The sight of her attitude once again rising to the surface eased some of the tension in Silas's body.

For too long now, she hadn't been her usual self, and Silas missed the carefree way Wren went about her life.

"Look." Wren pointed to the water below, a smile pulling her mouth wide.

Silas leaned over the rail and felt his own mouth pull into a smile. A pod of dolphins swam with the ship. They cut through the water effortlessly, their sleek bodies propelling them forward. Wren gasped in delight as one jumped from the water, arching high in the air before it dove under the surface once again. Silas couldn't help but stare at his mate. His chest ached at the sight of the joy shining in her eyes. He had seen so little happiness lately, and he knew the things they would face in the coming weeks would dull that joy again.

Pushing those thoughts aside, he watched his mate as she watched the dolphins. He wasn't aware of the others coming to stand beside them. His focus was solely on Wren. The shout from a crewmember drew his gaze away to the distance. Land appeared ahead. Alynthi Harbor was swiftly approaching as the ship continued on. He wished they had more time. More time to enjoy the carefree feelings they had just claimed. More time before the real world forced itself back into their thoughts.

Silas sighed and closed his eyes briefly. When he opened them, the joy was already draining from Wren's eyes as she too noticed the harbor coming into view.

"I'll make sure you get that joy back," he whispered as he made a promise to himself to do just that.

Wren narrowed her brows at his statement, but Silas just shook his head and placed a kiss on his mate's lips.

Chapter Sixteen

Wren made her way down the gangplank with Silas close behind. The arching bridges spanning the winding blue-green canals that usually brought her so much joy barely registered in her mind. With the approach of spring, colorful baskets of cascading flowers decorated every window and reflected off the surface of the water. For once, the sight of the capital city did nothing to ease her spirits.

General Bishop and Queen Elowyn waited just beyond the dock, their entourages clustered behind them. A figure broke ranks and prowled over the docks, black fur shining in the sunlight.

"Winston." Wren knelt on the sun-warmed wood and buried her face in the wolf's fur. The first stirrings of happiness she had felt since she had learned of the Eyeglass fluttered in her chest. "I met someone I think you would love. His name is Falkor. I believe you two could be fast friends." Winston's ears perked, and he tilted his head to the side, listening to every word she spoke.

Silas scratched Winston behind his ears before following Gabriel and Jerricha to the waiting crowd. With a last hug for her wolf, Wren slowly stood and joined them.

"I'm glad to see you home safely," the general said, clasping hands with Gabriel. Emotion filled his eyes as he looked upon Wren, but he said nothing. He ignored Silas and Jerricha completely.

"Were you successful in your quest?" Queen Elowyn had eyes only for Wren.

"We have the Crown, yes," she replied. She laced her fingers through Silas's and leaned against him. Despite taking a step back from filling the Crown, she was still exhausted and couldn't seem to catch up on any sleep on the journey home.

The queen didn't respond at first. Her gaze bounced back and forth between Wren and Silas, assessing and studying. When her gaze landed on the bit of tattoo peeking through Silas's shirt, her mouth tightened. Finally, resigned, she said, "It has been done, then. There is no going back to what you were before."

Wren knew immediately what her grandmother was talking about, and the implication had her straightening her spine. "There was never any chance of going back to what I was before, nor would I ever choose to if I could. Silas and I are mates and we had our tethering ceremony in Edein. In fact, you should all be thankful we are mates or else we would have no chance at winning this war. Without our combined magics, you would all be cattle up for slaughter. I will hear no more of this disparaging talk of him or my choice to be with him. The next person I hear make a comment about it will regret ever opening their mouth."

With her head held high, she brushed past the queen and the general, not deigning to look in their direction. Anger at the continued disrespect Silas received from them was burning in her gut. Silas had done nothing but show them respect and prove himself over and over, yet they continued to treat him like the enemy. She would not stand for it anymore.

You don't have to do that, you know. Silas caught up to her quickly and brushed his hand against hers. *What they say doesn't bother me.*

Yes, I do, because I know you won't. I don't know how you let them say the things they do. You deserve better than that.

He pulled her to a stop and made sure she was looking at him. *It doesn't bother me because I know it's not true. And the people who matter to me, the people I love and who love me back, they know the truth and that is all that matters. The only opinion I care about is yours. And maybe Jerricha's.*

She shook her head but felt her lips pull toward a smile at his last comment. *Well, I won't let them say those things. No matter what you say, I think the world needs to know how amazing you are.*

Why? So you can beat all the women off me with a stick? He winked at her and started walking, leaving her standing behind with her mouth hanging open.

Arrogant bastard.

His chuckle finally coaxed a smile out of her, and she hurried to catch up.

"So, this is the beautiful Alynthi?" he asked as they walked along the canal.

"It is." She looked around, seeing the familiar shops with wares displayed inside and the eateries with little iron tables and chairs out front under strings of lights. This little slice of heaven would be destroyed if they failed. The canals would run red with blood if they did not succeed in defeating the Dark Fae.

She paused in the middle of an arching stone bridge, leaning over the side to peer into the water below. The thought of failing had her trembling. "There is so much beauty here," she whispered. "So much life and light. So much to lose if we don't win."

Silas leaned against the stone wall with her, his arm brushing hers. She could feel his gaze on her, feel him probing at the bond, making sure she was okay. He said nothing but then again, there wasn't much to say. There were no promises he could make, no monsters to fight, no magic to wield that would change the situation they were in. He knew better than to placate her with words that weren't true. But his presence next to her, the reassurance of his support and love, was enough. It would have to be.

By the time they made it to the palace, Wren's feet were dragging. Between her fatigue from the constant use of her magic and the emotional battle waging in her mind, she was half-asleep walking. As they passed the door to the king's study, the general popped his head out.

"We're meeting now to discuss what happened and make plans. You need to be in here."

For a split second, Wren considered refusing. Not just to spite the man who she once considered her father but because she truly was exhausted. However, this was too important. They had a lot of information to go over and a lot of plans to make. She was gathering her resolve to head into the study when Silas stopped her.

"Not today. She needs to rest." He placed a hand on her lower back to guide her away.

The general narrowed his eyes at Silas. "She can rest later. Get in there. Now."

She knew that tone of voice—the voice that commanded armies and servants. Hearing it made her automatically retreat into little girl-mode—the desire to obey and be commended for it.

"She will meet tomorrow after she has had time to recover."

"Recover from what? Sailing across the sea on a ship where she could do nothing but rest?" The sneer on his face would normally make her see red, but as it was she could barely bring herself to care.

Silas stepped up to the general, back straight and shoulders squared. He looked in the general's eyes as he said in a low quiet voice, "Wren has been sacrificing herself for months. She has traveled through magical mist intent on tearing her apart. She has traversed through freezing cold mountains, crossed ravines, and climbed ledges to get that gods-forsaken Crown. She has thrown every bit of her magic into that Crown in order to keep your son safe, and in doing so she has worn herself into a wraith. She will meet tomorrow after she has rested."

Silas led her away without another word. Wren looked back once to see the general staring at him, jaw grinding back and forth. She didn't care. Once they were around the corner Wren took over, leading Silas through the palace to the rooms she stayed in when she visited.

"Thank you," she said quietly once they were behind closed doors.

"That's what I'm here for. To take care of you." He placed a gentle kiss on her forehead then pushed her toward the bedroom. "Now take your clothes off and go lie down."

She raised a brow at him. "I thought I was supposed to be resting?"

"I'm not going to ravish you," he said, although his eyes glimmered as if he was thinking of doing just that. "You really do need to rest."

She complied, taking off her travel-worn clothes as she went, leaving a trail of discarded clothing that looked for all the world like she and Silas had some fun on the way to the bedroom. A soft groan escaped her as she collapsed on the bed and curled onto her side. She hadn't realized just how tired she was. Silas joined her, tugging her back against his chest and wrapping his arms around her.

"Sleep, my love." He kissed her shoulder and tucked her hair behind her ear. "I'll be here."

* * *

Sitting in the king's study the next morning, Wren and her companions met with the general and Queen Elowyn. King Rodion, the king of Ellendyr, was on his way back from Tethoris, having left the city just before the Dark Fae attack. They had been discussing plans on infiltrating Valasia for the past hour, and Wren was ready to bang her head against a wall.

Everyone had an idea, each more outlandish than the last. Someone had suggested outright attack, another had suggested poisoning the water supply. Wren was about to suggest they all go jump off a cliff. She swallowed her annoyance and forced herself to listen until she couldn't stand it anymore. Her hand slamming on the desk caused them all to jump.

"This is ridiculous. These plans are only going to get us all killed."

"What would you suggest otherwise, love?" Silas's wry tone got a glare out of her.

"Leave the gods-damned thing there."

"Wren—" Gabriel began, but she cut him off.

"No. Don't placate me. You're not using the Eyeglass. End of story." She crossed her arms over her chest and glared at him.

Silas cut off whatever reply Gabriel was getting ready to say. "No matter if we use it or not, we need to get it out of Balor's hands. I know it's keyed to King Adriel's blood, but who knows what kind of tricks Balor has up his sleeve? It's too big of a risk to leave that kind of weapon in our enemies' hands."

Wren transferred her glare from Gabriel to Silas.

Don't kill me, love. You know it's true. His voice in her head was calm and soothing.

She gritted her teeth and relented. He was right but that didn't make her happy. If they had the Eyeglass, Gabriel would fight to get his hands on it. She couldn't risk that.

"Then what do you suggest, oh wise Shadow Caster?" Wren couldn't quite keep the sarcasm out of her question.

"A small group of us—no more than four or five—sneak in, get the Eyeglass, and sneak back out."

"He'll have it under heavy guard. How do you propose we sneak in and out?" Gabriel asked.

"Magic. We can use my shadows to cloak us and take the guards out. Wren can get the Eyeglass and we leave the same way we got in."

"That doesn't seem like a very sound plan." The general stared Silas down, a frown pulling his features grim.

Wren hated to admit she agreed with the general. Silas's plan sounded simple enough, but it left a lot to the imagination.

"I haven't heard you provide a better one," Silas challenged.

They stared at each other, neither speaking with words, but their eyes and postures spoke volumes.

"Enough," Wren cut in quietly. "It's the only plan we have. It will have to work—we'll make it work."

They discussed the plan further, hammering out details and deciding who would go. Wren withdrew into herself once again, and Silas kept a tight grasp on her hand. Waves of love crashed through the bond almost constantly. His attempts to keep her head above water were the only things keeping her afloat. Without his support she would have drowned by now.

The feeling of dread flooded her and she was unable to shake it. Her body felt heavy, like she was swimming in sludge and couldn't surface. The constant fear plaguing her was impossible to outrun. She couldn't remember the last time she felt carefree without the threat of loss hanging over her head.

When the discussion ended and everyone filed out the door, Gabriel tried to grab Wren's arm. She yanked out of his grip and started down the hall.

"Wren, stop!" Gabriel chased after her, grabbing for her arm again.

"Don't. I have nothing to say to you that you will want to hear."

"Stop being so selfish. That's not who you are."

His words drew her to an abrupt stop. "Selfish?"

"If we don't use the Eyeglass, we won't win this war. The world will fall to the Dark Fae. Are you really so willing to forsake the rest of the world just so one life is spared?"

"Yes," she hissed through clenched teeth. "And if that makes me selfish, if that makes me a monster, I will gladly accept that. The world can burn because if you die it wouldn't be worth saving anyway."

"We'll all die if we don't use the Eyeglass. You, me, Silas. None of us will survive."

"At least we'll die together, then."

She stormed off and heard his and Silas's soft, murmured voices as they stayed behind, letting her go off on her own. Outside the palace walls, Winston joined her as she trekked to the top of the hill that overlooked the city. This was the place she came to when she visited the city and missed the quiet solitude of Hillwood. She would sit atop the hill and trace the canals with her gaze, the blue-green water like ribbon twining between the buildings. The ferries and boats looked like ants swimming in the water from this distance, the people almost too small to make out.

As she sat on the hill with Winston by her side, she tried to sort through her thoughts and emotions. She hadn't meant to snap at Gabriel, but her anger was on a short leash. Everything was happening so fast. Before she knew it, the Eyeglass would be in her hands and Gabriel's life would be at risk. Before too long, all their lives would be at risk as they went up against the Dark Fae.

Was she really going to risk them losing the war to save Gabriel's life? On one hand, she knew she was being irrational. She couldn't really damn the world just to save him, because in the end he would die anyway. They all would. On the other hand, the thought of living without her big brother was crippling. She felt pulled in two different directions and the weight of those decisions was consuming her.

The sun was low on the horizon when she saw Silas climbing the hill, his long strides eating up the distance. She watched him approach, her gaze tracing his features and storing them in her memory. His broad shoulders and narrow waist. The black curls falling over his forehead and shading his beautiful green eyes. She devoured the sight of him as if she was starving and he was sustenance. In a way, she supposed he was her sustenance. At times, he was the only thing keeping her going.

Silas scratched Winston behind his ears and sent him off before sitting next to Wren. They sat in silence and watched the sun slowly sink below the horizon. The sky was a riot of color—orange, red, pink, and purple—and it stained the canal and the sea beyond the city like an artist's palette.

"What can I do to help you?" Silas's soft question broke the surrounding silence.

She didn't answer right away. There wasn't much he could do. He gently grasped her chin and turned her to look at him. His skin was warm as he brushed his thumb over her cheek and she leaned into his touch, closing her eyes.

"I hate seeing you like this. I hate the feeling of despair

coming through the bond. Please tell me what I can do. I will do anything to see you smile, even if it's just for a second."

"Make love to me," she whispered. "Make me forget everything for a little while. Let me get lost in you."

He lowered his head and brushed his lips against hers. "You never have to ask me for that."

His hands framed her face and the kiss deepened. He took his time, slowly drugging her with lazy swipes of his tongue. The grass was cool against her back as she wrapped her arms around his neck and pulled him down. The weight of his body settling on top of her helped to clear her mind of the fears she hadn't been able to get rid of. Before she knew it, her chest was heaving and her blood was boiling.

Silas broke away and moved to her neck, trailing kisses and nipping bites along her throat. Her hands found their way under his shirt and she skimmed them up his back, feeling his muscles shift beneath her palms. Only Silas could distract her like this—lost in his body and the sensations he drags forth.

Silas removed her shirt and the cool spring breeze teased her nipples, tightening them to peaks that Silas sucked into his mouth, the wet warmth a contrast to the chilly air. She pulled his shirt up and he stopped long enough for her to tug it off. He moved to her other nipple, laving it like he did the first. Her back arched off the ground and his arms came around her, holding her tight to him.

The feel of his skin against hers, his tongue teasing her nipple, had heat pooling in her core. She tried to squeeze her legs together to ease the ache building between them, but Silas's legs between hers prevented it. A whimper escaped her as her need continued to build, but Silas continued with his slow, teasing exploration of her body.

His fingers trailed down her sides and over her stomach, sparks igniting against her skin in their wake. He eased his fingers under the waistband of her leggings and sucked in a sharp breath as he felt how wet she was. He tugged her leggings off and threw them to the side before lying next to her, propped on his elbow.

Wren shamelessly let her legs fall open and felt herself flush with desire as Silas's gaze traveled the length of her body. He watched her with a hooded gaze as his fingers returned to her core. Lightning flashed through her veins as he worked his fingers around the bundle of nerves at the apex of her thighs. Her hips lifted, chasing his fingers, trying to get more of what she wanted.

Silas's eyes never left her as he slipped one finger inside, then another, watching as she writhed on his hand.

"Take what you want, love," he whispered hoarsely.

She did just that. Wren grabbed his wrist and held him in place as her hips moved, the desire in her climbing higher and higher. On the edge of release, she looked into his eyes. The stark want that burned in his stare sent her over the edge. She cried out as her release left her, her core tightening around his fingers. He brought her through it, and when she was limp and breathless, he finally removed his own pants.

The silken strands of his curls slid through her fingers, and she brought his head toward hers. They kissed deeply and slowly until fire again built inside her. She gasped as his arousal probed her entrance and her hips lifted of their own accord, inviting and begging. He slid inside slowly, and she felt everything as he filled her.

Silas's body moving in hers erased all thought. The bond between them was stronger than ever and she let his feelings of love and adoration fill the cold places within her. The build-up was slow, and she paid attention to every detail, every feeling, as her release rose like a cresting wave and crashed over her. Silas's release followed, and she held him through it.

They lay tangled together on the grass with the stars twinkling above them and caught their breath. No shadows hid them from view this time—it was just the two of them and the night sky. They said no words to each other, none were needed after what they had just shown each other. Wren was still terrified. She still did not know what to do about the Eyeglass, but the echoes of Silas's love were still traveling the length of the bond. It gave her strength, and she knew, no matter what happened, Silas's love would always be there.

Chapter Seventeen

This was the fourth time Wren had left the manor on some kind of mission. While the three times before bore a risk of danger, the prospect always held a touch of adventure. This time, it was different. Wren had lost all sense of adventure and excitement when leaving home. Each journey away had resulted in more heartache, and she knew this one would be the worst.

They had decided only five of them would go to Valasia to steal the Eyeglass. Silas, Gabriel, Aeron, and Hawthorne accompanied her. Jerricha had opted to remain at the palace. The Viking woman had retreated further inside herself, not unlike Wren had. Both of them were battling emotions dealing with Gabriel wanting to use the Eyeglass. While Hawthorne had wanted to remain behind, his knowledge of Valasia and the Library of Knowledge would be needed, so he had found himself atop a horse with the rest of them.

They were traveling hard and fast, climbing the mountains south of the pass to avoid any potential ambush set up by Balor and his Dark Fae. Wren was exhausted, cold, and sore. They left their horses in the foothills of the mountains and proceeded on foot. The terrain was treacherous and Wren had to rely on the boys more than she liked.

Snow had begun falling not long after they started the climb and it hadn't quit. It reached up to their thighs in some places, slowing them down. When they started, Wren had used her magic to melt the snow for easier climbing, but she soon became too tired to continue doing so. Gabriel did his best to forge a path for the rest of them to follow, but it was slippery and steep, and Wren sported many bruises and cuts from falling.

When they reached the top of the mountain, Wren sat to catch her breath. The air was thin so high up and Wren's gasping breaths clouded in front of her face in the cold. The view was spectacular. Mountains spread out on either side of them, the jagged peaks covered in snow. Before them, she could see the treetops of Valasia, massive trees with their red-and-orange leaves like a blanket of jewels covering the earth.

A piece of dried meat appeared in front of her face and she snaked her arm out of her cloak to grab it.

"Thanks," she mumbled as Silas sat next to her.

Wren watched her companions sit on whatever they could find—rocks, logs, tree stumps. Gabriel sat by himself, studying Valasia in the distance. Hawthorne and Aeron sat on a log together, engaged in a quiet conversation that had them both smiling and looking away from each other shyly.

Wren narrowed her eyes at them. "They have been getting along quite well, haven't they?"

"Who?" Silas followed her gaze to the two of them and snorted. "Thank the Gods. I don't think I could handle any bickering from anyone on this journey."

Remembering that Aeron hadn't confessed to anyone but her, Wren shook her head and hid her smile. She laid her head on Silas's shoulder and sighed.

"I am so tired."

He kissed the top of her head. "I know, love. Going down should be easier, hopefully."

Silas was both right and wrong. It took less energy to go down the mountain, however it was more dangerous. It was difficult to keep their footing. They frequently found themselves sliding down a few feet at a time, grappling to grab hold of anything around them to stop their quick descent. Silas kept close to Wren and did his best to keep her on her feet, although multiple times he accidentally dragged her down with him.

They were a quarter of the way down the mountain when Wren felt the ground trembling below her feet. Silas grabbed her arm and pulled her to a stop.

"Shit," he cursed.

Wren barely heard it. A roaring began behind them, higher on the mountain, drowning out his curse.

"Avalanche!" Silas yelled as he began tugging Wren to the side.

She whipped her head around and her heart stopped at the sight of the cascade of snow tumbling down the mountain. The tidal wave of power swept away trees and rocks. Everything in the path was destroyed. How would they survive that? Her companions quickly changed directions and began fighting their way to the side.

"Come on, Wren!" Silas urged her faster, trying to get them out of the avalanche's path.

They hadn't made it very far when the snow beneath her feet shimmied and bounced as it slid from underneath her boots. She struggled to keep running forward amid the pull of the snow that quickly rose around her. Silas changed directions again and headed for a tree, clearly realizing they would not make it out of the path in time.

He slammed her against the tree, wrapping her arms around the trunk with his own. His body pressed tightly against hers as he held them to the tree with every bit of strength he possessed.

The wave of snow as it hit them was so powerful it tried to pull Silas's body away from hers. Wren's scream was lost in the noise of cascading snow. Silas grunted and wrapped his leg around the trunk, further anchoring them to the tree. Snow crashed around them, tugging and pulling, trying to drown them. Wren focused on holding tightly to the tree as the snow quickly submerged them in a pile of white.

When the rumbling stopped and the tugging slowed, Wren opened her eyes. Complete darkness surrounded her. Snow pressed in on them, caging them. She tried to whirl around, but there wasn't enough room to move. Panic overtook her and her heart began stumbling in her chest. She couldn't seem to fill her lungs with enough air. They were going to suffocate.

It's okay. Silas's voice filtered through the bond, attempting to calm her nerves. *Don't panic, it will only make it worse.*

She tried to heed his words, but all sense of reason had fled. "I can't breathe, I can't breathe," she gasped.

Shh, it's okay, Wren. He managed to push enough snow out of the way to turn her around so she was facing him. He placed her hand on his chest. *Breathe with me.* He took deep breaths, his chest rising and falling under her hand.

Her eyes closed, and she focused on the feeling of his chest moving. Slowly, she matched her breathing to his and her panic ebbed away.

Once she was calm, Silas spoke into the bond again. *Use*

your magic to warm the surrounding snow. We'll be able to climb out.

Shame heated her face at her panic and how it made her forget she could use her magic to save them. She closed her eyes again and drew her magic up. Heat flared in her palms and she reached out to the snow on either side of them. Steam hissed where her hands touched snow. Rivulets of water ran down the sides of the snow packed around them.

Silas started digging where her magic had melted the snow and soon a hole appeared above them, bright sunlight shining through. Wren took her first deep breath since she saw the snow crashing down the mountain. It quickly faded, however, when she realized she had no clue if the rest of her companions were okay.

That thought spurred her forward and she drew up more of her magic, heat spiraling from her hands to soften the snow about them. Soon, Silas climbed out and he reached a hand down to help her.

On top of the snow once again, Wren looked around. A fresh blanket of snow covered everything. A few rocks and branches littered the ground and peeked out from the remnants of the avalanche. There was no sign of her companions.

"Gabriel!" She cupped her hands around her mouth and began yelling. "Aeron! Hawthorne!"

Silas joined her and they slowly made their way down the mountain, calling names and listening for any sign of life.

"Wait." She stopped and threw her arm out to stop Silas as well. "Listen."

Wren closed her eyes and focused on listening to the quiet surrounding them. A muffled yell came from their left. They scrambled over the snow, yelling and listening for the reply. Before long, Wren was using her magic to melt the snow once again while Silas dug. A pocket appeared, and she peered inside to see Aeron and Hawthorne huddled together in the tiny space.

"Thank the Gods for Sun Casters," Aeron said as Silas helped pull him to his feet.

Seeing they were okay, Wren had already turned her attention back to their surroundings. She continued calling for Gabriel, praying to every god she knew of that he was okay. They scoured the mountain until Wren was panicking once again. There was no sign of him. Tears fell down her cheeks and froze in the icy wind. She called his name until her voice was hoarse.

Finally, Aeron yelled, "Over here!"

Wren rushed to his side and dropped to her knees, her heart dropping with her. A boot was peeking through the snow. She used her magic again, heating her hands as she dug and dug. She found his head first and cried out. His eyes were closed and blood was frozen on his face from a gash on his forehead.

"Gabriel," she said, gently touching his cheeks. They were so cold. She used her magic to warm him. "Gabriel, wake up." He didn't move. She began scooping the rest of the snow away. She was relieved to see his chest moving, even if it was so slow. Aeron helped her dig and lift Gabriel from the snow.

Silas crouched next to Wren and placed his hand on Gabriel's neck. "His pulse is slow." His hand reached inside Gabriel's tunic, resting on his chest. "He's freezing. We need to get him warm."

Wren laid next to Gabriel, wrapping her arms around him. She covered him with her cloak and pushed her magic into him, urging it to warm her brother. Silas settled his cloak on top of them. Then Aeron and Hawthorne did the same. While the boys shivered in the stiff wind, Wren prayed and prayed.

"Please, Gabriel," she whispered. "I need you to wake up. You can't leave me."

She wasn't sure how long she lay there with her brother. Eventually, his breathing became steadier and his pulse got stronger. She pulled her magic back as she felt his body temperature rising. When he stirred, Wren almost cried from relief.

"Hey, big brother. Welcome back." She rubbed her eyes, trying to keep her tears from falling.

Gabriel groaned and sat up. He probed his head and winced at the gash on his forehead. "How long was I out? Is everyone else okay?"

"We're all fine," she replied. "You were out for a few hours." She reached into her bag and pulled out her waterskin and some dried meat. "Here. You need to get some strength back. Then we need to keep moving."

Being on the mountain was making her nervous. Gabriel getting hurt was too close for comfort and she wanted to be back on snow-free ground as soon as possible. Wren quickly cleaned Gabriel's wound as he ate. Once he gathered his strength, they were soon slipping and sliding down the mountain again.

Eventually, the snow disappeared and the ground leveled out. Wren huddled inside her cloak as the wind blowing off the mountain carried a chill that mirrored her feelings. The closer they got to Valasia, the quieter the group became—the severity of this mission was not lost on any of them. The uncertainty in the air was palpable. None of them could pretend this was anything short of incredibly dangerous.

A rider appeared in the distance and Gabriel called for a halt as everyone's hands went to their weapons. Wren relaxed as she saw Gabriel's shoulders lose their tension, and he walked forward to meet the rider. Her brother had sent scouts to the area a while ago to monitor Balor and Valasia. This must be one of them.

"The Dark Fae's presence extends farther than we anticipated," Gabriel said once he returned to the group. "We need to make camp here to avoid running into any Dark Fae scouts. Tonight, we can get a closer look before we make our move."

They set up camp in the foothills of the Ellendyr Mountains. Silas and Aeron set up wards with their magic to alert them of any unwelcome visitors while Gabriel and Hawthorne got a small fire going and hunted for food.

"Is it safe to have a fire this close to the Dark Fae?" Wren asked. She hated to voice the question—she was chilled to the bone and the heat the flames provided was heavenly—but if it was a risk, she would deal with the cold.

"I can shield the light and smoke," Silas answered, sidling close to her.

"That would have been handy the first time we traipsed through these mountains in the cold without a fire."

He bumped her shoulder playfully. "That would have exposed my magic. I couldn't have you running from me in fear, now, could I?"

"The sad thing is, I probably would have done just that. I was ignorant and learning you are Dark Fae would have terrified me."

Silas sat on the ground, pulling her down next to him. "It wasn't your fault. Deimos has done nothing except perpetuate the image that Dark Fae are evil."

"How many do you think would support you in your quest to remove him? How many are actually evil?"

He sighed heavily, thinking over her question. "I think a lot of them would show their support *after* Deimos has been removed. With him in the picture—and Balor and my uncle—

there is too much risk for them to rebel. They are scared, and the only thing they can do to stay alive is to follow him."

"Have you thought about what happens after we remove him? Someone will need to take his place."

"Why not you?" he asked. "You are their princess."

She glared at him and he chuckled.

"Kidding, sort of. I have thought about stepping in. I'm a direct descendent of Bhardyl so I have the blood to do it. But, do I want to?"

Wren stared at him as if she had never seen him before. "I had no clue you had ever thought about that."

"It was before I met you, honestly. After you came into my life my priorities changed. I wouldn't say no to taking up the crown, but only if it was something we both agreed on."

Silence descended around them as Wren stared into the fire.

"I can almost hear your thoughts. What are you thinking, love?"

Wren bit her lip and continued to stare at the flames. She wasn't sure she could voice aloud the thoughts running through her head. Instead, she sent her thoughts down the bond.

I am so incredibly selfish.

Silas turned to face her. *Why do you say that?*

I don't want my brother to use the Eyeglass, risking the entire world in the process. I refuse to take up the crown for the Light Fae. I am keeping you from taking up the crown for the Dark Fae. All because of what I don't want. I couldn't be more selfish.

I never said I wanted to take the crown, Wren. It's something I would be open to discussing. If you don't want me to, I wouldn't do it.

Tears blurred her vision making the fire blur into an

orange-and-red blob. "What if you resent me later for that? I can't be the reason you don't do something you want to do."

"I would never resent you." His brows drew down as he carefully asked, "Why exactly don't you want to be princess or queen?"

Just thinking about the responsibility and requirements required of royalty made her shoulders slump. She opened her mouth to respond but closed it again.

"Be honest with me, Wren. What is your real reason? It isn't because you don't want to lose your freedom."

Again, words bubbled up in her that she couldn't voice aloud. *Because I'm scared.*

Silas didn't say anything. He watched her as she sorted through her thoughts and came to terms with what was really on her heart.

What if I can't do it? What if I do something wrong? How do I know the correct decisions to make? It wouldn't just be my life I was risking, but the lives of all my people. I'm not ready for that kind of responsibility. I don't know if I'll ever be ready for that kind of responsibility.

Silas gently grasped her chin and forced her to look at him. "There is absolutely nothing you can't do. I have never once doubted your ability and I know if you took up your birthright, you would bring the world to its knees." His eyes were shining in the firelight and emotion swirled in their green depths. "Whatever decision you make, I will be next to you every step of the way. You won't ever be alone."

A tear dripped from her eye and he wiped it away.

"How can you be so sure?" Her words were so quiet they were barely audible over the fire.

"Because I have complete faith in you." He cracked a mischievous grin. "Besides, I think you would look amazing in a crown."

Voicing her fears didn't make them go away, but finally admitting to herself the real reason she didn't want to take up the crown was a relief. She felt lighter than she had in a while, even with the dangers they were facing in the coming days.

"Thank you," she whispered, "for listening and not judging."

He placed a gentle kiss on her lips. "I would never judge you for the way you feel, but I will do everything I can to make you see yourself the way I do."

The others began settling around the fire, and Wren cuddled close to Silas, leaning against his constant strength.

"As soon as night falls we will scout the perimeter of Valasia. We need to figure out guard rotations and any possible areas where we can enter the city," Gabriel said as he sat across from Wren and held his hands up to fire.

"Our best option will probably be going in through the treetops," Wren supplied. "That's how Silas and I escaped when Valasia was attacked. I imagine it's hard to keep an eye on both the ground and the trees with the number Balor has with him."

Gabriel nodded his agreement. "You're right. I think coming in from the top is the best idea. Hawthorne, where would the best drop-in point be?"

"Depending on what we find while scouting tonight, the southwest corner has the densest vegetation and will provide us with the most cover. It's a bit farther from the Library than I would like, but it's the best place to get into the city."

"Once inside, how do we get to the Library?" Wren asked.

"We stay in the trees using my shadows to hide us. We need to drop down to the ground level as close to the Library as possible," Silas said next to her.

"And the guards I'm sure Balor has guarding the Library?" she asked.

At this question, Hawthorne smiled. "There is a secret back

entrance no one knows about. It will most likely be unguarded and we can get in through there."

"Okay," Gabriel said. "Tonight I want Wren and Silas to take the northern border, Hawthorne, you take the western border, Aeron takes the eastern border, and I'll take the southern. We need as much information as we can get regarding the scouting rotation and timing of passes."

At his words, they all settled down around the fire, waiting for darkness to begin gathering intel.

Chapter Eighteen

With tired feet and aching muscles, Wren crept around the perimeter of Valasia with Silas. Shadows swirled around them, hiding them from enemy eyes. They were on their way back from exploring, having spent the entire night lying on their stomachs watching and timing the guard rotations. At one point, Silas had climbed into the trees to scout the higher ground and get a look inside the city.

The sun was peeking over the horizon when their little camp came into view. The rest of their companions were already back, having had a shorter distance to travel than Wren and Silas. Gabriel was settling down in his blankets while Aeron and Hawthorne were keeping watch. As Wren and Silas approached, Gabriel sat up.

"How did it go?" he asked. There were dark circles under his eyes and his cheeks were hollow. He looked as exhausted as Wren felt.

"It was fine. We had no problems," Silas answered. "We

have the needed information, but I think we all need to rest before we plan and make decisions."

Gabriel's jaw cracked wide open in a yawn. "That sounds like a wonderful idea."

Wren settled into the blankets next to the fire, fighting a yawn of her own.

"Come here," Silas whispered as he laid next to her.

She scooted into his open arms and laid her head on his chest. The rhythmic rise and fall of his chest and the steady thumping of his heart lulled her to sleep in minutes.

When Wren woke later, Silas and Gabriel were already huddled together discussing strategy with Hawthorne. Aeron was wrapped in his cloak, still asleep by the fire. Standing from her blankets, Wren draped her blanket over Aeron before joining the boys.

"I think Hawthorne's idea will work the best," Gabriel was saying. "After hearing everyone's reports, the southwest corner is the least defended, and with the vegetation and Silas's shadows to hide us, it will be easiest to slip in there."

Hawthorne nodded. "The hardest part will be dropping down behind the Library. We will be the most exposed at that time."

"I will do my best to keep us cloaked in shadow, but I have to be careful or it will look too unnatural and they will get suspicious." Silas draped his arm over Wren's shoulders and pressed a kiss to her temple.

"Okay," Gabriel said as he settled into soldier mode. "Aeron and I will remain in the trees to provide cover and monitor the lower levels while you"—a nod to Silas—"get Wren and Hawthorne to the Library through the back entrance."

"When do we leave?" Wren asked. Nerves fluttered to life in her stomach as reality crept in.

"Just before dusk. That will give us time to get into position. Once night has fallen, we will make our move." Gabriel looked each of them in the eye, weighing and assessing.

Wren marveled at how well Gabriel handled situations like these. Even knowing he had trained his whole life for this type of situation, it was something else to see him in action. His ability to read people and situations made him a powerful warrior and one day he would be just as deadly a general as his father.

Once the plans were made and discussed thoroughly, they sat around the fire and ate their meager meal of dried meat. Aeron woke and joined them and Gabriel filled him in on the plan. Before she knew it, they were putting out their fire and readying themselves to infiltrate Valasia.

The flutter of nerves in her stomach intensified as they made their way through the woods in silence. Everything depended on this mission. Wren's safety was a top priority, and all the boys were tense as they approached the entry point. If Balor captured Wren, he would use her to get the Eyeglass. They had left the Crown and the Sword behind to avoid the risk of the Dark Fae getting any more of the Artifacts.

Fear made Wren stumble in the oncoming darkness. Her stomach knotted painfully at the thought of being captured by Balor and being used against her will. A steady hand on her shoulder and a burst of reassurance through the bond from Silas kept her moving forward.

As they approached the southwest corner of Valasia, Silas cloaked them in shadows and used his magic to dampen sounds of their approach. The trees here grew closer together and the leafy tops obscured the little light from the moon. Gabriel stepped up to a large tree with low branches, perfect for climbing.

"Just like old times, Wren." He grinned at her, then quickly climbed the tree.

Aeron and Hawthorne followed, until just Silas and Wren waited on the ground.

"It is just like old times," Silas whispered in her ear. He wrapped his hands around her waist and lifted her up.

Memories of the night they were attacked in the woods flooded Wren as she climbed higher into the tree. She was thankful she wasn't injured this time. She made it to the top quickly, Silas joining them not long after.

The group made their way from branch to branch until they came to the edge of the city. The lights of Valasia still glowed in the darkness. Wren wasn't sure why that surprised her. She had imagined the city being dark and cold with the Dark Fae presence.

A patrol they hadn't expected was making its way along the wooden bridge closest to them. Gabriel held up his hand to call for a halt. Sitting quietly in the tree, they waited as the patrol passed.

A guard in the patrol stopped and looked directly at them. He squinted his eyes and peered into the darkness Silas had created. When the guard's brow furrowed and his mouth opened as if he would speak, Aeron held up a hand and pushed it away from him. Rustling leaves tore through the treetops as his magic created a diversion that caught the guard's attention.

They waited until the patrol passed, then made their way into the city, quietly crossing the bridges that connected the treetop buildings. Wren spotted more patrols on the ground level, but none of them looked up. If they had, they would have clearly seen bridges swaying under an invisible weight—something they hadn't accounted for.

Wren heaved a sigh of relief when they reached the bridge above the Library. They crouched around the platform, scanning all directions to make sure it was safe for them to climb down. When Gabriel gave the signal, Hawthorne shimmied down the tree. He reached the ground and peered around before signaling again, letting Wren know it was safe for her to climb down.

The bark was rough and bit into her skin as she made her way down the tree. Her heart was thumping madly in her chest the closer she got to the ground. For some reason it seemed safer to her up in the treetops—more escape routes if things went badly. As soon as her feet touched the ground, Silas began climbing down. He was standing next to her before she could blink, sword and dagger at the ready.

Hawthorne motioned them to follow him, and they skirted around the Library to the back side. Instead of stopping and facing the gray stone building, Hawthorne turned to a large tree. The base of the tree was wide enough to fit a carriage. He pulled a stone from his pocket—the same one used to open the front library door—and waved it in front of the tree.

The click that echoed in the quiet as a door unlocked sounded loud in Wren's ears and she tensed, waiting to hear signs of pursuit. When it remained quiet, Hawthorne pushed on the trunk of the tree and a door swung open, a faint glow from a torch shining in the darkness. The three of them slipped inside and the door snicked shut behind them.

"How many keys are there to the Library?" Wren whispered in the dim light as they descended a spiral staircase.

"Two," Hawthorne replied. "Unless Balor got his hands on the second, there is no way for them to get inside the Library."

"Let's assume he did and be prepared for anything," Silas said behind Wren.

The landing at the bottom of the staircase was small and dark, with another closed door leading to the main room of the Library. Hawthorne drew his spear and met Silas's gaze. A silent conversation passed between them before he gently eased the door open and stuck his head out. He motioned them to follow and slipped all the way out the door. Wren took a deep breath before following, daggers gripped tightly in her hands with her magic at the ready.

The Library was silent, the only sound their soft footfalls on the stone floor. Unease skittered down Wren's spine. It was too easy. She slowed and looked around, peering into the dark shadows that gathered behind shelves and in corners.

Something doesn't feel right. This has been too easy. She felt Silas tense behind her as she spoke down the bond.

I agree. Stay alert and let's be as quick as we can.

Hawthorne led them to a side room with an iron door Wren hadn't noticed the past times she had visited the Library. Using the same stone, Hawthorne unlocked the door and they entered. Wren stopped when she crossed the threshold. Sitting on a plinth in the middle of the room was the Eyeglass. There was no mistaking it—she could feel the raw magic of the Elementals who made it. It looked like a monocle made of black obsidian inlaid with bands of gold.

It was sitting on a bed of crushed red velvet with no case around it. As Wren stepped closer, she noticed a faint shimmer in the surrounding air. She raised her hand slowly, and carefully pushed through the almost invisible barrier. A shock traveled up her arm and into her chest, making her jerk. Her heart stuttered a few beats, and she gasped, her other hand pressing against her chest. Silas was immediately by her side, but Hawthorne held out a hand to stop him from touching her.

The sensation faded and Wren could press her hand farther through the barrier until she felt the cool stone of the Eyeglass against her skin. As she picked it up and held it to the light, the light filtering through fractured as if it was reflecting through a prism and rainbows danced on the surrounding walls.

"We need to keep moving," Hawthorne said quietly.

Wren put the Eyeglass in her pocket and drew her daggers again. She nodded and readied herself to step back out into the main Library. The sound of a door slamming in the distance made her jump. Hawthorne went to the door and peered outside.

"Shit," he muttered as he pulled Wren out the door and rushed back in the direction they had come.

Wren looked behind her as Hawthorne dragged her along, and she stumbled as her eyes met the cold dark gaze of Balor. She froze and her heart stopped as memories of being captured flew through her mind. Hawthorne tugging on her arm drew her out of her spiraling fear, but she still couldn't seem to make herself move as she stared into his eyes.

Silas pressed into her line of vision and his grim features and determination made her heart stop all over again.

"Go," he said to Hawthorne over her shoulder. "Get her out of here."

Wide-eyed, she stared at Silas as he readied his sword. "Silas," she breathed.

She was shaking her head no, readying an argument, when an arrow shot through the air. Hawthorne batted it away with his magic.

"Go!" Silas yelled before turning around to face off against Balor.

"No!" Wren struggled against Hawthorne, fighting his hold on her. She had to stay with Silas, she had to help him.

Arms grabbed her around her middle and lifted her off her feet. Hawthorne carried her through the Library, rushing through the shelves and displays of books and artifacts.

"Stop fighting me, Wren. And stop screaming. You're going to draw more attention to us."

He was right about the screaming, so she quieted, although inside she was still yelling. She reached through the bond but found the black swirling wall of shadows blocking her path to Silas. A whimper rose from her, and she had to close her eyes against the wave of fear that threatened to pull her under.

"Come on, we have to get you and the Eyeglass out of here." Hawthorne kept a tight hold on her arm as he opened the door to the hidden staircase and pulled her up and around the stairs.

At the top of the stairs, Hawthorne opened the door and made sure there was no one waiting. After determining the way was clear, he pulled Wren out the door and made for the tree once again. Before they could begin climbing, sounds of swords clashing echoed down from the treetop.

Hawthorne paused and looked around, his mouth pursed in worry. He bounced up and down on the balls of his feet as he ran through various escape routes.

"This way." He tugged Wren down the street, keeping to the shadows.

The sight of the shadows made her heart hurt. She once again reached down the bond for Silas, but she still couldn't sense him. That wall was impenetrable. The surroundings blurred together as she blindly followed Hawthorne, all her attention focused on trying to bust down that wall.

She followed down the street and through alleys, always keeping to the shadows. A sharp burst of pain bloomed in Wren's left thigh and she went down, hitting the stone hard. She held her scream in as she looked down at her leg. There was nothing there. She poked and prodded the area that hurt, but her leggings were intact, no hole in her leg, no blood.

Realization slammed into her and she gasped, jumping up and turning around. If she wasn't hurt, it had to be Silas. And for the pain to ricochet down the bond with him having blocked it off, the injury must be bad. Hawthorne cursed behind her and snagged her arm before she could get away.

"What are you doing?" he whispered.

"Silas is hurt. I have to get to him." She pulled her arm away, only to find Hawthorne's arms banded around her middle.

"I will carry you out of here if I have to," he growled in her ear as his arms tightened.

"I can't leave him here if he is injured." With her fear growing by the second, Wren pushed against Hawthorne, but he was too strong.

"He wouldn't want you running into danger to save him. He asked me to get you out of here if things went bad, and that's exactly what I'm going to do."

"You're asking me to leave my injured mate behind where he will surely be killed?" Her question was quiet and strangely calm.

As if sensing the dangerous ground he was treading on, Hawthorne paused before he opened his mouth to reply. Before he could say anything, rustling in the trees above them drew their attention. Wren adjusted the grip on her daggers just as a figure dropped from the tree. Hawthorne's spear was pressed to the man's throat before she could blink.

"Whoa, easy," Aeron whispered and held up his hands.

Hawthorne relaxed, his spear dropping from Aeron's neck, only for his shoulders to tense up again. "You're bleeding."

Blood was dripping from a hole in his shoulder and the front of his shirt was stained red.

Aeron looked down at his shoulder and shrugged, the motion causing him to flinch. "Arrow."

"Where's Gabriel?" Wren looked up into the trees but didn't see her brother.

"We were separated. Did you get the Eyeglass?"

"What do you mean, *separated*?" Hysteria was making her

louder than she should be, but at that moment she didn't care. Her mate and her brother were missing, one of them injured.

"Great," Hawthorne muttered. "You can get her out of here now."

Aeron looked between them, bewildered, and Wren took that moment of confusion to bolt. She turned and started running back in the direction they had just come. Limping from the phantom pain in her leg, she made it only four steps before hands latched on to her shoulders.

"Hold up, princess," Aeron said as he turned her around. "Where do you think you're going?"

"My mate is injured and fighting Balor. My brother is missing somewhere in the city. You cannot stop me from going back for them."

Aeron looked grim as he responded, "I'm sorry, princess. I can stop you, and I have to."

Wren didn't see the blow coming until it was too late to stop. Aeron's hilt connected with her head and she fell into his arms as unconsciousness took over.

Chapter Nineteen

The first thing Wren did when she regained consciousness was reach down the bond to Silas. She still felt nothing but that black wall of impenetrable shadows and pain. Gritting her teeth, she pushed herself into a sitting position, ignoring the throbbing in her head. The camp spun around in circles and she had to close her eyes to make the sensation of falling stop.

"Please don't run off yet," Hawthorne growled when he noticed her sitting up.

She peeked an eye open slowly and when the world didn't spin, she opened the other. Hawthorne was kneeling in front of Aeron with a bag of medical supplies open next to him. Aeron was shirtless and slouched against a tree, watching Hawthorne from the corner of his eye as he tended to his wound.

"How long have I been laying here uselessly while my family is in danger?" She couldn't keep the bite from her voice or from glaring at Aeron.

"Wren—" Aeron began, but cut off with a yelp as Hawthorne did something painful to his shoulder.

"How long?" Turning to face them directly, she crossed her arms and loomed as best she could while sitting on the ground.

Aeron sighed. "Twenty minutes. I didn't hit you that hard."

"Yeah, we'll talk about *that* later. Now, either you're letting me go back there to find them, or I will find a way to go without you letting me."

"You can't go back there and you know it," Aeron argued.

Wren growled in frustration and dug in her pocket, pulling out the Eyeglass. She tossed it to Aeron, who caught it with his free hand.

"There. That's what they want, right? If I don't have it, they won't want me."

"Put this away somewhere," Aeron hissed, shoving it back in her direction. "I don't care if you have the damn Eyeglass or not. Silas would never want you to put yourself in danger for him, and he would kill me if I let you go. So, no, you are staying here."

Wren refused to take the Eyeglass back, crossing her arms over her chest and opening her mouth to respond.

"Guys," Hawthorne warned before Wren could retaliate. He stood slowly and grabbed his spear, gaze pinned to a spot behind Wren.

She spun around, daggers drawn, and froze. Gabriel limped through the trees with Silas's arm draped around his shoulders.

"Silas," she murmured. Her daggers fell from fingers she could no longer feel as her mate limped his way into the camp.

He was bleeding profusely from a wound on his left thigh, the blood dripping down his leg in rivulets. The black curls falling on his forehead stood out starkly in the moonlight against his unusually pale skin.

Wren rushed to him and grabbed his face in her hands. "Silas." She couldn't stop the tears that blurred her vision. Relief and anger rose and fell within her as she realized he was going to be okay, along with the fact that he had almost sacrificed himself to save her.

He tugged her in for a one-armed hug, burying his face in the top of her head. "I'm fine. It's just a scratch."

"Never do that again," she breathed against his chest, ignoring his blatant lie about the injury. Looking up into his green eyes, her heart stuttered. They still had to make it through the final battle. The chances of her losing him, or someone else she loved, were too much to think about.

"Help me get him sitting down. We need to take care of his leg and get out of here as quickly as we can." Gabriel began shuffling Silas toward the fire, and Wren threw his other arm over her shoulder to help.

Once Silas was sitting by the fire, Wren lowered herself next to him and inspected the wound with Gabriel.

"What happened?" she asked.

"I forgot how dirty he fights," Silas grumbled. "Balor refused to let anyone fight with him. He seemed to want to make a point—that he was stronger than me. I was doing just fine, had the upper hand, and Balor must have signaled to one of his men. I got distracted and Balor got the hit on me." He cut off with a grunt as Gabriel began cleaning the wound.

"Where were you?" she asked Gabriel.

"Aeron and I were ambushed in the trees, but I saw you and Hawthorne leave and didn't see Silas with you. I made it to the Library in time or Balor would have won that fight."

Wren's heart stopped in her chest at her brother's words and she looked sharply at Silas. "I shouldn't have left you. I could have helped. Instead, Aeron knocked me out and carried me unconscious through the forest."

Silas glared at Aeron for a heartbeat before he sighed. "I made them swear they would get you out of there if something happened to me."

Her back straightened at his words. "Why would you do that?"

"It was dangerous back there, Wren. The safest thing was to make sure you got out with the Eyeglass."

"I could have given the Eyeglass to Hawthorne and stayed to help you. You didn't have to fight Ba—"

Silas shook his head and stopped her from saying more. "You couldn't have helped me. I needed you out of there."

"You don't think I can take care of myself in a fight? Is that what it is? Because I hate to break it to you, I'll have to fight in the battle with the Crown. And you know I can handle myself!"

"That's—" he cut off with a curse as Gabriel began stitching up his leg.

"Sorry," Gabriel winced. "Hawthorne used all the numbing agent on Aeron."

Hawthorne nodded and grinned. "I did. He can't handle stitches, apparently."

A blush crept up Aeron's neck and flushed his cheeks. "I don't like needles," he mumbled.

Wren's eyes didn't leave Silas during her friends' banter. She stood with her arms crossed and stared at him in disbelief. For all his talk of believing in her, he seemed to forget his words when they mattered most. With a shake of her head, she stalked off to the edge of camp and leaned against a tree.

Wren kept an eye toward Valasia. Balor would be quick to send out search parties, and they needed to be prepared. She was worried about Silas being able to travel soon, but they had little choice—he would have to suffer through. At this moment, she was more than okay with him suffering a little. She huffed in frustration at his words.

After some time had passed, Wren glanced over and saw

Silas shuffling toward her, a hand pressed against his bandaged leg.

He leaned against the tree, breathing heavily. "Can we sit? This thing is actually pretty painful."

It was his admitting he was in pain that got her moving. She helped him sit with his back against the tree, monitoring his facial expression the whole time. His lips were drawn and his eyes were tight. A slight sheen of sweat glistened on his brow once he was settled. She brushed his hair away and felt his forehead.

"I'm fine," he said as he captured her hand and placed a kiss to her knuckles.

Wren settled next to him and felt him roll the sleeve of her shirt up to expose her forearm and the mating tattoo on her skin. His finger traced the design and goose bumps rose on her flesh.

"It's not that I don't think you can take care of yourself," he began. "I've watched you train. I've sparred with you. I know what you're capable of." His finger kept tracing her tattoo. "It's just... It's not..." He trailed off and growled in frustration.

She had never seen him struggle to find words before.

He took a deep breath and tried again. "I'm worried about how I'll react with you fighting next to me."

"What do you mean?"

"I don't know if I can handle the distraction. I'm scared I'll be too worried about you and I'll lose my concentration. If something happens to you while we're fighting, I won't be able to focus on my fight. It will leave me vulnerable." He paused and looked at her, his green eyes so very serious. "I'm worried the same will apply to you. We are too much of a distraction to each other and it makes us vulnerable."

"You're going to have to get over that fear at some point,

Silas. We will have to fight side by side when the time comes to use the Artifacts."

His reply was so quiet she barely heard him. "I know."

"Why is the bond still blocked?" She reached out to the wall of shadows blocking him from her, running her fingertips along the smooth, swirling surface.

"Trying to keep the pain from making its way to you."

"It's that bad?" They were usually pretty good about keeping emotions and thoughts from the other person if they chose to. The only time it was difficult was when the thought or emotion was very strong.

"Getting better." He tried to give her a reassuring grin, but it fell short.

"I felt it happen," she whispered. "I thought I had been hit at first. Not being able to reach you was terrifying."

His arm came around her, and he pulled her against him. "I'm sorry, love. I'm so sorry."

They sat together in comfortable silence for a time, before making their way back to the fire.

"Is it safe to stay here?" Wren asked, looking around at their surroundings. They were completely open to any attack.

Gabriel nodded and handed Wren and Silas some dried meat. "My men are scouting Valasia and I have a few set up along the perimeter of our camp. We'll know if Balor is making a move on us."

"So, he is still alive?" Wren looked between her mate and her brother.

Gabriel grimaced. "Yeah, unfortunately, as soon as I made an appearance, he retreated."

Silas snorted. "Balor is confident in his skills, but he spooks easily. If he thought Gabriel and I could take him together, he wouldn't stick around."

Reluctantly, Wren settled next to Silas near the fire. Every noise she heard in the woods surrounding them caused her heart to lurch into her throat. After what felt like the hundredth time of jumping at a snapping twig, Silas nudged her with his elbow.

"Relax. Aeron and I both set up wards. If anyone we don't want gets too close, they will feel a sudden desire to turn away. No one is ambushing us in this camp."

She peered at him, studying his complexion and the strain visible on his face. "Are you sure you're okay enough to use your magic that much? Maybe you should rest." The back of her hand against his forehead told her he wasn't feverish, but he looked worn-out.

He groaned as he settled back on the grass, hands behind his head. "I'm fine, *Mother*."

Her look of exasperation rolled right off him, and he gave her a lopsided grin. Wren turned her attention to her companions. Since they had all regathered, she hadn't talked to any of them. She had been too focused on Silas to discuss what happened in Valasia.

"Are you all right, Aeron?" The white bandage adhered to his shoulder peeked through his shirt and she eyed it. A couple of inches to the left and it would have pierced his heart.

Aeron rolled his shoulder with a slight grimace. "Sore, but I'll be fine." He rubbed the back of his neck and peered at Wren sheepishly. "Listen, princess, I'm sorry I hit you. I did the only thing I could think of in the moment to get you to safety."

Wren gave an unladylike snort. "Don't worry about it," she said with a sweet smile. "I'll pay you back somehow."

Aeron visibly paled at her words. With his blue eyes wide in the firelight, he turned to her. "Please, have mercy on me. I was only following Silas's orders. I've said it before and I'll say it again. I'm too young to die!"

A chuckle across the fire made them all turn to look at Hawthorne.

"Sorry," he said through the chuckles. "I've just never met someone quite as dramatic as you, Aeron."

"Oh, yes you have," Wren mumbled under her breath and looked at Silas.

Hey, now. I am not dramatic. Silas's voice echoed down the bond.

Wren snorted and the sound seemed to bring everyone back to the importance of the moment. The levity in camp lagged and her companions all looked at her expectantly. Wren felt the weight of their task fall upon her shoulders once again.

"Don't look at me," she said, pointing to Aeron. "I gave it to him."

Aeron jumped as if he had forgotten she had tossed the Eyeglass to him earlier. After he scrambled in his pockets for a bit, he finally pulled the Eyeglass out. He gave it a cursory glance before tossing it back to Wren.

She caught it, the golden bands around the obsidian winking in the fire's light. As she turned the Artifact in her hands, studying the intricate details carved into the gold, she could feel Gabriel's gaze on her. She refused to acknowledge him, knowing what he was going to say the moment she met his stare.

"How does it work?" Aeron asked.

They all looked to Hawthorne, who preened under their gazes.

"From everything I have read and the discussions I had with Emperor Verellis, once the Eyeglass is on, it will display any wards and shields cast by magic users. The wearer can then disengage the wards and shatter the shields with just a thought." He paused before continuing, "It drains the user fast, though. Three hours max."

"That certainly sounds like it would come in handy," Gabriel said drily.

Wren curled her shoulders inward, shrinking in on herself. If only he would stop bringing it up, maybe she could forget the guilt she felt every time she thought about her coward's choice of saving her brother's life over the world.

Sensing her emotions taking a turn, Silas tugged on Wren's arm. "Okay," he announced. "Some of us need to rest before we break camp tomorrow morning."

She let him pull her down, careful of his injured leg. As he settled a blanket over them, his voice traveled down the bond.

We still have time. Don't think about it now. You will make the right decision in the end, whatever decision that may be.

She wished she had the same hope in herself that Silas had in her.

* * *

When the sun finally made its appearance through the thick clouds, Silas was gritting his teeth and trying not to show how much pain he was in. He kept the bond blocked. If he let that wall drop, Wren would immediately know he wasn't up for walking back to Alynthi yet, and they had to get moving. The longer they tarried in these woods, the greater the risk Balor would find them.

A whistle in the woods made Silas pause as he was slowly getting to his feet. With one knee on the ground, he drew a dagger and pushed himself to stand, gritting his teeth through the fiery pain lancing through his leg.

"It's one of my men," Gabriel said as he walked to the edge of camp.

A man wearing browns and greens emerged from the trees and greeted Gabriel. Silas relaxed and sheathed his dagger at his belt. With achingly slow steps, Silas made his way to Gabriel and the scout, however by the time he reached them the scout was turning away. There was no way he was going to be traveling today. The scout returned almost immediately, leading four horses.

Gabriel turned to Silas with a grin. "He saw two of our party were injured, so they stole a few horses for us."

Relief washed through Silas so fast his knees buckled. "Thank the Gods," he muttered. Now he just had to get in the saddle.

"We could only manage to get four," the scout said, handing the reins off to Gabriel. "We figured Lady Wren could ride with Lord Silas."

An unladylike snort behind Silas made him turn around.

"*Lord* Silas?" Wren pressed her lips together to keep her laughter in—and failed. She laughed so hard tears rolled down her cheeks. "I've never heard anyone refer to you as Lord Silas."

With a glare for his mate, Silas said, "Technically, I am a lord."

This only made her laugh harder and, to his dismay, Aeron joined in.

"Oh, come on, not you too?" he said to his friend.

"I know you technically are a lord, but it is kind of funny to imagine you acting as one." Aeron grabbed two sets of reins from Gabriel and walked away, shoulders shaking.

Silas snatched the last set of extra reins and pointed to the saddle. "Up," he said to Wren. "Before I throw you up there."

While Wren nimbly climbed into the saddle, Silas debated the best way to follow without giving her any sign of how badly he was hurting. In the end, he just had to grit his teeth and put his weight on his bad leg, supporting himself as much as he could with his upper body on the saddle. With a bracing breath, he swung his leg over and pulled himself up, grunting with the effort.

"Are you okay?" Wren asked, turning slightly in the saddle to see him.

He kissed her cheek and said, "I can't get anything past you, can I? I'm fine, love."

With everyone saddled and ready to go, the party headed south toward the sea, skirting the base of the mountains. Silas wrapped his arm around Wren's waist and tugged her back against his chest. They passed the time talking of nothing important, keeping the conversation light and carefree.

Aeron and Hawthorne rode up front next to each other while Gabriel brought up the rear, occasionally scouting behind them to cover any tracks. They made camp once, and Silas was grateful to get out of the saddle and stretch his leg. By the next morning, his Fae healing had kicked in and taken care of most of the pain.

It was midday when they rounded the end of the Ellendyr Mountains and the sea came into view. Silas slowed the horse and let the others trot on ahead.

"Remember the first time we passed this way?" he said in Wren's ear.

The surf crashed against the beach and the gray skies were angrier than they were the last time. The wind off the water was chilly and Silas wrapped his cloak around Wren, drawing her into his warmth.

"Seraphina was with us," Wren replied. Her gaze was distant as she looked out over the swater.

"Despite what had just happened, it was the first time I had felt at peace in a while."

Wren bit her lip and furrowed her brow. A thread of something bitter made its way down the bond.

"What's wrong?" He tucked a strand of hair behind her ear, only for the wind to catch it and rip it free again.

"Do you..." She trailed off, then took a breath and started again. "Do you remember what we talked about? The last time we were here."

Silas exhaled. "Yeah, I do."

"I'm sorry." She turned as much as she could in the saddle so she could look at him. "I know what I said—or rather what I didn't say—hurt you."

He remembered exactly what she was talking about. He had told her he had never imagined himself having kids, never imagined himself settling down, until he met her. She had said nothing. At the time, it had felt like a knife to his chest.

"Don't apologize for that," he breathed, the wind and waves almost drowning out his quiet words.

"I didn't know what I wanted." She shook her head. "No, that's not true. I knew what I wanted, but it scared me to admit it. I was so scared of getting hurt, so I pushed you away. I'm sorry."

Even knowing where they stood and how far their relationship had come since then, hearing those words lifted a weight he wasn't aware he had been carrying. He leaned forward and kissed her softly. When he pulled back, she smiled and placed her hand on his cheek.

"I want to have children with you. I want a house in the woods filled with the sounds of laughter and little feet. One day, I want all of it."

"Then you'll have all of it," he promised. "A house in the woods with a rain shower, ten kids, the whole thing. Maybe Winston will find a she-wolf and bring home pups for us to raise too."

"Ten kids?" She reared back with wide eyes. "I don't want ten kids."

"We'll see about that," he smirked and heeled the horse forward.

"No, we absolutely won't." She settled against him once again, then quietly added, "Three would be good."

He kissed the top of her head and promised himself he would make sure she got her happy ending.

Chapter Twenty

The palace was eerily quiet as Wren made her way down the halls, spinning the Crown in her hands absent-mindedly. The thud of her boots on the marble seemed extraordinarily loud; the echo ricocheted down the hall and back, making it sound like an army was marching rather than just her. Reaching down the bond, she could tell Silas was in a meeting with Gabriel and the general, most likely going over what happened on their journey to Valasia.

After they had returned to Alynthi, Wren had given the Eyeglass to Silas to guard and keep away from Gabriel. He had promised he would keep it out of Gabe's hands for as long as Wren was convinced that was the right route. She still didn't know what to do, and the implications for both decisions plagued her day and night.

Wren turned down another quiet corridor and peered behind her. The servants were all prepping for war, gathering and organizing supplies. The guards were in the training rings under the watchful eye of a Light Fae general from Valasia as well as Silas's old mentor, Torryn. Preparations for the battle to come were in full swing.

That was where Wren was headed—for training with Aeron. The training room in the palace was spacious and well-stocked, and Aeron had instructed Wren to meet him there in the morning to work on magic training. Any edge she could gain over their enemies would be advantageous.

Wren approached the large wooden door to the training room and pushed it open.

"Oh!" she exclaimed, jumping backward. "I'm sorry... I didn't... I'll just..." she stammered and backed up, heading toward the hallway again.

Aeron, who had Hawthorne pushed against the wall, pulled away and broke quite an affectionate kiss between the two. Red flooded his neck and cheeks, and his eyes, though glazed with lust, were wide with surprise. Hawthorne, to his credit, just smiled lazily and straightened his tunic.

"I'm sorry," Wren continued to stammer. "I'll just leave the two of you—"

"You're fine, Wren. I need to be about my business anyway." With a wink for Aeron, Hawthorne strode out the door with a swagger that spoke volumes.

Wren watched Hawthorne leave, a smile slowly spreading across her face. By the time she turned back to Aeron, she felt her lips pull into a full-blown grin.

"Well, well, well," she said, and waggled her eyebrows.

"Not a word." Aeron emphasized the threat with a finger pointed at her chest.

"At least tell me if it was any good?"

The blush deepened, and Wren cackled.

"I'll take that as a yes."

Aeron crossed his arms over his chest and stared at Wren.

She threw her hands up and said, "Fine, I'll stop. But let me just say I'm happy for you."

A grunt of acknowledgement was all she received before he turned and headed deeper into the training room.

The marble floors were shiny, reflecting the light from the large windows overlooking the front of the palace. Racks of weapons took up various positions in the open space. Straw-filled dummies lined one wall, targets lined another. One section of the room was designated for hand-to-hand combat with a soft mat padding the floor.

"So, what are we working on today?" she asked.

"Defense." Aeron stopped in the middle of the room and turned to face her.

"Why defense? Shielding was the first thing I learned."

"Not that kind of defense."

Before Wren could reply, Aeron hit her with a blast of magic so strong it threw her backward. She landed painfully on the marble floor and slid a few feet, Aeron's magic all the while pressing down on her. She smelled the ether of his storms, could feel the crackle of lightning in the air.

"Balor won't go easy on you. He will hit and hit hard. You need to be able to break away."

Wren groaned as Aeron's magic intensified. Pain erupted in her skull, like the change of pressure in the air before a storm, only magnified. Pressure on her chest made it difficult to breathe and Wren panicked. She reached for her magic, but it slipped through her fingers in her desperation to grab it.

Aeron took a step closer. "This isn't even half of what Balor will throw at you. Break away, Wren."

His slow approach and calm tone of voice twisted with her memories of Balor doing just this when she attempted to escape his captivity. Panic turned to outright fear as the press of his magic continued to grow.

Her head pounded in time with her racing heart. She felt warmth on her upper lip and knew her nose was bleeding from the pressure. Her bones ground into the floor under Aeron's assault. She dimly felt the floor rumbling underneath her. No matter how hard she tried, she couldn't reach her magic through her fear.

Suddenly, it wasn't Aeron standing in front of her. It was Balor, and he was going to kill her.

Wren gathered every bit of courage she could. With a scream, she reached deep inside herself and pulled up her magic. It released from her with a force that hit Aeron in the chest and threw him backward into a wall.

His body crashed against the marble, head smacking loud enough to echo in the room. The Dark magic surrounding her disappeared as Aeron slid bonelessly down the wall, landing in a heap on the floor. Wren lay on the floor, panting and pulling herself back together.

The door to the training room burst open and Silas rushed in. He paused for a moment to take in the scene, then rushed to Wren's side.

"What the hell happened here?" He helped Wren sit, then growled when he saw her bloody nose. "The entire palace shook like it was going to fall to the ground. And don't even get me started on what I was feeling through the bond."

Wren snapped her head in Aeron's direction as a groan sounded from across the room.

"Oh no. Aeron!" She scrambled to her hands and knees and crawled across the room to him.

By the time she reached him, his eyes were fluttering open.

"Are you okay? I'm so sorry. I didn't mean to do that. I just wanted to make it stop." She babbled as she brushed his hair away from his face. She probed the back of his head with gentle fingers. There was no blood, but he already had a knot forming.

"What's going on here?" Gabriel skidded into the training room, Jerricha following closely on his heels. He scanned the room for signs of trouble and, seeing none, relaxed.

"I'd like an answer to that question myself." Silas stood over Wren and Aeron with arms crossed.

"We were practicing our magic," Wren replied.

Silas raised one brow in question. "Why is your nose bleeding?"

"My fault," Aeron groaned from his position on the ground. "I pushed too hard."

"Why the hell would you do that?" Silas demanded. His eyes were like chips of emeralds, cold and angry.

"She needs the practice. She needs to be able to defend herself against someone like Balor." Aeron struggled to sit up and ended up propping himself against the wall with a wince.

"You should see a healer," Wren suggested. "You hit the wall pretty hard."

"No kidding," he mumbled with a grimace.

"I'm so sorry, Aeron. I really didn't mean to hit you that hard."

"It's okay. I was prepared for it. I knew I was putting myself at risk if I came at you the way I did."

Silas stood above them with crossed arms, gaze bouncing angrily between the two.

"Everything is fine, Silas," Wren said to him. "It's a good idea to prepare myself for any possibility."

Silas's expression lightened a fraction and his shoulders lost some of their tension. "I just don't enjoy seeing you hurt." He grabbed a cloth from a nearby cabinet and wiped under her nose. "You're right. It is a good idea, but I want someone else in here when you guys train. Just to make sure things don't go too far, for both your sakes."

"That's fair," she agreed.

"Let me get you to a healer," Gabriel said as he helped Aeron stand unsteadily on his feet. On their way out the door, Gabriel paused and looked back at the crowd in the room. "I think we all have been pushing ourselves to the limit. A break might be nice. What do you say to a beach bonfire tonight?"

Wren's eyes lit up at the idea. "Like we used to do years ago?"

"Exactly. Time for us to just relax and be with each other. No worries or talk of what's coming."

Jerricha smiled. "I like that idea."

"I do too," Silas added.

"Great. I'll get Aeron to a healer and get everything arranged. I'll see you all on the beach."

Jerricha followed Gabriel and Aeron out of the room. Wren looked at Silas and smiled.

"We used to have bonfires on the beach every time we came to Alynthi. It will be nice to forget about everything looming over our heads for a night."

"I couldn't agree more." He kissed her forehead and led her out of the room.

* * *

By the time Silas and Wren descended the stone steps cut into the side of the steep cliff, the bonfire was already raging. The beach was in a little cove, surrounded on three sides by trees and cliffs. The glow of the fire cast the surrounding area in orange light. Shadows flickered eerily on the cliff walls and deepened the darkness in the trees. A breeze off the ocean carried the smoke up and out of the cove, leaving the beach clear and chilly.

Jerricha and Gabriel were sitting by the fire, laughing at something Aeron said. Hawthorne sat next to Aeron, but

Wren noticed the discreet distance placed between them. A bottle of something Wren was sure contained alcohol was being passed around, thoroughly enjoyed by the company around the fire.

Silas grabbed her hand and tugged her forward. "Come on, love. They started without us."

Wren and Silas took a seat by the fire. The heat from the flames was welcome against the slight chill in the air. This far south, the weather was never too cold, but nights along the water could sometimes get brisk. Settling against Silas's side, Wren accepted the bottle and took a swig, choking as the liquid burned its way down her throat and into her chest. She didn't usually drink, but tonight was special.

The six of them sat by the fire, talking, laughing, and drinking for hours. The sun had long since set and the moon shone brightly in the cloudless sky filled with stars. Worries of what was to come were left behind. The heaviness weighing Wren down lifted. The overwhelming feeling of happiness settling in her chest overshadowed the fears and uncertainties she was used to feeling.

Late in the night, Silas leaned over and nuzzled Wren's neck. He kissed along her throat and up to her mouth. Wren melted against him, letting his solid strength hold her up, like she had done so many times before.

"I can't wait to get back to the palace," he whispered in her ear, tugging on her earlobe with his teeth.

Lightning shot through her veins and heat pooled in her core at the thought of what was to come. She pulled away from him and looked into his glazed eyes. They burned with desire, and her body answered in turn. She smiled slyly. The alcohol she had drunk made her feel brave and daring.

Her gaze dropped to his lips and she whispered back, "Who said we have to wait?"

Silas's chuckle slithered along her bones, causing her to shiver.

"As much as I enjoy that idea, I can't see you doing anything that brazen."

Those words were like a dare to her inebriated ego. She raised one brow as she stood and walked to the edge of the water, swishing her hips for extra emphasis. The waves tickled her feet as they crashed around her. Her stance shifted as the sand under her slipped away as the water receded. She could feel everyone's gaze on her, but the only gaze she paid attention to was Silas's as it burned into her back.

Turning around, she had eyes only for her mate as she slowly began taking her clothes off. A wicked smile drew her mouth up as Silas's eyes widened and his mouth dropped open. She heard Gabriel curse and the sound of crunching sand as he quickly left with Jerricha laughing and following him.

Silas stood and prowled toward Wren. His attention never wavered from her as her clothing dropped to the sand in a pile. Her gaze was riveted to him as well, as his hands began unbuttoning his shirt, exposing the black tattoo inked across his chest —the same one that graced her forearm. Their mating tattoos.

It didn't take long for Silas to stand before her, both of them completely naked. The moonlight gilded his skin and reflected in his eyes. She pulled his head down, kissing him deeply as she walked backward. The water rose around them, swirling and eddying as the waves crested and fell. Once they were deep enough, Wren wrapped her legs around his waist, pressing closer to him.

"That was quite a show you put on, love."

With desire burning through her, she couldn't even feel embarrassed for taking her clothes off in public in front of her family and friends. "I'm sorry, I won't do it again."

He huffed a laugh between kisses. "You do it as often as

you like. You won't see me complaining."

She pulled back, surprised. "You don't care if everyone saw me naked?"

His grin was wicked as he said, "They can look, as long as they know you are mine. I don't mind letting everyone know how incredibly lucky I am."

Silas cut off further conversation with a kiss so deep it left her seeing stars. His arousal pressed against her and she rubbed against him, eliciting a delightful growl from him. Her fingers slipped into his hair and she tangled her fists in his curls. She pulled back from the kiss, breathing heavily.

"I may be yours," she said breathlessly, "but you're mine too."

His eyes seemed to glow in the moonlight, the green shining so brightly. "Always," he said, his voice low and quiet.

She felt weightless in the water as Silas lifted her and slowly slid her down onto his arousal. She gasped at the pleasant stretch, the feeling of being filled by him. Her eyes closed and every other sensation awakened. She felt the warm water surrounding them, the gentle pushing and pulling of the tide as the waves formed and crashed behind them on the beach. The sound of the ocean, the breeze through the trees, and Silas's breathing all became a symphony in her ears. His skin was hot where their bodies met, both of them burning for the other.

She lost herself in the feelings, the sensations, the movements of Silas's body as he moved around her and inside her. The bond between them flowed brightly, and Wren sent every feeling and emotion she had down the chain toward Silas. His breathing hitched and he returned the favor, showing Wren everything he was feeling. Emotions rose and intensified between them. Knowing what the other was thinking drove them higher, pushed them closer together.

They came together, release rising through them like waves as they neared the shore before breaking. Wren clung tightly to Silas, her legs shaking as she wrapped them tighter around him. His broad hand stroked up and down her back, his calluses scraping gently. The ocean moved around them as they stood in the water wrapped in each other's arms. Wren laid her head on Silas's shoulder and closed her eyes.

She wasn't sure how long they stood together, but eventually Silas began walking them back to shore. She unwrapped herself from him but didn't let go of his hand. When they reached the beach, she bent to pick up their clothes. A soft sound drew her attention to the darkness near the cliff.

"What the..." Silas trailed off and his eyes widened as he stared at the scene before him.

Hawthorne was on his back in the sand with Aeron lying on top of him, both shirtless. Hands were roving and even though Wren couldn't see either of their faces, she could guess what they were doing.

Wren choked back a laugh as she quickly dressed, her clothes sticking to her wet skin. She threw Silas's clothes at him, and as he dressed, she walked over to the boys who were completely oblivious of her approach. She cleared her throat, then again, when neither of them reacted. Finally, she used her toe to poke Aeron in the side. He looked up at her, not completely registering what was happening.

"You boys might want to get a room," she offered. "Up to you though. Silas and I are leaving."

She didn't wait to see if they responded or took her advice. She pulled Silas to the steps, and they began climbing, emerging from the bliss that had been their night away from reality.

"What was that?" Silas asked. He kept looking behind him, his eyes still wide with surprise.

Wren laughed. "Exactly what it looked like."

"Aeron and Hawthorne? How long has that been going on?"

"Not too long, I think." She paused and turned to look at him, brows drawn down over her eyes. "Don't you dare judge them."

Silas held his hands up and shook his head. "No judgment. I just had no idea. Why hasn't Aeron ever said anything?"

Wren continued climbing, unsure how much she should tell Silas. In the end, she told him everything. It wasn't a secret anymore, and he was her mate. When they reached the top of the steps, she told him what Aeron experienced in the mist and the truth he later told her. Silas listened quietly until she reached the end.

"I never knew," he whispered. "I knew he didn't have the best relationship with his parents, and I knew Torryn killed Aeron's father, but I never knew why. I can't believe he never told me. Did he think I wouldn't accept him?"

"I think after everything he went through, trust was hard for him. Being hurt by the people who are supposed to love you unconditionally makes you fear trusting and ending up hurt again."

She was speaking from experience, and Silas knew that. He wrapped his arm around her waist and tugged her close.

"I love you unconditionally, Wren. I won't ever hurt you." He kissed her temple, and she could feel his amusement through the bond as he pinched her bottom.

She jumped and squealed, pulling away from him. When she looked back, her heart stuttered in her chest. His eyes shone with a mischievous light and he gave her a lopsided grin.

"Let's get back to the palace so I can show you how much I love you."

She practically ran the entire way to their room.

Chapter Twenty-One

Silas had just unbuckled the Sword from his waist and dropped it to the floor when there was a knock on the door. He had just gotten back from a day of training the soldiers with Torryn, as well as working on training with the Sword. Wren had left early in the morning to train with Aeron, and hopefully Hawthorne, since Silas didn't want them training without supervision anymore. As far as he was aware, they had been at it all day.

At the thought of Aeron and Hawthorne, he paused. He wished his friend had told him, although he understood why he hadn't. With the way they were raised and the implications that came from being gay, Silas probably wouldn't have told anyone either if the roles had been reversed. He was happy for his friend and he would support them anyway he could.

The knock came again and shook Silas out of his thoughts. He opened the door to find Gabriel standing in the hall, looking as exhausted as Silas felt.

"Hey, brother. Come on in." Silas gestured Gabriel inside and closed the door behind him. "Would you like a drink?"

Silas made his way to the little shelf of alcohol in their room and poured himself a glass.

"No thanks. It's weird seeing alcohol in here. Wren rarely drinks. It was a shock seeing her drunk last night."

Silas chuckled. "No she doesn't, and she hates it when I do." With that, he tipped his head back and downed the glass. The liquid burned its way down his throat and into his gut.

Gabriel smirked, but it quickly slid off his face. Silas took a deep breath before sitting in the chair opposite Gabriel. He knew what was coming.

"I need to use the Eyeglass."

Even though he knew this conversation was going to happen, it didn't make it easier for him. Silas closed his eyes and shook his head. "I can't give it to you."

"Come on, Silas. You know this has to happen. You know this is the best course of action. We can't let Wren make this decision."

"It's her decision to make," Silas countered.

"Is it though? What gives Wren the right to decide this?"

"It was keyed to her blood. Her ancestor spelled the thing to keep it safe. Her ancestor was part of the creation of the thing. It might as well be hers."

"What about her grandmother? Queen Elowyn is just as much a part of this, if not more."

Silas shook his head again. "I can't, Gabe. I'm sorry."

"You're not sorry yet, but you will be. You will regret letting her do this when everything falls apart on the battlefield. When we're losing and our people lay dying on the ground at our feet. You will regret this decision, but by then it will be too late." Gabriel pierced him with his blue-gray gaze. "Think about it, Silas. Really think about it. Take Wren out of the picture and the promise I know you made to her. You wouldn't hesitate to hand it over to me, would you?"

He wouldn't. He would have given Gabriel the Eyeglass immediately. It wouldn't have been easy—he didn't want to see Gabriel die. But in the end, one man's life versus millions? It wasn't a question. However, that wasn't the case. Wren was involved. He made a promise to his mate and he wouldn't break it.

Silas said nothing and Gabriel pressed his point.

"Look, I've come to terms with it. I have accepted my death. I've made my peace and I'm okay with it. Let me do this for everyone. Let me help."

"You're so ready to die? How can you be okay with that?"

Gabriel's eyes dulled, and he looked to the ground. "I don't want to watch as the people I love stay young and healthy while I grow old. I don't want to be remembered that way. I want to be remembered as I am now."

"I can't." Silas's voice was hoarse when he spoke. He hated doing this. He hated that he knew it was the right thing, but he wouldn't go against his mate. Maybe that made him selfish, but Wren would always come first. "It would kill Wren if I gave it to you. It would destroy everything we have, all the trust and love. I won't do that to her."

Gabriel stood in a rush, his chair scraping against the tile as it slid backward in his haste. "Wren will die. You will die. We are all going to die if I don't use the Eyeglass. Why can't you guys understand that? Nothing will matter anyway!"

Silas swallowed thickly. He never wanted to think of Wren dying. "I'll talk to her, Gabriel. But I won't promise anything."

Gabriel shook his head sadly before leaving without another word. Silas sat in the silence that followed with Gabriel's words bouncing around inside his skull. Unable to handle the thoughts, he poured himself another glass. He finished it in one gulp and poured another, which he promptly finished as well. The fourth glass he poured he took to the chair with him, taking small sips.

Bringing this topic up to Wren wouldn't end well. The decision was tearing her apart. He could feel the constant pressure she put on herself through the bond. It was something he wished he could do for her, make this decision for her and deal with the backlash so she didn't have to. But he couldn't. She had to do this alone.

With a frustrated growl, Silas tipped the glass back and finished it. The room spun slowly around him as he waited for his mate to return.

* * *

Silas had been drinking. She could feel it through the bond. Usually he would have a few and the bond would get fuzzy, his thoughts and emotions harder to discern. Tonight, however, as she made her way down the palace halls, Wren stumbled and pressed her hand to the wall to keep from falling. He must have drunk a lot more than a few glasses if she was feeling his inebriation this much.

When she opened the door to their room, she paused. He was sitting in a chair, elbows resting on his knees with his head in his hands. His curls hung loosely, covering his face so she couldn't read his expression. She tentatively stepped toward him and placed a hand on his shoulder. His eyes were bloodshot and glassy when he raised his head and met her gaze.

"How much have you had to drink?" she asked as she brushed his curls out of his eyes.

He looked at the empty glass in his hand and squinted one eye as if he was seeing double. "Five? Six?"

Wren pursed her lips and took the glass from him. She

filled it with water from the pitcher on the nightstand and handed it back. "Drink," she instructed.

He finished the water and sat back, head lolling against the back of the chair.

"What happened? What made you feel the need to drink so much that I can't even walk down the hall without stumbling?"

"Why are you stumbling?" His words slurred together, and he gave her a silly little smile.

She crossed her arms and stared at him hard. "The bond, Silas. I can feel it through the bond."

"Oh, that." He waved his hand dismissively.

"Yeah, that." She shook her head and tried to walk away. She didn't want to deal with him when he was like this.

With reflexes that should have been dulled because of the alcohol, Silas reached out and grabbed her arm, stopping her from walking away.

"Wait," he said and tugged her down to his lap. "We need to talk."

"It can wait until you're sober." She tried to stand, but he stopped her again.

"No, it can't." His eyes cleared, losing the glassy quality as he looked at her.

She felt through the bond some of the fuzziness lift, as if he forcibly pushed his drunkenness away. Unease settled in her gut. Whatever he had to talk about would not be pleasant.

"I talked to Gabriel tonight." He kept his voice quiet but firm. "He asked me to give him the Eyeglass."

"You didn't, did you?" Wren pulled back to look at him better. Was he drinking because he felt guilty about breaking his promise?

"No, I didn't break my promise to you, Wren. But we need

to talk about it. We really need to think about our decision and make the best one."

Her eyes filled with tears, but she blinked them away. "You think I should let my brother die?" Her voice broke, and she had to clear her throat to continue. "You think I should hand over the instrument that will kill him?"

Silas shook his head. "I'm just saying we should talk about both options, calmly. We need to make an informed decision, one not based on emotions. You know I will support whatever decision you make, but we need to think about the consequences of both choices."

"You think I haven't been thinking about the consequences? You think I haven't been slowly breaking inside because there is no good choice to make? Either way, I lose." She stood from Silas's lap and began pacing. The more she talked, the louder her voice got. It wasn't long before she was yelling. "How do I live with the guilt knowing I handed my brother the instrument that killed him? How do I live with the guilt knowing I let the entire world fall apart to save my brother's life, when in the end he will probably die anyway?"

Tears blurred her vision and she let them fall. They were angry and frustrated tears. Even with all the people surrounding her, her family and friends, her mate, she felt alone in the world. She was the only person who could make a choice that would ruin her no matter the decision she made.

"Everyone keeps telling me what to do. I keep hearing people say I have to make a choice. No one else will have to live the rest of their very long life with the guilt. No one else will have to look in the mirror every morning and see the empty shell of the person they used to be staring back at them. This is destroying me!"

"Wren—"

"I'm doing the best I can. I know it's not enough—it's never enough—but it's all I can do." She angrily wiped the tears from her cheeks. "I alone have to live with the consequences. The choice I make is the one I can live with the most. That's it. That's all I have."

Her shoulders slumped, the weight of everything pressing her down. She lifted her head and looked at Silas. He looked awful. Besides being drunk, he had dark circles under his eyes she hadn't noticed before. Strain bracketed his mouth and his green eyes weren't as bright as they usually were. The fight drained out of her, leaving her exhausted.

"I need to... I don't know. I need to go." She turned toward the door.

"Wren, wait."

She didn't stop. That feeling she got—the need to move, to run, to fly—was burning in her veins. In the hallway she took off, not caring who saw her running through the palace. She knew Silas wouldn't be able to catch up in his current state, and she wanted to put as much distance between her and everyone else as possible.

Wren headed for the back entrance, the one the servants used when deliveries were made. As she reached the gate that led to the back of the palace, she threw up a wall around the bond. She didn't want Silas following or telling anyone where she was.

The guards at the gate let her pass without questions. They knew as soon as she set foot outside the palace grounds, Winston would join her. He was as good a guard as one of them. Outside the gates, she let her muscles take over and she flew over the hills, Winston joining her immediately.

The farther she ran, the harder she pressed herself. It wasn't long before she had outrun all the thoughts that were constantly swirling in her mind. Her focus zeroed in on the burn in her muscles, her lungs pumping air in and out, her heart racing to keep up. This is why she ran. The only way to turn her mind off was to push her body to the limit, to focus on placing one foot in front of the other as she pushed herself to go a little faster, a little farther.

She didn't stop until her lungs felt like they would burst. She slowed to a jog, then a walk. A cramp had formed in her side and she pressed her hand to it, bending over, wheezing. Her legs were shaky and she let herself fall to the ground, the grass cool and damp with dew under her palms.

A wet nose nudged her neck and Winston whined, his sides heaving as much as hers were. Wren rolled over and laid on her back, one arm reaching out to pat the wolf on his side. She looked at him as he laid down with his head between his paws. The moonlight glinted off his black fur. She eyed the gray around his muzzle, something she hadn't noticed before, and her heart squeezed at the sight. She had never really thought about Winston aging. He had been with her for so long, he was such an integral part of her life, she had never imagined a time when he wouldn't be with her. But that day would come.

Just as it would come for Gabriel. Eventually, he would die —either using the Eyeglass, by sword, or old age. It wouldn't be easy to lose him. It wouldn't be easy to watch him grow old and frail—although she couldn't imagine him ever becoming frail, even in old age. Even knowing he wouldn't be with her for the rest of her long life, she still couldn't bring herself to hand over the Eyeglass. Gabriel dying when he was ninety years old to natural causes was something she could live with. It would hurt, and she would miss him dearly, but she could accept it.

Gabriel dying using the Eyeglass she handed over to him? That was something she could never live with. The guilt she would feel every day, the blame she would place on herself, would tear her apart. It was completely selfish, and for once, she didn't care.

Wren lay on the grass, watching the stars twinkle in the night sky. She smiled when one streaked across the blackness, the fiery white tail trailing in its wake. When she and Gabriel were younger, they would climb onto the roof of the manor and watch for falling stars. Gabe had told her once falling stars were spirits the Gods threw out of heaven. Wren had laughed, saying there was no way the Gods would ever be so cruel as to do something like that.

Now, watching the star streak across the sky, her smile faltered. The Gods could absolutely be that cruel. All she had to do was look at the world around her and know the Gods, if they even existed, had given up long ago. What else could explain the evil the Dark Fae wrought against the innocents of the human realm?

Wren sighed and pushed herself to her feet. Looking down at Winston, she whispered, "You ready to go back?"

They didn't run back to the palace, choosing to walk instead. She kept her thoughts focused on the surrounding land, the grass under her feet, the rocks jutting up from the ground she had to maneuver around. She kept her gaze trained on the sky, watching for more falling stars and wondering. When she died, would the Gods throw her out for her selfishness, for dooming the innocents of the world? Would she streak across the sky, a blazing light for the living to enjoy? Would anyone even be left alive to see it?

Chapter Twenty-Two

Dawn broke the next morning and Wren woke confused. She was lying on a couch and the bright morning sun was shining directly on her face. Blinking and shielding her eyes, Wren sat up, taking in her surroundings. The library. She had slept in the library in the palace. Confusion cleared as she remembered why she slept on the hard, uncomfortable couch instead of her warm, cozy bed. Her drunken mate.

When she returned to the palace the night before, she had no desire to see Silas. She didn't want to discuss the Eyeglass anymore, and she really didn't want to deal with his drunk ass. So, she made her way to the library and laid down on a couch in the back corner. She didn't think she would sleep, but surprisingly, she had.

Wren stood and stretched. Her muscles protested from sleeping on the hard surface, but she ignored them. Glancing out the window, she determined it was late enough in the morning that Silas should be out in the training fields, so she returned to her room, craving a warm bath.

In her room, she sat at the vanity and brushed her hair while the servants heated the water and poured it in the sunken tub in the bathing room. Once the servants had left, Wren ditched her clothes and gratefully sank into the lavender-scented hot water. Steam wafted around her as she laid her head back against the ledge and closed her eyes. Stiff muscles slowly relaxed, and the lavender eased her mind.

She hadn't been in the tub for long when she heard the bedroom door open and close. Boots thudded in the room and she held her breath, silently begging whoever it was to just leave. No such luck. A soft knock on the bathing room door made her groan.

"Go away. Please." She tacked on *please* and hoped it would be enough. Again, no such luck.

The door opened and Silas slipped inside, the steam billowing away from the draft as the door closed behind him. He said nothing as he sat on the floor next to the ledge of the tub, leaning against a wall. He stuck his hand in the water, idly swirling it around. His head fell forward and Wren had to fight the urge to brush his curls from his forehead.

Silas released a breath. "I'm sorry. I handled that all wrong." His green eyes met hers and they seemed to shimmer in the steam from the tub. "I had a long day, and talking with Gabriel..." he paused, searching for words.

Wren's brows furrowed. So rarely did Silas have trouble saying what he meant.

"I'm trying to hold everything together. I'm trying to keep everyone and everything organized. I'm preparing and planning and constantly thinking." He closed his eyes briefly and swallowed. When he opened them again, they shone with so much feeling. "I am doing everything I can to make sure you don't get hurt, to keep you smiling. It's not enough. I don't know what else to do and I hate that I'm failing you."

Wren sucked in a breath at his words. She reached down the bond to feel the sharp burn of guilt and regret. Before she could say anything, Silas continued.

"I couldn't take it anymore. After talking to Gabriel, I just kind of... snapped." He turned his gaze to his hand trailing in the water. "I am so sorry, Wren."

His broken, whispered apology was too much. She sat up and knelt in the tub next to Silas. Water sluiced down her arms and chest as she reached to take his head in both of her hands.

"You have not failed me," she whispered fiercely. "You are the only thing keeping me going every day." She waited until his gaze met hers. "I don't expect you to take away my pain. No one can, but you make it easier to bear. I would have bowed under this weight long ago if I didn't have you, so never think you have failed me."

Silas inhaled raggedly and closed his eyes against her words.

"I feel like I should be the one apologizing," she whispered.

His eyes popped open. "What do you have to apologize for?"

"I've been so absorbed in my own problems that I haven't thought about yours." She shook her head and snorted softly. "I really am selfish. I never thought about how much you are going through too, how much you have been doing and the stress you are under. I haven't been there for you, and for that I am sorry."

"Wren," he breathed. He brought his hands up and grasped her wrists gently. "You are not selfish. I have never once thought that. All of this was thrown at you unexpectedly. You never planned for this. You only wanted to know who you were, who your family is. All of this, all of the heartache, was never planned. You are doing everything you can, and I admire that. Greatly."

Wren's throat burned at his words. The fact he could dismiss how self-centered she had been ... she really didn't deserve him. He must have felt the change in her thoughts through the bond because his eyes sharpened.

"Don't go there, Wren. It's not true. Never think that."

Wren didn't reply. She stared into his eyes, the green so bright, and drew comfort from the familiar sight, from the strength of the bond between them. She wasn't sure who moved first, but their lips met, the kiss so soft and sweet it almost broke her heart. It didn't stay that way for long as Silas slid his hands up her arms and around her neck, threading his fingers through her wet hair.

The kiss deepened and Wren wrapped her arms around Silas's neck, answering the small bite Silas left on her lower lip by letting his tongue sweep in. She couldn't stop the moan that escaped. Feeling his shirt get wet from the water still on her skin, she pulled it over his head, briefly breaking the kiss. His mouth was on hers again immediately, and she tossed his shirt aside. Shivers erupted over her skin as his hands roamed over her bare flesh, his touch like a brand.

Silas trailed open-mouthed kisses down her neck, biting the spot where her neck met her shoulder. Wren's head fell back and her eyes closed, heat pooling between her legs. She clamped her legs together to ease the ache, and Silas's eyes lit up as he caught the motion. A wicked grin lifted the corners of his mouth as his hands slid from her back to the buttons on his pants. Wren was practically panting as he freed his arousal and tossed his pants and boots next to his shirt.

Wren lowered herself back into the water and gave Silas room to slip into the tub. He grabbed her arms and tugged her forward, wrapping her legs around his waist. She gasped at the feel of his wet skin against hers, and Silas claimed her mouth in another bruising kiss. It amazed her how easily he got under her skin, how quickly she burned for him. Only Silas could make her forget what waited for them. Only his touch, his kiss, made her burn.

Silas slipped a hand between them, trailing his fingers over her breasts, down her stomach, between her legs. She moaned as he pushed one finger inside and pulled it back out before adding another. Wren stopped thinking. She let her body take over, hips rolling, chasing the feeling lighting her up inside.

"I love you, Wren," Silas breathed against her mouth.

She captured his words, breathing them in and letting them fill the broken places inside her. She slowed her hips and looked at him. His beauty always took her breath away. She ran her hands through his hair, the curls glistening with drops of water and curling tighter than normal in the heat from the tub.

"Show me. Show me how much you love me." Her hands tightened in his hair, pulling gently on the strands. She knew those words would be his undoing, and she wasn't wrong.

His eyes seemed to glow with predatory intent as he lifted her hips and placed himself at her entrance. Wren's hands landed on his shoulders, feeling the muscles bunch under her fingers. With no warning, Silas slammed into her and Wren screamed, the pleasure almost too much to bear. He captured her bottom lip between his teeth and Wren clenched around him, drawing a groan from Silas.

Water splashed around them, the sounds mixing with Wren's breathy moans and Silas's growls. He moved harder and faster and Wren dug her fingers into his shoulders, riding the rising tide of fire that burned through her blood. Tension coiled tighter in her and she knew release was coming.

"Silas," she breathed.

"Not yet," he growled back.

His hand moved to her neck, and his grip tightened, drawing her gaze to his. She could do nothing as she was held captive in that green gaze, his hand holding her in place while his hips continued to pound into her.

It was too much. The pressure built, rising higher and higher. Her body was trembling as her need pushed against her.

"Please," she begged.

He tilted her head to the side and his teeth scraped along her neck before he clamped down, biting her. Wren screamed as her release tore through her, the tension exploding outward so hard she saw stars. She was barely aware of Silas's body tensing around her as he found his release.

When he fell still, her body slumped forward, all ability to move lost in the aftershock of what just happened. Little tremors continued to work their way through her as she laid her head on Silas's shoulder. Their chests rose and fell rapidly against each other. Silas wrapped his arms around her. She wasn't sure how he managed, seeing as her limbs were limp and unmovable.

Eventually, their hearts slowed and breathing returned to normal. Still, Silas held her close to him. His lips brushed her shoulder in a featherlight kiss that made her shiver.

"The water is getting cold," he said quietly.

"Yeah." Her voice was hoarse from screaming, and she had to clear her throat.

"We should get out."

"We should." But she didn't move. Instead, she snuggled in closer, tightening her legs around his waist.

He buried his nose in her hair and inhaled her scent. His chest rose with the breath he took, then fell as he exhaled loudly. He slowly stood from the water, keeping Wren in his arms. He lifted her out of the tub and set her on the ground. Grabbing a thick towel from the stack next to the tub, he wrapped her in it before wrapping another around his waist.

He took his time drying her off, then led her to the vanity and brushed the tangles out of her hair.

Their gazes met through the mirror, and she smiled. "Thank you," she whispered.

"For what?"

"For everything."

Before Silas could respond a knock sounded on the door. A growl rumbled out of his chest before he snapped, "Go away!"

The knock came again, louder this time, and Silas stormed to the door, throwing it open.

"What?"

Aeron stood on the other side, hand raised mid-knock. His eyebrows climbed to his hairline as he took in Silas standing in just a towel. His gaze flicked over Silas's shoulder to Wren standing in the bathing room door, also wearing nothing but a towel.

"Well," he drawled, "I was coming to yell at Wren for not meeting me for training, but I can see she was busy."

He smirked at Silas, and if Wren didn't know Aeron as well as she did, she would have thought he had a death wish.

Silas opened his mouth to reply, but Wren, sensing what was about to come out of his mouth, intervened.

"I'll be right there."

Before Aeron could answer, Silas shut the door in his face. Wren heard him laughing as he walked down the hall.

"You should be nice to your friends," she said as she walked to him, placing her hands on his chest.

"He's not my friend." A small smile pulled his lips up and his eyes danced with an inner light. He brought her hands to his mouth and kissed her knuckles. "I guess it's back to reality."

"I guess so." Wren stood on her toes and kissed him lightly. She turned to dress, but Silas's arm snagged around her waist and he pulled her against him.

"So," he murmured against her mouth, "did my actions show you how much I love you?"

She pulled out of his grasp and lifted one shoulder. "Maybe," she said coyly. Before he could grab her again, Wren rushed into the bathing room and shut the door.

She dressed quickly and braided her hair. When she left the bathing room, Silas was dressed and perched on the armrest of the chair.

"I'll walk you to the training room," he said and held out his hand.

She reached for it and intertwined their fingers. The walk to the training room was too short. Before she knew it, he was kissing her forehead and walking away. She watched him before joining Aeron, ready to work on her magic.

* * *

Wren and Aeron had been training for three hours. She was sweaty, disheveled, bruised, and bleeding. And that was with Hawthorne acting as chaperone. Aeron finally called for a break as he picked himself up off the floor, groaning at the hit Wren landed with her magic. It was one of a very few she had landed on him. The rest had been him drilling her with his Dark magic over and over again.

Wren stumbled to the table by the window to pour a glass of water. Her arms were shaking and more water landed outside the glass than in it. She glared at Aeron as he limped over, rubbing his backside.

"It's the least you deserve," she mumbled as she held her hand up, watching the tremors work through her arm.

"If you were faster, you wouldn't be so beat-up."

She was opening her mouth to give him a piece of her mind, but Hawthorne stepped between them.

"No fighting with words. You're doing enough of that with your magic." He leveled a hard stare at Aeron as if he were telling him to ease up.

About time.

Wren tipped the glass back and peered out the window. The sight that greeted her made her choke, water spewing out of her mouth and hitting the glass. She coughed and wiped her mouth with the back of her hand, grimacing at the tenderness of her lip.

"What's wrong?" Aeron peered over her shoulder. "Who is that?"

Wren's gaze landed on the man sitting atop a white warhorse, his shoulder-length brown hair pulled back from his face. She was too far away to see clearly, but she knew he had dark brown eyes, like melted chocolate. She also knew the sigil stitched on the breast of his cloak was a sword crossed over a round shield.

"Prince Castain," she replied. The man she was supposed to marry was dismounting in the courtyard, handing his reins to a stable hand.

Aeron glanced at her. "Isn't that your fiancé?"

Wren snorted. "Once upon a time, yeah, he was."

"Oh man, things are about to get interesting." Aeron chuckled as he walked away.

Wren contemplated sending a wave of magic to knock him on his ass, but she caught sight of Silas and Gabriel crossing the courtyard toward Castain.

"Shit," she mumbled. Spinning on her heel, she rushed for the door and sprinted down the hall. Servants no longer appeared shocked to see her running through the palace—lately it had become quite commonplace.

Wren took the stairs two at a time, skidding into the entryway wildly. She pushed the heavy front doors open and rushed out into the warm afternoon sun turning toward the courtyard. A small group of men were dismounting and Wren knew, without looking closely, the guards were not only guarding the crown prince, but the king as well. Her heart thundered in her chest thinking this could go one of two ways: Castain and his father would understand and forget the whole engagement, or they would be angry Wren had gone off and married, choosing a Dark Fae over the crown prince of Avisten.

She skidded to a stop in the courtyard, bumping into Gabriel who was chatting with Castain and the king. Silas stood at Gabe's side with a wry smile on his face. The smile dropped as soon as his gaze landed on Wren.

"What the hell?" he exclaimed, pulling Wren in front of him. He gently touched her cheek and frowned when she flinched. "If you say Aeron did this, I'm going to kill him."

Wren grimaced, feeling her split lip crack open and start bleeding again. "Please don't kill him. We need him."

Anger thundered down the bond, and Wren actually took a step back. "We don't need him that badly."

A throat cleared and Wren turned to find Castain and King Trion staring wide-eyed at her. She felt her blood climb up her neck and into her cheeks. In her haste to get to the courtyard, she had forgotten what exactly she looked like. She smiled sheepishly at the newcomers and patted her braid, attempting to tame the wild mess. It was a lost cause. She let her hands drop to her sides and straightened her shoulders.

"King Trion, Prince Castain." She nodded her head in their direction, the only acknowledgement she would give them regarding their titles and stations. She should curtsy, but seeing as she was wearing leggings and didn't particularly want to curtsy to them, she didn't. Not to mention she technically was a princess herself. The nod was more than sufficient.

King Trion's mouth tightened with distaste as his gaze

roamed over Wren, taking in her disheveled appearance and bloody lip. Her back straightened further and she lifted her chin. She would not let this man demean her.

"I was just welcoming King Trion and Prince Castain to the palace," Gabriel said as he placed a hand on her shoulder. "Rooms are being readied as we speak. My father and King Rodion will be eager to meet with you. Your men are welcome to the barracks or they may stay outside the gates with the rest of your army."

Wren's head snapped around toward Gabriel. Army? Had Avisten sent an army to aid Alynthi in the battle to come? Before she could open her mouth, King Trion spoke.

"Thank you for the welcome. We look forward to speaking with King Rodion and your father as well."

His voice made Wren shiver. The deep baritone was gravelly and cold. His eyes were just as icy as he once again looked at Wren. She couldn't read the expression, but she didn't like it. King Trion turned and headed for the palace, following a servant who would take him to his rooms. Prince Castain remained behind and Wren finally let herself look at him.

He looked like she remembered, only older. His brown hair and eyes, tan skin, and wide shoulders were the same. His mouth was curved down in a frown as he looked at Wren, absent-mindedly rubbing his shoulder.

Wren fought a grin as she realized that was where she had stabbed him the last time she saw him. Amusement filtered through the bond and she realized she must have projected that memory to Silas.

Castain finally smiled and inclined his head, the smile not reaching his eyes. "It's nice to see you again, Wren. I must admit I missed you."

Chapter Twenty-Three

Wren barely contained the snort at Castain's words. He missed her? The last time she saw him, she shoved a dagger in his shoulder for saying something about women not being able to handle blades.

Now his gaze traveled over Wren, lingering on her leggings and the bruising no doubt gracing her face. His mouth ticked up in a small smirk as he finally met her gaze. "Nothing to say?"

Wren gave him an overly sweet smile. "Have you met Silas?" She reached behind her and pulled Silas forward to stand next to her.

"I... uh... yeah." Castain glanced between them, his brow furrowed.

Wren linked her arm through Silas's and gazed adoringly into his eyes. "He's my mate," she said before glancing back at Castain.

She had to bite her lip to keep her laughter from escaping. Castain's eyes widened comically, and his gaze bounced back and forth between Wren and Silas before he turned to Gabriel.

Silas's amusement intensified through the bond. *Was that really necessary?*

Her eyes narrowed on Silas. *Yes, it was. Now, be quiet.*

Silas chuckled, and Castain's gaze snapped to him.

"Yes, well," Castain said, straightening his shirt and adjusting his cloak. "I'll just go find my father." He turned to Gabriel. "I'll see you in a few minutes."

Wren watched Castain stalk off and smiled. Gabriel turned toward her and gave her a stern look.

"Really, Wren?"

"That's what I said," Silas muttered.

Wren huffed and started walking away. "I'm going to go clean up. Do not start that meeting without me."

"Wouldn't dream of it," Gabriel said as he and Silas returned to the training fields.

Wren returned to her room and finally got a good look in the mirror. She grimaced at her reflection, wincing at the slight pain in her lip and cheek. Aeron hadn't gone easy on her today again. The first time Hawthorne had attempted to step in, Wren asked him not to. Unless Aeron was about to kill her, she didn't want Hawthorne stopping them. It was the only way she would get stronger. The only way she could face Balor and not freeze in fear.

Wren filled the basin with water and used her magic to heat it. A cut split her bottom lip, as well as her right eyebrow. Her left cheek was already turning purple. And that didn't count the multiple aches and pains she felt in her arms, legs, and ass. Aeron's magic had given her quite a punch in the stomach and taking a deep breath still hurt. She wondered if she had a broken rib or two.

The door opened as she was cleaning the cut on her lip and she met Silas's glance through the mirror.

"Before you say anything, I'm fine." She dropped the cloth in the water with a splash and turned to face him.

His gaze roamed over her face, cataloging her injuries. Anger, worry, and love warred for attention through the bond as he stalked across the room to stand in front of her. He reached behind her and grabbed the cloth, tilting her head to the side with his other hand.

"I know you're fine, but that doesn't mean I enjoy seeing you like this." He dabbed at her eyebrow with the cloth. "Wasn't Hawthorne there while you trained?"

"Yes. I told him not to interfere unless Aeron was about to kill me." She said the last bit sarcastically. She highly doubted Aeron would get that carried away.

Silas sighed and gave her a wry smile. "Why am I not surprised to hear that?" He dropped the cloth back in the water and reached for a tin of salve. He spread the ointment on her cuts, his thumb lingering on her bottom lip.

Heat pooled in Wren's stomach at Silas's hooded gaze.

"I'd kiss you right now, but I doubt that ointment tastes very good." He gave her a boyish grin and slid his hands around her waist, tugging her close. "Can I just make one request?"

"You can. Doesn't mean I'll listen."

He huffed a laugh on top of her head. "You can be so infuriating," he mumbled against her hair. "Please, just be careful. Don't push yourself too hard. I understand how important it is for you to continue to grow and learn to master your magic. And I'm all for you strengthening and using whatever you have in your arsenal. It's just important for you to not drain yourself. I know you're still feeding the Crown and I don't want you to overdo it. You need to be strong when this battle happens."

She pulled back enough to look at him. The concern she felt through the bond and saw glittering in his eyes made her heart skip a beat. He was right, and she knew it. She also knew she had been pushing herself, but seeing and feeling his concern made her realize she needed to be more careful.

"I know," she said quietly. "I will, I promise." She felt the relief through the bond, as well as some of the tension ease out of his shoulders.

"Thank you." He placed a kiss on top of her head. "Now, how about you change and we head down for that meeting? I'm looking forward to seeing more of your fiancé."

Wren pulled back and smacked his chest, but like he always could, he made her smile.

* * *

Wren and Silas entered the council room hand in hand. The general and Gabriel sat next to each other, talking quietly with Queen Elowyn. Jerricha, Aeron, and Hawthorne did the same farther down the table. King Rodion was seated at the head of the table flipping through reports. It had been a while since Wren had seen him and she suddenly felt a flutter of nerves in his presence. The last time she saw him, she was his niece. Now she was no one of importance.

The sound of the door closing behind them drew everyone's head in their direction and Wren paused briefly before taking a seat opposite Gabriel. The king's gaze was a brand upon her she did her best to ignore.

"If you are sitting in on this meeting, I expect you to behave." The general's words made her back stiffen, and she had to bite back the words that came to her mind.

A soft chuckle came from her left, and the king said, "When has she ever behaved?"

It wasn't his words but his tone that cooled her anger. There was nothing mocking in it, only a sense of fondness.

Wren slowly turned her head and looked at King Rodion. His brown eyes were lit with something she couldn't place.

"As we all now know, you are not truly my niece, but some things are hard to forget. While you may not be my niece by blood, I still consider you my niece by heart."

Wren's eyes welled with tears. She had never enjoyed the idea that being the king's niece made her a pawn to be used for political warfare. However, the king had always been kind to her. As she was growing up, he had acted like a doting uncle rather than a king. One who not only overlooked her and Gabriel's antics but often encouraged them. His words made her realize she didn't want to lose that uncle.

"I also hear congratulations are in order," he continued as his gaze moved past Wren and settled on Silas. "I assume Wren's father already spoke to you about what would happen if you hurt her."

Silas snorted. "Hardly," he muttered so quietly she wasn't sure anyone heard.

The king apparently did because his eyes widened, and his gaze slid to his brother in shock.

"Don't worry," Wren cut in before anyone could throw out any more angry words. "Gabriel took that upon himself." The memory of Silas's black eye and Gabriel's subsequent broken nose rose to the surface.

Across the table, Gabriel grinned at her. "That I did." He rubbed his nose before continuing, "and those warnings are unnecessary. Silas is the last person who would ever harm Wren."

"That is good to hear," the king said and settled back in his chair.

The doors to the council room opened once again and cut short any further conversation. King Trion and Prince Castain entered with a few of their men trailing behind. It didn't get past Wren that they were the only ones armed. As soon as King Trion noticed Silas seated next to Wren his lip curled back in disgust.

"I didn't realize we were letting just anyone in this meeting," he said as his gaze traveled over the rest of Wren's friends.

She bit her tongue but said down the bond, *Clearly we are because we let you join.* She saw Silas press his lips together out of the corner of her eye and amusement flickered down the bond.

"King Trion, Prince Castain. You are welcome at my table," King Rodion said. His eyes hardened, and he continued, "as long as you keep your opinions about my guests to yourself."

Castain stiffened but sat with a nod at the king of Alynthi. His father joined him and folded his hands on top of the table, pointedly ignoring Wren and the rest.

"We are more than grateful to you for bringing your troops with you," Gabriel said, ever the one to keep the peace. "We were worried you hadn't made it out of Avisten in time."

"We barely made it out," King Trion said. "The little news we have received from home is not promising. I am afraid we will, and have already, lost many to the Dark Fae."

A stone settled in Wren's stomach as everything else fled from her mind. The reason they were meeting came rushing back at his somber words. Innocents in the path of the Dark Fae, gone before anything could be done.

"I am truly sorry to hear that." King Rodion leaned forward in his seat. "When the time comes, you have as much support from Ellendyr as we can spare."

The words left unspoken didn't go unheard. No one knew what kind of support Ellendyr would be able to provide at the end of this.

Gabriel cleared his throat, and everyone looked at him. "I have received news from one of my men. Balor has left Valasia as it no longer holds any importance to him." He glanced at Wren when he said this. "He is moving his men across the Ellendyr Mountains. I believe his goal is to meet up with his father and combine troops."

The breath in Wren's lungs burned at his words. It didn't come as a surprise, but hearing it was still terrifying.

"They will look for a place to make a stand," Silas added. "And if I know my uncle at all, which I unfortunately do, he will make it along the border of Ellendyr and Avisten. The ground is flat and the mountains to the north provide an escape route only the Dark Fae can safely cross."

Castain's head jerked in Silas's direction and his mouth dropped open in shock. "Your uncle?"

"Silas's uncle is King Deimos's advisor," Gabriel clarified.

King Rodion's face darkened, red suffusing his cheeks and neck. "You are Dark Fae?" He turned to glare at King Trion. "You knowingly let a Dark Fae join this meeting?"

Castain's gaze remained on Wren, shock and disbelief warring across his features. As she looked at him, she saw the shock drop away, replaced by ugly rage.

"You chose a Dark Fae over me?" he almost growled the words.

Wren sighed. She had hoped it wouldn't come to this, but she wasn't surprised. Castain had always been vain. Her ending up with Silas, a Dark Fae, would surely hurt his ego. Wren sensed more than saw her friends tensing down the table. King Rodion remained relaxed in his chair, but his eyes were chips of ice as he stared at Castain.

King Trion placed a hand on his son's arm. "That is another discussion we need to have." He turned to King Rodion. "Your niece never fulfilled her end of the agreement. I understand it was because she is a Light Fae and you were concerned with how we would react to that. Seeing as everything that is taking place, having a Light Fae wed into the family would be more than acceptable."

Wren sat up taller and tried to process what he was saying. She almost couldn't believe this conversation was happening. The Dark Fae were on their doorstep. The entire world was at risk of being destroyed, and they wanted to talk about Wren's broken engagement to Castain? It was absurd. Silas placed a hand on her leg under the table, squeezing gently.

King Trion continued, "As far as I'm concerned, the marriage can still take place." He eyed Wren, his gaze traveling over her body. "Of course, a few things will have to change. We would not let a princess of our country dress or behave the same way you have."

Wren's eyes about popped out of her head. Her knuckles turned white as she gripped the arms of her chair. "The marriage absolutely will not take place. End of discussion." She turned to her uncle. "Now, may we resume with more important matters?"

King Rodion smiled warmly at Wren. He held a hand up, halting whatever acidic comment was about to spew from King Trion's mouth. "Even if I had the inclination to agree with you, Trion—which I do not—I believe it is too late for any marriage between Wren and your son. Wren and Silas completed the tethering ceremony already. Correct me if I'm wrong, Queen Elowyn, but I believe that bond far supersedes that of a marriage bond and cannot be undone."

Queen Elowyn nodded her head at King Trion. "You are correct. Nothing will come between a couple who has completed a tethering ceremony. Not even death."

Chills skittered down Wren's spine. Death was all too likely in the coming days and she didn't particularly enjoy the reminder. However, her grandmother's words warmed her heart. Queen Elowyn was less than supportive of her relationship with Silas, but it seemed she drew a line where Wren was concerned.

"Now," King Rodion announced, "we may move on to more important matters. That is, unless you do not wish to continue this alliance? Although, from what Gabriel has said, I do not believe you can cross the border back into Avisten."

"You still haven't enlightened us as to why you are allowing a Dark Fae to join this meeting. You may find it acceptable for your niece to tie herself to the enemy, but I object to allowing them to hear of our plans." King Trion stared down King Rodion, the challenge clear in his eyes.

King Rodion sighed heavily and ran a hand down his face. "I shouldn't have to explain to you why I let anyone sit in on the meetings I have called. Silas and his companions are more than welcome at my table, having proven themselves time and again. Now, this meeting will continue or you may leave."

The Avisten royals looked less than pleased to have been so thoroughly dismissed, however, they had little choice. King Trion gritted his teeth and nodded his head jerkily. Castain stared at Silas and Wren, pure loathing in his gaze.

Silas gave Castain a small smile and placed his arm along the back of Wren's chair, idly toying with a strand of her hair.

Quit antagonizing him. Wren pinched Silas's leg in warning.

Ouch. His head dipped to her ear and his warm breath shivered across her skin as he whispered, "Not antagonizing. I just can't keep my hands off you." *And this is the least indecent place I can touch you with people around.*

Blood crept into her cheeks at the same time her toes curled in her boots. *You need to learn to control yourself.*

Oh, I've tried, love. If you weren't so beautiful, it wouldn't be a problem.

Wren hid her smile behind her hand and forced herself to tune in to the conversation at the table.

"Ellendyr's armies have been training with the Light Fae, as well as the few Dark Fae on our side and the Elementals who sailed back with us from Edein," Gabriel was saying. "Having the Dark Fae here has been invaluable in teaching our men how to defend against their magic, as much as we can. Silas and I have come up with a strategy we think will be the most successful. Of course, it all comes down to the use of the Artifacts."

"The Artifacts?" King Trion glanced at Gabriel.

Wren pushed thoughts of Gabriel's unspoken words about the use of the Eyeglass aside while he educated the Avisten royals on the Obsidian Artifacts. She had made up her mind and nothing would change that. Luckily, Gabriel didn't mention the Eyeglass nor the drama it had caused between them.

Discussion lasted long into the evening. Dinner was brought in, although most ate only a few bites. Castain remained quiet through the meeting, even though Wren frequently felt his stare across the table.

The sun had long since set, and Wren was exhausted. She wasn't used to these types of meetings and the worry that came with it was burrowing deep in her bones. Not caring what people thought, she scooted her chair closer to Silas's and rested her head on his shoulder, seeking the comfort his touch and presence brought her. With his arm around her, she could focus on the conversation again, pushing her fears aside once more.

By the time King Rodion called an end to the meeting, everyone was looking as exhausted as Wren felt. They had discussed strategy and made back-up plans, but so much was still uncertain until King Deimos made his move. Silas said it wouldn't be long before he did. Most likely when Balor and his men joined up with the king's army.

As Wren and Silas made their way to their room in silence, the words spoken and unspoken in the meeting vied for attention in Wren's head. "How much time do you think we have?" she asked him quietly.

Silas squeezed her hand before replying, "Gabriel said it will take Balor a week to reach Deimos. After that"—he released a deep breath—"two days, three at the most. Deimos is already in Tethoris. If he were smart, which he is, he will have already begun moving his men to the border."

Wren's heart sank in her chest at his words. Fear so potent blossomed within her and she stumbled. When they reached their room and the door closed behind them, Wren spun to face Silas. She stood on her toes and laced her fingers in his hair, bringing his head down to hers.

"Make me forget," she whispered against his lips.

As Silas lowered his mouth to hers, he did just that.

Chapter Twenty-Four

The next week passed in a blur of training, planning, and strategizing. Preparations were underway for the armies to march, servants were packing supplies, and orders were being given. Wren and Silas spent every night together trying to forget what was looming on the horizon. During the day, they rarely saw one another, both busy with their own training.

"Take a break," Aeron said, picking himself up from the ground. They were training outside today as the weather was nice and Wren was tired of looking at the same four walls.

Wren grinned at him. "You just want a break because I'm actually beating you."

Aeron gave her a bland look. "I'm letting you win, princess."

Wren and Hawthorne both snorted at his comment, but she was glad for the reprieve. Even though her skill with her magic was improving, she found herself on the ground more often than not and she had the bruises to prove it.

Wren headed to the big training ground where Silas was

training the human and Light Fae armies on defending against Dark Fae magic. He split his time between that and working with the Sword, and as a result he was usually exhausted come nightfall.

Silas was finishing an exercise with a group of humans, and Wren watched as he wielded his magic. As always, when she saw him fight, he stole her breath. Powerful muscles shifted under his clothing, flexing as he easily avoided a strike. His movements were fluid, like water flowing over rocks. Shadows whipped out of him faster than she could follow, and it was a testament to his skills as a trainer that all the men avoided the first strike. They weren't so lucky on the second attempt. He made it look effortless and beautiful.

He called for a break and as he prowled off the field, his gaze snagged on Wren. He made his way to her and pulled her in for a hug.

"Ew," she squealed, and pushed him away. "You're sweaty."

He chuckled and tried to pull her in again, rubbing his sweat-soaked curls on her face. "That never bothers you at night." His voice was midnight silk and made her stomach flutter.

"That is different," she exclaimed, jumping backward away from him.

He laughed but relented. Someone tossed him a towel, and he quickly wiped the sweat off before taking her hand and leading her away down the path behind the palace.

"How's training going?" she asked, looking behind them at the mass of human men working through drills.

"Actually, they are doing really well." He sounded surprised and also respectful. "Most of them are spending extra time on the field, getting in as much practice as they can."

Wren didn't have a chance to respond. Before she could even open her mouth, Silas turned the corner and tugged her into a shadowy alcove. She managed a surprised gasp as he pressed her against the cool stones, and then his mouth was on hers. She immediately melted against him, her body responding to him in a primal way.

Silas slid his hand up her arm and around her neck, cupping the back of her head as he pressed her harder against the wall. Wren's senses zeroed in on the way his body felt against her, all the hard planes and angles against her softer curves. The sound of clashing swords and the shouts of men could be heard in the distance, and the risk of being caught only heightened her arousal.

These moments with Silas were what she lived for. The distraction from the impending battle and the way she could get lost in him, even if just for a moment, was something she would never take for granted. Time was never guaranteed, and she was determined to make every second count.

Silas slipped his hand under her shirt and Wren moaned against his mouth, which only seemed to fuel his actions. His hand slid up her ribs and cupped her breast, his thumb rubbing over the peak, making Wren's back arch off the wall. Her hands shot to his hair and she tangled her fingers in his curls, tugging gently. A sound vibrated in the back of his throat that reminded Wren of a large cat, a mix between a growl and purr.

Emboldened by that sound and wanting to live in the moment, Wren slid her hands down his back and around his waist, fingers slipping under the belt and waistline of his pants. His warm skin against her fingers and the feel of the ridges of his muscles caused tingles to dance over her fingertips. She rolled her hips, feeling his arousal low against her stomach.

Silas broke the kiss and pulled back far enough to look at her face. Her body trembled at the fire burning in his eyes, eyes that were almost pure black and shadowed under his thick lashes.

"If you don't stop touching me like that nothing is going to stop me from burying myself so far inside you that you'll be feeling me days later." His voice was barely recognizable, low and gravelly, and it rolled over Wren's skin and sank into her bones.

"That doesn't sound like such a bad thing," she breathed. Her tongue flicked out and traced up the column of his throat at the same time she moved her hand lower in his pants. His arousal twitched against her stomach and she gave a throaty laugh against his neck.

"Oh, it definitely isn't a bad thing," he said against her ear.

That thumb continued to move back and forth across her nipple, making it hard for her to focus on his words.

"However, this alcove is not the most hidden and anyone could happen upon us," he continued.

"Since when are you the voice of reason?" Her fingers slipped a little lower, teasing the soft skin above his arousal. She stood on her toes and whispered in his ear, "I want you to fuck me against this wall, where anyone could see us."

"Fuck," he growled. Her words undid him. Shadows fell around them, providing a semblance of privacy.

He pulled her leggings down, freeing one of her legs and tossing her boot to the side. He undid the belt and the laces on his pants in record time, and Wren wrapped her legs around him. Their joining wasn't slow or sweet. He filled her in one hard thrust and Wren's head would have hit the wall behind her had Silas's hand not been there.

The stones were hard and dug into her back, but she barely felt them as Silas pounded into her repeatedly. He stretched and filled her in the most amazing way. She felt every inch of him inside her as his scent and taste invaded her other senses. His shadows were cool and slick on her heated skin as they danced around them.

Tension coiled low in her stomach, and she gripped his hair tightly, pulling his mouth to hers. Wren fractured around him and all her senses dimmed except the feel of herself coming undone. She recognized the feeling of Silas tensing as he also found his release.

She collapsed limply against his chest, her head on his shoulder. The only thing keeping her legs wrapped around Silas were his arms—if it weren't for him, she would have slid bonelessly to the ground. Both of their chests heaved as they caught their breath. Slowly, sound returned and Wren could hear the clash of swords and the shouts of men training through the shadows still swirling around the alcove. Her cheeks heated at how brazen she had been, but she quickly pushed embarrassment aside. She wouldn't let propriety ruin what had just happened.

Silas gently lowered her to the ground, and she had to hold on to his shoulders as her knees shook. His grin was wicked and all-knowing as he waited for her to get her balance. Once she was steady, Silas knelt in front of her and helped her put her foot back in her leggings and boot, then pulled her leggings back up her legs, placing a kiss on her thigh.

"I have no clue what got into you," Silas said between gentle kisses, "but I'm not going to complain. Anytime you want me to fuck you against a wall where anyone can see us, you just let me know."

"You have such a filthy mouth," she mumbled, not able to meet his eyes.

His fingers wrapped around her chin gently and forced her to look up into his bright green eyes. He raised one brow as he said, "I believe it was your mouth that got us into this situation."

Wren tugged her shirt straight and tucked a loose piece of hair behind her ear. "Yes, well." She brushed past Silas, parting the shadows.

The bright sunlight caused her eyes to water after being surrounded by Silas's shadows. Blinking rapidly, she jumped back as the shape of a person took form in front of her. She continued blinking, hoping doing so would change what she was seeing.

"Prince Castain," she said, crossing her arms over her chest. "What are you doing here?"

Castain's gaze flicked behind her where she knew Silas had let the shadows disperse. His gaze returned to Wren and he smirked. "I was walking by when I heard something. I was worried some poor girl was being taken advantage of." His eyes darkened and his smirk turned into a sneer. "I see now it was just you whoring yourself out to the enemy."

Out of the corner of her eye, she saw Silas tense. His hand dropped to the Sword and she could feel his magic rising inside him as he took a step forward. All she did was put her hand on his arm and he stopped—he released his grasp on the Sword and his magic calmed. Wren stepped around him and looked up at Castain.

She gave him a small shake of her head. "Jealousy does not become you, prince."

His brown eyes flared and anger simmered in their depths. His mouth opened and Wren had no doubt he was about to spew something toxic she had no desire to hear. With a flick of her fingers, she used the seed of Dark magic that was planted within her when she bonded with Silas. Shadows swirled out of her fingers and covered Castain's mouth, silencing whatever he was about to say.

"There is nothing you could say that would remotely interest me." Wren breezed past Castain, Silas following on her heels. The sight of the crown prince trying to pull the shadows away from his mouth while his fingers went right through them would be a source of entertainment for her for years to come.

Silas nudged her with his shoulder as they walked back to the training fields. "Remind me to never make you mad."

Wren snorted, but through the bond she felt his approval and amusement.

They slowly made their way to the training fields, neither one wanting to part ways. Wren held tightly to Silas's hand, ignoring the worry that tried to seep in and erase the pleasure she had just experienced.

Silas noticed it first. He stopped walking, and a pulse of dread crept down the bond, making Wren's steps falter. She glanced up at him, ready to ask what was wrong, but his gaze was trained on the sky. Resolve steeled his features and he looked down at Wren, swallowing thickly. Wren quickly turned her attention to the sky. A falcon swooped down, powerful wings beating as it raced for the training field. Wren knew who the falcon was looking for.

They hurried their steps, reaching the training field and weaving through the soldiers, who were oblivious to what was happening. They approached Gabriel just as the bird took off with a flap of wings that ruffled Gabriel's blond hair. He unraveled a small roll of parchment, eyes scanning the contents. Wren held her breath, her grip on Silas's hand threatening to break bones. She watched as Gabriel's face paled and he lifted his eyes. His gaze landed on Wren and the grim set to his mouth and the concern in his eyes caused the world to tilt around her.

Gabriel transferred his gaze to Silas. "It's time."

Chapter Twenty-Five

The march to the border of Ellendyr and Avisten was a somber one. Wren and Silas rode at the front with both kings, Queen Elowyn, the general, and Gabriel. The army was divided into three sections—the mounted unit, the foot soldiers, and a special unit of scouts Wren nicknamed the assassins. Light Fae and Elementals were interspersed among the humans strategically to bolster the human army, as well as provide extra protection.

When they reached the location where they would make their stand, tents were set up and cook fires started. They had somehow beaten the Dark Fae, something that made everyone nervous. King Deimos had plenty of time to get his men to the location, and Wren couldn't help but wonder why he was taking his time. Silas believed it was a ploy to drum up anxiety, to make them nervous and jumpy. It was working.

Sitting around a campfire with her closest friends and family, Wren made sure she was in the moment. This could be the last time they were all together and she didn't want to waste a minute of it worrying about tomorrow. There was little laughter but conversation flowed freely. Stories were being shared—real and make-believe. Despite everything, despite the fact they were sitting in a war camp, Wren felt relaxed while she leaned against Silas and ate her stew.

That is, until a falcon cried above them, circling until Gabriel raised his arm. The bird landed and Gabriel removed the thin parchment, reading quickly.

"They will be here by nightfall tomorrow." He scanned his companions sitting around the fire. "I expect Deimos will make his move the following morning."

The stew Wren had eaten turned into a lump in her stomach. So much for relaxed feelings and no thoughts of the days to come. Silas's arm tightened around her shoulders.

"Yeah, he will," Silas confirmed. "He will use the cover of night to send some men over to scout our camp to get a read on what we have, and our overall morale. He will try to find anything he can use against us."

Gabriel stood. "I'll have our scouts prepared to keep an eye out for anyone who doesn't belong."

The scouts he spoke of were not just scouts. Wren had nicknamed them the assassins for a reason. They were stealthy, silent, and incredibly deadly. They were trained in all ways of death and destruction, as well as spying. Their job during the battle was to gain any intelligence they could on the enemy's movements before it happened. And if the opportunity arose, they would take a life in the process.

"So," Wren said quietly, staring at the flames dancing in front of her. "This is it."

Silence settled around their fire as each of her companions lost themselves in their own thoughts. Wren did her best to keep her feelings from traveling down the bond. She didn't want Silas to know how terrified she was. It wasn't her own death that scared her though. The thought of losing someone she loved was overwhelming. The thought of losing Silas was crippling.

What happened during this battle would shape the future of the world and Wren's choice to not use the Eyeglass was a tremendous risk. Even knowing that, she couldn't bring herself to hand it over to Gabriel, and she absolutely hated herself for that. Her mind was made up though, and she would not change it.

Silas stood and reached a hand down to pull Wren to her feet. They didn't talk as they made their way to their tent. There wasn't much left to say. Wren laid down on the pallet, and Silas settled in behind her. His warmth surrounded her and his scent of leather and pine blanketed her. With his arm around her and his chest against her back, Wren fell into a fitful sleep, although she was content to lie awake in the safety and comfort of her mate's arms on this night.

* * *

Wren stood atop the hill overlooking the Dark Fae army spread before her. The sheer size of the army dried her mouth and caused her stomach to sink to her feet. Turning her head, she looked to the right where the human and Light Fae armies were waiting in position. It wasn't hard to notice the difference in the size of both armies.

"There has to be twice as many of them," she said thickly, attempting to work moisture into her mouth.

"They don't have the Artifacts though. We have that advantage, at least." Silas stood next to her, his hand gripping hers tightly.

She looked into his green eyes, unable to hide the fear from him. It seeped through the bond no matter how much she tried to contain it. Silas turned her away from the sight in front of them, so the only thing she saw was him. He placed his hands on her face, his thumbs gently rubbing across her cheeks. His green eyes were duller than normal and the serious set to his features only intensified her nerves.

"No matter what happens down there," he said quietly for her ears only, "nothing will keep me from you. Not even death."

Wren sucked in a breath at his words. She didn't want to think about his death. Not now, not ever. But especially not before a battle that most likely would end poorly for them.

Silas continued, "You are the light I am drawn to, the light even my shadows don't hide from. However today ends, it won't be the end of us. Nothing can destroy what we have. And if one of us falls today—" he cut off as his voice broke and anguish so sharp shot down the bond. "If one of us falls today, it's not the end. It will never be the end. We will see each other again in the afterlife."

Silas's anguish collided with hers and Wren found it hard to draw breath. Tears burned the back of her throat and blurred her vision. She tried to say something, but her words got stuck and no matter how she tried to force them out, she couldn't.

Silas pulled her close and rested his forehead against hers. "I love you, Wren."

He kissed her softly and Wren's heart broke. It felt too much like a goodbye, as if he knew one of them would not survive the day. She couldn't handle it—the fear and heartbreak was too much.

She was trying to hold herself together when a sudden blast of energy rocked over the hilltop, knocking Wren and Silas to the ground. Silas curved his body around hers instinctively, protecting her from the fall as well as whatever danger caused that blast. She lay on the ground, panting and staring wide-eyed at Silas.

"What was that?" she asked.

"I don't know." He lifted himself to his elbows and scanned her face and body for injury. Finding none, he stood and pulled her to her feet.

Wren looked over his shoulder as Silas turned toward the direction the wave had come from. The ground seemed to tip precariously under her as her gaze landed on Gabriel. If Wren had felt fear before, it was nothing compared to what blasted through her seeing her brother on the ground, hands and knees planted in the soft grass of the hill.

She ran forward and fell to the ground in front of him. Her hands shook as she reached for his shoulders. Gabriel groaned in pain and his hands fisted in the grass. Wren couldn't see what was wrong, but his head was bowed and a puddle of red was quickly forming below him.

"Gabriel, what happened? Where are you hurt?" Her voice shook as much as her hands.

Wren looked at Jerricha, who stood next to Gabriel. Her face was pale and her eyes were wild. Wren had never seen her so undone before.

"What happened?" Silas placed a hand on Jerricha's shoulder, causing the woman to jump.

Before she could respond, Gabriel lifted his head and Wren's fear turned to ice in her veins.

"No." She lost her balance and fell backward, shaking her head as if she could clear the sight from her eyes.

Gabriel had fitted the Eyeglass to his eye. Wren could do nothing but stare as the blood dripped down his face where the Eyeglass had impaled itself into his eye, golden spikes digging in and grabbing hold. She stared in horror as his blue-gray eye turned white, the pupil completely disappearing.

Gabriel shuddered and wiped the blood from his face. "I'm

sorry, Wren." His voice was hoarse, but he didn't sound apologetic at all. "It had to be done."

Wren whipped her head in Silas's direction. If he had given Gabriel the Eyeglass, despite her wishes, she was going to kill him. Angry words died on her tongue when she saw Silas's shocked face, his hand on the empty pouch at his side.

"He didn't give it to me," Gabriel said. He slowly stood from the ground, unsteady on his feet. Jerricha jumped forward and grabbed his arm to steady him. "I took it without his knowledge. This isn't his fault."

Wren was speechless as she stepped backward, away from Gabriel. Her emotions were a whirlwind inside her. She didn't know how to feel. Angry, sad, scared, betrayed. Why would he do that? Why would he let himself die and leave her to live without him? She didn't know what to do or say, so kept slowly retreating until she bumped into Silas. She blindly reached behind her until she grasped his hand, squeezing tightly.

Aeron and Hawthorne appeared on the hill, drawn by the blast of power that had rocked the hilltop when Gabriel placed the Eyeglass to his eye. Wren didn't even notice them as she stared at her brother, trying to wrangle her emotions into a semblance of calm. Right now wasn't the time to be angry. Once she left this hilltop, she wouldn't see Gabriel alive again.

Her heart cracked open, and all her fear and despair spilled out. Tears she could no longer hold back flooded her eyes and flowed over, rolling down her cheeks. A sob racked her chest and her legs gave out. She collapsed on the ground with her shoulders heaving as her heart bled. Gabriel knelt in front of her and wrapped his arms around her. His embrace only made her cry harder. She would never receive another of his hugs again. She would never again look into his eyes and see the sparkle of mischief that so often got them in trouble.

"Why?" She clung to his shirt. She could feel the blood dripping off his face onto her hair. "Why are you doing this?"

"Because you have to live, Wren. All of you have to live." His voice caught, and he held her tighter.

"But what about you? You have to live too."

"Only to die in a few short years while everyone I love continues to live on, young and healthy. This is for the best, Wren."

"No, it's not," she cried. "Those few short years were still years I would have my brother at my side."

"I'll always be with you, Wren. Nothing will ever change that." He pushed her far enough away to look into her eyes. "The only thing in my life I was ever truly proud of was being your brother." He wiped away her tears as they began flowing even harder. "You are an amazing woman, and I know you will continue to do amazing things. Don't let this stop you."

"Gabe," she could barely get the word out through her sobs.

"I love you, little sister."

Her world fell apart at those words. She didn't know how she gathered herself back together, but she knew she had to tell Gabe she loved him too.

With a deep breath, she opened her eyes and looked into his good one. "I love you too, big brother," she whispered.

Gabriel helped her to her feet and turned to Jerricha. Wren's heart broke all over again at the look on Jerricha's face. Gabriel was her brother and losing him was going to be unbearable, but Jerricha was losing the man she loved. She wouldn't even let herself think about what that would feel like. Instead, she turned to Silas and buried her face in his chest, slowly pushing her feelings deep inside until she was numb.

Everyone on the hill gave Jerricha and Gabriel privacy while they said their goodbyes. Hawthorne approached Wren, his face carefully blank.

"Can you put a shield around yourself using your Light magic?" Hawthorne asked Wren. At her nod, he turned to Silas. "Can you put one around yourself with your Dark magic? I want Gabriel to use the Eyeglass to break your shields, so he knows what he's looking for."

Wren shuddered but drew her magic up and created a shield of light around herself. She felt it sink into her, a warm tingling sensation skirting across her skin.

Once Gabriel and Jerricha joined the rest of the group, Hawthorne instructed Gabriel on how to use the Eyeglass. "Do you see anything when you look at Wren and Silas?"

Gabriel's white-eyed gaze landed on Wren and she had to look away.

"Wren has a white aura around her and Silas has a black aura. Is that their shields?" He turned to Hawthorne with one raised brow.

"Yes. Shields will look like auras around us. White for Light Fae and black for Dark Fae. Now to break a shield, I'm not positive, but I think you just look at the person and will it to break." Hawthorne shifted on his feet while biting his lower lip, but his interest zeroed in on the Eyeglass impaled in Gabriel's eye. "The Eyeglass has gone behind your eye, most likely into your brain, which is how it will kill you. It will know your thoughts and will make them happen."

Jerricha made a sound in her throat and closed her eyes. Wren squeezed Silas's hand. Neither of them wanted to hear of Gabriel's death.

Gabriel's focus returned to Wren and Silas, and before Wren could blink, she felt something snap inside her. Her shield broke, the magic sucking back inside her so fast she doubled over, grabbing her chest as pain erupted. Silas grunted behind her, and she knew he felt something similar. The pain faded quickly and Wren straightened, her shield gone.

"That was unpleasant," she murmured. She felt Silas shaking himself behind her, throwing off the unwanted sensation.

"It worked?" Hawthorne's eyes lit up and his mouth parted in shock. "That is amazing. Remember, the more you use the Eyeglass, the more of your energy it will drain. Wait until absolutely necessary to use it."

Gabriel nodded and turned to the others. "Okay." He slid into his role, the role he had been training for his whole life. "Does everyone remember the plan?"

Everyone nodded and the reason they were all gathered on the hilltop returned to Wren. The sun was high enough for the armies to see on the lower ground. Even now, Wren saw movement and knew it was only a matter of time before the Dark Fae made their first move.

"All right then, everyone to their places." Gabriel gave Wren one last look before turning away and heading down the hill, Jerricha at his side.

No goodbyes were said. Wren wouldn't have been able to handle them. Instead, she straightened her shoulders and turned to face the Dark Fae army. She and Silas would remain on top of the hill until the right moment, then they would join the armies on the ground. They hoped to flush out the three men who would not survive this day. King Deimos, Prince Balor, and Silas's uncle.

Gabriel and Jerricha were going to be stationed on another hilltop—a change from the original plan of them being on the ground in the thick of things. Now Gabriel would need the high ground to use the Eyeglass. Hawthorne and Aeron had positions on the ground near Queen Elowyn to keep her protected. Of course, Wren's grandmother would also fight in this battle, as she had just as much to lose as the rest of them.

A ripple of magic washed over the Dark Fae, spreading out

and growing until it encompassed the entire army. Wren felt the darkness in that ripple. She knew it was her father's doing—a shield to protect his men. She tried not to think about Gabriel using his energy to take that shield out and failed, as that ripple of magic shattered. Gabriel had used the Eyeglass, and the shield was thrown back to Deimos, wherever he was.

A shout from the back of the Dark Fae army was followed by bows raised and arrows nocked. Another shout and the sky was darkened by the cloud of arrows released by the Dark Fae, heading toward the Light Fae army.

It had begun.

Chapter Twenty-Six

The last and only battle Wren had experienced was a blur in her memory, overshadowed by the image of the arrow protruding from Silas's chest. As she stood on the hill and watched the armies come together, it felt like the first time she had witnessed such a thing. Even as high up as they were on the hill, the sounds of metal clashing, men shouting, and horses whinnying was deafening.

Wren spotted Queen Elowyn at the front of a group of Light Fae, with Hawthorne and Aeron close by. Her heart stuttered as she watched her grandmother take down Dark Fae as if it was no work at all. Wren had known her grandmother was trained to fight, but she had never witnessed it. Wren looked away, unable to watch as worry grew at the thought of losing her grandmother too. She couldn't lose her entire family in one day. She wouldn't survive that loss.

Silas was a solid wall of confidence next to her as he observed the battle raging below them. Wren couldn't help but fidget, feet shifting nervously in the grass as her eyes darted back and forth, taking in all the surrounding sights. She tried and failed to remember what it was like the last time when she had walked onto the battlefield to join Silas. There was nothing in her mind but crushing fear at the memory of Silas dying. She prayed to any god who would listen that she wouldn't have to go through that again.

Time moved strangely. It felt like she stood on that hill for hours while at the same time, it felt like everything had just started. Wren glanced at the sky and saw the sun had moved quite a bit. It was well past midday. Silas handed her a water-skin and she took a small sip. Her stomach felt like it would revolt at any minute.

Her gaze wandered again, checking in on her friends and family. She couldn't see Queen Elowyn, but King Rodion was swinging his sword with a strength that looked like it would never flag. The sight of bodies strewn across the ground, broken and bleeding, was a knife in her chest. How many would die this day? How many loved ones would be mourning come the rising sun?

Silas tensed next to Wren and she followed his gaze to the middle of the Dark Fae army. His uncle, Vidar, sat atop a horse, wielding a sword and cutting down humans as if was enjoying it. He probably was. Silas unhooked the Crown from his belt and handed it to Wren.

"Are you ready?" His gaze never left his uncle. Hate simmered in his eyes and Wren was surprised his uncle couldn't feel it.

She took the Crown, the obsidian cool in her palms as it sucked in the surrounding light. She said nothing, just placed the Crown upon her head. It felt surprisingly weightless and the echo of the magic she had fed it settled into her bones. Ready to be used.

Together, Wren and Silas made their way down the hill. The closer they got to the action, the louder the noise became.

Wren wanted to cover her ears. She wanted to block out the sounds of men dying and horses screaming. The scent of iron permeated the air as human and Fae alike lost their life-force. Her palms were sweaty on the hilt of her daggers and she tightened her grasp, afraid she would drop one the first moment she engaged with the enemy.

A Dark Fae soldier spotted them and rushed forward. Silas smoothly slid in front of Wren and met the Fae head-on, Sword sparking against the iron sword of the enemy. It took him seconds to disarm his opponent, another second to slide the blade into his heart. The body crumpled to the ground and Silas continued on without a backward glance. His goal was obvious—take out his uncle, end the man who had brutalized and murdered his mother.

Wren skirted around the body and hurried to catch up to Silas. Her eyes were wide as she scanned for an attack. Silas appeared lost in his revenge, unaware of his surroundings as another Dark Fae approached. Wren didn't hesitate. She flipped her dagger to grasp it by the blade and threw it. The dagger spun end over end through the air before lodging in the man's throat. Wren released a breath as he fell to the ground, grabbing his throat to hold in the blood as he choked and coughed. She hurried to pull the dagger out, ignoring the sucking sound as it slid free of his neck.

Somehow they made it across the field with no further confrontation. Wren was jumpy. Every sound of blade against blade stopped her heart. She felt an invisible sword on the back of her neck, waiting constantly for it to fall. She wasn't sure she had taken a full breath since they left the hilltop.

Silas's uncle spotted them from atop his horse and a slow grin spread across his blood-splattered face. He dismounted, never taking his eyes off Silas, and approached.

"I have been waiting for this moment for years," his uncle said with a voice hoarse from yelling commands.

"Funny," Silas replied, "so have I. Ever since you let your men rape my mother."

His uncle's smile grew impossibly more delighted at Silas's words. He took one step forward, then jerked back, free hand going to his chest. His eyes were wide and wild as he looked at Silas.

"Impossible," Vidar breathed.

Wren had felt the ripple of power. The sign Gabriel had once again used the Eyeglass to take out Silas's uncle's shield.

Silas chuckled darkly and hefted the Sword. "Let's get this over with."

Vidar charged forward without warning and Wren fell back, giving them room and not wanting to be a distraction to Silas. She monitored the surroundings to ensure no one inter-rupted. Every clash of their weapons as they came together stopped her heart. Silas was fast, the Sword a black blur as he pushed his uncle back, forcing him to defend against the onslaught. His uncle was strong though, and managed to get a few swipes inside Silas's guard, causing him to jump back to avoid the sharp edge of his blade.

Wren had no doubt Silas could use the Sword to channel his magic and end the fight immediately, but neither Fae used his magic. This was personal for both of them. She knew Silas wanted to feel the blade pierce his uncle's chest, slide through skin and muscle and watch the life leave his eyes.

Something behind Vidar caught Wren's attention at the same time another ripple of magic washed over the field. Toward the back of the army, King Deimos sat atop his horse, no sword in his outstretched hand, but Dark magic flew from his fingers sharper than any blade. The ripple of magic from the

Eyeglass hit him, and Wren watched as he reacted to his shield being destroyed.

This was it. Now was her time. She glanced at Silas who was still engaged with his uncle. She would have to go alone.

* * *

Silas grunted as he met his uncle's attack. Damn, he hit hard. He wasn't sure how long he had been battling Vidar, but he was starting to notice the fatigue—his as well as his uncle's. The Sword was somehow lighter than a normal sword, despite being made of obsidian, and that gave him an edge. If his arms were feeling tired, he knew his uncle's had to be as well.

For the hundredth time, he considered using his magic. He could end this thing right here, right now, but something always stayed his hand. He needed to do this without magic. His revenge was so close he tasted it and he could swear he felt his mother's presence surround him, giving him strength.

With renewed energy, Silas charged forward. He feinted right and when Vidar moved to block, Silas shifted his weight, ignoring the ache in his left thigh where his uncle had landed a hit earlier. With the dagger in his left hand, Silas swiped low and fast, feeling the blade catch as it tore through clothes and skin. It wasn't a terribly deep wound, but it would be enough to slow Vidar down.

His uncle cursed. Blood flowed between his fingers as his free hand pressed against his stomach. His gaze flew to Silas's, the pure anger and hate almost smade Silas take a step back. "You'll pay for that," he growled.

Vidar lunged forward, but Silas was expecting that. He knocked the sword away and kicked his booted foot out, connecting with his uncle's knee. Silas heard the crack as

Vidar's kneecap shattered. He screamed and fell to the ground, sword still grasped in his hand.

"Let me guess," Silas said as he prowled over his uncle. "I'll pay for that too?" He smirked as his uncle attempted to crawl backward away from him.

Finally, Silas let his magic flow through the Sword. The emerald on the pommel grew bright, wisps of green light radiating from it, and dark shadows swirled through the blade. Faint traces of light, like fireflies, flickered in the shadows. Wren's magic mixed with his.

Vidar's eyes widened at the sight, and he froze.

"You deserve so much more pain than this," Silas said quietly as he crouched next to his uncle.

Vidar, with one last burst of energy, swung his sword arm attempting to slice Silas's head from his body. He was too slow. Silas ducked and shadows shot from him, pinning Vidar to the ground.

"I still think of that day," Vidar laughed roughly. "Your mother's pleas as she begged for you still echo in my mind. I still see her tears as they slid down her cheeks. The only thing I regret is killing her so quickly. The entertainment she provided will never be forgotten."

The rest of the world faded away. The battle raging around him disappeared as Silas stood. Ice coated his veins at the same time fire burned through him. He trembled in rage as he leveled the Sword at his uncle's heart.

"This is for her," he said quietly.

He took his time, slowly pushing the tip of the Sword through his uncle's clothing, skin, muscle. The scream that ripped from Vidar's throat would stay with Silas for a long time. With a final push, the blade pierced his heart. His uncle gasped, body attempting to jerk in the shadow bindings. Silas didn't take his gaze off his uncle's eyes as the light slowly faded and the last breath left his lungs.

He tore the Sword from his uncle's chest and let his magic fade. Chest heaving, he stared at the body for a moment, letting the realization sink in. He'd done it. He had avenged his mother. A weight he had been carrying for years lifted from his shoulders.

The Sword hung limply in his hand at his side as he turned, looking for Wren. He didn't know how much time had passed while he fought his uncle. The battle still raged on around him. From what he could see, the human army was holding their own. It actually surprised him how many Dark Fae he saw lying on the ground. All that time training the humans had paid off.

All thought of the battle fled his mind when he realized he couldn't see Wren. He turned around, eyes scanning everywhere, but she wasn't here. His breath got stuck in his chest. *Where are you?* He fired the question down the bond. He waited impatiently for a response but none came. *Wren! Where are you?* Still nothing.

His exhaustion was forgotten as panic seized him and he took off running, thigh screaming in agony as he headed for the hill to get above the crush of bodies. By some luck he stumbled into Aeron, who was fighting one of King Deimos's generals. Aeron's sword arm hung limply at his side, his sword held in his left hand. Silas skidded to a halt next to Aeron, breathing heavily.

"Need some help?" he asked.

"Nah, I got this," Aeron replied as he clumsily parried a thrust by the enemy.

Silas snorted. "How many times have I told you to train with your left arm as well?"

"I'm ignoring you right now," Aeron shouted as he jumped

back, narrowly missing being disemboweled. "In case you haven't noticed, I'm a little busy."

"Oh no. I noticed." Silas spun and threw his dagger, taking down a Dark Fae about to land a killing blow on a human. "Still don't need any help?"

Aeron growled, jumping back again. "Fine. A little help would be appreciated."

Silas grinned and retrieved his dagger. "At your service."

Together, he and Aeron made quick work of the general.

"Have you seen Wren?" Silas asked when the fight was over. His chest was heaving, but it wasn't from exertion. Every second the bond was silent was tearing him apart.

"Last I saw her, she was heading to the back of the Dark Fae army. I thought I glimpsed King Deimos. I would have gone after her, but I was otherwise engaged."

Fear momentarily froze him at Aeron's words, and his heart dropped into his stomach. *Wren, I swear if you get yourself killed, I am going to be so pissed.* Still nothing from the bond. Silas shook off his fear and took off running through the battle again, dodging swords, arrows, and fallen bodies. He had to get to his mate.

Chapter Twenty-Seven

Wren stood in front of her father and found herself at a loss for words. She had imagined this moment many times, and each time she had something to say to him. Something to show him how she felt about him, how she hated that his blood flowed through her veins. But standing here, a battle he created raging around them, she had nothing to say. She felt exhausted, sad. Even her anger had burned away.

Deimos smiled kindly at her. She tried not to notice how his eyes crinkled at the edges, eyes that were almost the exact shade of blue as hers. His sword was still sheathed at his hip. He was the type of man who wouldn't bloody his hands. He would use his magic to end lives instead.

"My daughter."

"I am not your daughter," she spat. "I have never been, nor will I ever be, your daughter."

Anger flared in his eyes but was quickly replaced by something else, something she couldn't interpret.

"You are so much like your mother."

"Don't speak of her!" His words fanned the flames of her anger, and once again, it burned in her chest. "You have no right to talk about her. You are nothing more than a rapist, forcing yourself on her to create something to use against her, against the entire world. I won't be used that way."

Deimos's eyes went distant. "I cared for her," he said quietly. The sounds of battle around them almost drowned out his words. "Lyra was beautiful, fierce, and stubborn. I believe with time she could have come to love me."

Wren snorted at that impossibility and his eyes focused once more, gaze latching on to hers.

"There is no way she would have ever loved you. She ran from you to protect her child. To keep you from getting the Eyeglass, she was prepared to take her own life, and mine with it. She was terrified of you. Terrified of what you would do to the world. There was never a chance of love and you are delusional for thinking there was."

Deimos narrowed his gaze on Wren. "You are exactly like her. Too bad you didn't take after me."

"I thank the Gods every day I'm not like you." Wren adjusted her grip on the handles of her daggers.

Deimos noticed the movement and smiled. This smile was anything but warm. "Plan on using those on me?"

She didn't respond, only shifted her stance as Gabriel had taught her to do.

"Even with that Crown"—his gaze flicked up to the Crown resting on her head—"you won't be able to defeat me." Deimos swung his leg over the saddle and gracefully landed on the ground, hand resting on the pommel of his sword.

"We'll see about that."

Wren tapped into the Crown and felt the power swirling inside. She had been filling it with her magic but hadn't noticed how much she had given it. The rush of power filling her veins almost sent her to her knees. Wren knew, even with all her weapons training, she could never take her father in hand-to-hand combat. Unfortunately, she had never seen him use magic before, so she was at a disadvantage there. He had to be powerful, but she had the Crown.

Light magic gathered in her palms and she imagined it growing hot. Her palms heated and tingled, and Wren tensed as she threw the magic forward. Deimos had expected it. He blocked the light with a blast of Dark magic that made Wren take a step backward.

"You'll have to do better than that," he chuckled.

Tapping into her training with Aeron, Wren created a sword of light. Glowing suns decorated the hilt, and the blade was sharper than any steel. It was warm in her palm and lighter than air, but she knew it was solid and she knew it would hurt. She couldn't beat him with just any sword, but a magic sword? That she could do.

Her father's eyes widened as she rushed forward, sword raised. He recovered quickly, drawing his blade and meeting her attack head-on. Light flared as steel sword met sword of magic. The force of the hit rattled Wren to her bones, and she knew she would have to end this quickly. She would tire much quicker than him if all of his hits were that strong.

Deimos pressed forward, and Wren stumbled back as his blade cut into her left bicep. She gasped and watched as blood welled along the cut.

"End this now, Wren." Her father lowered his sword and shook his head. "I don't want to hurt you. Join me. Together, we could do amazing things. At my side, you could become the princess you were always destined to be."

"I'll die before I ever join you."

Wren charged forward, knowing Deimos would raise his sword to block her attack. Grabbing his shoulder with her left arm, she ducked under his arm and pulled herself around. She raised her sword, ready to shove it through his back, but his magic threw her backward. Her breath whooshed out of her as she landed hard on the ground. She cursed herself. How could she have forgotten about his magic?

As Deimos stalked forward, she felt his magic gathering around him, and she panicked. She forgot about Aeron's lessons as she struggled to draw air into her lungs. In desperation, she shot a beam of light straight for his chest. He knocked it aside with another wave of magic that pressed Wren harder to the ground.

"I see you won't stop this pointless attack." Her father actually had the audacity to look sad as he stood over her. "I'm sorry about this. Truly, I am."

He raised his sword and pointed it at Wren's chest. Desperate to save herself, she tried to draw her magic to her, but it slipped through her fingers as she watched the point of the sword draw closer. She wanted to close her eyes. She didn't want to see her death slowly approaching, but she forced them open.

At the last second, she reached down the bond. *I love you, Silas.*

* * *

Silas raced through the throng of warriors, not seeing the fighting taking place around him. His eyes were scanning, gaze bouncing around frantically, looking for Wren and Deimos. As he neared the back of the Dark Fae army, he caught sight of the king standing tall, looking down at something. Silas couldn't see Wren, but he had a sinking feeling that she was what Deimos was looking down on.

As he pushed through the last of the soldiers blocking his view, Wren's voice traveled down the bond.

I love you, Silas.

He saw her at the same moment, on her back with a sword pointed at her chest. Fear and regret shone in her stormy blue eyes. His heart stopped. His breath lodged in his throat. Instinct took over. He flipped his dagger, grasping it by the blade. His muscles strained in his arm as he cocked it back, then released. The dagger flew true, hitting the king's blade and knocking it to the side. The sound of metal hitting metal was loud in Silas's ears, second only to the sound of his breathing.

Deimos whirled around, his eyes wide in surprise. One look at Silas and Deimos's eyes narrowed in anger.

"You have been nothing but trouble," Deimos stated, bringing his sword around and angling it at Silas.

"Something I am quite proud of." He smirked and saw Deimos's anger rise a notch. Behind Deimos, Silas noticed Wren climbing to her feet. He kept his gaze focused on the king, not wanting to draw attention to his mate. "So, are we going to do this?" Silas hefted the Sword and filtered his magic through it.

Deimos opened his mouth to respond, but the only thing to come out was a choked sound and a spray of blood. Silas jerked as he saw the tip of a blade protruding from the front of the king's neck. Deimos's hands scrabbled at the tip of the blade. His wide eyes met Silas's as he coughed, frothy blood splattering his lips. The king of the Dark Fae fell to his knees revealing Silas's mate standing with a bloody dagger in her hand.

Wren stepped around her father, coming to stand beside Silas. He couldn't take his eyes off her. She didn't appear to have any major injuries and his racing heart calmed.

"That is for my mother and all the innocent people you

have killed." Wren stared down at her father impassively as he continued choking on his blood.

It was not a quick death and Silas placed his hand on Wren's shoulder as they watched King Deimos suffer until his last breath.

Silas felt Wren shudder and he pulled her into his arms, inhaling her scent and further calming his heart.

"Are you all right?" he asked.

She didn't respond, but he felt her head nod against his chest.

Pushing her away far enough to look into her eyes, Silas said, "You have to answer me next time. I was out of my mind with worry."

"I'm sorry," she said quietly and placed her palm on his chest, right over his heart. "I didn't want to distract you."

He shook his head and pulled her against him again. Low laughter filtered through the trees behind Wren, and Silas froze. Emerging from the shadows was the last person he wanted to deal with. Shoving Wren behind him, he drew the Sword again.

Balor stepped from the shadows, an evil grin pulling the corners of his lips up. "I guess I should be thanking you." He glanced at Deimos's still body on the ground. "With him out of the way, I am now king. King Balor. It has a nice ring to it."

"Enjoy it while you can," Silas said. "I have a feeling you won't be king for long."

Balor chuckled and quick as lightning, his magic shot out, shadows sharp as blades heading straight for Wren. Silas had anticipated this and deflected Balor's attack, shoving Wren back and out of the way.

This would not be a pretty fight, but Silas was ready. The Sword was primed and he wouldn't let Balor walk away with his life this time.

* * *

Wren barely caught herself from falling to the ground as Silas pushed her out of the way. The Crown atop her head tilted forward, blocking her view of Silas and Balor. She quickly pushed it back up and her breath caught in her throat.

That fast they had engaged. Shadows ripped out of both of them and swords clashed as they came together and broke apart. A rogue shadow snapped in her direction and she threw up a shield of light, watching the shadow burn away as it came into contact with it. Wren took a few more steps back, putting distance between herself and the fight going on in front of her. There was no way she could join in the fray. Both Dark Fae were too skilled with sword and magic. She would just be a hindrance and distraction to Silas. Still, she kept her eyes on the fight and her magic ready. If any opportunity presented itself, she would take it.

The intensity of the fight stole her breath and stopped her heart. Silas had an edge over Balor using the Sword, but Balor was well trained. Both men sported minor cuts, but neither could take control of the situation. Wren bounced on her toes and worried her lip between her teeth. If she had to guess, Balor had been sitting at the back of the army, not engaging in any of the fighting. He was fresh and well rested. Silas, on the other hand, had been fighting fiercely and would tire quicker than Balor. Wren winced as Balor landed a slice on Silas's thigh, the one that already looked to be bleeding. Silas stumbled but remained upright.

A flash of something caught Wren's eye. She turned in time to see a storm cloud of magic slam into the back of Silas's knees. Wren screamed as he fell to the ground, knees slamming into the dirt. Another Dark Fae emerged from the trees, smiling from ear to ear. Silas's words from before came back to her, how Balor didn't fight fair. This was just proof of that.

Fire erupted in her veins and she drew her magic from the Crown, filling her to bursting with bright, hot power. She unleashed the magic at the Dark Fae emerging from the trees. It struck his chest and incinerated him on the spot. When the light faded, nothing but a pile of ashes blew on the wind.

Wren's attack didn't distract Balor from Silas. When she turned her attention back to her mate, she found him on his knees with Balor slowly approaching. Wren readied her magic again—she wasn't about to let Balor hurt him. Dark magic shimmered in the air as Balor and Silas both gathered their magic to them. Silas was tiring though, and Wren could feel how much stronger Balor's magic was at the moment.

As Balor sent his magic forward, barreling to Silas, Wren screamed. Someone came running into her field of vision. She wasn't able to see who it was until they jumped in front of Silas. Balor's magic slammed into him and blew him backward.

Wren gaped at the sight of the general lying on the ground, feet from where he blocked the blow meant for Silas. She stared, not understanding what she was looking at. Her confusion lasted only a second, however, before she pulled herself together and turned back to Balor and Silas.

Both Dark Fae were similarly stunned. Silas stared at Wren as if he was waiting for her reaction. Balor stared at the general, confusion clouding his features as if he couldn't understand what had happened. Wren shook herself into action. Using Balor's distraction, she pulled up as much magic as she could as quickly as possible. Silas, sensing her plan, did the same.

Together, Wren and Silas sent wave after wave of magic toward Balor. Wren concentrated her light and heat, a beam of pure white light striking him in the chest at the same time Silas's shadows circled Balor and squeezed. The anguished scream of pain coming from Balor almost made Wren stop, but she kept her magic flowing. It flowed until there was nothing left of Balor, not even ashes on the wind. Her magic had burned him up completely.

Wren sank to her knees as exhaustion swept through her. The only time she had used that much magic at one time was when Silas had been shot during the last battle. This time, with the use of the Crown, she could remain conscious, but her muscles trembled and her breathing was labored.

A soft groan came from her left. Wren's head whipped toward the general and found him somehow still alive. She crawled over to him, her feelings a tangled mess. The general looked at her through dimming blue-gray eyes.

"Wren," he gasped. His voice was hoarse and filled with pain.

He tried to reach for her and instinct had Wren grabbing his hand in both of hers.

"Why did you do it?" Maybe it wasn't the best question to ask as he lay there dying, but she couldn't help it. She had to know why he had saved Silas's life.

"Because—" he cut off, coughing wetly. After he caught his breath, he continued, "I have a lot to make up for and saving"—more coughing—"saving your mate is the first step in making things right."

Wren's eyes burned but no tears came. She shook her head, unsure what to say to the man who had once been a father to her.

"I am sorry for everything." His labored breathing increased. "I am proud of the woman you have become. And I —" The general's body was racked by coughing, his eyes dimming further. "I love..."

Wren wasn't breathing. Her gaze landed on the general's chest, silently urging it to rise again, but it didn't. The general was still, his chest no longer rising and falling. His blue-gray eyes were dull and staring blankly at Wren. He was no longer alive. He had been about to tell her he loved her, and Wren hadn't said a word to him.

Even now, holding his hand with the skin quickly cooling, she couldn't bring herself to feel anything. Wren wasn't sure how to feel after everything he had done to her, all the things he had forced her to do, and the person he had attempted to mold her into. Gratitude filled her for saving Silas's life. She would forever be thankful for that, but everything else? She didn't know.

Silas's hand on her shoulder drew her out of her thoughts.

"Are you okay?" he asked quietly.

Wren shook her head. "I don't know."

Silas pulled her to her feet and she turned to face him. They said nothing, just stared at each other. The battle was still raging around them. Wren took a deep breath, filled her lungs, and prepared herself to turn and look at the battlefield. The sense of despair welled up in her at the sight of all the bodies lying on the ground. So much death and still more dying. It wasn't over yet.

"You know what you need to do," Silas said, eyeing the Crown on her head.

So much death, and she was about to add to it. Resigned, Wren tapped into the Crown, filling her veins with the soft flutter of wings. The flutter increased, the flapping becoming incessant, and heat built as she continued to pull more from the Crown. She was vaguely aware of a soft light emanating from her body at the amounts of magic she was pulling in.

Silas stood at her back, but she was barely aware of his presence. The shock wave rippling through the armies and knocking her backward into Silas was the only thing that registered in her magic-filled brain. Tears pooled in her eyes, knowing that wave of magic came from Gabriel using the Eyeglass. Knowing that large of a shock wave had to have been the last of his energy. Gabriel had just sacrificed himself to take out the rest of the shields, giving Wren the opening she needed to use the Crown.

With her body humming and filled to bursting with the magic in her veins, with her heart breaking, Wren released the magic. It rushed out of her in a wave of bright white light washing over the battlefield. The wave harmlessly passed through the humans, Light Fae, and Elementals. It didn't touch the Dark Fae on their side. But the enemy, where that light touched, just disappeared. Nothing left but a shimmering dust that faded quickly.

As the last of the magic left Wren's body, consciousness slipped from her grip. She felt Silas's arms around her as he gently lowered her to the ground, then nothing.

Chapter Twenty-Eight

Sound returned first and Wren almost wished it hadn't. The moans and cries of pain from the soldiers surrounding her made her wish for unconsciousness. Her head was resting in Silas's lap and his fingers gently brushed the strands of hair that had escaped her braid. She ached all over, like the time she had a fever as a child. Every movement caused her to wince. Her mind hadn't quite caught up to everything yet and she floated in the fog that surrounded her.

Thoughts swirled around in her head. No rhyme or reason to the pattern. She had killed her biological father—she felt no sadness at that. The general had died saving Silas's life—that thought brought confusion. She still didn't know what to think or how to feel. How would Gabriel handle hearing of his father's death?

"Gabriel!" Wren gasped and sat up so quickly the world spun around her. She grabbed her head and forced the dizziness away. Gabe had used the Eyeglass. Her brother was gone.

A sob climbed up her throat, but she swallowed it. Her legs shook under her weight as she tried to stand.

"Whoa. Slow down, love." Silas grabbed her arms to steady her, then tried to wrap his arm around her waist for support.

Pushing out of his grasp, Wren forced her legs to work and took off at an awkward run. She didn't see the dead and dying on the field. She didn't hear the cries of the wounded or smell the blood and rot in the air. Her only thought was getting to Gabriel. Was he already gone? Would she have time to say goodbye?

By the time she reached the hill Gabriel had been stationed on, her lungs were screaming for oxygen and her legs burned from how hard she had pushed them. Standing at the bottom of the hill and looking toward the top, Wren whimpered but straightened her spine. She focused on placing one foot on the hill, then the next, then the next. Silas's presence next to her fortified her further, and before she knew it, she was cresting the top of the hill. The sight before her drove her to her knees.

Jerricha—the strongest woman Wren had ever met—was leaning over Gabriel's body, shoulders shaking from the force of her tears. A keening sound came from the woman's mouth, a sound Wren would hear in her nightmares. Wren stared at Gabriel's unmoving body and pain like she had never felt pierced her chest.

He lay on his back, his blond hair spread out behind him. Blood soaked the front of his shirt and had dried in a trail down his face from the Eyeglass. His skin was white, all color having already faded, and the worst part was the chest that no longer rose with breath.

Wren couldn't breathe. She stared at the scene in front of her not knowing what to do. Tears filled her eyes and blurred her vision before silently spilling over and tracking down her cheeks. Silas knelt next to her, his hand on her lower back a warm comfort. Distantly, Wren noticed others arriving on the hilltop—Aeron, Hawthorne, and Queen Elowyn. The mood was somber, the sound of Jerricha's crying cutting through each person's heart.

Eventually, Aeron approached Jerricha and gently pulled her away from Gabriel's body. She didn't fight him, and Wren wondered what was going through her head. If that had been Silas lying on the ground, she would have been clawing her way back to his body. Instead, Jerricha collapsed against Aeron, all her energy spent.

Hawthorne approached Gabriel and knelt next to him. He tentatively grasped the Eyeglass and tugged. The Eyeglass popped out of Gabriel's eye with a wet slurp. Bile burned the back of Wren's throat at the eyeball dangling from the Artifact. She turned her head into Silas's shoulder to avoid the image.

At first, Wren noticed nothing out of the ordinary, however Silas's body tensing next to her brought her head up. The leaves on the trees fluttered in the wind—wind that hadn't blown all day. The breeze picked up and the loose strands of her hair whipped in front of her face.

The wind kept growing stronger, and it didn't take long for Wren to realize the wind was blowing toward Gabriel's body. All around the hilltop, it was as if a magical force were sucking the air from around them, drawing it toward Gabriel. The force buffeted against her and she was pushed forward onto her hands. Silas covered her body with his own, forcing her head down.

The wind roared around them for what felt like hours when it was probably only seconds. As the last of the gusts faded, Wren lifted her head to look around. The others on the hill were similarly on the ground, protecting themselves from whatever had just happened. A shocked gasp drew Wren's gaze in Jerricha's direction. Her eyes were wide, hands covering her mouth, and she stared at Gabriel with a mixture of despair and hope.

Wren's gaze flew to her brother and echoed Jerricha's gasp. She pushed Silas off her and rushed forward. Gabriel was moving. His chest was moving, his head turning from side to side. She avoided the gruesome sight of his empty eye socket and placed her hand on his forehead. The skin was warm, the white pallor now the soft peach of the living.

"Gabriel?" she whispered, tears once again blurring her vision.

Jerricha fell to the ground on the other side of Gabriel. Her eyes shone with hope Wren knew was mirrored in her own.

Her gaze sought Hawthorne, and she asked, "What's happening?"

Looking as shocked as the rest of them, Hawthorne could only shake his head. The bloody Eyeglass was still in his hand, eyeball still dangling from the Artifact.

Queen Elowyn approached, silent as a wraith, and knelt next to him. Her hands glowed as she hovered them over Gabriel's body. The queen's lips parted on a soft inhale.

"Unbelievable," she breathed. Looking toward Hawthorne, then Silas and Aeron, she said, "Don't you feel it?"

Silas and Aeron came closer, brows drawn low over their eyes. Silas jerked back first, followed by Hawthorne and Aeron.

Silas's wide green eyes slid to Wren. "He's not human anymore. Gabriel is Fae."

Queen Elowyn shook her head. "Not just Fae. He is an Elemental."

* * *

Elemental. The word bounced around in Wren's head as she sat in a plush chair in Gabriel's room at the palace. She didn't understand what had happened, even after Hawthorne explained. The Eyeglass took Gabriel's mortal life, just like they had been informed it would. What hadn't been explained or expected was that Gabriel would then become an Elemental Fae. Maybe Emperor Verellis didn't even know that would happen. How it had happened, Wren still didn't understand, but as she kept watch over her brother, she was thankful it had.

Gabriel hadn't woken up yet, but he continued to breathe steadily. Wren and Jerricha had taken up positions in his room, neither speaking but both watching each rise and fall of his chest. Silas and the others had been meeting in the council room with King Rodion and King Trion, discussing injuries, deaths, and future plans.

Wren glanced at Jerricha. The Viking-like woman had finally given in to the battle she had been waging with sleep. Her chair was next to the bed, Gabriel's hand held in hers, her legs tucked under her. Wren yawned. She wasn't faring too well in her own battle against sleep. She wasn't sure she had ever felt this exhausted—physically and emotionally. So many thoughts battled for dominance in her head—the general's death, Gabriel's death and subsequent rebirth, and her father's death at her hands—but she refused to give any of them the time of day.

The door to Gabriel's room opened, and Silas entered. He knelt next to Wren's chair, placing one hand on her knee. He looked at Jerricha and Gabriel and pitched his voice low so as not to wake them.

"You need to rest, Wren. And we need to take care of that gash on your arm."

She had completely forgotten about that injury. Despite the truth in his words, she shook her head. An irrational fear bubbled up that if she took her eyes off him, Gabriel would stop breathing again.

"You can barely keep your eyes open. Come on, come to bed. If anything changes with Gabriel, someone will come get you. I promise." He stood and gently pulled her to her feet.

She let him, only because she didn't have the energy to fight him. He led her out of the room and through the halls, which were eerily quiet despite the number of people in them. Healers and servants rushed from room to room, taking care of the injured and dying. Wren wanted to ask how many lives had been lost, but she couldn't get her mouth to move. Exhausted. She was so exhausted.

Once in their rooms, Silas helped Wren out of her bloody clothing and led her to the bathing chamber. Gooseflesh pimpled her skin and she wrapped her arms around herself. Silas draped a soft blanket over her shoulders and gathered the things he needed to care for her wound. While he did that, servants appeared with buckets of hot water and filled the sunken tub.

"In." Silas removed the blanket and ushered her into the tub.

The heat wrapped around her, easing muscles she hadn't realized were tight. Sinking farther into the tub she released a breath and closed her eyes. She startled at the feel of a rag on her skin as Silas washed her. Tears pricked the corners of her eyes at the gesture. Silas was just as exhausted as she was. This was the last thing he needed to do for her.

"Silas, you don't have to—"

"I know, but I want to." He smiled sweetly and her heart fluttered. "Let me do this for you."

Swallowing, she nodded and relaxed into the tub, letting Silas wash the blood and dirt of the day off her skin. He cleaned and bandaged her wound, which had already dried and scabbed over. He let her soak for a few minutes and she must have dozed off, because the next thing she knew, he was kneeling next to the tub, gently shaking her.

"Out." He held open a towel and wrapped it around her as she stood.

Wren let him carry her to the sink and set her on the counter. She had no energy left to stop him as he dried her off and brushed out her hair. When he was finished, he picked her up again and carried her to the bed. The mattress felt divine as she sank into the soft feathers and she couldn't stop from groaning in pleasure.

Silas quickly undressed and settled behind her, pulling her into his arms and covering them with a blanket. She was asleep before the blanket settled around her shoulders.

* * *

A soft knock on the door woke Silas hours later. He quietly eased out from under the blanket without disturbing Wren and pulled on a pair of pants. Aeron greeted him when he opened the door. He had a cut above his left eyebrow and a bandage peeked out from under the collar of his shirt.

"Everything okay?" Silas asked and leaned against the door frame.

"Yeah, I just wanted to let you know Gabriel is awake." Aeron glanced into the room at Wren sleeping on the bed. "I didn't know if you would want to tell Wren."

Silas shook his head. "She'll probably kill me when she finds out, but I'm going to let her sleep. Thanks for letting me know though."

Aeron grinned. "Oh, she will definitely kill you. Make sure I'm around when she finds out. I'd love to watch her take a bite out of you."

Silas gave Aeron a bland stare. "Is there anything else?"

"Actually, there is." He sobered quickly. "Queen Elowyn wants to talk to you."

Silas groaned. "Of course she does. I can already guess what she wants to say to me." He turned back into the room to grab a shirt and pull his boots on. Wren shifted on the bed and he froze, silently urging her back to sleep. There was no way she had slept long enough with everything she had gone through during that battle. He relaxed as she settled again, sighing softly and snuggling under the blanket.

Aeron led him to the king's office and Silas's hands grew sweaty. This felt far more formal than he would prefer. As he entered the office his heart rate increased as well. King Rodion and King Trion were also waiting for him in addition to Queen Elowyn.

"Good luck," Aeron whispered before ducking out the door and closing it behind him.

Silas froze at the sound of the door snicking shut. What did the rulers of three of the four realms of Sorentiv want to talk to him about? His stomach turned over at the possibilities.

"Please, have a seat." Queen Elowyn gestured to an open chair. Once he was seated, she continued, "I'm sure you are wondering why we brought you here. However, before we begin, I would ask how my granddaughter is doing."

"She is doing as well as can be expected," Silas answered. "She's sleeping right now. I don't think she has had much time to process everything that has happened."

Queen Elowyn nodded. "Thank you for taking care of her."

Shock made Silas rock back in his seat. Wren's grandmother had made it known many times that she did not approve of her granddaughter mating Silas. That she would thank him—in front of others, no less—was astounding.

"I see my gratitude surprises you." She smiled. "I will admit I wasn't happy with Wren's choice initially. However, you have proven yourself many times over. I don't think there is anyone else who would be so attentive or care so deeply for her. I know it's a little late, and technically not needed, but you have my blessing."

Silas was momentarily speechless, a feeling he wasn't used to. Finally, he shook himself and placed his hand on his heart. "I appreciate that. *We* appreciate that."

"Well, now that's settled, we can discuss what we really called you here to discuss." The queen sat back in her chair and clasped her hands in her lap. "With King Deimos and Prince Balor out of the picture, there is an opening to be filled."

This is what he was afraid of. Silas closed his eyes and shook his head. "I can't." He opened his eyes to see all three rulers staring him down. He shifted uncomfortably in his seat.

"Why ever not?" Queen Elowyn sat forward, gripping the arms of her chair. "You are a descendant of King Bhardyl. The very blood flowing in your veins gives you the right to sit upon the throne."

"Wren doesn't want that life. I won't force her into it by taking up a crown."

Queen Elowyn made a noise that sounded an awful lot like a harrumph. Not a very queenly sound. "Forget about what my granddaughter does and doesn't want. What do you want?"

He really didn't know. In the past, he had thought about taking the crown from Deimos. When he and Torryn had begun this insane venture of trying to overthrow the king, it was something they had often discussed. But meeting Wren had changed everything for him. As soon as he met her, his plans changed. He still wanted to change the way the Dark Fae lived. He wanted to create a place and a people that were valued and respected, not feared and hated. But Wren wanted to live a quieter life, a life where she could make her own choices, and he respected that.

"The thing is, I can't just forget what she wants. She is my mate and she means everything to me. The reality is whatever decisions we make, we make them together. So, my answer is no."

Something like respect shone in Queen Elowyn's eyes, but it quickly turned into annoyance. "I assume you won't try to convince her to take up her birthright?"

Silas smiled wryly. "Do you think Wren can be convinced to do something she doesn't want to?"

The queen snorted, and the sound was so similar to the one Wren makes that Silas did a double take. She looked at Silas once more. "Are you sure that is your decision?"

"I am." And strangely enough, he was sure. He didn't need the crown to be happy. He only needed his mate.

Chapter Twenty-Nine

Wren spent the next three months helping the healers with the injured, mourning with the families who had lost a loved one, and sorting through her own emotions. She was now on a ship sailing around Ellendyr to Valasia.

She felt no guilt over her role in Deimos's and Balor's deaths. She did, however, feel constant guilt over the many Dark Fae she had ended with her last blast of magic. Silas claimed it was the only way to end the battle, but she couldn't help but question that. It was something that would sit on her conscience for the rest of her very long life.

The memory of the general's death and his last words drove her from sleep many nights. Silas was always there to talk her through it, but her feelings never became less tangled. She hurt too much to forgive the general for what he had done when she was younger. She still had too much anger inside her when she thought about the ways he had betrayed her. Did his sacrifice at the end change any of that? She still didn't know, and she wasn't sure if she ever would.

Knowing the Dark Fae had been stopped was a relief. The world could move on from their vicious rule. Already she had heard of smaller towns bringing out their hidden trove of books and history. It was a slow process, but it was a start. It was a process Wren felt called to do more about. This feeling, coupled with the consideration of her birthright, was like a constant cloud hanging over her head. It was one reason she had decided to travel to Valasia.

The sound of retching filled the air and drew Wren from her thoughts. She turned from the view of the ocean to find Aeron leaning over the railing of the ship, emptying the contents of his stomach.

"Really, Aeron?" she asked as she crossed the deck to him. "We aren't even that far out in the ocean. You can see the shore from here."

Their journey to Valasia would hopefully be less dangerous than their journey to Edein Island. So far, they hadn't even lost sight of the land as they sailed around Ellendyr.

Aeron's only response was to groan and tighten his grip on the railing.

"Here, these will help." Hawthorne appeared and handed Aeron a peppermint candy, the only thing that seemed to settle his stomach. "Poor thing will never make a good sailor."

Aeron's curse was cut off by more heaving.

"Well, you have fun with that," Wren said, wrinkling her nose.

Hawthorne's chuckle followed her across the deck. She descended the ladder to the main deck and the sight of two shirtless men sparring greeted her.

"Come to enjoy the view?" Jerricha asked as Wren sidled up next to her.

"Half of it," Wren replied. "I don't really enjoy seeing my

brother shirtless and sweating. Just as I'm sure you don't enjoy seeing your cousin the same way."

Jerricha snorted. "You are right about that."

"He's getting better." Wren watched Gabriel defend against Silas's attack. The black eye patch covering his missing eye gave her brother a roguish appearance.

"He is. I think training with Silas has helped him gain some of his confidence back."

Wren was glad to hear that. Gabriel had been struggling after he lost his eye. He seemed to think it made him less of a man, even though everyone around him told him otherwise. When Silas had suggested training to reorient himself to fighting with a limited field of view, Gabriel hesitated at first. Jerricha had been able to talk him into it, and it had made a world of difference, much to Wren's relief.

"Still no developments on the magic front?" Wren asked.

"Nothing. Hawthorne said he might not have any magic. It makes sense if he doesn't. The Eyeglass wasn't infused with magic like the Sword and the Crown. I still don't understand how it brought him back as an Elemental to begin with."

"Me neither, but I won't complain."

Jerricha agreed, and they sat on the railing of the ship and watched their men train.

* * *

Valasia looked quite a bit different from the last time Wren had visited. The burned-out husks of buildings had been torn down and new structures were popping up to replace them. Skeletal trees still remained throughout the city, blackened and charred from the fire. Wren knew the trees would remain. The Light Fae would let nature take its course unless a tree was at risk of falling on the city.

Wren and Silas were ushered into Queen Elowyn's personal sitting room, a room she had never seen on her first and only visit to Valasia. The room was a surprise to Wren. She had expected over-the-top opulence, but the queen opted for simple elegance. The room put her at ease and made her feel welcome, as did the queen standing in front of a large window overlooking the river.

"I am so glad you came to visit," her grandmother said with a smile and open arms.

A few months ago, Wren would have balked at a hug from the woman standing before her. Now she welcomed it. "Well, to be honest, we're not here for just a simple visit," Wren admitted before sitting in a cream-colored chair.

"When is anything ever simple with you two?" Elowyn smiled and pulled Silas in for a hug as well.

He stiffened at the contact at first, but quickly relaxed and hugged her back. Wren could feel his shock and amusement through the bond. She waited until Silas perched on the arm of her chair and her grandmother settled in a chair across from her.

"I have a question I have been wanting to ask you," Wren began. "Now that the threat of the Dark Fae has been taken care of, what did you plan on doing with the Library of Knowledge?"

The queen's eyes sparkled with interest. "I haven't been able to devote as much thought to that as I would like, to be honest. Rebuilding has taken longer than I had originally hoped. Did you have something in mind?"

Wren took a deep breath, soaking in Silas's steady presence for reassurance. "I want to redistribute the items in the Library and return them to their cities and towns of origin. I also want to help cities create and rebuild libraries. It's important for people to learn and understand their history, as well as begin recording their own history for the future."

She fell silent and waited for her grandmother to respond. Despite the pride she felt from Silas, she twisted her hands in her lap nervously.

"I think that is a great idea," her grandmother said.

Wren's head popped up. "You do?"

"Absolutely. I couldn't agree with you more. Do you have any plans on how to go about starting this?"

"I thought creating committees to take on various tasks would be the best way to handle it."

"I'll arrange for you to meet with the head librarian to start forming committees." Queen Elowyn smiled at Wren and there was no denying the pride that shone in her eyes.

Wren took another breath. What she planned to say next was hard for her. Even Silas didn't know what she was planning. "There is one more thing I wanted to talk to you about."

Silas's head turned in her direction, curiosity sliding down the bond.

"I'm ready to take up my birthright."

The reactions of the people in the room couldn't have been more different. Silas's jaw dropped and he stared at Wren in incredulity. Queen Elowyn smiled broadly, her eyes misting over at Wren's words.

"Are you serious?" Silas blurted. He searched Wren's face with wide eyes.

"I'm sorry I didn't tell you," she said to him. "I really just decided to do it. It felt right."

A smile lifted the corners of his mouth. "Don't apologize, love. I'm proud of you."

"I always knew you would make the right decision," her grandmother said.

"You're okay with Silas being prince even though he is Dark Fae?" she asked cautiously.

"Oh, I have an even better idea." The smile her grandmother gave them caused butterflies to take flight in Wren's stomach.

"What idea?" Silas asked flatly.

"I think it's time to get rid of the distinction between Light and Dark Fae. It has done nothing but hinder our growth and harm us. We, as a race, are simply Fae."

Wren exhaled loudly at the queen's proclamation. "You want me to be princess to all Fae?"

"No. I want you to be queen to all Fae. With Silas at your side as king."

Neither Wren nor Silas spoke. Their shock and confusion bounced down the bond, compounding with each other. Wren knew her mouth was hanging open in a very unladylike manner, but she couldn't seem to close it.

"I'm sorry," Silas said, "I must have misheard you."

"You did not mishear me," Queen Elowyn clarified. "It is time for change. The Fae as a race have been failing. Our lives are shorter, fewer children are brought into the world, and bonds and mates are almost unheard-of these days." Her gaze slid back and forth between Wren and Silas. "You two have already ushered in change. Not only have you stopped the Dark Fae from destroying the world, but you share a bond that is incredibly rare, even more so because you are Light and Dark Fae."

She stood from her chair and glided to the window. "We cannot keep going on as we have been. Wren, you were right when you first came to me. We need to unite the Light and Dark Fae, and what better way than getting rid of the labels altogether?" She turned from the window and smiled at them.

"Already you have broken barriers that have been in place for centuries, and it's not just you two. I saw Hawthorne getting off the ship with a certain Dark Fae at his side. If anyone can unite the Fae, it is you."

"And you think we need to be king and queen to make this happen?" Wren ignored how squeaky her voice sounded. She couldn't believe she was hearing these words from her grandmother.

"I don't think you *need* to be king and queen, but I *want* you to be." Queen Elowyn returned to her seat and sat on the edge. "I know exactly what you're thinking, Wren. You're thinking you aren't ready for that. You're thinking you do not know how to be a queen. But I disagree with you. You are more than ready, and you won't be alone. I will be here to guide you both every step of the way."

Wren turned to Silas, whose expression was as shocked as hers. "I think we need some time to think this over," she said quietly.

"Of course. Rooms have been prepared. I'll have refreshments sent up shortly." She stood as Wren and Silas stood. "And Wren, your mother would be so proud of you."

* * *

"She would throw out that last bit about my mother. Anything to get me to agree to this crazy idea."

The door closed behind Silas and his silence made her pause. The entire way through the village, up the stairs, and across the bridges, Silas was quiet. Even the bond felt quiet.

Wren turned to her mate, who was leaning against the closed door. "What's going on in your head right now? You are unusually quiet."

A small smirk appeared and he pushed off the door, prowling toward her. "I'm just wrapping my head around calling you 'my queen.'" He clasped her face in his calloused palms.

Wren ignored the shiver his thumbs swiping across her cheeks created and pulled his hands down. "I think now would be a good time to be serious. My grandmother's plan is insane, right? We can't rule over all the Fae, can we?"

Silas shrugged as he smiled down at her. "Why not?"

"Why not?" she exclaimed, her voice rising in volume. "Why not? Because... because..." Words failed her as she couldn't think of any good reason they couldn't rule the Fae. Her first excuse was them not knowing a thing about ruling, but her grandmother took care of that by saying she would help guide them. "Ugh!" She threw her hands up and walked to the window.

Silas's warmth washed over her as he approached and ran his hands down her arms. She appreciated his silence as he let her work through her thoughts. Finally, she leaned her head back against his chest and sighed.

"This is what you wanted when you joined with Torryn, isn't it? To change the way the Dark Fae lived and were seen by the world. To become king. It was always me holding you back from that."

"Whoa, slow down." Silas turned her to face him. He stared into her eyes, his usual lighthearted expression replaced by a very serious one. "You have never held me back from anything. I already told you, my priorities shifted when I met you. You will always come first, no matter what else happens in my life." His thumb traced her bottom lip and his gaze followed the path before returning to her eyes. "Don't worry about what I want, Wren. What do you want? Really think about it, because no matter what you choose, I will be right next to you the entire way."

"What if I make a mistake?" she asked quietly. "What if I do something wrong?"

"Do you think in all the years your grandmother has ruled she never made a mistake?" His fingers brushed her jaw before tucking a strand of hair behind her ear. "You might not have trained to become queen immediately, but you trained to be a princess. If you had married Prince Castain, you would have become queen eventually. That you are worried about making mistakes tells me you will be a good ruler." His smile was the sun itself as he said, "I have complete faith in you, Wren. I know you can do this. Together, we can do this."

Tears burned her eyes as she looked up at her mate. "How did you get to be so perfect?" she whispered through the thickness in her throat.

"I was born this amazing." He gave her one of his signature half smiles before sobering. "Do you want this, Wren? And not because you think it's what I want, but do *you* want it?"

Taking a deep breath, she gave him a wobbly smile. "Yes, I do."

His smile was wicked. "I can't wait to tell Aeron he has to call me 'Your Majesty.'"

A laugh bubbled up Wren's throat, and she couldn't keep it back. She laughed and felt a weight lift off her shoulders, not realizing how much this decision had been plaguing her.

"Come here, my queen." Silas's eyes burned as he pulled her against his chest. "Your king demands you kiss him."

"Well, how can I refuse an order from my king?" She stood on her toes and pressed a soft kiss to his lips.

"What kind of kiss was that?" he asked when she pulled away.

The gravel in his voice caused her toes to curl in her boots and the intensity of his stare stole her breath. When he lowered his mouth to hers, all thoughts of crowns fled and fire ignited in her veins. He claimed her mouth and soul and she let him, losing herself in the love of her mate.

Chapter Thirty

"You look beautiful, Wren. So much like your mother." Queen Elowyn adjusted the straps of Wren's gown and blinked to clear the tears in her eyes.

"Thank you." Wren stared at herself in the mirror. Her eyes were larger than normal and lined with kohl. Rouge had been brushed on her cheeks and lips, giving her a rosy appearance. "I wish she were here today. I wish I could have known her."

"She really would have been so proud of you for everything you have done. I am just as proud."

Now it was Wren's turn to blink back tears. The skirts of her gown swished as she turned to hug her grandmother. "Are you sure you're okay with me taking over? Are you ready to step down?"

Queen Elowyn laughed and waved a hand. "I am more than ready. My rule has been long enough. I have always wanted to take up gardening. Maybe I will in my spare time."

Wren laughed at the image of her regal grandmother

kneeling in the dirt and cultivating flowers. She turned back to the mirror for one last glance at the dress her grandmother had brought in early this morning.

The dress was composed of nude tulle underskirts with white floral lace bodice and skirts over the tulle. The sleeves that draped off her shoulders were white floral appliqué. Blush-colored tulle attached to the skirts at her left hip and around her back to her navel, leaving the floral lace of her left hip exposed. It was a beautiful gown. A gown fit for a queen.

Adjusting the skirts of the gown, Wren released a breath. "I'm ready."

Queen Elowyn walked with Wren through the village, her final job as queen before passing the crown to her granddaughter. Fae not attending the ceremony bowed their heads in respect of their queen and future queen. Luckily, Wren had gotten ready on the ground level of Valasia so she didn't have to climb down stairs and ladders in her gown. Her thoughts were all over the place as she made her way to the throne room. Her palms were sweaty and her heart was racing in her chest. Was she really ready to take this on?

As the throne room came into view, she saw Silas standing out front and her worries immediately eased. Her gaze traveled down the length of his body and she smiled. He looked incredibly handsome, dressed in all black with gold-stitched accents. Wren pursed her lips. For once, his curls were tamed back and not falling into his eyes

A slow smile spread across Silas's face as she approached, and his eyes seemed to glow a vibrant green. "You look stunning," he said, and kissed her cheek.

Wren narrowed her eyes at him, then reached up and ruffled his hair, sending his curls falling to their usual disarray. "That's better. You look wonderful now as well."

One brow rose as he brushed a curl out of his eye. "Unbelievable," he muttered. "I spent more time on my hair than I have in my entire life, and you show up and ruin it."

"You didn't look like yourself." She rose on her toes and kissed him. "Are you ready?"

"I'm ready if you are."

Silas threaded his fingers with hers and opened the massive wooden door. Wren's nerves returned as she saw the room packed wall-to-wall with Fae. Her breathing became uneven and her palms once again started to sweat. She tried to pull her hand out of Silas's grasp so he wouldn't feel how clammy it was, but he tightened his grip.

Relax. I'm right here.

Silas's voice down the bond helped her take a deep breath. Butterflies still danced in her stomach and she was glad she had eaten nothing this morning or she would make quite the first impression on her subjects.

Her gown hid her shaking knees as she climbed the stairs to the dais where an ancient-looking Fae stood in white robes. Wren and Silas stood before him, the eyes of all of Valasia at their backs. The Fae began speaking and Wren tried to focus on what he was saying, but his words entered her ears then got lost in the swirling thoughts she wasn't able to calm. She forced herself to pay attention when the celebrant turned to Silas, a golden knife in his hand.

"Repeat after me: I, Silas, swear on my blood and honor to uphold the laws of the Fae, protect the innocent, and judge fairly the accused. I swear on my blood and honor to rule the Fae with strength and fairness, honesty and loyalty."

Silas held out his hand and the Fae sliced down his palm with the golden knife. Blood welled ruby bright and Silas squeezed his fist, letting his blood drip onto the dais. He repeated the words, his voice ringing sure and strong.

The celebrant lifted a golden crown from the throne and

placed it on Silas's head. "I present to you, Silas, king of the Fae."

Wren jumped when the Fae behind them roared their approval. Every Fae in Valasia knew what Silas had done during the attack on Valasia, as well as during the battle. There was no doubt as to their support for him. When the celebrant stepped back, Silas looked at Wren and winked. She had to bite back a laugh, and she knew he did that on purpose to calm her nerves.

With the golden knife once again in his hands, the old Fae stepped up to Wren. "Repeat after me: I, Wren, swear on my blood and honor to uphold the laws of the Fae, protect the innocent, and judge fairly the accused. I swear on my blood and honor to rule the Fae with strength and fairness, honesty and loyalty."

Wren swallowed when the knife sliced into her skin. As she squeezed her fist to let her blood drip on the dais, she wasn't sure she was breathing. She repeated the words in a breathy voice, not near as sure or strong as Silas's had been.

The old Fae lifted another golden crown from the throne, smaller and daintier than Silas's, and placed it on her head. "I present to you, Wren, queen of the Fae."

Their subjects' cheers were just as loud for her as they had been for Silas. Wren inhaled and turned to Silas. His smile was brilliant, and he took her hand in his and turned them so they faced the audience. The cheers grew louder and Wren couldn't help but smile at their outward joy. She saw her grandmother standing just below the dais, tears in her eyes and a smile on her face. Gabriel stood next to Elowyn, and the pride he felt was obvious to anyone who looked at him. Behind them, their friends and family stood—Jerricha, Aeron, and Hawthorne—all of them smiling widely.

Elowyn approached and curtsied. "Your Majesties, it is

customary for the newly crowned to meet in the council room, where you will be introduced to everyone of importance."

She led them to a door behind the dais that opened to a small hallway. At the other end of the hallway, another door opened into a large room with an oval table. Wren and Silas each took a seat, followed by a line of people who had followed them in. Wren once again felt completely overwhelmed. She tried to focus, but too much information was being shared and she felt like a balloon filled to bursting. She really hoped Silas was paying attention. Wren mentally shook her head at the great start she was making as queen.

When the meeting finally ended, Wren and Silas made their way to their room for some time alone and to process what had just happened.

Wren sank into a chair by the fireplace and groaned. "Is it always going to be like this? I have no idea what just happened."

Silas chuckled and removed his jacket and boots. "It will get easier. I'm sure it's going to be crazy for a while." He knelt in front of Wren and slipped his hands under her skirts to remove her shoes. "We have some open positions we will need to fill. General of the army and captain of the guard being the two most pressing. I'm sure you have some ideas for who you want in those positions."

"Gabriel, of course. He has trained his whole life to be general of King Rodion's army." Wren paused and bit her lip. "That is, if he wants to take it. With the whole thing with his eye, I have a feeling he might try to refuse. He will probably think he isn't capable enough to do it."

Silas snorted, and his hands moved from her feet to her calves. "He is more than capable of doing it, one eye or none. Jerricha will convince him, I'm sure. And what about the captain of the guard?"

"Aeron. I wouldn't trust anyone else."

Silas groaned. "Must you choose Aeron? I'm not sure I can stand being in his presence that often."

Wren kicked him lightly and he caught her foot, eyes heating as he trailed his hands farther up her leg.

"Yes, I must choose him." The breathless sound of her voice shocked her.

He gave her a wicked grin and looked at her through hooded eyes. "Guess I'll have to learn to deal with it."

His hand traveled higher, curving to the inside of her thigh.

"Guess you will," she said. She shifted in the seat, opening her legs wider for him.

Silas's eyes twinkled as his fingers brushed against her core. "Just imagine all the places we can hide in this city with nothing but my shadows to hide us."

Wren couldn't help it. She laughed at his words. Leaning forward, she kissed her mate, feeling the same love and joy from the bond that she was feeling in her heart. This new journey would not be easy, but with Silas at her side, as well as the rest of her friends and family, it was a journey she was excited to be on.

END

Acknowledgments

I am so incredibly honored you have stuck with me through the release of my first duet. None of this would have possible if I hadn't had the support and kind words of my readers. Thank you.

I also have to thank my husband for giving me the time I needed to get this book written and his unconditional support.

To my parents, who *hopefully* still haven't read book one.

To my Mom's Who Write Facebook page, you ladies have helped me in so many ways. I couldn't have done it without you!

About the Author

Whitney L. Spradling is a full time Occupational Therapist and autism mama, who has had a dream to write and publish a novel since she was a little girl. She lives outside of Cincinnati with her husband, son, and two cats. When she is not writing she can be found in her craft room making custom tumblers, or curled up with a good book and a cup of coffee (or glass of wine).

Also by Whitney L. Spradling

The Obsidian Artifacts

The Obsidian Sword

The Obsidian Crown

The Cursed Realms

Of Flames and Curses (coming March 2023)

www.ingramcontent.com/pod-product-compliance
Lightning Source LLC
Chambersburg PA
CBHW021221310726
48971CB00006B/1647